Acclaim for Julie Kramer's

STALKING SUSAN

Finalist for the Minnesota Book Award

"A dazzling debut. . . . It's hard to believe that *Stalking Susan* is Kramer's first novel. Her confident, witty writing style is as fluid as it is flawless. . . . Readers who enjoy novels by authors like Janet Evanovich will soon be stalking Julie Kramer." —*Chicago Tribune*

"*Stalking Susan* by Julie Kramer introduces Riley Spartz, a Twin Cities TV reporter who's determined to get her story—if it doesn't get her first." —*Parade Magazine*
(*Parade* Pick for Summer Suspense)

"*Stalking Susan* is fast, edgy, and even nerve-wracking with its pacing. Add another author to the must-read list." —*Crimespree Magazine*

"Great characters and a well-constructed, chilling plot make this a thoroughly satisfying novel. Riley is a character you will love, and this page-turner is difficult to put down. It ranks as one of the best debut novels I've encountered." —Jo Peters, *Romantic Times*

Julie Kramer

STALKING SUSAN

Julie Kramer is a television news producer for
NBC's *Today* show, *Nightly News*, and *Dateline*.
Prior to that, she was a national award-winning
investigative producer for WCCO-TV in Minneapolis. She lives in White Bear Lake, Minnesota, with her husband and sons.

www.juliekramerbooks.com

STALKING SUSAN

STALKING SUSAN

A Novel

JULIE KRAMER

ANCHOR BOOKS

A Division of Random House, Inc.

New York

FIRST ANCHOR BOOKS MASS-MARKET EDITION, JUNE 2009

Copyright © 2008 by Julie Kramer
Excerpt from Missing Mark *copyright © 2009 by Julie Kramer*

This book contains an excerpt from the author's forthcoming novel, *Missing
Mark*. This excerpt has been set for this edition only and may not reflect the
final content of the forthcoming edition.

This is a work of fiction. Names, characters, places, and incidents are
either the product of the author's imagination or are used fictitiously. Any
resemblance to actual persons, living or dead, events, or locales is entirely
coincidental.

The Library of Congress has cataloged the Doubleday edition
as follows:
Kramer, Julie.
Stalking Susan / Julie Kramer.—1st ed.
p. cm.
1. Women television journalists—Fiction. 2. Serial murderers—
Minnesota—Minneapolis—Fiction. 3. Minneapolis (Minn.)—Fiction.
I. Title.
PS3611.R355S73 2008
813'.6—dc22 2007034712

Anchor ISBN: 978-0-307-38851-3

www.anchorbooks.com

Printed in the United States of America
10 9 8 7 6 5 4 3

IN MEMORY OF MY FATHER,
HARRY KRAMER,
FARMER AND STORYTELLER

AND ALSO
TO THE LATE ANGIE KIMBALL
NIECE TURNED ANGEL

STALKING SUSAN

CHAPTER 1

So the deal is this—any cop who tickets me for a moving violation gets an "attaboy" from the chief and a day off duty, off the books. To their credit, most cops know this is not fair play, but there's still enough of them out there who like the idea of a day off without their wives knowing about it that I keep a close eye on my rearview mirror and a light foot on my accelerator, careful not to let the speedometer of my Mustang sneak past thirty.

I've been on guard against Minneapolis cops since the police chief put a bounty on my "pretty little head" two years ago. He was good and pissed after I did a TV story about some of his officers sleeping in movie theaters and hanging out in strip clubs instead of patrolling the downtown streets. He got even more pissed when I reported other cops falsifying overtime after a tornado blew through town. You'd think by now the man's job would be on the line, but the chief apparently knows some dark secret about the mayor, who reappoints him to a new term every three years.

I knew all this from a source I was rushing to meet.

When the public thinks source, they think Deep Throat. Don't get me wrong, for a journalist, a high-level source is the ultimate rush. But you can't spend your news career waiting for a mysterious cliché in a trench coat to whisper state secrets. A low-level source with remarkable access can do almost as much damage. Give me a secretary with a straight-and-narrow conscience, working for a boss with a crooked soul, and I'll give you a lead story for the late news.

What bosses don't understand is that whistle-blowers don't call reporters first. They call us last. Only when they are completely disillusioned by the knowledge that going through the system doesn't work do they turn to us: the media. That's when we turn scandal into ratings and ratings into money. If I sound jaded, that's a shameful, recent development.

I hit the gas. Speed down the freeway ramp off Lyndale Avenue and onto the interstate. Here's where I make up lost time. City police don't usually make traffic stops on freeways and I'm not worried about the State Patrol. More than a year ago, I became untouchable in Minnesota. Every State Patrol officer from International Falls to the Iowa border knows my name and face. If I'm inadvertently stopped, they apologize sincerely and send me on my way.

My name is Riley Spartz. I'm a television reporter for Channel 3. I'm thirty-six years old, but on a good day I look a decade younger. A big plus in a cutthroat business. Beyond the obvious advantage of youth meaning a longer shelf life, strangers tend to underestimate me—thus I've broken more than my share of exclusives and won more than my share of awards. But none of that matters when contract time comes around.

Then, all any news director wants to know is "What have you done for me lately?" Being objective, I have to admit, lately I haven't done shit.

When I first started out in this business, I considered news the stuff that happens to other people. I know better now. I understand why some folks consider news just another four-letter word.

I WAS ACROSS the Mississippi River and had already claimed the back row of seats when Nick Garnett walked in the Highland Theater in St. Paul. I gave him the aisle since his legs are longer. The afternoon matinee wasn't scheduled to begin for a half hour so the theater was empty.

"Been waiting long?" he asked.

"A few minutes."

"Sorry. I got lost on the way." A top Minneapolis homicide detective, Garnett was more talented at telling good from evil than north from south.

"Why did we have to meet all the way over here?" I asked.

"So we won't run into anybody who knows us."

The overhead lights dimmed on the art deco décor but only Garnett's boss would consider our meeting illicit.

"Unfortunately that rules out all the fancy-pants hot spots where you like to hang out," he continued.

"It also rules out all the dives where you mooch free food 'cause you're a cop."

I'm always surprised how many restaurants will trade coffee and a burger for police presence.

"Not for long."

Garnett had a big retirement bash set for tonight. I wasn't invited, though we'd known each other nearly half his career. For the best sources, public credit can be hazardous to their jobs. Garnett didn't relish being reassigned to rounding up drunks for detox, so our friendship remained our secret.

We'd first met when I was a rookie reporter covering a small-town fire in southern Minnesota. The blaze started in an apartment building and consumed city hall, a hardware store, and the town diner before firefighters got it under control. Ends up, the local police chief set the fire so he could rescue his girlfriend, who lived in an upstairs apartment.

She'd dumped him the weekend before and he figured playing hero might win her back. The plan was ending as happily as a fairy tale, except that a security camera mounted on the service station across the street recorded video of the chief carrying a gas can into the apartments moments before the blaze began. Garnett had slapped the cuffs on his boss and done a perp parade in front of the courthouse. A couple years later, Garnett took a street job in Minneapolis, moving up the ranks to homicide.

"I still don't see why I can't come to your party," I said. "I'd like a chance to roast you and toast you. What are they going to do if I show up? Fire you?"

"I don't need the grief."

He'd had enough of the inside politics involved in fighting big-city crime. Garnett had landed a lucrative private sector job as head of corporate security for the Mall of America out in Bloomington. So at age fifty, still in decent physical shape, and with just barely graying hair, he was taking an early retirement package. It came with a cushy public sector pension.

"I'm leaving at the top of my game," he said. "I don't need any whispers. I don't need any finger-pointing. And I sure as hell don't need my new bosses knowing about you." He gave me a look that meant he meant business. "And from now on you can leave your hidden camera home when you step on my turf."

"What? The Mall of America is my favorite under-cover shopping spot."

The Mall of America is the largest indoor shopping complex in the United States. Something like 520 stores. Fifty restaurants. Fourteen movie screens. Very upscale. Minnesota-based Northwest Airlines even offers special rates for day trips so shopaholics from as far away as Tokyo can afford to fly in for a holiday spending spree. An added bonus: no sales tax on cloth-ing purchased in Minnesota.

I used the mall as a backdrop for several consumer investigative stories. I often shoot undercover video with a hidden camera, just one of the modern tools of the TV trade not available to Edward R. Murrow. Early on, I'd mounted a bulky black-and-white camera in an oversized briefcase. Next came a lipstick lens in a Coach purse. But technology improved so much that now I'm able to shoot color video with a pinhole-size lens hidden in an ink pen, watch, brooch, button, or even a pair of glasses.

A wire runs from the lens to a small video recorder I carry in a fanny pack around my waist. I tape a tiny microphone to the V of my bra. I'm a B cup, ample enough to hide the mike, but not so voluptuous that the audio is muffled. Luck and a whole lot of duct tape keep the operation inconspicuous. I was not eager to give up the Mall of America. So I told him that.

"Yeah, but I gotta show I'm doing something," Garnett said, "so in addition to increasing security, I'm going to cut down on negative publicity about the mall. Besides, you're going to be too busy working on your next big scoop to have time for stories about shoppers being cheated out of a nickel."

"Hey! That pricing error story was good TV. It won a lot of awards. My motto is, if you can show ten thousand folks getting cheated out of a nickel, that's as good as showing one guy getting bilked out of five hundred big ones. Also more relevant to a wider audience. Anyway, I don't have a next big scoop."

"You do now." He pulled a fat file from his briefcase. By now other movie patrons were shuffling around, looking for seats. I considered pretending to make out with Garnett so no one would want to sit by us, but he definitely wasn't my type, plus that could create a whole new set of problems.

We both acted like we were getting together to celebrate his new job, but we both knew he was there to prop me up. This was no business meeting. This was one friend healing another's pain. My career was in the toilet. Going from star to slacker wasn't working for me, and Garnett could tell.

"I know it's not the same, Riley, but you helped me through my divorce when things got wacko. I'd like to help you." He paused, then said with exaggerated emphasis, "After all, tomorrow is another day."

"Vivien Leigh, *Gone With the Wind,* 1939," I answered.

Garnett and I were both film buffs and occasionally met in shadowy theaters to pass documents and catch an action flick or drama. Never a date movie. We'd developed a routine of him weaving famous movie lines into our conversations, and me guessing the actor, picture, and year. Not as difficult as it sounds, because I associate films with historical and breaking news events. For example, *Gone With the Wind* debuted the year Germany invaded Poland. And *Stand by Me* came out the same year the Space Shuttle *Challenger* exploded.

Our rule to avoid reruns: no matter how appropriate the circumstance, Garnett can utter a line only once. The man has patience; in all the years I'd known him, he'd never used Rhett Butler's scandalous farewell with me. I'm sure there were times he was tempted, but I suspect he didn't want to waste the line on a mediocre moment.

"My life's not your life," I said. "And as for tomorrow

being another day, my tomorrow is really no different from my yesterday."

I shook my head, still bitter about being single again. Angry the way my marriage ended.

An old priest I knew from my farm girl days suggested that forgiving those who hurt us can lead to inner peace. Trouble was, I wasn't interested in peace. I craved revenge. On my good days, I'm an edgy chick with a temper. I didn't like that I still didn't like sleeping alone. I was also embarrassed to admit that I missed my husband, even though I'd found plenty to complain about when he was around.

Garnett pressed the file at me along with a tiny flashlight. "Have a look while I get us some snacks. But don't look so close you lose your appetite."

He left me alone with the file. It read SUSAN. I flipped through the police reports and the crime scene photos.

The truth was, I was desperate for a big scoop.

I had just come back to work last week following a three-month personal leave spent trying to get my personal life back together. I worried the time off might have been a mistake. I had always considered the key to keeping my world in order was never letting my personal and professional lives get out of whack at the same time. Now I was trying to get them both on track simultaneously. An overwhelming challenge.

Garnett returned during the previews with two large plastic cups of soda pop and a giant bucket of popcorn.

I took a handful to be polite and got extra butter all over my fingers. Luckily, he brought extra napkins. I said nothing, accepting him for who he is—a man who considers potato chips his favorite vegetable and chocolate-covered cherries his favorite fruit.

"Who's Susan?" I finally asked.

"Which one?" Garnett pulled a newspaper clipping from the folder. The headline: "Body Found by Lake Calhoun." He said, "Check the date."

I moved the light beam to the top right corner. "November 19, 1991." He handed me another article, printed the next day, that identified the victim as Susan Chenowith. "Okay," I said, "tell me the story."

"Not yet." He stacked another clipping on top: "Unidentified Woman Strangled," it read.

I jerked slightly when he pointed at the date. November 19, 1992. Exactly one year later. "This is sort of weird."

"Don't get me started." He handed me a follow-up article that identified the second dead woman as Susan Moreno. "Okay," he said to me, "now *you* tell *me* the story."

I paused, my eyes moving back and forth between the two headlines in front of me. "They're both named Susan. They were both murdered. Same day, a year apart." Up on the silver screen the movie began, so I lowered my voice. "A serial killer stalking Susans?"

"Don't go writing your promo before you've got the facts," he warned. "I don't know what it means. I can't prove they are even related, though I spent a few years trying. But I also can't walk out the door knowing no one else is going to bother. So I'm giving you a copy. Have a crack at it."

Garnett's cell phone rang during the opening credits. An older man a few rows in front of us turned to glare. "No cell phones," the man hissed. He had no clue he was hissing at a cop. Garnett wore a dark suit and tie, nice enough for the street, but not good enough for on air.

He pulled out his badge, shined the light on it and then in our hisser's eyes. "Police business."

His phone rang again, the same generic ring tone as the day he bought it. He liked blending in, whether it be clothes, cars, or cell phones. He glanced at the number. Then he flipped open the receiver and I watched as he listened to whoever was on the other end. "Okay. I'm on my way," he finally said.

I didn't ask for details. If he could tell me, he would.

"I'll be back." He imitated the husky voice of a postapocalyptic cyborg. Pitiful.

"Arnold Schwarzenegger, *The Terminator,* 1984. That the best you got? You are so incredibly lame."

"I wanted to start you back slow until you get your confidence. When I'm convinced you can handle blockbusters again we'll move on to independent art films. And since you did so well in today's competition, I'll leave you our feast." He shoved his popcorn my way.

Some feast. A pail of grease. I shook my head and motioned thanks, but no thanks.

"Call me when you've had a chance to look through the file," he said. "I'm interested to see if there's anything I missed. And when you talk to the department, don't let them know you have it."

Then he pulled me close to whisper in my ear. "Be careful on this one."

I shrugged. "I'm always careful." But that wasn't exactly true, and he knew it.

"This is a bad unsub," he told me. "Unsub" is cop talk for "unidentified subject." I love cop talk. "Real bad," he said again for emphasis.

"They're all bad," I replied.

"But this one might be a cop."

Before I could press him further about this juicy little nugget, Garnett grabbed his briefcase and his greasy popcorn and left me alone in a dark theater in St. Paul. Holding a cold case file.

CHAPTER 2

A garbage man found Susan Chenowith's body in the alley behind a two-million-dollar mansion on Lake Harriet. The date was November 19, 1991. The sky was more dark than light that morning. He put the brakes on his twenty-five-ton rig and got out to examine the bundle blocking his route. His breakfast beat the sun up that morning. The garbage man staggered to a back door. Began pounding. Then he heaved again.

The crime scene photos made me flinch as I paged through the file, now spread across my desk at Channel 3. I shut my office door so the rest of the newsroom wouldn't see what I was working on. The photos were in color as well as black and white. The color pictures were to preserve evidence: the crime scene and the body as it actually looked when it was discovered. The black-and-white copies were backup, in case the murder went to trial and the judge ruled color to be too inflammatory for the jurors—an argument defense attorneys routinely make.

Susan Chenowith's discolored face and protruding tongue screamed strangulation. I scanned the death certificate and read the words "asphyxia" and "homicide."

Susan was twenty-six years old. She worked the day

shift as a waitress at Peter's Grill, a landmark Minneapolis diner that serves comfort food to downtown crowds. On that salary she still lived with her parents in south Minneapolis. Her parents told investigators she had never come home after her shift. It wasn't typical for her to stay out all night, but it sometimes happened. So they hadn't worried about her—until it was too late to worry about her.

Dark hair. Blue eyes. But no beauty. Certainly not now, but not even before her fatal encounter. I picked up a snapshot the cops probably showed witnesses as they tried to retrace her final steps. On her best day, Susan was fairly ordinary looking. That might explain why no one reported seeing her after she got off her shift. People tend to remember beauty or the beast. Folks in between can count on a degree of invisibility. Good for villains; bad for their victims.

The medical examiner's report detailed bruising around her vagina and concluded she had been raped even though no semen was found. No semen meant no DNA. If the killer had left a little something behind, this might have been a whole different case. Garnett could have sent a sample to the state crime lab, where nearly forty thousand felons have their DNA on file. And not voluntarily either. DNA is a biological blueprint that can lead to a name, which can lead to an arrest, which can lead to a conviction. Hell, without semen, the cops can't even be sure the killer is male.

Susan died wearing Kmart clothes. I don't mean

they were necessarily bought at Kmart, but they looked like average, run-of-the-mill clothes. The kind Martha Stewart wouldn't be caught dead in. Tan pants made of a poly-cotton blend. I examined a photo that showed a full body shot. There was a dark stain, maybe blood or maybe mud, near her crotch. A royal blue button was missing from her brown and blue striped sweater. Her shoes were black loafers. The police report noted a shoulder bag found near her body held a black skirt and white shirt, which her mother explained she always changed into at work.

Garnett had run a search under her name and date of birth. An NCIC search. That's a national crime identification computer that can call up a national rap sheet. Criminals can run from their past, but they can't hide from it. Her name came up blank. No drugs. No prostitution. No criminal record whatsoever. Susan Chenowith stayed away from trouble, but trouble had found her anyway.

EXACTLY ONE YEAR later, a man walking his dog found Susan Moreno's body slumped against a small pine tree near the beach on Lake Calhoun. She wore a raincoat over a short denim skirt and a purple tank top with spaghetti straps.

A vice cop was the last known person to see her alive. Nine hours earlier, he had stopped her for soliciting near the corner of Franklin and Chicago. He ordered her into the backseat of an unmarked car, but she raced off, disappearing into the Phillips neighborhood, a run-down part of town frequented by runaways. Each block has CONDEMNED signs on deteriorating duplexes with peeling paint and broken glass. That doesn't stop squatters from moving in when they need a temporary place to crash.

Many of the residents are Native American, drifting back and forth between the poverty here and the poverty on the reservations in northern Minnesota. Children in the Phillips neighborhood have a higher incidence of fetal alcohol syndrome and lead poisoning than anywhere else in the state. Many skip school. The ones who don't, show up for the free lunch, not the free education.

Susan Moreno's rap sheet was long for a teenager. Prostitution. Theft. Drugs. I searched through the pile of papers and found her juvenile mug shot. Sixteen years old with tangled blonde hair. A hard life, but a soft smile. The crime scene photos were a harsh contrast. This Susan had also been strangled. Her face was Viking purple and she had some sort of ligature around her neck. Her eyes were rolled back into her head. One photo showed a close-up of a tattoo on her shoulder. Susan ♥ Sam.

Sam seemed like a good place to start. The police apparently agreed. I flipped through several sheets about a man named Sam Fox, age twenty-three. Arrested for burglary, assault, drugs, DWI. Damn. I felt like crumbling the pages when I got to the part about him being in jail on the date of the murder. November 19, 1992. No alibi is as ironclad as a man behind iron bars. The cops had interviewed him anyway. They noted he seemed saddened and stunned by his girl-friend's death. He had no idea who might have wanted her dead.

Neither did her father. He hadn't seen her for four months, and then only because she'd drifted back home one afternoon looking for money. I read a brutal line in the investigative report where her dad told police, "The street swallowed her up because she was unholy."

Most likely she had fallen victim to a violent john. With no public outcry, police are less likely to devote resources to low-life cases. A fact of the street.

Susan Moreno had also been sexually assaulted before she was murdered. Again, no semen. She was wearing a leopard print thong under her skirt, but no bra under her tank top. I shuddered as I read that her matching bra was actually the murder weapon. Occa-sionally the forensic guys can pull a print off skin, but it was hours too late for that in either of the SUSAN cases.

In both of the murders, police recovered micro-scopic fibers on the victims' clothing, but analysis of the fibers showed them to be different so they couldn't link the two cases. Without a suspect for comparison purposes, the fiber evidence was fairly useless. As years passed, the murderer or murderers were likely to buy new cars, move to different apartments, tear out old carpet, and destroy any forensic connection they once had with their victims.

These murders were also difficult to solve because the police had only one crime scene in each case, yet clearly more than one crime scene existed. What the cops actually had was the body disposal site. The Susans had been killed elsewhere, the bodies transported in motor vehicles. That meant possibly two additional crime scenes that might have yielded better evidence, if only they'd been located.

I'd covered enough murders and read enough crime manuals to know that homicide cops classify murderers two ways: organized and disorganized. This was an organized killer, able to plan, escape, and keep his mouth shut. The homicide closure rate is much easier with disorganized killers, who typically leave loads of clues in one place and will often confess when confronted.

I set the papers down, feeling energized for the first time in months. SUSAN had stopped being a file and started being a story. A compelling story even if I didn't find any new evidence. A story could bring tips. Tips could bring answers. The beauty of that, then you had another story. I glanced at my watch, checking the date. October 17, 2007.

I started writing the story in my mind. *"A deadly anniversary is approaching."*

I charted the cases with black marker on white boards.

SUSAN CHENOWITH 1991   SUSAN MORENO 1992

In life, the victims didn't seem to have had much in common beyond their name. A sixteen-year-old hooker versus a twenty-six-year-old waitress. One blonde, the other brunette.

SUSAN CHENOWITH 1991	SUSAN MORENO 1992
AGE: 26	AGE: 16
WAITRESS	RUNAWAY/PROSTITUTE
BRUNETTE	BLONDE

In death, however, the two women shared much. Under each name, I wrote the murder clues:

DEATH DATE/NOVEMBER 19	DEATH DATE/NOVEMBER 19
NIGHTTIME	NIGHTTIME
STRANGLED	STRANGLED
RAPE	RAPE
NO SEMEN	NO SEMEN
MINNEAPOLIS LAKES	MINNEAPOLIS LAKES

Another parallel seemed obvious: both women had disappeared from one of Minneapolis's poorest neighborhoods; both were dumped in one of the city's wealthiest. Maybe the killer was trying to send a message.

CHAPTER 3

The vocabulary of TV news tends to be morbid. "If it bleeds, it leads" is the philosophy in many newsrooms for determining which story gets the best play. To name a story is to "slug" it. Unwanted silence during a newscast is "dead" air. If you don't want any audio, you "kill" the sound. Unedited videotape is called "raw." To edit it, you "cut" it. And you don't just take pictures of something, you "shoot" it.

I headed for the tape "morgue," the archive where television stations store old news tapes. Even without that name, it's a spooky place. Especially at night.

Usually the only video that gets saved are the scenes that actually make it on the air, a fraction of what is shot each day. The raw tapes are recycled after a week, used over and over again until they're too ragged to shoot new stories on. Tape costs money, so news directors are always pressuring reporters, producers, and photographers to dump used tapes back into circulation. Typically the only tapes spared are those the station attorney has decreed must be packed away for years in case of a lawsuit. These are often sensitive, sometimes sensational, investigative stories we might need to defend in court someday. I've got about thirty boxes of tapes and notes stashed away, but I haven't been sued yet. That gives the newsroom bean counters a false sense of security, so occasionally they try to get their hands on those tapes and I have to rat them out to our lawyer.

Every once in a while an enterprising video editor bucks the system and starts a tape box for big stories, or little stories that might get big. After all, it would be a bummer to find that a serial killer has been piling up corpses while the cops kept quiet; but it would be an even bigger bummer to find out that the only video your newsroom has of the murders is a couple of fifteen-second shots of a body bag surrounded by police tape. Or worse, a couple of fifteen-second shots of a wooded area surrounded by police tape. Or even worse than that, fifteen-second shots of boring cop cars parked on the street.

I knew that was about all I'd find in the on-air tape, so I was hoping for raw tape. Besides providing more video for my story, raw tape might contain clues from the crime scenes. About five years ago, I got lucky and found raw tape of the funeral of a family killed in a house fire. When police arrested the arsonist a year later, bingo, I matched his mug to one of the mourners.

If bystanders gather at a murder scene, the police routinely photograph the crowd because they know killers sometimes become gawkers.

It was a long shot, but I scanned the back shelves for a cardboard box with a promising label. I'm no intern— I never expected a box labeled SUSAN MURDERS to jump out at me, and it didn't. But I didn't find anything

even remotely promising, like LAKE HARRIET HOMI-
CIDE or FRANKLIN AVENUE HOOKER.

The light was dim; tape morgues don't get windows.
They're typically basement corners, or interior storage
rooms nobody else wants. Invariably, they have bad flu-
orescent lighting that buzzes and cuts in and out. After
about fifteen minutes, my eyes ached. I was ready to
reach for the doorknob when I noticed a battered box
on a top shelf. IRON RANGE FIREBOMB. It was dated
well over a year ago.

Suddenly I felt a chill, as if I was standing in the
county morgue amid dead bodies, not dead tapes. I
never covered the firebombing story, yet I was familiar
with it, like almost every journalist in the country.

No surprise the box existed. After all, the story had
won nearly every award in broadcast news from
Peabody to Emmy to Murrow. Big-bucks political con-
sultants were using it as a textbook case to teach their
clients how not to act in front of TV cameras.

As I pulled the box from the shelf I knew that, for
me, it was Pandora's box.

RAW TAPE CAN trigger raw emotions. Top-notch TV
news producers know this. They use that power to move
viewers to tears. I had been in the business long enough
to know that if I put that firebombing tape in a video
viewing machine, thirty seconds later I just might be
the one reaching for a tissue, bawling my eyes out.

I carried the box down the hall to a closet-sized room
and shut the door. I wouldn't be doing this if it wasn't

late at night and the newsroom wasn't empty, except for a college student hired to listen to the police scanners and dispatch a sleepy photographer at the first sign of spot news. Inside the box I found a dozen videotapes. I was interested only in one.

I put it in the viewing deck and hit *play*. The tape began to roll.

The camera is on Minnesota governor Rocky Johnson. Voters love Governor Johnson almost as much as the camera does. He's a large man with thick wavy hair and a professional smile. But he's not just a pretty political face: his background made him electable and his charm appears to be the ticket to making him reelectable.

Governor Johnson didn't avoid Vietnam like some politicians. He trained as a Green Beret, though he's fuzzy on whether or not he actually saw combat. The media has pretty much had to take his word for it, because a 1973 fire at an army storage center in St. Louis, Missouri, destroyed rooms of military records, including his.

The election is a few months away. On the tape he exudes the confidence of an incumbent and front-runner. The previous week's poll put him fifteen points ahead of his challenger, Lester Muller, a family farmer from southern Minnesota with character but no charisma. So far his campaign slogan, Les Is More, had earned him less support and more ridicule.

Free publicity is on Governor Johnson's itinerary

today. A Channel 3 camera crew is following him, shooting cover of backslapping and baby kissing for a behind-the-scenes campaign piece. Governor Johnson is touring the newly opened Iron Range Regional Center, which he touts as a "cooperative venture between public and private forces." The Iron Range covers much of northeastern Minnesota. Since mining went bust, the area's future is financially bleak. But the Range got a fat government grant for this "building of the future," and Governor Johnson is here to take credit. It's a shrewd political move because the Iron Range is the strong arm of the Minnesota Democratic-Farmer-Labor Party.

There's a saying in state politics: as goes the Iron Range, so goes the election. The Range was the last area in Minnesota to switch from hand-counted ballots to electronic tabulation. Because of that, their returns always came in last. The joke was, the Rangers are still waiting to see how many votes they need.

The Iron Range Regional Center is located outside the small town of Finland, population 603. Rugged and isolated, it's in one of the last parts of Minnesota to be settled. Immigrants from the old country founded it in the late 1890s and kept the name so they'd never forget their roots. The town's biggest attraction before the Iron Range Regional Center was a purple and green wooden statue of Saint Urho who, legend has it, chased the grasshoppers out of Finland.

The Center houses a day care center, a senior center,

a coffee shop, a barbershop, a bait shop, and a county licensing bureau where folks can get marriage licenses, auto licenses, boat licenses, fishing licenses, and, most important, hunting licenses. In northern Minnesota, every pickup truck has a gun rack and the right to bear arms is the only right anyone within a hundred miles gives a damn about.

Governor Johnson is greeting veterans at a reception in the senior center. A thin old man in a loose-fitting World War II uniform offers him a moose burger and they kid each other about war. The governor gives the crowd the standard "All veterans are heroes and our nation must never forget them." The camera pans the knotty pine-paneled room as the vets applaud. The décor is early hunting lodge: deer and moose heads mounted on the walls along with Minnesota's state fish, the walleye. Governor Johnson pauses between handshakes to point his thumb and forefinger at the head of a twelve-point buck. "Bang, bang, bang," he says. "Get you next season."

The camera catches Sergeant Hugh Boyer, the governor's bodyguard and driver, breaking his usual stoic stance to roll his baby blue eyes.

I rewound the tape and watched it again. Boyer and I shared enough off-the-record chats about Governor Johnson that I know that he knows the governor is so very full of shit. The only one who doesn't know that is the governor. Even so, Boyer should be smarter than to let it show in public.

Boyer used to be the state's top highway crash investigator and having him babysit Governor Johnson was a waste of talent. He was temporarily drafted for the bodyguard job a year earlier when the gov's main muscle got caught driving drunk one weekend. The State Patrol bosses suspected that Boyer was a media source, though they preferred to call it violating the Minnesota Data Practices Law, an act punishable by a thousand-dollar fine and up to ninety days in jail.

"They're just doing this to flush you out," I told him. "They'll set you up with an irresistible but fake tip to see if it shows up during sweeps month. Then they'll have the proof that you're a leak."

"You're probably right, Riley," he said to me. "But it's a chance to get out of writing up fatals for a few months."

Protecting the state's highest elected official is just a minor duty of the Minnesota State Patrol. Their most visible role is cracking down on speeders, but officers also investigate fatal traffic accidents. Boyer, their best accident reconstructionist, could read skid marks like a TV anchor could read a teleprompter.

We had met four years earlier after a rock star's stretch limo hit a school bus. I could see how tracing small body outlines in chalk on blacktop roads might start to wear on a guy, but I was still sore when Boyer decided that the best way to avoid being caught leaking stuff to the media was to stop leaking stuff to the media.

On the tape, the governor moves down the hall. So does the camera. A sign reads BILL'S BARBERSHOP. The shot is wide and wobbly because the photographer, Chuck Hudella, is trying to get ahead of the group by walking backward. He doesn't notice, in the far corner of the screen, Governor Johnson carelessly giving press secretary Poppy Jones a little squeeze on the ass. Body-guard Boyer apparently does and gives a slight shake of his head toward the governor, who responds by briefly flashing what looks like his middle finger. None of this made news because what happens later on the tape made everything else irrelevant.

The governor gives a high five to a three-year-old boy getting a crew cut. The kid is perched on a board across the top of the barber chair. Suddenly the boy slides out of frame as an explosion rocks the room.

The camera shuts down briefly. Screams are the only thing heard when the tape rolls again. It's dark and dusty.

"What's goin' on? Anybody know what's goin' on?"

I can't see who is yelling, but I recognized Chuck's voice. The old-time photog had a reputation among the reporters at Channel 3 of being difficult to work with because he disliked using a tripod—a fault that some-times resulted in shaky stand-ups. Stubbornly, he'd brace his elbow on the hood of a car and call himself a human tripod. But no cameraman's shoulder could have withstood that blast.

I easily pick Chuck's voice out of the din, louder than the others, because he's closest to the microphone. "You people, clear out." Somehow he manages to keep the camera rolling.

Boyer pushes the governor into the hall. "Move it." His deep command echoes through the pandemonium. Barber Bill is carrying his young customer. The little boy's face is bleeding, his haircut half finished. "Everyone, keep moving." Boyer's voice grows urgent. My heart starts to beat faster.

They are about fifteen yards away from the door and their escape when a wall caves in. More dust. More screams. High-pitched and frantic. The camera swings wildly. Under a pile of debris I see Poppy Jones's shapely ass, but not much else of the press secretary.

"Back." Boyer coughs. I can't see him because of the heavy dust.

The governor knocks the old veteran down as he tries to move farther from the rubble.

"My hip!" the old man cries.

The camera follows Governor Johnson around a corner. A young woman is surrounded by children—none looks older than five. She's holding two kids in her arms and more are pressed against her legs.

"The day care's on fire!" Her face is streaked with dirt and tears. The children, wide-eyed, tremble.

Boyer, still broad and strong from his days as a high school linebacker, heaves the old veteran over his shoulders. He motions for everyone to head in the other direction to the senior center. As they move down the hall, sunlight from a picture window shines through smoke.

"Stop," the day care woman cries. "Becky's missing. There's supposed to be nine kids. We've got to go back."

"Which way?" Boyer asks.

The governor shoves him. "We can't go back, we have to get out."

"You get them out. I'll find the little girl." I note the nonnegotiable tone in his voice. Gently, Boyer sets the old vet down and makes a promise. "I'll come back for you."

"No! You have to stick with me." The governor thrashes his arms. His speech turns shrill and desperate, almost on the verge of a tantrum. "It's your job to get me out. So go do your job."

Boyer pushes him against the wall and a rifle from a Civil War display about the First Minnesota Volunteers falls down. "You want out. I'll get you out." He picks up the antique firearm and smashes the window, then knocks Governor Johnson backward through the broken glass. The ground is about twenty feet below.

He instructs barber Bill and the day care lady to lower the kids out the window. My throat tightens as Boyer disappears back into the smoke.

"Hurry." The woman sobs. "She's only two."

The tape continues to roll on chaos and confusion as the kids are dropped outside. "Run," the grown-ups tell them. "Get away from the building."

"Him next." Chuck puts his camera on the floor to help lower the old vet down. They don't realize he's already in cardiac arrest. For the next ten seconds, all I see are feet.

Another explosion. Then all I see is black.

A few seconds later the tape goes to snow. That's what TV journalists call it when the pictures suddenly stop and all that shows on the monitor is white-and-gray static. I reach for my purse and pull out, no, not a tissue—I have no tears left.

What I pull out is a wallet-sized wedding photo of Hugh Boyer and me.

THE NEXT DAY searchers found my husband's body in the rubble, a dead toddler clutched in his arms.

Perhaps now you understand why I have what amounts to a get-out-of-jail-free card from the Minnesota State Patrol.

They also found the bodies of the day care lady, barber Bill, and Chuck Hudella. His crumpled camera lay nearby, the videotape inside.

Now you understand why Governor Johnson got what amounts to a get-the-hell-out-of-office card from Minnesota voters.

Minnesota has a national reputation for the highest voter turnout. It's a matter of state pride. While the rest of the country struggles to get 40 percent to the polls, Minnesota can count on at least 75 percent of its voters to do their patriotic duty. On the Iron Range, the figure is closer to 90 percent.

This election set two state records: highest turnout

and lowest showing by a major-party gubernatorial candidate. Governor Johnson finished the night with just 17 percent of the vote.

Voters might have been able to forgive him for acting like a coward while campaigning as a war hero. But they could never forgive him for being a big fat liar.

You see, a few hours after the building collapsed, the governor figured the only surviving witnesses to his meltdown were all under the age of five and would probably remain traumatized through grade school. With his press secretary dead, he held a news conference that was carried live by every TV and radio station in the state, as well as by CNN, FOX, and MSNBC.

Tape of that news conference was in the box, too. But I didn't bother looking at it. I remembered the sound bites, which played over and over on the news. The governor had worn a sling on his arm and tears on his cheek. He had sobbed about his own survivor's guilt.

"I should have perished inside with them. But my close personal friend, Hugh Boyer, forced me out. He told me, 'Governor, my job is to keep you safe.' And he literally pushed me out the window to keep me from helping evacuate the children."

That scenario meshed with what witnesses saw from the parking lot; so that scenario led the newscasts—until Channel 3 got Chuck's camera back.

LIFE WOULD HAVE been easier for Governor Johnson if the firebomb had been an assassination attempt.

Then he might have landed some public sympathy. After all, it wasn't his fault the Iron Range Regional Center collapsed—at least not directly. The person most responsible was Roger Meyerhofer. But he was dead, and folks needed someone alive and kicking to blame.

At the same moment the governor was high-fiving the little boy in the barber chair, Roger Meyerhofer drove his '83 Ford Ranger pickup through the Licensing Bureau wall on the other side of the building. He had a full tank of gas, plus a full load of chemical fertilizer. Kaboom.

Meyerhofer was fed up with the bureaucrats inside because they wouldn't give him a hunting license. They told him there was no point in him having a hunting license because, being a convicted felon, under state law he couldn't carry a gun until ten years after his probation was up. That wasn't going to happen until 2011. Meyerhofer had been ticketed for poaching deer that season and was supposed to serve a month in the county jail, starting the next day. Authorities had already confiscated his rifle, otherwise he probably would have shot the place up instead of blowing it up. He died instantly along with three government employees and a pregnant teenage couple who were there getting a marriage license.

There were twenty-three other people in the Iron Range Regional Center that day. They might all have got out alive, except for the person second most responsible for the tragedy: Frank Skaw.

His role didn't come out until months later when authorities concluded the investigation. Skaw was the beer-bellied Iron Ranger in charge of the construction project. Turns out, he had skimmed part of the grant money and used steel beams that didn't meet code.

And in a classic what-goes-around-comes-around twist, the investigation also uncovered that Frank Skaw won the bid in the first place because he was a big campaign contributor to Governor Johnson.

So when Roger Meyerhofer crashed his truck, he started a chain reaction through the entire building that ended thirteen lives, one political career, and my marriage.

The person next most responsible was me.

I was the reporter who broke the story about gun-wielding felons and hunting licenses the year before. I'd had our newsroom computer genius cross the state criminal database with the state hunting license database, popping hundreds of names, including Meyerhofer's. My report clued state law enforcement officials that some dangerous dudes were packing heat, and put political heat on them to stop it.

So in a way, crazy old Roger Meyerhofer was my fault. Of course, I was the only one who blamed me; but anyone would understand why I've been messed up for the last year or so and why the Susan story might be just the thing I needed to rescue myself from the emotional disorder of my life.

CHAPTER 4

One quick glance in the mirror the next morning and a quick step on the scale confirmed the status quo: I'd let myself go in the personal grooming department. I wasn't used to looking like the "before" picture. Sallow complexion. Shapeless hair. Drab brown. No highlights. I definitely needed a trip to the salon. But cosmetic fixes are easier than making over damaged psyches. I practiced smiling, closemouthed as well as with teeth.

Knowing the right break could turn today from a research day into an on-camera day, I added powder, blush, and my favorite rust-colored lipstick to my reflection. Mascara around my brown eyes, a dab of foundation over a small scar at the corner of my left eyebrow, and I was ready for air.

Surveying my closet, I selected a loose-fitting vintage jacket made of black wool to hide the fact I was still down fifteen pounds. The loss didn't bother me, but I tire of people telling me I look too thin. Don't they know the camera adds ten?

Most days, television reporters need to look good only from the waist up, so I slipped on a pair of jeans and headed out the door.

BEING A GEEK is better than being a nerd. Nerd suggests uncool while geek implies shy genius. Lee Xiong wasn't just any geek. He was an alpha geek.

"I got a job for you," I told him that morning in the newsroom. He was hunched over one of his computers and didn't look up.

"I already have a job, Riley."

Geek isn't really a job description. Technically Xiong was a news producer, but the bulk of his workload consisted in keeping the newsroom computers running. Just as magicians love pulling rabbits out of hats, he loved pulling clues out of computers.

My trip to the tape morgue the night before had yielded nothing but heartbreak. As I had predicted, the only tape saved from the Susan slayings was what had aired the day after the murders. The camera never got close enough to capture any actual evidence. Just police and police tape. Thirty-five seconds total. Shot from a distance. If I was going to break any new ground, I'd have to look in places the cops hadn't. I thought I'd start with a kazillion gigabytes of death records.

Like thousands of other Hmong, Xiong had come to St. Paul as a child from a refugee camp in Thailand after the Vietnam War. His parents kept their old country ways, but Xiong was young enough to grow up on Saturday-morning cartoons and American video games. He excelled at computer training and landed a job at Channel 3, where he developed a knack for crunching obscure numbers into meaningful stories.

His most vivid coup occurred a few months back when the I-35W bridge in Minneapolis collapsed during rush hour and fell into the Mississippi River. While most journalists chased heroes and victims, Xiong analyzed bridge inspection data and produced an unsettling, widely copied story about the safety of America's bridges.

Reclusive, like most geeks, he dressed more like Mr. Rogers than a recent college graduate. His only fashion flair was his funky wire rim glasses. On his desk sat a souvenir photo of him and Eeyore taken at Disney World several winters ago during spring break. He preferred e-mail over face-to-face communication, but since I hadn't bothered him for several months, and since I didn't feel like typing up a ten-page memo, I simply pulled up a chair and gave him the verbal backstory on the Susans.

"Interesting," he said.

"I want to look for others."

"Others?"

"Other victims," I told him. "Other Susans. I want to look for a pattern. If I find more murders, it'll be harder to dismiss these two cases as coincidence and it may become easier to connect the dots."

"Well, we still have the death certificate database," he said.

A few years back we had used that information to match death certificates with voting records for a story on voter fraud. We called it "Dead Man Voting." We found cases of people casting ballots from the grave in tight local races. While Minnesota allows more flexibility than most states when it comes to registering on Election Day and absentee balloting, election law does insist that each voter have a pulse.

"I bought even more," Xiong said. "So we can check thirty years of records starting in 1976. It won't take any longer than running the last decade."

Besides name and date of death, the computer records contained other useful fields: date of birth, cause of death, zip code, race, and marital status. In all, more than a million deaths.

"Let's check the death date of November 19 without a year, so we can be open to whatever comes up," I suggested.

"All homicides? All Susans? What are we looking for?"

"Let's do a run of all Susans who died on that date, in case a murder fell through the cracks. Then let's do another run of all homicides that day in case the Susan name is a fluke."

"National or just Minnesota?"

I hesitated. If we searched too narrowly, we might miss the big picture. If we searched too wide, we might be overwhelmed by unrelated cases. It's much easier to find a needle in a pin cushion than in a haystack.

"Take Minnesota, Wisconsin, Iowa, and the Dakotas," I decided. "If we find any leads, we can always expand our search."

"I'll split the name field into two new fields," Xiong explained. "First and last names. That way we can do a unique breakdown on the Susan theory. I need to write a program and let the computer run. Then clean the data. Might be done sometime tomorrow, but that does not mean we will come up with anything. Also, did you run this by Noreen?"

Noreen Banks, our news director, had a talent for spotting talent. She could look at an anchor audition tape and predict which blonde with the earnest eyes and sparkling smile would click with viewers in which market. Corporate bigwigs in the television news business highly value that particular skill. But when it came to deciding what story should lead the ten o'clock news, Banks untraditionally favored warm and fuzzy tales of small children and cute animals over the lurid lore of crime and punishment.

"Did Noreen approve?" Xiong repeated.

"Not yet," I said. "I'm waiting to flesh out the story more before I pitch it. I hate to get her hopes up if I can't deliver."

Actually, I was waiting to see if Noreen might possibly win the lottery and move to Polynesia, or if her appendix might suddenly rupture, or if she might even meet Mr. Right and become a stay-at-home trophy wife. I didn't care which as long as she didn't let the door hit her on her way out.

Noreen Banks surrounded herself with a team of news managers who had no clue as to why the term "totally destroyed" is redundant. I suspected she hand-picked her staff to make herself feel smarter. The average tenure for a television news director is just over eighteen months. Live by the ratings; die by the ratings. Banks had two years under her belt at Channel 3, and so far the ratings were on her side. Turns out Twin Cities viewers embraced warm and fuzzy, and under Noreen, Channel 3 moved from a solid third place in the market to a close second. The only way she'd likely leave the newsroom was a promotion to general manager. The big office upstairs.

"Don't wait too long." Xiong nodded. "She makes me justify everything I do."

He dismissed me by leaning over his screen to write computer code, which might as well have been Latin for all it meant to me. I felt a flash of geek envy, and then I left him to the solitary click-click of his keyboard.

CHAPTER 5

Susan Chenowith's parents had an unlisted telephone number. That gave me a good excuse for not calling them before knocking on their door. Trial and error had taught me it's usually better to just show up. Calling first gives them a chance to hang up, or a reason not to answer the door, or maybe time to change their mind. But since Ken and Tina Chenowith didn't know I was knocking with questions about their dead waitress daughter, they didn't hesitate to open the door.

"You're here about Susan? Ken," she called out, "a reporter's here about Susan."

If I can get someone to open the door, I can usually get invited inside. If they offer me coffee, that usually means they'll eventually go on camera. That last part is crucial. No video, no story. Newspaper reporters have it easy, they can land a story without leaving their desk.

Things went well on the Chenowith doorstep and five minutes later, Ken and Tina and I were having coffee at their kitchen table. They hoped I had found their daughter's killer and were clearly disappointed that I was asking the same questions the police had asked fifteen years earlier.

"If they had any leads, they never told us," Ken said.

"I hope it was a stranger," Tina said. "I hate to think

it's someone we know. That would make it worse, if it was somebody we had ever shaken hands with or smiled at. I couldn't bear that."

I heard sound bites as she spoke. Sound bites are the magic part of an interview. The words that make it on the air. A good sound bite can make pain real. It can leave a viewer breathless. An interview can stretch an hour without ten seconds of magic, but Tina spoke magic fluently.

"Sometimes I watch men on the street and wonder, was it him? Or was it him?"

"I'd kill the guy if I knew," Ken said.

I didn't doubt him. A former construction worker, he still had burly shoulders, strong hands, and a lot of body hair. His bulk made his wife's petite frame seem feeble. But while her voice was strong, his was low and slow, that of a broken man.

She handed me a picture of Susan. "She was wearing this exact raincoat that night."

I recalled the raincoat from the crime scene photos. It was knee length and tan. "May I make a copy of this?"

"Take whatever you want," she said. "Maybe someone will see the story and come forward."

"She didn't deserve to die like that," Ken said.

Susan was their only child. They had her late in life and their modest south Minneapolis rambler, while not a shrine to Susan, was proof enough of her existence. Eight-by-ten school photographs from kindergarten to high school hung in two rows down a long hallway.

As a child, she smiled a shy, crooked grin. As a teenager, her smile was closemouthed and self-conscious. If her family had money, she'd have had braces by fifth grade, perfect teeth by eighth.

I listened as they told me about a girl who wasn't smart or social, but was friendly enough if someone was friendly first.

Yes, Susan dated. But while her friends became fiancées and brides and mothers, Susan remained simply their daughter. From time to time, she would be somebody's girlfriend and he would pick her up at the door. But those relationships generally measured weeks, not months.

It's possible she had been on her way to meet someone that night. Her parents had stopped asking, and Susan had stopped telling. She was the kind of waitress who could flirt well enough for tips at a casual diner, but not at an upscale restaurant. For her, waitressing was a dead-end job in more ways than one.

Her bedroom was as it had been the last night she left home.

"We talk about clearing out her stuff, but can't seem to do it," her mother told me, almost apologetically.

"I know how hard it can be to let go," I said. Boy, did I know. Boyer's State Patrol uniforms were still hanging in my closet. His golf clubs sat in the garage. Everything was where he had left it. Except his gun. I keep that under my bed. Loaded.

I opened the closet and found several black skirts and white shirts.

"That's what she wore waitressing," Tina said. Pinned to each shirt was a black plastic nametag reading SUSAN.

KEN AND TINA held hands tightly as they sat on the tattered couch. They slouched down more than I liked, but it was important that they be comfortable. They'd sit higher if we used the straight-back chairs from the kitchen, but they'd also be tense.

I wanted the interview to be emotional. That means, I wanted them to cry. This, after all, was television.

I phoned Malik Rahman and told him to bring in the camera. He'd been waiting on standby outside in the van. He did a careful job with the lighting, pulling the living room drapes shut and then setting up two light stands with a rose gel over the bulbs. The shot felt warm and the room looked rich. He eliminated the shadows on their faces. I wasn't crazy about the two-shot because Ken was so much taller than Tina, but Malik convinced me it would work.

I briefly rested my hand on theirs and assured them we could stop the interview at any time, but this was their chance to tell viewers how special Susan was.

"Remember the interview is taped, not live. If you stumble, just start over."

The secret to getting an interviewee to cry is trust: making them feel safe. If you've frightened them or made them nervous, it won't work. Their words will seem stilted. You can't scare someone into crying on camera. It's also important that they not look directly at the lens, otherwise they'll have an unnatural, deer-in-the-headlights appearance. I instructed Tina and Ken to look only at me and ignore Malik.

Our audio check found a low buzz coming from their refrigerator. I unplugged the appliance and put my car keys inside to remind me not to drive off without plugging it back in.

I set a box of tissues between Susan's parents, and then we started.

They were good talkers. They had waited more than a decade for someone like me to knock on their door and clip a microphone to their collars.

"Susan was our life," Tina began.

I had asked them not to speak with any other media until after Channel 3's story aired. Other stations often try to undercut a competitor's exclusive by airing a "spoiler" ahead of time. Sometimes newsmakers, either to be polite or to go for maximum exposure, decide to talk to all the media. This often backfires, diluting their story because no station feels ownership. Instead of being one channel's lead story they get short shrift in multiple newscasts.

This television business may seem calculated, but I have personal limits that have evolved from reconciling what I do for a living with how I live with myself. For example, I won't seek an exclusive in the case of a missing person, when time is critical. A family facing that horror needs all the publicity they can get. They can't risk turning down *any* interview, because that station or newspaper just might be the one that leads to the tip that brings the return of their loved one. I carry enough job-related guilt; I don't need that on my conscience.

Since I was the first reporter to contact the Chenowiths since their daughter's death, they readily agreed to stick by me.

"I can't solve her murder," I explained to them. "But I can make sure she's not forgotten." For them, that was good enough.

"I feel like we're not a family anymore," Tina went on. "A family should be more than two people."

The magic came with my fourth question: "What was it like when the police came to your house that morning?"

There was a long pause. "Our world ended," Tina told me, the camera rolling. "A policeman saying 'murder' and 'your daughter' and our world ended."

Tina began to weep. Ken wrapped his hairy arms around the mother of the murdered waitress and leaned his cheek against her forehead.

"Sound up, tears," I thought in TV lingo, hating and congratulating myself at the same time.

CHAPTER 6

'd seen it before and I had experienced it personally. The loss of a loved one can cause survivors either to turn their back on religion, or to seek solace in it. I'd done the former. Susan Moreno's father apparently had chosen to embrace God. He lived alone in a split-level home in the old part of Bloomington, an inner-ring Minneapolis suburb. The living room décor was biblical. Crucifixes and Madonna figurines. A sanctuary to the loss of his sixteen-year-old daughter. But I misjudged what that loss was.

"Oh, my life did not end when Susan died. My life ended when she was born."

My shock did not thwart him.

"My wife died in childbirth. Susan killed her mother."

I couldn't speak, and that doesn't happen too often. I wasn't sure if I was more disturbed by his words, or by his candid delivery of them. I looked away from him, toward a wall where a baby sampler hung. It read SUSAN and was embroidered with white lilies, her date of birth, and her weight and length.

"Susan means 'lily,'" Tim Moreno said. "I only keep that because my mother made it. Lilies symbolize purity."

So Susan meant "lily." I made a mental note to research name origination as a possible clue. I had always associated lilies with death. Just as I was thinking he must have named her as a constant reminder of his pain, he explained that Susan had been his grand-mother's name. He stressed that the choice had ended up being a poor one for his daughter.

"Susan wasn't pure," he told me. "She was Satan's whore. That's why she died."

"She didn't deserve murder."

"Neither did Christ. But as He rose again, so shall she, if forgiven by the Lord."

He didn't offer me coffee, he wouldn't go on camera, and he didn't seem to care whether her killer was ever caught or not.

"Leave now, TV lady."

I wished I could cry for Susan Moreno; her father apparently never had. But I hadn't cried for anyone, even myself, in months. Years ago I had realized one of the reasons I stay in this business is selfish. Like a leech, I feed off the emotion of others. Their sorrow, their pain, their anger satisfies an emptiness that used to bring me to tears when I sat alone in a viewing booth replaying their interviews. That Tim Moreno felt none of these things unsettled me. I'd cried plenty in the days after my husband died. Since then, nothing. I was in search of a good cry, but couldn't seem to find one.

"I'll let you know if I learn anything." I always like to leave the door open for a return visit.

His final words to me: "If He wills."

As I walked down the driveway, moonlight reflected off a large garden of white lilies.

CHAPTER 7

The Moreno house was just minutes from the Mall of America, so I stopped by to see how Garnett was adjusting to his first days on the job, and to fill him in on the chase.

The Mall of America put the Minneapolis suburb of Bloomington on the world retail map in 1992. More than 4 million square feet of entertainment and shopping space. Complete with an indoor amusement park and a giant aquarium stocked with sharks. Last Valentine's Day a couple even got married underwater, live on the *Today* show.

I couldn't help noticing the signs posted on the doors: MALL OF AMERICA BANS GUNS IN THESE PREMISES. Similar signs greet visitors of churches, restaurants, and other buildings throughout the state. Years ago Minnesota Republicans got a conceal-and-carry law through the legislature by burying it in a natural resources bill along with ice fishing, snowmobiling, and litter. Any establishment that didn't want armed customers posted the signs and hoped for the best.

Outside Garnett's office, twenty monitors for a hundred security cameras filled the wall. Not fuzzy black-and-white images like you see in banks and gas stations, but crisp color pictures as good as any police mug shot. Some screens were divided into quads, but the click of a mouse could bring any of them full screen and enlarge the image.

Two security guards monitored the monitors. One was a young black guy with muscles and attitude. The other guard had a gray balding head, like a Franciscan monk. They glanced up as I moved by, then returned to switching the screens from camera to camera. First a food court, then an escalator, then a parking ramp. I felt myself getting drowsy watching them.

"How do you keep from zoning out?" I asked them.

The older guy laughed. "Don't try to watch everything. Just watch for what don't belong."

"Like some of the juvies," the younger guy added.

In its early years, MOA had become a popular and convenient hangout for gangs because it was on the downtown bus lines and it was open late. Skirmishes became frequent; shoppers became nervous. Not wanting turf wars over Legoland, the mall had started a "safety policy." After four in the afternoon on Fridays and Saturdays, anyone under sixteen has to be accompanied by an adult.

"We spot 'em, we radio the bouncers." The young black guard waved an impressive walkie-talkie in my face. "Trouble spots are always up on screen."

He pointed to an eye-level row of monitors. One showed the area by Johnny Rockets restaurant. Another, just outside the Paul Bunyan flume ride. Others showed skyway entrances between the mall and parking ramps. "Most of the other cameras rotate through the screens, unless we see something that needs closer inspection."

The console in front of him looked like a video game board. He pushed a lever and a camera zoomed in close. Another lever shifted the scene sideways.

"Pay no attention to the man behind the curtain," Garnett said, as he walked up behind us.

"Frank Morgan, *The Wizard of Oz,* 1939," I replied. "The guys here were just giving me a behind-the-scenes tour."

"Don't give away all our secrets," he told them.

The rest of the administrative staff had gone home a few hours before. He ushered me into his office overlooking the roller coasters of what used to be called Camp Snoopy. Partially unpacked boxes filled one corner. Propped on a shelf, a plastic sign read REMEMBER, WE WORK FOR GOD, the motto for Practical Homicide Investigation. I recalled it from his desk at the cop shop.

"Better security than even the Indian casinos," he said. "And we need it. With a name like Mall of America, we're not only a tourist destination, we're a terrorist target. A symbol of conspicuous consumption in America's heartland. Wouldn't have half the problems I've got if they'd called it the Bloomington MegaMall."

"You probably wouldn't be making half the money you are either. I bet it's a nice bump from the public payroll." I noticed the suit and tie he wore were nicer than his usual wardrobe. Good enough for on air, even.

"Nice hours. Better benefits. Extra vacation. You might want to pick up an application on your way out, Riley."

"Come on, Nick, you know only TV can satisfy my ego," I teased him. "Really, you didn't take all your vacation as a cop, what makes you think you're going to take even more now?"

"Then I had a job I couldn't bear to leave. Now I've got a job I can't wait to leave."

"Then how come you're still here tonight?"

"Just getting the lay of the land so my instincts will kick in if I need them."

"A little while ago my instincts were telling me to stay far away from Susan Moreno's father." I briefed him on my encounters with the Susan families. Garnett knew the players; he'd met them years earlier when their anguish was rawest.

"I'm guessing Mr. Moreno wasn't terribly heartbroken when you told him his daughter was dead," I said.

"I thought he was nuts then, no reason to change my diagnosis now."

"Did you ever look at him as a suspect?"

"Yes. He is delusional, just the kind of guy who'd kill 'cause the voices told him to do it. No one could vouch for where he was that night. But when folks like him are pushed, they usually confess their sin. Remember, she'd also been sexually assaulted, and I just didn't see him good for that."

"How come you never told me about the Susan cases earlier?"

"There are lots of cases I never told you about. The chief didn't buy a connection, and I didn't have any proof to sell it otherwise."

"So you think the name and date might just be coincidence?"

"Might." He nodded. "Except there was one other thing that made these cases different. I'd be willing to connect the killings based simply on that."

"What?"

"The victims were re-dressed."

"Re-dressed?"

"Yeah, the killer put their clothes back on after."

I thought back to the crime scene photos and realized he was right. I wondered what else the file told him that my eyes had missed. "How unusual is that?" I asked.

"Different from most homicides I've worked."

"And why would he do something like that?"

"It could be part of his signature."

A signature is something a perpetrator feels compelled to do. It goes beyond what's necessary to commit the crime. Often it has a sexual component. Murderers change their MO as they learn better ways to kill, and better ways to stay ahead of the police. But signature may reflect an inner need they can't change. Signature can also be a clue that catches a killer.

"That re-dressing stuff wasn't in the news stories," I told him.

"We held it back as something only the real killer would know. It wasn't difficult; neither case got much publicity."

The brutal images from the file lingered in my mind. "But you're telling me and I'm a reporter."

"Yeah, I'm going to trust that you see the sense in keeping a few things off air. But I also want you to understand why my cop gut is telling me this is the same killer."

"Sometimes my reporter gut tells me things, too. What does the chief's gut say?" I asked.

"Police chiefs don't have cop guts. They're administrators. The last thing the chief wants is a serial killer on the Minneapolis chain of lakes. Most of the money in this city lives on that water. If our guy had been snatching victims from that neighborhood instead of dumping them there, we'd have heard a whole lot more commotion."

"So the chief isn't covering anything up; he just doesn't want to find evidence of a Susan killer?"

"He didn't encourage that direction of the investigation."

"Did he discourage it?"

"When he heard the addresses, he showed up at both crime scenes, Mayor Skubic by his side, probably to make sure the deceased wasn't a campaign contributor. Police procedure calls for as few folks behind the tape as necessary. Yet he VIPs them through, they get in our way, muck with the evidence. Their very presence could contaminate the crime scene and complicate the investigation."

"That's why you never let us reporters back there."

"Right. If anyone drops fibers or leaves a print, it's one more person to eliminate, and a sharp defense attorney can use it to embarrass us. The chief knows better; you don't see him out on location when it's a drive-by shooting in north Minneapolis."

"Bosses are hell in the field," I agreed. "But pragmatically, I still don't understand why any killer would take the time to put a victim's clothes back on."

"That's why it's so unusual," Garnett said. "Psychopaths often like to leave their victim naked. Accomplishes two things. Shocks whoever finds the body. Plus, as a practical matter, nudity cuts down on the amount of evidence they leave behind. If it were me, I'd have thrown the body, naked, in the lake. That takes care of fibers and hair evidence."

"So the killer was taking a risk. Why?"

"Might be trying to undo the violence. Restore the victim's dignity. I'm trained in reading evidence, not Freud. But if our unsub is a serialist, a profiler could have some insight. I'd say the perp was bolder the second time around. He didn't just dump the body. He displayed it. He propped it against a tree because he wanted it to be found, and quickly."

"But why?" I asked. "There're places within a half hour of here where a body would never be found. At least not until hunting season."

"Might be remorse. Maybe he wanted the body to have a proper funeral. Clearly, he felt comfortable in that neighborhood and didn't worry about attracting attention. If we play the odds, he's probably a decent-looking guy."

"How come?"

He shrugged. "Ugly serial killers have a harder time attracting victims."

"You're terrible."

"I'm not joking. Look at the stats. Look at their mug shots. But my hunch is that deep down, our unsub is a show-off."

"I thought you thought he was a cop."

"Cops are the ultimate show-offs," he answered. "Though that's not why I think he might be blue. Our guy left no DNA, nothing for the forensic team. Might suggest some familiarity with crime scenes. Could be on the processing end, like a cop, or could be on the receiving end, like a con."

"What does that mean?"

"Might have been questioned in an earlier crime, like rape. Might have had to give samples. Might have even spent time in prison. Might have learned how to be more careful next time."

I was absorbing this information, playing with it in my mind, as Garnett continued.

"There's another reason he might have a law enforcement connection." He lowered his voice. "The year after the second Susan, I set up an anniversary stakeout around Lake Calhoun. Waited all night with a couple of unmarked squads."

"And?" I pressed.

"Nothing. All quiet. Nobody died that night, at least not from foul play. But some of the guys at the local precinct were joking about it ahead of time, thought it was a waste of time. If the killer was one of us, he might have heard about the sting. Chief didn't think it was a good use of resources. After that, I kept it hush-hush."

"Hush-hush?"

"Every November 19, from midnight till dawn, I go on stakeout cruising the lakes. But not this year. This year, I'm retired."

"If this were an Agatha Christie book, you'd be the killer because you're the least likely suspect."

As Garnett smiled, he shrugged his shoulders. "Better check me out, Riley. Like I said, he might be a cop."

CHAPTER 8

SUSAN CHENOWITH 1991   SUSAN MORENO 1992
RE-DRESSED   RE-DRESSED

I had just written RE-DRESSED under both victims' names on the SUSAN charts the next morning when I heard my office door open. Noreen Banks stood there, unsmiling, her arms folded over her chest. She cleared her throat to ensure my complete attention.

The most disconcerting thing about having Noreen as my boss wasn't that she was younger, but that she was more attractive. Good-looking enough to be in front of a camera, or even behind an anchor desk. Black hair. White skin. Ruby lips. Stunning like Snow White, but with a heart like the Wicked Queen. Noreen must have sensed viewers would detect that flaw, so when a management job opened early in her career, she took that path and never looked back.

She had little tolerance for her reporters and anchors looking hagged out on the air; if she could look like a million bucks, so could the talent.

"Well, Riley Spartz, perhaps you'd like to tell me what you're working on?" She spoke in a staccato fashion, clipping each word like a TV remote control.

"A 40 share," I answered. Now I had her complete attention.

In TV news, a 40 share is the Super Bowl of ratings. It means 40 percent of the television sets being watched in your market are tuned to your story. I used to score the big four-oh a couple times a year, but with the increase in cable and satellite programming, along with online news, competition is intense, a 40 share scarce. Noreen looked understandably skeptical; while a Minnesota Vikings–Green Bay Packers football game could still deliver even a 60-share audience, holding those viewers through a newscast never happened.

"I heard you were shooting yesterday," she said. "You know I give you enormous latitude to chase leads, but when equipment and other staff are involved, I need to approve the story first. It's a question of resources."

"I understand completely." I spoke in my smoothest Miss Congeniality voice. "An opportunity came up yesterday, a family was willing to go on camera and I wanted to move fast before they changed their mind. I was hoping to catch you after the morning meeting."

I spent the next ten minutes bringing her up to speed on the Susan story, steering her through the characters, driving home the emotion. Five seconds later, she slammed the brakes on the whole thing.

"No. I don't like it."

"What? What's not to like? Come on, Noreen. It's got mystery, it's got suspense, it's got November written all over it."

November is one of the three major ratings months in television. Some folks call it "sweeps"; others call it

"The Book" and they're not talking about the Bible either. During those weeks, stations try to spike the numbers by heavily promoting exclusive stories. Higher ratings mean higher commercial rates. Ka-ching. Ka-ching.

"You know how I feel about showcasing senseless violence," she said. "It also seems dicey. You're always talking about how critical the first forty-eight hours are after a homicide, how if the police don't nail it by then, forget it. These cases are more than a decade old. It doesn't sound like the police even care anymore. Why should we?"

I didn't know whether to be more amazed that she actually remembered anything I said, or that she twisted my words to dismiss the Susans.

"Noreen, we should especially care in cases where the cops don't. So victims aren't forgotten. So justice has its day. I already have the story," I insisted, over and over. "This isn't a question of throwing a lot of time and money at something that might not make air. This cold case is hot. And it's ours."

I almost said mine. That would have blown it right there. I needed her to think of us as a team and I needed that to happen now. Once we moved to a formal story meeting with her minions, they would echo her objections, fawn over her decisions, and make it impossible for me to change her mind.

"This is the kind of story where we might take some heat from the cops, Noreen. I need you behind me.

Without your support, this story might go untold and families might be left without any closure. You're right, we shouldn't jump on it just because it's a ratings bonanza. But we shouldn't turn our back on it either because it might be difficult. There's a chance to do some good here."

My news director paused as if flipping a mental coin. Heads, do the right thing. Tails, do what's easy and uncontroversial.

"All right. All right." Noreen finally caved. "There probably are a lot of viewers named Susan. Good thing it's not something like Mildred or Priscilla. We'll slate it for the November book. There's still some open nights because most of the staff's been working on folos to the broken bridge, but frankly unless someone leaks something juicy, there's not enough fresh elements there to fill sweeps."

The biggest story in Minnesota history and I had sat it out. If I hadn't been depressed before, I certainly was then. Like viewers across the country, I'd watched the life-and-death stories of rescue and recovery unfold on live television, followed by finger-pointing and politics. Now it was a matter of waiting for the National Transportation Safety Board to determine the cause. Then the media could jump back into the blame game.

"You need to work on something besides this old murder case," Noreen continued. "I know you're just getting back, but I need you to turn more than one project for November."

"Absolutely." I reverted to my smooth Miss Congeniality voice. "I'll make some calls and work up a list of story ideas by the end of the day."

"Actually, Riley, I already have an idea for you."

This couldn't be good. Noreen was a desk head, meaning she had little experience in the field, thus no idea of what it really took to get a story on the air.

"I was going through the tip calls," she continued.

This could only be bad. I knew what kinds of calls came in on the station tip line: neighbors yelling about barking dogs, old ladies complaining about kids knocking over garbage cans, a whole lot of he said/she said from shoppers who didn't save their receipts.

I tried a subtle evasion tactic. "I hate to just swoop in and take the good tips before any of the other reporters get a chance."

"Don't worry," Noreen said. "I checked with them and they're too busy, so it's all yours."

"Thanks." *I'll bet they're too busy,* I thought as I practiced my closemouthed smile. I'll bet they turned it down because they knew a dog when they smelled one. "What is it?"

"A man took his dog to be cremated and thinks he didn't get the right ashes back. See what you can find out. Do some undercover sting or something. Put them to the test. You love those kinds of stories."

"You want me to kill someone's pet as part of a consumer test?"

"No. That would be bad for the station's image. It's

traumatic for an owner when a pet dies, so if someone's deceiving people, we need to put a stop to it. You're the reporter, you figure it out."

She handed me a computer printout of story tips. One circled in red. Name. Phone. Something about a dog. I promised to get right on it.

"There's something else we need to discuss," Noreen said. "Please come with me."

Ominous. I followed her through the newsroom, past the assignment desk to her fishbowl office with the glass walls on each side to allow the troops to see, but not hear, her hard at work. That didn't stop those outside the glass from trying to read the lips, facial expressions, and body language of those inside the glass. So I put on my poker face, took a chair across from her desk, folded my hands on my lap, and waited for her to begin.

"This is an important ratings book for the station, but it's also an important ratings book for Riley Spartz. I want to remind you that your contract is up in ninety days."

That explained why she wanted me on her turf for this conversation. I was glad I was wearing makeup.

"Under the contract terms, I have to notify you at this point whether or not we intend to re-sign you."

My contract was not the standard TV news boiler-plate. It was a four-year deal negotiated by Noreen's predecessor, who valued investigative stories above all others. What he viewed as a shrewd move to prevent me from jumping to the competition, she viewed as a sweetheart deal.

My contract kept me out of the clutches of the newsroom assignment desk and put me in a special projects unit where I worked on longer, high-impact stories. That meant, unless the sky was falling, I didn't have to chase storm clouds or liquor store holdups and I didn't have to report live shots on the first day back to school. It was the difference between being a pawn on a chessboard and being a bishop. Oops, the queen was speaking.

"We do intend to renegotiate, but I want to be clear that I can't offer you the same contract in terms of money or assignment. We're looking at changing direction here at Channel 3."

Do not think about this now, I told myself. Think about something else. Think about whiskers on kittens. No, I reconsidered, that's probably what Noreen was thinking about. So I thought about a 40 share instead, thanked her for letting me know where she stood, and walked outside for some fresh air.

CHAPTER 9

Law enforcement widows are well provided for, so while I didn't need Channel 3's paycheck, I needed the job just the same. Since I didn't have anyone to come home to, work was a reason not to come home.

I realized that I'd been a widow almost as long as I'd been a wife.

Plenty of women in this world are prettier, smarter, and sexier than I am. But I'm a good package. My single days had stretched on—not because I was short on men—but because I was short on time. A loose woman on a tight schedule, that was me. Dinner dates fell victim to spot news. I was desperately seeking love at first sight, and it just wasn't happening. I was beginning to write off the whole concept as an urban myth.

I wound up marrying Hugh Boyer because I was afraid to fly.

I'd known Boyer on the beat for a few years. Our paths had crossed on several road tragedies where I watched him reduce twisted metal to math and assign blame. Like a truck driver who dozed off after too many hours behind the wheel. Or a teen who hit the brakes too late because of a cell phone call. Even a cop who collided with a day care van during a high-speed chase. Boyer gave answers to families in grief.

We were friendly, sometimes flirty, but there was no simmering undercurrent of longing. I'm not sure why not. I know women who would have deliberately driven into a speed trap just for a chance to meet a tall, lean law enforcement machine like Hugh Boyer.

Certainly Hugh posed a conflict of interest professionally. Journalists aren't supposed to get involved with people we might end up covering as news. But I could have rationalized my way around that. After all, ethics didn't stop me from ultimately marrying the guy. I think I was just too busy writing scripts, taping stand-ups, and doing live shots to imagine him without his uniform. My day was spent on deadline; by night, I was dead tired.

"These skid marks tell the story," I once explained to viewers, as I knelt in the center lane of a busy blacktop road while traffic whizzed uncomfortably close to me and the camera.

As I started enterprising my own stories, the car crashes got handed off to rookies. I hadn't seen Boyer for more than a year. Fate in the form of a late-night 911 call brought us together.

"I've . . . I've been hit by a deer . . . I mean I hit a deer," I sobbed to the emergency operator from my cell phone.

One minute I was driving, okay speeding, down Highway 96 near Dellwood. The next minute I had venison frying on the hood of my car. My windshield shattered, a hoof hit me in the shoulder, and the deer's head stuck through the glass on the passenger side. My attacker had antlers, so I knew I'd landed a buck. The deer shuddered and thrashed a couple times, then was still.

I gave my location over the phone, then touched my face. Sticky. Blood from the broken glass. Thousands of Minnesota motorists hit deer each year; hundreds are injured; a handful killed. Belted in, I wasn't badly hurt, but I was as freaked out as I had ever been because the deer seemed to be staring accusingly into my eyes.

Boyer was the closest unit, so he was dispatched to "assist hysterical motorist who hit deer."

I struggled to open the door because my hands were slippery. I fell out of the car and tumbled into a muddy ditch just as Boyer pulled up. He parked his squad car so the headlights shone in my direction, then rushed over, helping me to my feet. I started crying harder and he held me tight until I calmed.

"I'm bloody," I apologized. As I looked up, we recognized each other. It should have been one of those magic moments when two people become one in the moonlight. But then he opened his mouth, and not to kiss me, either.

"Want me to call a tow truck or a camera?" He had an annoying habit of thinking he was funny when he wasn't. "Did you get the license plate on that deer?"

"Shut up, Boyer." I pushed him away. Now I was steady, no longer shaky. "Good thing you're a cop 'cause you couldn't make it as a comedian."

"Good thing I got thick skin. Thick as deer hide." He whistled when he saw the size of the stag. "Nice rack," he said. "The deer. Don't want any complaints about comments offensive to women."

"None taken," I said, stiffly. "Just get Bambi off my car."

He counted the antler tips one at a time. "Wow. A ten-pointer. Drivers are allowed to keep a deer if they hit it. Nice trophy. Good eating."

His eyes sparkled at the prospect, but I didn't want to see a deer ever again. Dead or alive. The idea of consuming my attacker was revolting.

"Don't have to decide right now." He opened his trunk and unrolled a tarp. "I'll write you out a possession permit." I turned away when I saw him take out a large hunting knife to gut the animal. "You can think it over."

He hoisted the deer onto his shoulders and dumped it in back. Slammed the lid. Turned to me and said, "Maybe we ought to stop at the ER and have you checked out."

Boyer let me ride shotgun, but wouldn't turn on the lights, even though I asked politely. While he radioed to have my car towed to a body shop, I called the station to explain my vehicle versus venison encounter and let them know I wouldn't be in the next day. The emergency room doctor gave me two stitches over my left eyebrow, determined I had no concussion, and then sent me home to rest. It was past midnight when Boyer and I pulled into my driveway.

"Thanks, Boyer. I'd ask you in for coffee, but you probably have miles to patrol before you sleep."

"Actually, I got off a couple hours ago."

"Above and beyond. Now I feel guilty. You definitely deserve coffee."

"I didn't have anywhere I needed to be."

"Do you have anywhere you need to be now?"

He followed me inside to the kitchen. We both grabbed a Summit beer from the fridge and headed for the living room. He admired my painting of a bare-breasted mermaid hanging over the fireplace and I admired his gun. I hit the gas switch for flames and was rewarded with instant atmosphere. Between laughs and liquor we became entangled on the couch.

The fire shone on our faces, and for the second time that night we had a chance at a Hollywood moment. This time, instead of saying something stupid, he kissed me. And I kissed back. Forget love at first sight, this was love at first . . . well, touch.

I SHOOK HIM awake early the next morning and made him move his patrol car a half mile away so my neighbor Mrs. Fredericks wouldn't think I was sleeping with a cop.

"Let's do something this weekend." He put his arms around my waist as I stood at the kitchen counter buttering toast.

"I'm out of town," I replied. "Investigative reporters' conference in Las Vegas."

His disappointment seemed genuine, and that cheered me.

"It really is a lot of work once you get there, but it's the getting there that's the hardest part."

"Need a ride to the airport?" he asked.

"What I might need is to have you put me on the plane at gunpoint. But I suppose airline security might have a problem with that."

He raised an eyebrow, but said nothing, and because he didn't ask, I told. It wasn't like I had anything to be ashamed of—lots of people hate to fly. With great difficulty, I can get on a commercial airliner. As for a small single-engine plane, forget it. This fear means I'm not network material. On a clear day I get that my career is more likely to crash and burn because of my phobia than I am to crash and burn because of an airplane malfunction. But most days I'm not that clearheaded. In network news, competitive advantage often comes down to how fast the assignment desk can get someone to the scene of a breaking story. If you're a reporter for one of the big three, you spend more time in the air than on the air.

"I'll drive you," he said.

"Thanks, but it's an early-morning flight. I'll just take a cab."

"No, I mean I'll drive you to Vegas."

We left the next morning. Four days later we were husband and wife.

CHAPTER 10

I walked a couple miles through downtown Minneapolis, lingering at the farmers' market on Nicollet Mall. Squash, potatoes, and other fall food beckoned from the small booths. I continued through Loring Park, savoring the crisp Indian summer weather before heading back to Channel 3. I slipped in the security desk entrance to avoid walking past Noreen's office, since being blind wasn't one of her shortcomings.

Once again, I faced the SUSAN chart, as if staring at it long enough might produce physical evidence linking the two murders.

I'm experienced enough to concede that what I was searching for might not exist.

I unloaded the interview videotapes of Susan Chenowith's parents from my black bag so I could log them later in the day. For daily news stories it's much faster to just pull a sound bite and drop it into the script. For investigative stories, I like to transcribe each interview verbatim, because sometimes something crucial hinges on a remark that didn't seem significant at the time.

I pulled the raincoat photo her mother had given me from my notebook. So this is what Susan Chenowith wore the last time she left home. I added the picture to her homicide file, then stopped, a bit puzzled. She wasn't wearing a raincoat in the crime scene photos. Wrong Susan. The raincoat was on the second Susan's body. Side by side, the coats looked identical, but the style—tan, knee length, belted—was commonplace.

RAINCOAT? I wrote on the wall chart.

"LET ME GET this straight." Garnett paused on the other end of the phone line. "You think the unsub took a raincoat off the first victim and put it on the second victim one year later?"

"Maybe."

"Too wild. You'd have to be talking about a perp with the sophistication of the Zodiac Killer."

Every homicide cop in America knew about the Zodiac, the killer who took credit for seventeen murders in California in the late 1960s. He taunted police and media with dozens of letters containing codes and a trademark salutation: "This is the Zodiac speaking . . ." While the crimes appeared random, the killer insisted he picked his victims based on their astrological signs. Evil and elusive, the Zodiac was never captured. The cases were never cleared.

"It's the first possibility of physical evidence linking the cases," I said. "Maybe the killer wants us to know. Remember the show-off factor you were pushing?"

"Show-offs aren't that subtle. He'd be much more in our face. The raincoat can't be proven. We aren't dealing with first graders whose mamas write their names inside their clothes."

"Where would the raincoat be today?"

"Homicide case? No statute of limitations? In the property room. That stuff is saved forever."

"Can you get me in to see it?"

"I'm off the force," he argued. "You'll have to take it up with Chief Capacasa, and lots of luck there. He's an amateur chess champion, so he's always a move ahead of everyone."

"Well, eventually he'll know about the story because I'll need an interview. So I guess it's sooner rather than later."

"Later is better. Do some more legwork before you start pissing off the top brass."

"All right, I won't head for the cop shop yet, but when I get there, I'm going to mean business."

"Fine," Garnett said. "I suspect these cases can't be cleared unless you figure out whether there's a significance to the name and date. November 19 clearly means something to him. It might be a stressor connected to his past. And who was Susan? A girlfriend who dumped him? A mother who didn't love him? If the victims were not random, these were not simply crimes of opportunity. That means these women were preselected. Stalked."

"Give me cop talk. You know how I love cop talk. What else would that tell you about the killer?"

Garnett paused before answering. "That he's

disciplined. An annual kill seems to satisfy him. That's a long cooling off period between crimes. And he didn't overkill his victims either. He used enough force to get the job done. Mission accomplished. No mutilation. No frenzy. That might suggest he wasn't emotionally involved with them. Probably views women as objects. Disposable."

"Ish," I groaned. "Don't give me cop talk anymore."

I DOUBLE-CHECKED my list of loose ends and focused on Susan Moreno's old boyfriend, Sam Fox, her tattoo namesake. Being in jail the night of her murder proved he didn't do it, but that didn't mean he might not have an inkling neither he nor the cops had appreciated back then. I e-mailed Fox's name and date of birth to Xiong and asked for a full background check.

Then I dialed Susan Chenowith's parents. Tina answered the phone on the first ring. I'd assured them I would stay in touch, but neither of us expected my next call to be this soon or about such an odd query.

"The brand of her raincoat?" She repeated my question. "Actually I do know. It was a London Fog. She bought it used at the Salvation Army store on Nicollet. I remember she paid four dollars. It looked practically new. You'd be surprised all the nice things people donate there. After your visit my husband and I even discussed taking some of her things there. It feels like it might be time."

I asked her to hold on to their daughter's things just

a little while longer—until after the story ran. I couldn't risk their giving away potential clues, and I couldn't judge what might end up being important.

Xiong must have had light duty that day, because he'd already sent me the information on Sam Fox by the time I hung up on Tina.

Fox, who'd had a history of drugs, alcohol, and petty crime right up to the night of his Susan's death, hadn't been arrested since. If he was currently in a Minnesota prison, there should be one more arrest. My first hunch was that he had moved out of state and I might need to appeal to Garnett to have one of his buddies run an NCIC for me, since only cops can access the national crime database. But as I paged through the file, it hit me that Fox might have accomplished the impossible: he might have gone straight.

Turns out, he had a valid Minnesota driver's license, owned an older model Nissan, worked at the Best Buy in Brooklyn Center, and held title to a small house in Richfield with a woman named, eerily enough, Susan Fox.

THE BEST BUY telephone operator confirmed it. "Sure, Sam Fox is working today. He'd be happy to help you." She assumed I wished to buy a new stereo or refrigerator from my favorite sales guy—especially since I didn't mention my name or television affiliation.

I didn't spot him right away when I entered the

store. He looked older and cleaner than his mug shot. He was losing his hair in the front and wore a Best Buy polo shirt with a nametag reading SAM. I also noticed a ring on his left hand.

Sam worked in home electronics. He was disappointed to find out I worked in television news, and that I was not there to purchase a sixty-inch HDTV screen with 1080p resolution, even though they had a great sale going on and an attractive financing plan.

"I'm here to talk about Susan Moreno."

His eyes appeared puzzled, like he'd forgotten his old girlfriend from the streets. He took a step backward and bumped into a DVD display of the latest Harry Potter movie.

"I know she's a name from the past," I continued, "but she used to be important to you."

"I know who she is," he answered. "But I don't know why you're here."

"I'm working on a story about her death. Looking for justice. Trying to make sure murders aren't forgotten by the police or the public."

"I haven't forgotten her."

"That's good, but you probably haven't thought of her in a while."

He laughed with a snort and rolled up his shirt sleeve to unveil a matching tattoo: Sam ♥ Susan.

"My wife thinks I got it for her. Early in the courtship. Because I knew she was the one. Who can fight fate? And you better not rat me out, either."

"Don't worry," I told him, "it's not the kind of thing I need to put in the story."

As we walked down the TV aisles, he talked about Susan Moreno. Much of what he told me I'd already read in the police report, but some was new. Like how she had rebelled to try to shatter her father's indifference. Or how she had looked for love on the streets that she was denied at home. And how the two of them had planned to start a splendid life together, just as soon as they got straight.

Her life ended before that could happen.

When the cops told him about her murder, he told me he had vowed to keep that pledge. I complimented him, sincerely, not just reporter shtick. After all, he lost his love and pulled himself together. I lost my love and fell apart.

But nothing he said seemed to contain any motive or clue about her murder. Occasionally he and his girl had grabbed a bite to eat at Peter's Grill, the same diner where Susan Chenowith worked. But that seemed to be stretching things, since most folks, including me, who live or work in downtown Minneapolis are also regulars. Even President Clinton ordered lunch there on one of his trips through town. (A Canadian bacon and egg sandwich, Coke, vegetable soup, and apple pie. Now known on the menu as the "Clinton Special.")

I referred to a short list of questions I had scribbled beforehand in case I got only one chance at Sam. "Do you think her father might have killed her?"

"Nope. Too much bother for him. He'd have pre-ferred to let the Lord sit in judgment of her."

"Most likely a john then?"

He flushed, embarrassed at his former girlfriend's occupation. "She kept telling me she was going to stop. Trick gone bad—I know that's what the cops think hap-pened. But she was savvy. I never believed it."

I showed him a crime scene photo of the raincoat with his girlfriend's head tastefully cropped off. He didn't react.

"Did she ever wear a coat like this?" I asked.

"Not that I ever knew. Why?"

"It's what she was wearing when the police found her body."

"I've never seen it before. Did it belong to the killer?"

"I'm not sure, but it's definitely a woman's coat."

"Could her killer have been a woman?"

I shrugged and we left it at that. Sam Fox was the kind of knucklehead Noreen would bemoan my wast-ing time or lunch on. News directors prefer that reporters wine and dine top-level sources, because they think the investment is more likely to pay off with top-rated stories. They don't realize the invisible bum on the street corner sees plenty. Cops understand this, and have long cultivated a diverse array of nitwit snitches. So as part of my knucklehead outreach pro-gram, I gave Sam a business card with my cell phone number, and he promised to call me if he remembered anything interesting, as long as I promised never to call his house.

I felt a little better knowing someone had wept for Susan Moreno.

FRANKLIN AVENUE IS six miles of diversity linking Minneapolis and St. Paul. Called the Twin Cities, they're not identical twins: Minneapolis, corporate; St. Paul, quirky. Franklin Avenue used to be a main thoroughfare, passing through rough neighborhoods and rich neighborhoods, until Interstate 94 cut neighborhoods out of most commutes.

Vice cop Pete Terrell let me ride in the back of his undercover car while he pointed out the place where he had last seen Susan Moreno on November 19, 1992. It was one of the rougher stretches of Franklin Avenue.

"Sounds like a long time ago," I told him. "What do you remember about that night?"

Malik rode in the front videotaping our conversation. I'd set up the ride-along with the police department in the guise of researching vice. I had waited until dark because I wanted the video to match the time frame when Susan had disappeared. Casually, I had asked Terrell whether he'd ever been involved in any murder investigations.

"I wouldn't remember most hookers ten years later, but when she showed up dead the next morning, it did kinda stick in my mind. Yep. I kept thinking she traded her life to avoid a night in jail. Wrong choice."

"What was she wearing when you stopped her?"

"Slutty street outfit. Short and tight. That's what sells."

"How about a raincoat?"

"Raincoat?" he asked. "I'm not following you. It wasn't raining that night."

I already knew that because I had one of the station meteorologists check the National Weather Service records.

"Was she wearing a raincoat anyway?"

"No. That would defeat the purpose." He spoke slowly as if talking to a child. "Hookers don't wear raincoats. If she'd had a raincoat on, I wouldn't have given her a second look and neither would any john."

I caught a glimpse of myself in Terrell's rearview mirror. Ugh. No one would give me a second look either. Splotchy skin, snarly hair. Definitely a long day. Good thing Noreen wasn't around to see me.

MALIK WANTED TO grab a late dinner at the Black Forest, an old German restaurant a few miles from the station. I craved their spaetzle and cheese casserole so it seemed as good a time as any to brainstorm story logistics.

Malik brought his camera inside with him and set it on a chair at our table. Channel 3 had recently reverted to unmarked vehicles after a string of break-ins and equipment thefts. The head of the promotion department bemoaned the loss of station logos displayed as our vehicles traveled around the state, but our photo chief insisted that the only thing marked vehicles advertised was that expensive camera equipment was kept inside.

I ordered a glass of white wine from the Rhine Valley and Malik called for a St. Pauli Girl Beer. We discussed how best to visualize the Susan story, and we agreed he would swing by both grave sites the next day and shoot the names and dates on the markers. Thirty seconds of b-roll was better than nothing, and I knew he'd come back with creative and artsy shots we could dissolve-edit between to create mystery.

"It's good to be working together again." Malik raised his glass. "I heard you were off writing a book."

That was a rumor I had started to explain my absence from Channel 3, and to keep other rumors from spreading. I'd been in a physical tailspin. Anyone with eyes could have seen that. What I wanted to keep under wraps was the psychological effect of the Iron Range firebomb. "Nope, just chilling."

"Cut the shit, Riley. So you needed some time to sort things out. You're back now. You're among friends. Lean on us if you need to."

I regretted not having returned his calls while I was off. Malik Rahman was an all-American nice guy who, during recent years, had been frequently mistaken for a terrorist—especially when he was videotaping exteriors of federal buildings, like the FBI office in downtown Minneapolis. His mother had never traveled outside the state, but had married a man from Pakistan while they were students at the University of Minnesota.

"Missy wants you to come over for dinner some night."

Malik had married his high school sweetheart after serving a short stint as a video photographer in the U.S. Army shooting propaganda films for the military. His wife and their two kids waited for him each night after the news. Suppertime. Bath time. Bedtime. Ratings months played havoc with their suburban bliss, but Missy swapped whatever overtime he racked up for a new household appliance. This month, he explained, she had her eye on a new clothes dryer. Let the long hours begin.

"Hey, I ran into Noreen after our shoot yesterday," he told me. "She wanted to know what I was out on. Hope that didn't create trouble."

"No more than I should have expected. My contract's coming up and she's playing wicked witch."

"She'll fold once she gets a chance to see you in action. Unfortunately, she came on board the station just before you were going under. But I have a feeling about this story. Let's not settle for the hack version. Let's break some real news."

So that's what we toasted to. Breaking news.

MALIK PULLED INTO the driveway next to my house, a small English tudor in the Tangletown neighborhood of south Minneapolis. Stately, well-maintained houses set on curvy streets lined with mature oak trees. A harvest moon shone overhead. A perfect autumn night.

"Ever think of selling?" he asked. Mine was the smallest house on the block, one street over from a bus stop, and would likely net multiple offers the first day of listing. I bought it four years ago when I signed my last contract. Since then the housing market had skyrocketed, and I already had six figures of equity. Cashing out would be simple, and starting fresh might be smart.

"Can't leave. Too many memories."

"Must be bad memories. Keeping you up at night. You look like crap."

"The good ones make the bad ones worth it."

As Malik drove off I allowed myself the indulgence of reliving a good one as I walked toward the door, fallen leaves crunching under my feet. I'd always considered carrying the bride over the threshold a corny tradition. "The neighbors will laugh," I had told Boyer. I pivoted away, keeping the pile of suitcases on the sidewalk between us. "Just carry the luggage."

"Why? You afraid they might think we're married?"

A fairly traditional guy, Boyer didn't realize he was marrying a fairly untraditional gal, until moments before we said "I do."

"What do you mean there's not going to be any Mrs. Boyer?" He had noticed me writing "Riley Spartz" on the marriage license. "It's who I am." I gave him a quick kiss on the lips. "It doesn't mean I won't love, honor, and cherish you."

"Aren't you supposed to obey me?"

"That's not part of the vows anymore."

"Well, I better never catch you using the name Mrs. Hugh Boyer undercover to sting anyone."

Definitely a marriage mismatch, so why did we do it? How does that song go? Something about getting married in a fever . . .

"Maybe I can't make you call yourself Mrs. Boyer, but you're not going over that threshold without me."

He chased me around the yard, scooped me up in his arms, and proceeded up the porch steps in triumph. He planted a deep kiss on my mouth before waving to Mrs. Fredericks who was watching from her window.

CHAPTER 11

Last night I dreamt I went to Manderley again."

Just kidding, but I did dream incredibly vivid dreams of my years with Boyer, complete with color, touch, and sound. When my alarm woke me at seven, I opened my eyes and thought, "What would Daphne du Maurier do?"

If she had written *Susan* instead of *Rebecca,* the tale would hinge on a terrible secret.

If Agatha Christie had told the story, red herrings would distract the reader from the truth.

As I lay in bed I fantasized being Sherlock Holmes in a silk smoking jacket, without the silly pipe. Whether I possessed the intellectual heft and deductive reasoning of Sir Arthur Conan Doyle's legendary detective remained questionable, but a girl can dream.

"Elementary, my dear Noreen." My accent needed work. Most people don't realize Holmes's creator never wrote his trademark quip. That dialogue actually came from an old movie.

Then, in an unwelcome twist, E. C. Bentley's hapless gentleman sleuth came to mind so I prayed, "Just don't let me end up like Philip Trent and get it all wrong."

Scholars consider *Trent's Last Case,* written in 1913, the first modern mystery novel. A wealthy financier is murdered at his country estate and Philip Trent, a bungling newspaper reporter, cracks the case . . . or so he thinks, until the final pages when the perpetrator sets him straight over dinner.

I sympathized with Trent. As a journalist, I lacked a novelist's freedom. I was bound by facts. "Just the facts, ma'am," as Garnett would say, quoting Dan Aykroyd in *Dragnet*, 1987. The movie, not the old TV series. Me, I'm more of a bookworm, but since so much of what the studios put on the big screen springs from the pages of best sellers, I'm an ample match for his challenges.

I'd converted one of my guest rooms into a library with walls of fiction and nonfiction. My favorite shelves housed what I called my "dusty books," best sellers from yesteryear. None is a first edition, but each is a first in its own way, a pioneer in a specific genre or storytelling technique. Published in 1841, Edgar Allan Poe's "The Murders in the Rue Morgue" is literature's first locked-room mystery. *The Moonstone,* written by Wilkie Collins in 1868, takes its place as the first detective novel. Agatha Christie's *The Murder of Roger Ackroyd* was significant in 1926 as the first murder mystery in which the narrator "did it."

My literary interests are wider than crime; I admire the imagination and influence of any breakthrough author. My collection includes the first science fiction novel, *From the Earth to the Moon,* written by Jules Verne in 1865; as well as the first western, *The Virgin-*

ian, written by Owen Wister in 1902. I glanced over to my bed stand and saw my current read, *The Castle of Otranto,* by Horace Walpole. Published in 1764, it's the world's first gothic novel. If nightmares find me, look no further.

I showered, dressed, and brought the *Star Tribune* inside. I skimmed the headlines on the front page and Metro section, but didn't see much that wasn't on the budget yesterday for our late news.

I poured a cup of black coffee, put a bagel in the toaster, and logged on to my computer to check my e-mail before leaving for work. I opened a message from my computer guy, Lee Xiong, downloaded the attachment, and found a death certificate, dated the year before my first dead Susan.

Susan Redding. November 19, 1990. Duluth, Minnesota. Homicide. Strangled.

DULUTH IS A couple hours north of the Twin Cities if you drive fast. And because it was all freeway, I drove fast. Very fast.

I called the Duluth Police from my cell phone. Bingo. The case investigator still worked there. "Why are you calling about Susan Redding?" he asked. "That's a long time back."

"Long story. And it's going to take more time to explain than I'm comfortable going into while driving and talking on a cell phone. Can I fill you in when I get there?" That explanation, plus my bad connection, with the added bonus that I was buying lunch, satisfied him for the moment.

Malik sprawled out in the backseat asleep for the last forty minutes. He had learned to nap on demand in the military, a skill I envied. During sweeps, he liked to bank sleep when he could because he knew of the toll the edit booth would take on him later in the month.

I don't mind driving the station's minivan. I enjoy sitting up high on the road and I'm not bothered that my wheels look like a mom mobile. It's roomy, anonymous, and good for surveillance. A woman in a minivan parked in a residential neighborhood attracts less suspicion than a man, particularly if the vehicle has dark glass. Sometimes I even put cleats and shin guards in the front and a car seat in the back to complete the soccer mom ruse. And I'm not above borrowing a niece or nephew if I need a child prop.

"Are we almost there yet?" a groggy voice called from behind.

"Twenty minutes," I assured Malik. "We're closing in on lunch."

"I want walleye."

"Then you shall have it."

Walleye is Minnesota's official state fish, but ironically most of the walleye consumed in Minnesota is actually shipped in from Canada. A while back I'd done a Channel 3 investigation that found that much of what restaurants bill as walleye is really zander, a less desirable fillet. The outcome didn't matter much to me, since I don't like fish. But viewers apparently do, because the story got great numbers and even a mention on the front page of the Minneapolis newspaper.

I told Malik we'd be dining with one of Duluth's finest in the hope of getting some inside info on their Susan investigation. We needed to build a relationship with him, because cops typically distrust outsiders, and the media even more so. While we were in town, we also needed to shoot cover.

"Better to overshoot than undershoot." I passed a road sign reading DULUTH 19 MILES. "Especially since we're not sure where this fits in."

He nodded. "Nice daylight. Let's tape the cop interview outside, if he'll do it. I hope he's wearing his uniform."

"Viva Las Vegas" played on the radio and I flashed back to my honeymoon road trip three years earlier.

"Bright light city gonna set my soul . . . Gonna set my soul on fire." To my delight, Boyer did a fairly good imitation of the King.

Seventeen hundred miles with a man you've really known only a couple days is usually a bad idea. I'd won the skirmish over luggage because I needed clothes for work and play. After all, I reminded him, this was a business trip.

He won the next round at the car rental counter. Since I still had a deer-shaped dent on the hood of my Jetta, I'd rented a vehicle with unlimited mileage.

"What kind of car?" Boyer asked.

"Midsized," I answered.

"You don't even know what kind of car? Hell, it's probably your father's Oldsmobile."

"The problem being?" I asked. Yes, my tone was huffy.

"The problem being I'm not driving a Ford Taurus to Vegas."

The car rental agent intuitively understood the needs of a man who puts fifty thousand miles on a Crown Vic each year in the line of duty. They discussed Land Rovers versus Jaguars before settling on a Ford Mustang convertible. After all, Boyer reminded me, this was a vacation.

A global positioning system was mounted under the dash. Neither of us had used a GPS before. I typed in the conference hotel address.

"Right turn in one quarter of a mile," the car told us in a monotone computer chick voice. About fifteen seconds later, it continued, "Right turn approaching."

"Don't need that," Boyer said.

"Turn now," the car demanded, as we prepared to turn south onto Interstate 35.

"Shut up," he told the car. "All I need to know is we drive south for a few hours, then west for a whole lot more."

"Hey, check this out," I said. The GPS had computerized yellow pages for all major cities. Hotels. Restaurants. Gas stations. We could even store and recall previous addresses and routes. "This way we can find our way home again."

"Sure thing, Gretel. GPS is the new bread crumbs."

Suddenly Malik and I were in Duluth and I left visions of Vegas behind.

From the south, our first glimpse of Duluth was a magnificent aerial view after the road climbs onto a hill overlooking the port city. Duluth, the largest inland seaport in the world, used to be the shipping gateway for the iron ore industry. Now grain has replaced iron as the primary export. Our next impression was an unsightly maze of freeway overpasses as we drove into town. But whenever I reach the shore of Lake Superior, I'm always dazzled. Looking over the greatest of the Great Lakes is like looking over an ocean. No wonder Superior is immortalized in poems like *The Song of Hiawatha* and songs like "The Wreck of the Edmund Fitzgerald."

I turned the van into Canal Park, the city's showcase waterfront designed with walking and bike paths, a small lighthouse, Lake Superior Marine Museum, and an aerial lift bridge to let large ships and barges pass. I parked in front of Grandma's Saloon & Grill. Great food, but the restaurant is best known for sponsoring a scenic North Shore marathon that delivers nine thousand hungry and thirsty runners to its door fifty yards from the finish line each June.

Lieutenant Dexter Finholt was examining the trademark antique bric-a-brac that decorated the walls of Grandma's when we entered. He was in uniform and Malik carried a camera, so they sized each other up immediately. I introduced myself.

"That so?" he said. "How'd you get a name like Riley?"

I was used to the question. I explained that my parents had promised my great-grandfather that if I was a boy they'd name me after him. I turned out to be a girl, but they bent the rules because his health had so deteriorated in the months before my birth it became clear I was the only great-grandchild he would ever hold.

"I don't remember him," I said. "But there are lots of pictures of us taking naps together."

Malik and I settled comfortably into a booth with the lieutenant and they ordered the walleye shore lunch while I went for a cajun chicken and wild rice specialty. Then we turned to the subject of Susan.

"Well, Lieutenant Finholt," I began, "like I said on the phone—"

"Call me Lieutenant Dex," he said. "Duluth's a small town compared to where you're from. We're a little more laid-back."

"Sure. Thanks, Lieutenant Dex. The story is a bit convoluted, maybe even crazy."

"Crazy is what she does best," Malik interrupted. "Followed by convoluted." I kicked him under the table even though I knew he was just trying to loosen up our lunch guest.

Lieutenant Dex laughed, but I was about to find out the joke was on me. "We sure don't get as many murders as you do down in the Cities, that's for sure. What makes this one so special you're all the way up here after so long?"

"We're following a possible pattern. Name, date,

mode of death." I gave him a thumbnail sketch on my two Susans. "We're here to look at whether your killer might be our killer."

"Nope. You've come a long way for nothing."

"How can you be so sure?"

"All right, let's review the facts. The first Minneapolis murder happened the year after ours. The second, two years later. Right?"

I nodded.

"That seals it for me," he said. "Our killer's doing life in Oak Park Heights State Prison. Our investigation's long over."

My fork froze in midair and my voice cracked in midsentence. "Are you sure you got the right man?"

"You betcha," he laughed. "This was a pretty straightforward case. They can't all be as complicated as the Congdon murders."

He was referring to Duluth's most famous homicide, the death of the elderly Elisabeth Congdon, more than thirty years ago. What initially appeared to be a bungled burglary ended up being a scheme to speed up an inheritance from the wealthiest woman in the state.

While that case possessed so many twists and turns even Court TV couldn't resist the story, Lieutenant Dex insisted that his Susan murder was open and shut. "Opened a cell and shut the door."

"Did he confess?" I asked.

"Nope, but they don't usually. We made a strong circumstantial case."

I should have known this information before we hit the road. It reminded me that I wasn't quite at the top of my game. Instead of spending a few hours researching the case, I had assumed it was unsolved. Malik gave me a look. If we'd been alone, he'd have given me the lecture I'd given him many a time, drummed into my head by a University of St. Thomas journalism professor: When you assume, you make an ass out of you and me. To get the point, it helps to write it out on a blackboard: ass u me.

"I'll make it simple, here's what happened," Lieutenant Dex continued. "Susan Redding was strangled in her home by her lover. Friends of both told us there had been tension because he wanted her to leave her husband. She apparently enjoyed a little on the side, but also enjoyed the lifestyle that came from being a doctor's wife. Jury came back the same day. Guilty as charged."

"Did you check out the husband?"

"You betcha. Airtight. A local psychiatrist, down in Minneapolis doing some consulting work for the county at the time of the murder. Goes down a couple days each month and picks up some of their patient load. His alibi holds. Didn't even know about the affair till we told him. Pretty devastated. Yep he was."

We taped a brief interview outside, with Lieutenant Dex standing in front of his squad car with downtown Duluth in the background, but we weren't sure if it would ever hit air. I rode back to the cop shop with him, while Malik drove around town taping skyline shots, the lift bridge, exteriors of the crime scene, and the cemetery headstone. Since the case was closed, there was no problem getting a copy of the police reports. Next I walked to the St. Louis County courthouse and had the clerk of court copy much of the trial file while I left Garnett a voice message about my wasted day. A few blocks farther along I checked the newspaper microfiche at the Duluth library for stories about Susan Redding's life and death.

I had accumulated an impressive stack of paper by the time Malik and I headed south to the Twin Cities. I made him drive so I could start sorting through the mess.

"Feels like a dead end," he said.

"Maybe." I shrugged. "Maybe not."

"Not to play pessimist, but how is this not a dead end?"

"It's not a dead end if we've stumbled onto an innocent man doing life for murder."

CHAPTER 12

The headline on Susan (O'Keefe) Redding's obituary read "Miss Duluth." The photograph featured a young woman wearing a dazzling tiara and a sparkling smile. The fine print included such details as preceded in death by her parents, survived by husband, Dr. Brent Redding, a list of civic accomplishments, and memorials preferred to St. Luke's Hospital.

While we were in Duluth I stopped at St. Luke's. The receptionist told me Dr. Redding was out of town. According to the police file, Dr. Redding was a respected psychiatrist. No surprise then that his home phone was unpublished, otherwise he'd have patients pestering him day and night. I called Xiong to run a property check and learned that Dr. Redding had sold the house where his wife had died and he had bought a ground-floor town house in a renovated brick warehouse near the hospital. I walked around the back and admired a small greenhouse porch. His was the only name on the mailbox, so it seemed unlikely he'd remarried. I left no messages, figuring I'd wait to see where the trail led first, and also because I prefer looking people in the eye the first time I meet them.

Like when I was face-to-face with Dusty Foster, lover and killer of Susan Redding. A window of prison glass separated us. Inmate on one side, visitor on the other. Chatting on the telephone. Malik shot it all, since we weren't sure whether prison officials would grant us an encore visit.

"I didn't do it," he told me. "But no one believes me." Foster had worked landscaping and home maintenance for several wealthy families in the area. A handyman. He had met Susan Redding on the job, apparently proving himself handy where it mattered most. Now in his midforties, he'd spent nearly fifteen years behind bars at Oak Park Heights, where Minnesota houses its most dangerous inmates. Dusty was kind of cute, in a Ted Bundy sort of way, except for an obviously broken nose he'd gotten in a prison scuffle shortly after he was incarcerated. His arms and shoulders rippled muscles, so he likely lifted behind bars to stay hard and discourage altercations.

"You understand why you were the prime suspect in her death?"

"I was their only suspect. Yes, we were sleeping together. But I didn't kill her."

"The jury thought otherwise. They seemed swayed by your brother's testimony that you told him even though you and Susan weren't married, you were going to hold her to the 'till death do us part' clause."

"A joke. I would never have harmed her."

"Because you loved her too much?"

He paused. "I've had a long time to think about this. Susan was a hard person to love. I wanted to be with her, but I don't think either of us really loved the other. We each had something the other craved."

"What was that?"

"She was the hottest thing I'd ever met. Red hair, green eyes. She got better-looking each year. Like she knew the secret of eternal youth. She was actually more lovely the day she died than the day she got that damn beauty crown. I mean, you're a good-looking babe, but you're no Susan."

Malik risked shaking the camera shot just to kick me under the table. I elbowed him back. Having a lifer who hadn't been with a woman in so many years tell me I'm good-looking but . . . would be a blow to most women's self-esteem. However I'm a pro; I just kept the questions coming.

"You saw her the morning she died. A neighbor saw you go in the house around nine but didn't notice when you left."

"I admitted everything to the police. Susan and I messed around that morning. Then I drove up the north shore and went hiking. She'd have gone with me, because her old man was out of town, but she had a big charity event that night and needed the afternoon to get dolled up. Next day I heard she was dead."

"No one saw you during that time?"

"No. Bad for me, my alibi couldn't be verified. My fingerprints were all over the place. Friends of ours misunderstood some things we each said, and the cops came up with a story of 'If I couldn't have her, no one could.' "

"You said she gave you beauty. What did you give her?"

"A secret. She lived the high life with the doc; with me she got to sample low life. She discovered she liked sweating and sneaking. She may not have been ready to leave the marriage, but neither of us felt our thing had run its course."

Foster had nothing to lose in talking to the media. If he was lying, we were an interesting distraction to his otherwise predictable day. Lieutenant Dex acknowledged that Foster had passed a lie detector test, but the results weren't admissible in court, and anyway Foster wouldn't have been the first psychopath to beat a polygraph.

"What're you doing here?" Foster asked. "And how come it seems like you might believe me?"

So I told him about the other Susans.

"I want a new trial." His face looked relieved, genuinely. "I've already done too much time behind bars for a crime I didn't do. At last this nightmare is over."

"Unless someone confesses, I don't see you going anywhere. There's no proof. And it's not like there's police or prosecutorial misconduct."

"I'm calling my lawyer."

"Great. Tell him to let me know if he has any ideas. I'm going to keep plugging away. But I didn't come here to get your hopes up, I came here for a story."

The guard indicated time was up. He put the cuffs on Dusty and led him away. Dusty looked back and tried to tell me something, but since he was behind the glass, off speaker, I couldn't understand his words.

———

"YOU GOTTA BE kidding me," Malik said when I told him about our next stop. "We're interviewing some guy about his dead dog?"

"Listen, I can't risk Noreen howling at me the next time I walk into the newsroom. This story was a direct order and I have no choice but to roll over."

"Well, this dog better not be named Susan."

Before Toby Elness could share the sad tale of Fluffy, his recently departed bichon frise, we had to meet the rest of the family: a German shepherd named Shep, a husky named Husky, a labrador named Blackie, seven cats named after the seven dwarfs, a pair of hamsters named Giddy and Gabby, and an aquarium of fish, all of whom had names, too, like Bubbles and Fishlips.

When Toby first opened the door, I expected him to own a basset hound, because that's what he looked like. Sad eyes, droopy face, long earlobes, short legs.

Toby's wife had left him four years earlier. In the divorce settlement she got a hefty bank account, the car, and half his pension. He held out for custody of the animals, a house heavy with mortgage and pet odor, and the ashes of Terry, their deceased tiny terrier.

"We had him cremated and kept his ashes in a small box in her underwear drawer," he explained.

"Her underwear drawer?" Malik repeated.

"It was her idea; he always liked to sniff her crotch."

Malik didn't say anything, and neither did I. Toby was another knucklehead Noreen would normally roll her eyes at, except that they obviously shared a penchant for pets.

"Why do you think these aren't Fluffy's ashes?" I tried to get the story back on track.

Toby set two small boxes on the coffee table.

"Fluffy was bigger than Terry, but as you can see, the amount of Fluffy's ashes is much smaller than Terry's."

"Is it possible that the bichon frise just looked bigger 'cause of all its fur?" Malik asked. I flashed him a please-don't-encourage-him look.

"No. Fluffy definitely weighed more than Terry. And if you open the two sets of ashes, they don't physically look the same. Fluffy's don't look like real ashes."

Malik moved in for a close-up shot as Toby opened the boxes. One set looked like . . . charred ashes, I guess. The other set looked more like cat litter mixed with sand.

"Where did you have the bodies cremated?" I asked.

"My veterinarian took care of the details. Fluffy was eighteen years old and needed to be put to sleep." Toby rubbed a tear from his eye. "I paid $160 for a private cremation. I didn't want Fluffy's ashes being mixed with the ashes of other animals. The vet made the arrangements, took care of transporting his body, and I picked up the ashes the next week. I should tell you, it wasn't the same vet for both dogs. My old vet retired; this new one I don't like as much. Blackie and Husky and Shep always growl at him."

"Did you tell your vet you're worried about the ashes?"

"No. I'm considering dropping him. I think Blackie and Husky and Shep were trying to tell me something. I wish I had listened."

"All right, for now, don't say anything," I told him. "We don't want him to get suspicious. Give us some time to see what we can find out."

We videotaped old photographs of Fluffy and Terry in happier times. I wrote down the veterinarian's name and address. While we were packing up our gear, I got an idea.

"Hey Toby, can we take Fluffy's ashes with us?"

Toby frowned. "I'm not sure I'm comfortable letting them out of my sight. They're all I have left of Fluffy."

"Come on, you're not even sure they are Fluffy. We'll bring them back."

Shep rubbed his back against my leg and licked my hand.

"Well, nobody tried to bite you," Toby said. "So I guess you're okay."

IT WAS A few miles before either Malik or I could speak. We kept our eyes on the road straight ahead. Finally Malik couldn't stand it any longer.

"How big a fight do you think his ex waged to get custody?" He burst out laughing, then choked a couple times.

"Maybe I should drive." I slapped him on the back and grabbed the steering wheel. "Give you a chance to get it out of your system."

"I'm fine." He straightened up in his seat again. "You planning on scattering those ashes somewhere?"

"No. We're taking them to an expert."

Journalists don't personally know much about anything. All we know is what people tell us. A lot of what people tell us isn't worth dog shit. But I was no more going to air a story about Toby Elness's cremation speculation without getting independent corroboration than I was going to offer to pet-sit for him Thanksgiving weekend.

CHAPTER 13

The morning news was under way when I walked into the newsroom. Noreen Banks sat at her desk, on the phone, monitoring our rivals while speaking to the control room.

I winced as I heard her telling Channel 3's producer "to put more energy in the last block of the show." My old news director insisted that our work product be referred to as a "newscast," not a "show." We're not entertainment, we're news, was his motto. I tried sharing this philosophy with Noreen once, but suspected if I brought it up again it would be our last conversation.

I stuck my head in her office, knowing now was not a good time for her to talk. "Got some *very* nice sound on the dog cremation story." I used my best boss suck-up voice.

She gave me a thumbs-up and I moved on to the computer center to thank Xiong for Susan Redding's death certificate. He was working on a script for the noon newscast. He told me to check my e-mail.

When I returned to my office, I made a new board for my new victim.

SUSAN REDDING 1990
AGE: 28
DOCTOR'S WIFE

REDHEAD
DEATH DATE/NOVEMBER 19
STRANGLED
LOVER CONVICTED/MAINTAINS INNOCENCE
DULUTH HOME

I set her chart next to the Susan Chenowith and Susan Moreno boards, then logged on to my computer. Seven e-mail messages. I skipped over likely spam and one from my sister to click on Xiong's e-mail. I found myself staring at another death certificate.

Susan Niemczyk. November 19, 1994. Rochester, Minnesota. Suicide. Suffocation.

"ALSO SIGNIFICANT IS what I did not find," Xiong explained. "No other Susans murdered on that day anywhere else in the country. It's less coincidental we should have a cluster here."

Xiong showed me the results on his computer screen. He had found other Susan deaths on various November 19s, but they appeared to be from accidental or natural causes such as car crashes, cancer, or heart disease.

"I threw you the suicide because, well, you never know." Xiong hesitated. He looked uneasy about the subject. I wondered how much he knew about what had happened with me. And if he knew, how many others did too?

"It's okay," I assured him. "I'm okay." Most of the

newsroom thought I had simply taken time off to grieve. My family knew the truth. So did the station bigwigs. Even though I assured them I would never have gone through with it, they weren't satisfied until I admitted myself—okay, forced by their intervention—to the Mayo Clinic psych ward. There, surrounded by some seriously troubled patients, and some seriously patient therapists, I had found my way back.

Xiong avoided eye contact with me, but continued talking. "I remember what you said about a possible murder slipping through the cracks."

This time I did some research before flying out the door for southern Minnesota. Nothing in the online newspaper archives, except an obituary that listed Susan Niemczyk's parents and a sister. With a name like Niemczyk it wasn't hard to locate addresses and phone numbers. Lucky for me, they lived in the Twin Cities: her mother in northeast Minneapolis, her sister in St. Paul. I decided not to contact them just yet and dialed Rochester Police instead.

The officer who handled the case had retired five years ago, but the desk sergeant gave me his name: James Anderson. Tough break for me; it's the Minnesota equivalent of writing John Smith on a motel ledger. Minnesota has deep Scandinavian roots, having been settled 150 years ago by sons of Ander, sons of John, and sons of Carl. My hunch is 25 percent of Minnesotans have last names ending in "son."

I couldn't find a phone listing for Anderson in

Rochester, so I asked Xiong to run the name through his computer databases. Cops like to keep their home addresses and other personal information private. But Channel 3 had copies of state driver's licenses and vehicle registrations. If those didn't work, we could fall back on the hunting and fishing license files. Finding cop addresses in that bunch was like shooting fish in a barrel; cops always use their home address rather than risk their hunting license renewal going astray. If we still came up empty, we could search for Officer Anderson in our criminal records database. I hoped that wouldn't be necessary; he'd be in a foul mood if he was in jail.

"First I will run death records to make sure he is still alive," Xiong said. "If I find no trace of him there, we will look in snowbird states."

Seemed as good a plan as any. Just then I heard my name paged over the newsroom loudspeaker. "Riley Spartz to the news director's office."

I didn't think I was in any trouble, but I'm often the last to know, so I headed to Noreen's office to see what it would take to get her off my back this time. Turns out, she just wanted more details on the dog story.

"I'll level with you," I told her. "I'm not saying it's not a story. I can make it a story. But our tipster seems a little flaky."

"In what way?"

"A little doggone crazy." I filled her in on Toby Elness's domestic zoo.

"He sounds like he has a good heart," she said. "I hope you're not judging him harshly because he cares for animals."

"Not . . . at . . . all." I stammered the words as I tried backtracking.

"Excuse me." Noreen's secretary, Lynn, interrupted us on the speaker phone. "The president of North Country Bank is on the line. They caught Mike Flagg going through their garbage dumpster."

"Not again." Noreen put her hands over her face. "Put him through."

Flagg was last year's hotshot hire: smooth, handsome, with the kind of year-round tan only money can buy. From what I'd seen of him on air, he was a cross between a tattletale and a playground bully. Most irritating was his tendency to do crime victim interviews with an exaggerated "let me feel your pain" gimmick.

He was careful on air to refer to himself as "Michael" Flagg. "Mike flag" is TV jargon for the 3-D plastic station logos clipped onto microphones and shoved in the face of whoever is being interviewed. News folks generally dislike them because they focus viewers on the station logo rather than on what is being said. Promotion folks generally like them because they focus viewers on the station logo rather than on what is being said. The stations here in the Twin Cities used to have a gentleman's agreement of "no mike flags" at news conferences to avoid a mishmash of channel numbers and network symbols. One of the first moves Noreen made as news director was ordering flashy new mike flags for each of the photographers. Our competitors quickly followed suit, so a mike flag war, with each more cheesy and obnoxious than the next, is currently being waged in the Minneapolis–St. Paul news market.

Noreen grimaced as she took her phone off speaker mode. "Hello, Mr. Kahn, how are things at the bank . . . I'm so sorry for your inconvenience . . . Yes, I'll speak with him . . . I understand completely . . . Thank you."

"Dumpster diving?" I asked.

"A reporter at his old station did a story about financial institutions not shredding sensitive customer records. He's trying to see if it's a problem here."

"It was a problem here," I told her, "until about four years ago when I first did the story. Then everybody else in the country copied it. Now it's not such a big problem."

"Oh." Noreen seemed startled, like she'd forgotten why I was in her office. "That's good to know."

I sure wasn't going to remind her that she had been on the verge of reprimanding me for snickering about Toby Elness. She shuffled through some papers on her desk, apparently trying to recall just what I had done to vex her. I decided to jump in first.

"We were just talking about the need to shoot enough tape on the pet story so promotion would have plenty of animal shots to work with."

"Yes," she agreed. "Don't skimp on video."

THE FLASHING MESSAGE at my desk, like most of my phone calls these days, came from my family, checking up on me. My mom had the station 800 number and didn't hesitate to use it. I suppose a mom message is better than no message, but a reporter is only as good as her next story, so I was anxious for old sources to start calling with new ideas. Except most wouldn't realize I was back at work until they actually saw me back on the air, which wouldn't happen for another couple weeks.

I marked the best sound bites from Toby Elness's interview and added more details to the SUSAN boards. Writing VEHICLE under the unsub column didn't require any Sherlockian skill, but I vowed to keep track of all clues, no matter how obvious or obscure. Clearly, our Susan killer had access to wheels.

The phone rang. This time, not Mom. A computer voice said, "You have a collect call from Oak Park Heights prison." Short pause.

"Dusty Foster." Slowly and deliberately, Dusty said his name.

After another brief pause the computer voice continued, "Will you accept the charges?"

"Yes," I answered. Outsiders can't call prison inmates. And for obvious reasons, inmates can only dial numbers collect, from a preapproved list. Cell phone numbers are not allowed.

"Hello, Dusty. How's it going inside?"

"Same as it's gone the last fifteen years. How's it going outside?"

"Better than inside, I'm sure."

"How about your investigation?"

He craved encouragement, but I made no promises. I'd rather have him calling out of boredom than out of false hope. "I put a call in to your attorney. He's sending you an authorization form to sign, then he'll get the old files up from storage."

"You do believe me, don't you?"

"Dusty, we've been through this. The state proved you're a murderer. I'm open to the possibility you're not. That's the best I can do."

"My mom wants to talk to you."

"I already have a mom" would have been my reply in most cases, but I took her phone number because I sensed another television interview ending in a mother's sobs. Here we go again: sound up, tears.

IN ADDITION TO the police and court records, I'd found several articles about Susan Redding in the *Duluth News-Tribune.* She and her doctor husband had been married four years. No children. A feature profile talked about her earlier reign as Miss Duluth, and her later charity work at the hospital, a local church, and the university.

When Susan Redding failed to show up at a fundraiser for the University of Minnesota-Duluth that night, a friend had called her house. When no one answered the phone, the friend stopped by and discovered Susan's partially clothed body. At ten o'clock at night the front door had been unlocked. Rigor mortis was complete, so the medical examiner put the time of death between ten in the morning and one in the afternoon.

The cops in this case clearly had more evidence to work with than did the detectives working the other SUSAN cases. The body had been left where it had fallen, not dumped elsewhere. The crime scene was indoors, easy to secure. And witnesses whispered about a secret lover with a predictable motive.

"Sorry to bring up these memories after so long." I was speaking to Laura Robins, the friend who had found Susan Redding's body. I dialed the phone number listed on her police statement, expecting it to be outdated. She answered on the first ring.

"This is a surprise, but I'll try to answer some questions. Why are you calling now?"

"I'm comparing and contrasting some other murders that happened around that time. Other cases, other women, some similarities. You'd be surprised how vulnerable we all are to violence." I didn't want to get too specific right away. "How long did you know Susan?"

"Are you going to put what I say on TV?"

"Right now I'm just trying to get some background on the case. I've already talked to Lieutenant Dex, but I'm looking for some personal insight. For me to include what you say on TV, I'd have to interview you on camera. I'm not exactly sure where this story is headed, but if you told me something and it ended up being important, I would probably call you back and ask if you'd be willing to do that. That's not a decision you have to make yet. Right now, it's just you and me talking."

"All right, I just wasn't sure how that worked. Susan knew more about the TV business."

"Really, how's that?"

"She worked as a reporter at one of the local stations here in town. It was only for a year, right out of college. What she really wanted to do was work her way up to the anchor desk, but her boss pretty much told her to forget it."

"With her looks? She'd be a standout in a small market like Duluth."

"She sure was, but she had a squeaky little girl voice that was real irritating. I was her friend, so I got used to it, but her boss said no market was small enough to overlook that."

"Yeah, most people don't realize it, but in broadcasting, voice can matter more than face." I was fortunate to be an alto.

"She complained about the long hours and bad pay. Susan barely made ten grand a year. Can you believe it?"

Sadly, that was a typical paycheck in small-market television stations then, and the economics aren't much better today. As market size goes up, so does the money. New York is market 1. Minneapolis is market 15. Duluth is market 137. North Platte, Nebraska, is market 209. The smaller the market, the bigger the number. In markets under 100, a station receptionist can earn more per hour than a rookie reporter, yet a news director might get a hundred audition tapes for a single general assignment reporter opening.

"She also griped about having to write her own copy," Laura continued.

That was also typical of many new hires. Just one of the reasons most wouldn't last.

"What was Susan like as a person? Everyone remarks on her appearance. I'd like to get beyond that."

"Susan never let anyone forget she was a beauty queen. As the years went on, it got tiresome. I mean it wasn't like she was Miss America."

"Did you ever have any doubt Dusty Foster did it?"

"None. She told me he was possessive. She wanted to end it but was afraid he'd tell her husband. That seemed to worry her more than anything."

"Did she have other affairs?"

"If she had cheated before, she didn't tell me. Your mayor knows more about her early years."

"My mayor?"

"Mayor Skubic in Minneapolis."

"What does he have to do with any of this?"

"He was her college sweetheart."

"Really? Karl Skubic?"

"They were both UMD Bulldogs. He played hockey,

she was on the ski team. He drove up for the college fund-raising dinner the night her body was found. We had all reserved a table together. He was disappointed she didn't show."

"OF ALL THE gin joints in all the towns in all the world she walks into mine." Nick Garnett held a beer at the bar in Hooters at the Mall of America.

"Humphrey Bogart, *Casablanca,* 1942. What are you doing in Hooters?"

"I'm a man. What are you doing in Hooters?"

"Looking for you. Your surveillance duo ratted you out."

"Technically, I'm still on duty. There've been complaints about some of the clientele and a certain lack of management response. I figured I'd sit back and get a firsthand look. Of course, you're blowing my cover."

"Sorry, hope nothing else gets blown here. I realize the view isn't as good back in the corner, but maybe we can talk shop for a minute."

He picked up his beer and a plate of chicken wings and mozzarella sticks and we shuffled over to an empty table. I ordered a glass of house red.

"Here's that Duluth case I was telling you about." I handed him a copy of the Susan Redding file, and he went straight for the crime scene photos. A wide shot and close-up showed her body sprawled on the bedroom floor.

"Oh look, the chalk fairy," he said, scornfully.

"The what?"

"See the chalk outline around her body? Amateurs. They're lucky the judge didn't rule the photos inadmissible."

"What's wrong? I've seen that on TV."

"Just what we need, cops getting homicide investigative training from Hollywood. It's important that the first officers who arrive preserve the scene and not change anything until after the photos have been taken. When the detective arrives and asks, 'Who contaminated the crime scene?' suddenly nobody wants to take credit. Must have been the chalk fairy."

"Sounds like something from Neverland."

"Well, if you're waiting for me to say, 'Do you believe in fairies? Clap your hands,' forget it. The only time it's permissible to make a chalk outline is if the body has to be moved before the scene can be processed. Like the victim is still alive and an officer gets there just ahead of the ambulance. Obviously we don't want anyone going from 'likely to die' to dead while we wait for a camera."

Garnett slid the photos back inside the file. "I'll read through this, see if anything jumps out."

"I might have another."

"Another drink?"

"Another Susan." I filled him in on Susan Niemczyk, the Rochester suicide. So far there wasn't much to tell. "Might be nothing."

"Might." Garnett nodded. "But if it's something, more cases could make the pattern clearer."

"Or more complicated."

"Those would be the two possibilities."

Sherlock Holmes's satisfaction in battling Professor Moriarty came from a yearning to confront an antagonist who was his intellectual equal. Not me, I hankered for dumb villains.

"Why am I always involved with smart bad guys?" I asked Garnett. "Why can't I investigate more idiots?"

"Comes down to math," he said. "Remember? The police catch the idiots in the first forty-eight hours after a crime. We don't need the media for those cases. By the time you get involved, the dunces are already behind bars."

I threw down a few bucks for a tip. Garnett gave the waitress a once-over and uncharacteristically left a five spot. Even though the timing didn't feel right, I blurted out a question that had been bothering me.

"Nick, why did you quit the cop shop? You belong in the field, not in a shopping mall."

He raised an eyebrow, as if in disdain. "This isn't just any shopping mall. This is the Mall of America."

"You know what I mean."

"I had my reasons."

"What reasons were they?"

"My reasons."

When reading his mind didn't work I tried staring him down. Nothing.

"If they ever become your reasons," he said, "you'll be the first to know."

CHAPTER 14

A nother e-mail from Xiong, another death certificate. It was like being spammed by the grim reaper. Rochester police officer James Anderson died three years ago, across the river in Hudson, Wisconsin. Heart attack.

Since dead men tell no tales, that left me no choice—I would have to call Susan Niemczyk's family.

I dreaded calling families of suicides. Media doesn't usually treat these deaths as news, so I worried about stirring up feelings of guilt, especially after so many years. Talking to families of homicides—solved or unsolved—didn't bother me at all. I told myself I was bringing closure, and in one case I had even brought justice.

I deviated from my normal method and made first contact by telephone instead of cold knocking on the door because I wanted them to feel in control. It's easier to slam down a phone than to slam a door in someone's face. After about ten rings I was ready to hang up when Susan Niemczyk's mother finally answered. I introduced myself and earned a long pause. To fill the silence, I explained my interest in her daughter's death.

"I'm so sorry to be calling after all this time." I concluded my pitch and waited, this time for her to fill the silence, or to hang up. Her words finally came, but hesitantly, as if each was an ordeal.

"Susan's death was a final exit suicide. I don't approve, but I've accepted it."

I was confused. "What do you mean, final exit?"

Again, she spoke slowly. "You really don't know?"

"I'm afraid not."

"If you had called back then, I wouldn't have talked. I couldn't have talked."

She agreed to let me stop by at seven that night and ask some questions. I thanked her, then I dialed Garnett.

"Ever hear of a final exit suicide?" I asked him.

"Yeah. Surge of them in the first couple years after the book came out."

"What book are we talking about?"

"Called *Final Exit.* Written by the guy who founded the Hemlock Society. Tells terminal cases how to bag it. Literally. Why do you want to know?"

"It might be related to that new Susan I was telling you about. Susan Niemczyk."

"Okay. Do some research and call me when you're up to speed."

I found plenty of background online. *Final Exit* had topped the *New York Times* Best Sellers list in 1991. It was a how-to guide for an individual to end his or her life. The recommended tools seemed to be a combination of prescription drugs, alcohol, and a plastic bag over the face. Occasionally a murderer tried to stage the crime scene to look like just such a suicide.

Malik stuck his head in my office. "Still got that ten o'clock shoot?" The clock read 9:35 a.m.

"Yeah, I just got distracted for a minute. Let's get moving."

We headed for the basement garage, climbed in the van, and drove toward the northern suburbs. We pulled into the driveway of the Happy Paws Resting Stop. Besides being a lovely pet cemetery, the establishment also offered cremation services. I fumbled around in the backseat before finding Fluffy's box of ashes. "Keep your voice low and respectful," I warned Malik.

Charles Raverty owned Happy Paws and had agreed to examine Fluffy's ashes and give us his expert opinion. He also happened to be the past president of the Pet Cremation Society of America. Malik had the camera rolling when Raverty opened the box of ashes.

"What's this?" he asked. "Some joke?"

"Dog ashes," I answered. "One of our viewers paid 160 bucks for them."

"These are not cremains." His voice was definitive. "This is some kind of cruel scam."

I explained the history of the ashes, and then he explained the vulnerability pet owners face when the time comes to put down a beloved companion animal. He also gave me the name of a Texas laboratory that could analyze the ashes for us. Raverty agreed to keep quiet until we had a chance to talk to our veterinarian. I smiled, anticipating that interview.

"What's next?" As we drove away, Malik drew me back to our current dilemma. "Want to go talk to the vet?"

"Not yet," I replied. "We need to sting him first. Know anybody with a dying pet they wouldn't mind letting us play guinea pig with?"

"I'm making a prediction right now. That ain't going to happen."

"Wait, we might not need it. I just got an idea. Keep driving."

"What direction?"

"Doesn't matter. Just head out of town."

We drove till we ran out of blacktop and hit gravel. Then we drove some more.

MALIK AND I sat in the front of the van outside Dr. Petit's vet office, having a minor disagreement on our next course of action.

"I'll wear the watch," he insisted. "You carry the dog."

"No, you carry the dog, I'll wear the watch."

"The camera's in the watch and I'm the photographer, so I should wear the watch. You'll probably just end up tilting the watch wrong and shooting the ceiling."

That was a common problem with hidden cameras. In this case, that would be especially unfortunate because we wouldn't easily get a second chance.

We had driven nearly fifty miles of country roads before we had happened upon Lucky, our roadkill collie. I didn't want to risk ruining the shot, so I agreed to let Malik wear the watch.

We had actually been looking for a cat, or a smaller dog, but after driving by dead raccoons, woodchucks, and even a Canada goose we felt lucky to find the collie. We convinced ourselves this could be lucky for him, too. So we named him Lucky and crossed our fingers. He had no collar. The farmer down the road didn't recognize him, but explained that city folk often dumped unwanted pets in the country to fend for themselves.

"This way, at least, he'll get a decent burial," Malik said.

"Actually," I admitted, "he might not get a decent burial, but whatever happens can't be worse than rotting by the side of the road."

MALIK'S PHOTOGRAPHY GEAR and Lucky's body took up most of the space in the back of the van, but I crawled in anyway for a quick change. I pulled a ratty sweatshirt over my head, pushed my hair up under a baseball cap, and put on a pair of dark glasses to cover my presumably red, swollen eyes.

Malik put on the watch cam, checked the pinhole lens, and made sure the black cable ran from the watch up his shirtsleeve, and then down into a waist pack where he kept the recorder and battery. Then he opened the back hatch of the van and placed Lucky in my arms.

I struggled to get my balance, and made a pouty face at Malik. "Dr. Petit's going to think you're a jerk making me carry a heavy dog all by myself."

"I'm going to tell him you insisted 'cause he was *your* dog, sort of like Old Yeller."

He put his finger to his lips, hit the record button on the camera, and zipped the fanny pack shut. That's our "tape's rolling" signal to zip our lips.

Many TV crews have seen their careers end because of what was said on the outtakes of hidden camera footage. Libel lawsuits have been lost, not because of what was reported in the actual story, but because of what the reporters or photographers said while they were walking in to get the story or walking out after they got the story.

Viewers see only what the station broadcasts, but jurors may see all the raw tapes and hear plaintiff's lawyers argue not just about hidden cameras, but about hidden motives. Talk like "I really want to get these guys" or "Wasn't it great when that slimeball lied?" or "This is going to push the ratings through the roof!" will make a jury pile on punitive damages faster than the judge can pound his gavel for order in the court.

So Malik and I avoided any chitchat as we walked into Dr. Petit's veterinary clinic. The receptionist took one look at Lucky and quickly ushered us through the waiting room, past a lady holding a tabby cat and past a man with a colorful bird in a cage. Dead dogs probably aren't good for business.

I glanced at my watch as we waited in a small room without windows. Lucky's body lay on a metal table covered with white paper. A Purina Dog Chow poster featuring small photos of different breeds hung on the wall along with a copy of Dr. Petit's veterinary diploma.

As the minutes ticked away we became nervous. We had an hour-long tape and we had already used at least ten minutes of it. We were gambling we could wrap up the shoot before the tape ran out. Our other option was to try to rewind the tape now, before anyone came into the room. I shook my head at Malik, not wanting to risk being caught with a camera in the clinic. We'd also be wasting Lucky.

Another five minutes passed. Malik coughed and gestured toward the bag. It was a tough call. I was on the verge of signaling to him to rewind when the door suddenly opened.

"Who have we here?" Dr. Petit's eyes opened wide. His head seemed too wide for his body. He looked like a tall, skinny owl. His voice dripped with sympathy. A couple times during our visit I coyly pretended not to hear him so he'd repeat himself so we could make sure the hidden microphone picked up our exchange. Malik placed his elbow on a table as a makeshift tripod and rested his chin on his hand. The watch stayed steady, pointed at Dr. Petit.

"A terrible end to a fine animal," the veterinarian said. His calm, professional manner contrasted with the comical necktie he wore featuring a dog chasing a cat up a tree.

We informed Dr. Petit that we were friends of Toby

Elness, that Lucky had been hit by a car, and that we were hoping he could help us get him cremated. All true. He assured us he would handle the arrangements for an individual cremation, and that we could pick up the ashes in a week.

"Some people like to keep the ashes as a physical reminder of their pet," Dr. Petit said. "Others prefer to scatter them somewhere special. Cremation is a wonderful way for you to honor Lucky."

We knew Dr. Petit didn't have a crematorium in his office, so we waited outside to see where he would take Lucky. Malik's camera was perched on a tripod in the back of the van, but there was no action. We parked so we could see the front and back doors of the clinic. Closing time came and went; we watched him and his staff lock up and leave.

Back in an edit booth at the station, Malik put the digital videotape from the bag cam in a deck and hit *play*. We held our breath until we were certain we weren't looking at one of those unfortunate undercover lapses of video without audio, or audio without video. The light was good. The sound was good. Especially the part where I counted out eight twenty-dollar bills and placed them in Dr. Petit's hand. The glint in his eyes at that moment could not be mistaken for sympathy.

CHAPTER 15

"Roadkill?" Noreen put her head on her desk. She was a sucker for animal stories. *So much for our out-of-the-box thinking.*

"This way," I explained, "we can assure viewers no dogs were killed for the making of this story," I explained.

"Yeah, 'cause we used a dog already dead," Malik pitched in.

"This is horrible," she screamed. "Why didn't you check with me first?"

Noreen should have known the answer. Not checking with her gave her plausible deniability. Meaning if this story blew up in our faces, she had an out and would keep her job while our butts would be fired. Plausible deniability is a valuable gift.

With no thank-you forthcoming, I returned to the salt mines of TV news: logging tapes. I ducked into a claustrophobic viewing room but I ducked back out when Mike Flagg threw me a dirty look. He was already inside, showing the new newsroom intern the computer transcription program. In the dimly lit room, I could swear he rested one hand on her thigh as he patiently demonstrated how to fast-forward.

So Malik and I headed out to meet with the family of Suicide Susan.

Joyce Niemczyk's address was an assisted-living facility in northeast Minneapolis. The neighborhood had hit bottom a decade earlier and was now considered fashionably funky. Inner-city housing values had soared. Ethnic immigrants brought new energy to this neglected pocket of Minneapolis. Somali restaurants with spicy foods and women in colorful head scarves decorated Central Avenue.

Malik and I rang Mrs. Niemczyk's doorbell. "Come in," a voice called out. A wooden buffet with stained-glass doors was the focal point of the room. My eyes passed over it and instead focused on a dark-haired woman, younger than I had expected.

"Mrs. Niemczyk?" I asked.

"No, I'm her daughter, Sharon."

An older woman emerged from around the corner, moving toward us, haltingly, in an electric wheelchair. Thin, elderly, taut. A look about her hinted at lost beauty until an awkward grimace unexpectedly crossed her face.

"This is my mother, Mother, Ms. Spartz." Sharon introduced us. "She asked me to join you."

"Oh. I recognize you from the television," Mrs. Niemczyk said. Her voice shook when she spoke and her arm jerked stiffly, twice.

The women bore no family resemblance. I noticed two framed graduation photos on the buffet. The blonde woman in one picture was stunning, clearly her mother's daughter. The brunette in the other was ordinary looking, clearly Sharon.

"Fraternal twins," Mrs. Niemczyk said. "Susan looked like me. Beautiful on the outside. Cursed on the inside." Then she laughed and started to choke.

Sharon slapped her upper back. "Mother." Though Sharon didn't say it, her tone was the kind a parent might use to indicate "I'm warning you" to a child.

Mrs. Niemczyk ignored her daughter. "Sharon takes after her father. The lucky twin. The curse missed her."

"Oh, Mother, please."

"What curse?" I asked.

"The family curse," Mrs. Niemczyk answered sluggishly, not for drama, I realized, but because that was simply the way she spoke. "It killed Susan."

I became confused. "I thought Susan killed herself."

Mrs. Niemczyk's neck gave another seemingly uncontrollable yank. Her shoulders shrugged stiffly. "She did, because of the curse."

"Mother's talking about Huntington's disease. Susan inherited the gene from her. She started showing symptoms about five years before her death. An occasional facial tic. A dancing step. She mentioned the disease in her suicide note. Frankly, we were stunned. I was closer to her than anyone and I still don't believe she took her life."

"I never gave her the impression my life wasn't worth living," Mrs. Niemczyk said. "I never did."

Talk of Susan's photo gave me an opening to ask if

Malik might bring the camera inside to take a picture of her picture. It's a good way to get folks used to the camera before turning it on them.

While Malik set up the tripod, Sharon explained that Huntington's disease was a rare, inherited neurological disorder. Patients progressively declined physically, intellectually, and mentally. Carriers of the disease had a fifty-fifty chance of passing it on to their children. And worst of all, Huntington's has no cure.

"I'm so sorry," I said, because I had to say something, and in tough jams where nothing can be done, "sorry" is sometimes the safest thing any of us can muster.

Neither mother nor daughter replied. I was sure they'd heard the sentiment plenty of times before. Sharon reached for a cardboard box and set it on the dining room table. I took a seat and Mrs. Niemczyk moved her wheelchair to the other side. I wanted to open the box because Susan's name and the date of her death were handwritten on the side. Patience, I cautioned myself.

"What do you know about Susan's death?" Sharon asked. Enough time had passed that she was able to speak matter-of-factly.

"Just what I read on the death certificate and in the obit. Suicide. Asphyxiation. There weren't any newspaper articles, but that's pretty standard in suicides. They seldom get media attention."

"Why are you here now?" Mrs. Niemczyk asked.

"I'm working on a story that involves the deaths of other women, and I found some similarities. My first call was to the detective assigned to her case, but he died a couple years back."

"Did these women kill themselves?" Sharon asked.

"No, but I'm wondering whether the police ever investigated Susan's death as anything but a suicide?"

"I wanted them to," Sharon said, "but they said the trail ended with her."

"She was not a happy person," her mother acknowledged.

"That was no secret," Sharon agreed, "but we clearly misjudged the depth of her depression."

"I know this is painful," I said, "even after all this time. But how exactly did she die?"

"She died in her hotel room," Sharon explained. "Susan was at an education conference in Rochester. She was a high school teacher and attended it to learn more about disadvantaged students. She liked networking with colleagues and listening to the lectures."

"Wouldn't you think that with her being surrounded by all those people, someone would have noticed she seemed suicidal?" her mother asked.

"Mother, we couldn't tell, how could they be expected to?" Sharon explained that, while her mother's twitching, jerking, and grimaces—classic Huntington's symptoms—hadn't started until she was middle-aged, Susan's had begun earlier. Doctors had predicted that Susan's form of the disease would ultimately be more severe.

"They especially warned us that victims sometimes turn to suicide, but Susan's signs weren't that bad yet."

"We vowed never to take that step," Mrs. Niemczyk said. "She and I."

Sharon nodded. "She told me that, too. But Susan's personality was definitely changing. At times she seemed paranoid."

"Was she in a personal relationship with anyone?" I asked.

"Not then," Sharon said. "Even though she was a teacher, she wasn't a terribly social person. What she enjoyed most about her work was the one-on-one student contact."

"She kept men away," her mother said.

"Mother," Sharon corrected her, "Susan had romances."

"She wasn't emotionally invested. Not like you. You have a husband and kids. She feared passing on the curse."

To me, the curse was sounding self-fulfilling. But I knew better than to say that aloud, especially since Sharon was opening the box.

"The police found these things in Susan's hotel room," she said.

I saw a copy of *Final Exit* sticking out from behind a pile of papers.

"She left three letters." Sharon held them up. "A personal one telling us she loved us but didn't love life, a legal-sounding one saying no one else knew about her decision to end her life or helped her in any way, and a brief note to the hotel staff apologizing for the shock and inconvenience."

The box also included the police and autopsy reports. As I rifled through the pages, I found a heavy envelope. Inside was a gold heart-shaped pendant on a fine chain. Engraved on the front of the pendant was the name SUSAN.

"She was wearing that jewelry when she died," Sharon said. "At least that's what the officer handling her case told us."

"Lovely," I said. "Is it a family piece? It looks like an antique."

"Never seen it before," Mrs. Niemczyk said. "We considered burying it with her, but decided to dress her in a topaz birthstone necklace I'd given her."

"It feels like real gold." I tried handing the pendant to Sharon, but she pulled her hands away.

"Put it back," she said. "I don't want to touch it. Somehow it seems tainted."

I put the jewelry back inside the box with all the papers. The two agreed to let me take everything home, sort through the items, and return them later. Malik and I also videotaped a camera interview with them about Susan: their daughter and sister.

"We've accepted her death as a suicide, only because the police insisted," Sharon said.

"I'd like to know what really happened in that hotel room," her mother added. An awesome line, but delivered so slowly I wasn't sure we'd be able to air the sound bite.

The drive back to the station was subdued. I envied Malik; when he reached home he would not be walking into an empty house.

"Suicide is lonely." The words sounded superficial and obvious. I regretted saying them aloud.

"It better be lonely," Malik replied. "I don't have to be a cop to know someone's looking at a murder rap otherwise."

CHAPTER 16

The front desk buzzed me the next morning in my office. "Guest in the lobby."

"Get a name?" I wasn't expecting anyone, and experience taught me nothing good walks through the front door unannounced.

"Dr. Brent Redding."

Him I wanted to talk to, but I had hoped to do more digging first. His beauty queen wife's murder measured high on my intrigue scale. That her former flame Minneapolis Mayor Karl Skubic had been in Duluth the day she died was not lost on me as a possible clue.

Dr. Redding's combination of horn-rims and tweed was attractive in an academic way. He'd aged well since his wife's death and didn't look much older than he did in the newspaper photo I'd copied from the Duluth library. His hair was a shade between blond and white. He was about half a foot taller than I. A thin build, but he looked like he might sport some strength beneath his sport coat.

I shook his hand and sat with him in an alcove off the lobby. I didn't invite him back to my office because I didn't want him to see the SUSAN charts. For amateurs, the inside world of TV news can sometimes be too much like watching sausage being made.

"Ms. Spartz, I understand you are trying to free my

wife's killer." He didn't have to say it in such an accusatory way.

"I don't have the kind of power to free anyone," I replied. "And you can call me Riley."

"You may call me Dr. Redding."

Okay, if that's the way he wanted it. "Well, Doctor, I'm looking at some unsolved homicides, and stumbled onto your wife's case. I'm not sure how, or even if, it fits in my story."

"My wife's death was a tragedy, not a story. Calling it a story trivializes it, Ms. Spartz." Dr. Redding's voice sounded sharp, and he clipped each word as if not wanting to waste any extra ones on me.

"I'm sorry for your loss, but your wife's murder was a story long before I came along." My voice sounded defensive. And I felt defensive for sounding defensive.

"That story has already been told," he reminded me. "It had an ending. I had accepted it. Now you're trying to rewrite it for ratings."

"Ouch." I wasn't poking fun at him because he was a doctor. I said "ouch" because it was hard to argue with such a logical comeback. I apologized again, then uncharacteristically acted on an impulse to reach for his arm. I wasn't flirting to get information, though sometimes I do. This was sincere. I understood his grief better than most people. Redding snatched his arm away.

"What gives you the right?" He had an affected way of speaking that made me feel he thought he was better than me. He probably was.

"Listen, I knew when you and I spoke it wasn't going to be easy," I said. "But it wasn't something I was trying to avoid either. I looked for you when I was in Duluth. I planned on calling you at St. Luke's today since your home number isn't listed."

He listened but didn't say anything.

"Since you saved me a drive back to Duluth, how about I buy you a cup of coffee and we talk things through?"

The disadvantage of snooping around a small market like Duluth is, everybody knows everybody else. Lieutenant Dex had called Dr. Redding before I'd even left the city limits. He'd also apparently checked with some law enforcement buddy at Oak Park Heights prison and confirmed that Dusty's mom was no longer the only name on his visiting list. I didn't doubt Dr. Redding would provide Lieutenant Dex a full report of his conversation with me, but sometimes reporters have to give information to get information.

So in between eating deli sandwiches on a bench at an urban park along Nicollet Mall, I shared more details about the case than I really wanted to.

It didn't work. He told me about the important good he does for his patients, the worthwhile committees he serves on to help troubled teens throughout the state, and how highly educated he was, but he wouldn't tell me much about his deceased wife. And nothing I said was going to get him to go on TV.

"I prefer listening to speaking," he said. "You might

say I'm a professional listener. Part of the job qualifications. You, however, seem to be a professional talker."

I've been called worse. "The person I'd really like to talk to is your wife, but since she can't speak, don't you think you might speak for her?"

"We each leave a certain legacy behind us when we die, Ms. Spartz. This is not what she would have wanted."

He didn't seem upset anymore, just sort of pompous. He wiped his mouth with a napkin and started lecturing me about the correlation between violence on television and crime. As if I, by my occupation, might share some blame for his wife's homicide.

Fortunately for me, I didn't need his permission to get pictures or video of Susan. Our local network affiliate in Duluth had plenty from the time she worked there, and even more from her murder coverage. Visually, I had nailed the story. I was about to write off our meeting as a necessary but unproductive block of time.

"What about her old college boyfriend, the mayor?" I asked.

"What about him?"

"He was in Duluth the day she died. Were they still friends?"

"Not really. They were friends with some of the same people, so occasionally they would run into each other at social events. They were always cordial."

"How about you? Were you friends with him?"

"No. He had a dark side that I saw through Susan.

The fact that she could share a drink with him at a university function was proof of her forgiving nature and healthy attitude."

"What did she have to forgive him for?"

He paused for nearly half a minute. I'm sure of the time. TV journalists are a good judge of thirty seconds, because that's the standard commercial length. Half a minute is a very uncomfortable pause. Most people on the listening end would nervously try to fill the silence with chatter, but I've found such a pause sometimes signals that important information is near. If you're quiet and patient, the answer to the question might be worth the wait. I just might be a professional listener after all.

"Patient confidentiality prevents me from speaking," he said. "I'm afraid I've said more than I should, and I'm going to stop now."

"Are you speaking as a doctor or a husband?" I lowered my voice to add some good-natured drama. "Do you know what you know because she was your wife, or because she was your patient? Seems like there might be enough ambiguity there for a little chit-chat?"

Dr. Brent Redding, licensed psychiatrist, was not amused.

"We have strict professional ethics. I'm not going to take offense because I could hardly expect a reporter to understand."

"But what about the ethics of dating patients?"

I shouldn't have gone there, especially since I wasn't exactly pure when it came to dating sources, but since he wasn't going to be cooperative, there didn't seem to be much downside in pissing him off.

Except his voice turned low and scary. "Now I will take offense. It's none of your business. And perhaps you should consider that the man you're attempting to free might actually be safer behind bars."

He threw down his napkin and left without saying good-bye, leaving me to ponder whether he had just threatened his wife's killer.

"I'M WARNING YOU, it's disgusting."

Malik cued up the videotape he had shot that morning while parked in the alley behind Dr. Petit's veterinary clinic.

"Maybe you should look at this later, after your lunch has had time to settle," he cautioned.

With a setup like that, I could hardly wait to press *play*. A battered garbage truck was parked by the back door of the vet office. A short, fat man came out with an armload of something. I couldn't tell what it was until he flung it into the back of the truck.

"Was that a dead cat?" I asked.

"It sure wasn't a flying squirrel," Malik answered. "Kind of bent and crooked though."

The man went back inside and came out again and threw another dead cat. Rigor mortis had made its corpse bent and crooked, too. The man wore a tight

T-shirt. Each time he flung an animal corpse into the truck, his shirt pulled up and revealed a floppy belly. His jeans rode below his protruding stomach, so when he turned away from the camera, we got an eyeful of his butt crack.

"I told you it was disgusting," Malik reminded me. "Talk about a wardrobe malfunction."

Next the man tossed a small mixed-breed dog, its limbs frozen at right angles. He followed up with the mangled corpse of a pit bull. When the man came out again, he carried a larger load that I had no trouble recognizing: Lucky. His body hung limp. Rigor mortis must have passed. The man heaved Lucky into the back hatch, slammed the rusty gate shut, then climbed in the driver's seat.

Malik had followed the truck and shot similar stops outside an animal shelter as well as an agricultural university where the man struggled to load a dead sheep. He drove out of town, and, for reasons I couldn't fathom, stopped to toss in a roadkill skunk, then finally pulled into a fenced area in an industrial park. A large chimney spewed grey smoke from a warehouse. Malik stayed back, but the camera zoomed in until we could read the sign: VALLEY RENDERING PLANT.

I HAD JUST finished some Internet research on "rendering plants" and "pets" when Noreen buzzed me to come to her office for a story update.

Since she asked for it, I gave it to her, in greater

detail than usual. Bottom line: instead of getting an individual cremation, Lucky was part of a mass meltdown, and likely turned into lipstick, cement, ink, or perhaps (dramatic pause) even pet food. "It's a dog-eat-dog world out there," I said, concluding my presentation.

Her face ashen, Noreen waved me out of her office. It didn't take an investigative reporter to see she lacked the stomach for this part of our business. About ten minutes later, feeling a twinge of guilt, I went back to remind her about the circle of life and that even some old horses went to the glue factory when their time ran out. But my news director was nowhere to be found.

"Where's Noreen?" I asked Lynn.

"She went home sick."

So I called it a day, climbed into my Mustang, and went home, too. Cars meant more to Boyer than to me, so as a wedding gift I let him trade in my newly repaired Jetta for faster wheels. I gunned the gas fondly, just thinking of him.

I phoned Garnett from the car and asked him to look closely at Dr. Redding's alibi for his wife's murder.

"He seems awfully tight with the Duluth investigator and adamantly opposed to reopening the case," I said. "I'd like to make sure nobody overlooked the obvious."

"I'm one step ahead of you. The husband was definitely meeting with patients in Hennepin County when his wife was killed. One hundred forty miles from the scene of the crime. Multiple witnesses. Hate to say this, Riley, but the guy they got behind bars looks good to me."

"Yeah, well, I'm going to keep digging. Seems like the three Susans have to be connected somehow. And if they are, I don't see how Dusty Foster can be guilty."

I also filled him in on Susan Niemczyk, or Suicide Susan as I called her—not the most sensitive nickname, but the four cases had started to blur together, and I needed to keep them straight in my mind.

So Susan Redding became Duluth Susan.

Susan Chenowith, Waitress Susan.

Susan Moreno, Sinner Susan.

It may sound cold, but journalists often develop verbal shorthand for story subjects, not to be callous, just expedient. It's a solid solution as long as you don't put any nicknames in writing and you learn to bite your tongue around outsiders.

Because it was so dissimilar to the others, I was tempted to discard the Niemczyk case, especially since I had done some research and learned that victims of Huntington's disease have a suicide rate nearly eight times the national average. Odds were, Suicide Susan did kill herself. But the Suicide Susan box beckoned me to the living room where I left it the night before. I cleared off an old Shaker coffee table so I could sort the papers into piles.

Amid old magazines I found a scrapbook my sister made after Boyer's funeral. I had paged through it once

with her looking on, murmured the proper appreciation, and hadn't opened it since. She had included
funeral photos, condolence cards and letters sent by
friends and family, news articles detailing the tragedy
and obituaries from the *Star Tribune* and the *Pioneer
Press*.

"Minnesota State Patrol Sgt. Hugh Boyer died in the
line of duty June 13, 2006."

June 13, 2006—the date of our second wedding
anniversary.

Boyer and I were packed for a trip to Chicago to celebrate two years of mostly wedded bliss, actually make
that one year and 364 days. He'd tuned up the car for
the eight-hour drive . . . when a story I was working on
threw a wrench in our travel plans.

"Just two more days," I pleaded.

I had a pattern going on a consumer fraud investigation and needed to play out one more sting for the
whole thing to tie together. A delay meant a break in
the pattern and I'd have to start all over, which might
scrub the whole project. "This story is so close to going
from a B to an A," I told him. "Then I won't have to
sweat about work all summer." In this exigent business, you're only as good as your last story, and my last
story was just so-so.

"What about us?" Boyer asked.

"*Us* will always be there. Chicago will still be there
two days from now."

"I don't want to wait two days. I've got the time off.

You've got the time off. We've even got tickets to the Cubs game."

"I know. I know. But I've got two weeks invested in this story."

"Yeah, and I've got two years invested in this marriage and I want my annual payoff." He grabbed me, kissed my neck, and playfully nudged me toward the door.

"Please, honey," I said. "We can still celebrate tomorrow night and just hit the road a little later. Romantic dinner, candles, champagne." I kissed him back and seductively nudged him away from the door. "I could wear your uniform."

"Forget it." He turned away and headed up the stairs. "If you're going to work, I'm going to work. I'll take the Iron Range trip with the gov tomorrow. I'll see you in two days. Maybe you'll be ready to leave by then."

We went to bed angry.

SUICIDE SUSAN'S COPY of the book *Final Exit* was not page worn, which made her death seem impulsive instead of deliberate. Her suicide notes were exactly by the book, as her sister, Sharon, described. I glanced at the education conference schedule, then set it aside to read the police and autopsy reports.

Susan had washed down Seconal and phenobarbital, strong sedatives, with a great deal of vodka. Then she had placed a plastic bag over her face. The maid found her in her hotel bed the next morning. Susan was fully dressed. The dead bolt had not been turned. The medical examiner determined she had probably had sexual intercourse the day she died, though he found no semen on her body. His report said her pelvic area was swollen and red. A flag to me, since the woman Susan Niemczyk's mother and sister described didn't seem prone to one-night stands.

The police had looked for homicide clues, but hotel rooms pose special investigative problems. With so many people passing through, fingerprint, hair, and fiber evidence can be hard to connect to anyone except a registered guest or hotel employee.

Hotel bedspreads aren't usually washed between guests, so it's not unusual to find multiple semen stains from previous trysts. My colleague Mike Flagg had even aired a sweeps piece on that very topic and found five stars didn't guarantee clean linen. He rented local hotel rooms ranging from sleazy to swanky, shined ultraviolet lights on the bedspreads to spot the stains, then followed up with chemical analysis. He even called a raunchy talk radio guy the morning of his airdate to promo the piece with bawdy guy humor.

I started a board for Suicide Susan.

SUSAN NIEMCZYK
AGE: 36
TEACHER

BLONDE
HUNTINGTON'S DISEASE
SUICIDE/FINAL EXIT
ROCHESTER HOTEL

In the bottom of the box I found the Susan pendant along with a convention nametag reading HELLO MY NAME IS SUSAN NIEMCZYK. I held the items in my hands, recalling the name SUSAN pinned to a waitress's blouse, and SUSAN tattooed on a runaway's arm. Could they have been advertisements, attracting a killer's interest?

CHAPTER 17

Normally I wear contact lenses, but this morning I was wearing my brainy-girl glasses for my meeting with Police Chief Vince Capacasa at the cop shop. I wanted to impress him as a serious journalist.

"You can't be serious?" the chief said. "Evidence stays in the property room. Evidence is not a prop for TV ratings. No raincoat. Now move along."

A marble chess set sat on the credenza behind his desk. I also noticed a game already in progress on his computer screen; his long-distance opponent probably on hold until I left.

"Now Chief," I began.

Chiefs dig it when reporters call them Chief. They view each utterance as a frank admission that they outrank you.

"I'm coming to you for help," I continued.

Appealing for help that only they can provide also appeals to their ego.

"Open investigation," he told me. "No comment."

"This story might enable you to close your investigation."

Often if the cops think there's something in it for them, they'll play ball.

"Unlikely. Move along," he repeated.

None of my tactics was working, so I dangled a chance to go off the record.

"This is not an ambush. I didn't come here with a photographer to try to catch you unprepared about a cold case. The door's shut. It's just you and me in here, Chief." I emphasized his title again.

"Don't you have some live shot you need to get to?" he asked, sarcastically. "The TCF Bank in the Cub Foods in White Bear Lake got robbed today. Why don't you stand out in front of it and talk about dye packs and an undisclosed amount of money?"

"You'd just love it if I reported about crime outside of Minneapolis." I leaned across his desk and stared him straight in the eye. If they won't play softball, sometimes you have to play hardball. "You can't get rid of me that easily. This story is slated for air. You can look like you're cooperating, or you can look like you're stonewalling."

He leaned across his desk and held my gaze. Our faces were about a foot apart. Once again, I was glad I was wearing makeup.

"If you have evidence of a crime, you're legally obligated to turn it over."

"I don't have evidence. All I have is a hunch."

"Maybe you should just tell me your hunch instead of worrying your pretty little head."

So much for the power of brainy-girl glasses. The chief leaned back in his chair, the pleased expression of checkmate on his face.

Damn it. I was going to have to level with him.

"REMEMBER OUR DEAL," the chief said. "No match. No story."

He'd scoffed at my theory that the raincoat found on Sinner Susan actually belonged to Waitress Susan.

"And if it does match," I answered, "I have a story and you have a serial killer."

Much better deal for me. If I lost I'd simply scramble for another sweeps story. But if he lost he'd be fending off political trouble forever because serial killers don't just kill people; they kill tourism. And right now the movers and shakers of the Twin Cities were preparing to host the Republican National Convention. Traditionally, Minnesota's considered a Democratic stronghold; but Republicans have bigger expense accounts. And Scandinavians are nothing if not practical.

The chief unfolded the raincoat and laid it on the conference table. Most definitely an anticlimactic moment. The label read London Fog and it looked like virtually every other London Fog raincoat ever sewn. Nothing unique. Nothing memorable. Certainly nothing identifiable. I had a feeling this showdown might end badly for me.

"Can you check the pockets?"

I had promised not to touch anything; the chief had promised to let us roll tape. Malik knew the drill: no matter what the cops said during the next few minutes, he was not to stop rolling unless I said so.

One at a time, the chief turned the four pockets inside out. Empty. Empty. Empty. A blue button.

"That's all," said the chief. "Satisfied?"

The room was quiet. My mind was reaching. For what, I didn't know, but I sensed I was close to something critical.

The button was small and royal blue. It clearly did not belong with the raincoat. Color crime scene photos slowly came into focus in the back of my mind and transformed into one of those rare "aha" moments. Waitress Susan lay dead in the alley, wearing a blue and brown buttoned-up sweater. One button was missing. A small royal blue button.

"I'm satisfied."

CHAPTER 18

I suppose it's egotistical to think you can recognize evil by staring it in the eye, but it panned out for me five years ago in the case of a missing seven-year-old girl down by Mankato. Her mom's boyfriend postered the town with her picture, and he organized extensive searches. He also creeped me out big-time during an interview, and I sensed he was hiding something. Ends up, it was her body.

Identifying a villain with eye contact—it's just a theory—is certainly not foolproof. And the truth is, I'd been fooled more times than not. There had been the Munchausen mom in Brainerd, Minnesota, four years ago. She looked me straight in the eye and swore she had no idea why her daughter was always sick. I believed her. And don't remind me about that high-flying St. Paul attorney who killed his wife last Valentine's Day. He was *so* the perfect source: so charming, so connected, so good on camera. I never once sensed scoundrel in his soul.

Despite my uneven track record, I still wanted to test my premise on Mayor Skubic. I couldn't shake his personal connection with the first Susan and his proximity to the crime. The trick was looking deep into his eyes without him smelling suspicion. I knew just the right time and place.

Mayor Skubic would be home Halloween night, handing out treats to the kiddies and handshakes to their parents. In Minnesota all politicians from the governor on down view Halloween as prime campaign time, second only to donning a plaid shirt and sweating in a Fourth of July parade. Some elected officials also help serve Thanksgiving dinner in homeless shelters, but that's because they're hoping to get on TV on a slow news day, not because they expect to win an election with the indigent vote.

When I offered to take my niece and nephew trick-or-treating, my sister, Robyn, seemed skeptical.

"Aren't you busy with ratings?" During sweeps I usually swept family under the rug. But with no kids of my own, and none likely now, I missed them.

"I can take one night off. I haven't seen them for ages."

"Come on, Mom," pleaded Darcy, age seven. "We never get to do anything."

I cheated by having them listen in on the upstairs phone.

"Robyn, maybe you can offer to work that night and trade for a Saturday off." She's a nurse at a local hospital and, like me, works her share of weekends.

"Please, Mom, can we?" asked five-year-old Davy.

"All right," she agreed.

So I had my props. All I needed was a costume.

Mayor Skubic was dressed in a white hockey goalie mask, like Jason in the horror film *Friday the 13th.* Elsewhere that might be a poor costume choice for a politician. Most go for Uncle Sam or a rubber mask of whoever's currently occupying the White House. But Skubic had been a college hockey hero and hockey rules in Minnesota. One of our competitors once aired a story showing undercover video of underage hockey jocks buying drinks in a local sports bar without getting carded. Viewers called in angry at the station for violating the players' privacy. So no surprise, nobody seemed bothered that one night a year the mayor resembled a serial killer. The rest of the year he resembled a paunchy, aging athlete, but that didn't require any special costume.

His mask made eye contact more difficult than I had expected. I was glad I went with my second choice for Halloween costume. I had almost worn a Lone Ranger mask and Boyer's State Patrol uniform with my hair tucked under his hat. Instead I put on a nurse's uniform I spotted hanging in my sister's coat closet when I picked up the kids. I added a toy stethoscope that belonged to my niece, a big red wig Boyer had given me as a joke, a white half mask, and a heavy dose of fuchsia lipstick. Not a chance I'd be recognized. Especially not as part of this trio. Davy wore a coonskin cap and a fringed suede shirt my sister had sewn. Darcy wore a tiara and a yellow princess dress. They both carried pillow cases in anticipation of a heavy haul of candy.

Halloween is no time for an elected official to go cheap with tiny Tootsie Rolls or SweeTarts. Mayor

Skubic shrewdly handed out full-size candy bars made by Minnesota-based Pearson Candies. He curtsied in front of Darcy, gave her a Nut Goodie, and tossed a Salted Nut Roll in Davy's bag while singing about Davy Crockett, a rifle-wielding politician and king of the wild frontier.

When my turn came, the mayor held my toy stethoscope against his heart. "I think it might be broken," he said.

"It's not real," I answered.

"I meant my heart." He dropped something in my bag. Later I found a Skubic campaign button and his business card with a phone number scribbled on the back. I'd rather have a Mint Pattie.

So what *did* I see in his eyes?

We had maintained eye contact for less than ten seconds. He looked away first, not that it was a contest. His eyes definitely burned—but most likely from a jack-o'-lantern reflecting from the kitchen bay window—not with evil, but reflecting his supposedly broken heart.

Like I said, it was just a theory.

I DIDN'T WANT to linger on the mayor's block, so we hit a handful of houses there then drove to another neighborhood and started fresh. It wasn't even six o'clock, plenty of time to make good on my promise to net Davy and Darcy enough candy to last till Christmas. Call me Aunt Santa.

"You tell me when you've had enough," I told them, noting their already bulging bags.

"We're not tired," Darcy said.

Davy agreed. "I'm strong."

A small house down the street captured their attention. Decorated with pumpkin lights, bats hung from strings, and ceramic black cats adorned the sidewalk.

"Wow." Davy moved toward the action. "It looks scary."

"Let's go," I answered.

A line of children, mesmerized by the haunted house décor, stood in front of us. As we got closer I watched the man handing out popcorn balls and felt certain I'd met him before.

"Come back anytime," he told the trick-or-treaters.

I guessed he was in his midthirties. He wore thick glasses and a black cape. He didn't need a mask because a reddish scar stretched across the bridge of his nose. My memory clicked. When we reached the door, I stooped down, pretending to tie Davy's shoes, but actually keeping my eyes pinned to the man's feet. I spied a monitoring bracelet around the guy's ankle and knew I needed to call Xiong.

I herded my niece and nephew back to the car and told them I'd give a prize to whoever had the most Reese's peanut butter cups. They started counting in the backseat while I hit Xiong's number on my speed dial.

"It's Riley. Can you call up the Minnesota Corrections

Web site? I have an address I need to check on the sex offender's database."

"I'm in the middle of a story for ten," he said. "Can't you do it yourself?"

"I'm out of the office, trick-or-treating. It's a long story. This could be big."

I gave him the address and waited.

"Hey Aunt Riley, so far I have six Reese's and Davy only has four."

"Interesting, honey. Keep counting."

Xiong confirmed that the address matched that of Paul Friendly, a level 3 sex offender, convicted of molesting boys. In the legal world of sex crimes, level 3's are deemed most dangerous, most likely to reoffend. A few years ago I'd covered a community meeting where residents protested his moving into their neighborhood. Headlines and promotions read along the lines of "Friendly Unwelcome." Apparently he had moved again. Inconspicuously. The idea of him handing out Halloween candy repulsed me.

"Now Davy has more than me."

"Keep counting." I called the Channel 3 assignment desk to fill them in and page Malik to meet me a couple blocks away. I took off my wig, put a jacket over my nurse uniform, and rubbed off the lipstick. It might be Halloween, but I didn't want to look like a clown when I confronted Mr. Friendly on camera.

"We're done, Aunt Riley. Guess what? Davy and I have the same amount."

"That's great. Why don't you count MilkyWays next?"

"I want to go to more houses," Davy said.

"We'll do that later," I said. "A friend of mine is coming to take our picture at the scary house."

"We get to go back?" Darcy asked.

"Sure do."

Malik groused about shooting late on Halloween. "I got kids, too, you know."

I apologized. "This is a once-in-a-year opportunity. We've got to get this on camera now."

First Malik shot wide from the back of the van, videotaping the line of kids lured by the elaborate decorations. We wanted a close-up of Mr. Friendly, so Malik put on hat cam—a baseball cap with a pinhole lens in the front and a cable through the back. It wasn't great for low-light situations, but we had no choice.

"Come on, kids." I considered leaving them in the car, but decided I better keep them in sight. Technically, I was a babysitter, not a reporter. "You can each get another popcorn ball, but then wait behind me while I talk to that man. I need to ask him some questions."

Malik signaled that the camera was rolling. He turned his head back and forth to get some nice cover of children wearing football jerseys and dinosaur outfits. Just as we reached the steps, our man told a young boy dressed in camouflage, "Come visit again."

Mr. Friendly patted Davy on the head. "You must live nearby. I think this is your second time here tonight."

"No," Davy said, "my aunt just wants to talk to you." He pointed at me. Damn. Kindergarten curriculum must not include undercover skills.

"Really." Mr. Friendly looked warily at me.

"That's right. You're a level 3 sex offender." I didn't ask it, I said it.

He didn't deny it. The mom and pop crowd in the yard gathered to listen.

"I'm Riley Spartz from Channel 3. You're Paul Friendly and you're not supposed to have contact with children."

"They're approaching me. I'm not approaching them."

"Let's see what the Corrections department has to say. If luring kids with candy isn't violating the letter of your parole, I'm sure it's violating the spirit."

"It's Halloween. Everybody's handing out candy."

"You're not everybody."

"Excuse me," said the father of a boy wearing a Spiderman suit. "Did you say he's a sex offender?"

"Level 3."

His fist hit Mr. Friendly's face a split second later making a crunching noise and squirting blood onto Darcy's yellow princess dress. She screamed and dropped her bag of candy. Davy started to cry. A woman wearing Playboy bunny ears kicked Mr. Friendly in the crotch. I overheard someone in the back calling 911. Malik and I each grabbed a kid and raced for the van. He heaved the big camera onto his shoulder just in time to roll tape of somebody's grandma throwing a pumpkin through Mr. Friendly's front window.

"BASICALLY, YOU STARTED a riot." Noreen relished playing Monday-morning quarterback. "But you did beat the competition."

"Only because she *started* the riot," said Miles Lewis, Channel 3's media attorney. "Of course she beat the competition." He was a short black man in a fancy suit. Him being in the news director's office didn't bode well for me.

Actually, I'd hoped to do more research and hold the story a few days until the first night of the ratings book. But two squad cars responded and the other stations followed on the heels of their sirens. I scrambled to feed tape back from a Channel 3 truck and do a live shot for the top of the news. Noreen was right about the competition. We had the story. They had the aftermath.

"It's just too bad we weren't able to promote it," she continued. "An early show tease or prime-time spot would have let viewers in on our scoop."

Malik and I suffered a setback when we discovered our hidden camera tape didn't have audio. Technical gremlins must have been out Halloweening, so I had to paraphrase for viewers Mr. Friendly's explanation of why he wasn't scum. What we did have on tape was literally a knockout: an exclusive shot of fist slamming face.

"The story's got legs," I said. "I'm happy to do some follow-up stories."

"That's what we need to talk about," Miles said. "It might be better to hand the story off to someone else."

"No way. It's my story. I found it."

I also lost it.

Trouble was, Mr. Friendly's attorney called Noreen earlier that morning, using big lawyer words and threatening to sue Channel 3. Even Miles called that idea laughable. More problematic for us, Mr. Friendly wanted to press criminal charges against his attackers. Our tape was potential evidence and Malik and I, potential witnesses.

Two things stood in our favor. Even if we had to give up the raw tape, our shot wasn't wide enough to capture the gentleman who had thrown the first punch. And if called to testify, I honestly couldn't remember what he looked like.

"Honestly."

"You're sure?" Miles asked.

"Absolutely. It was dark. I was distracted by my niece and nephew."

"That's another thing," Noreen said. "I don't want you taking young children along on stories. Ride-alongs need to be in college. Station policy."

"It didn't start out as a story," I insisted. "It started

out as a family outing. If it weren't for them, we wouldn't have the story."

"Whatever," she scolded me. "Don't let it happen again. And I think Miles is right. You've become a part of the story. We need to assign another reporter."

Just when I thought nothing worse could happen, she told me to give the tapes to Mike Flagg. "His dumpster-diving story fell through and he needs another project."

WHEN I GOT back to my desk I had a message from my sister, peeved. Okay outraged, because, in her words, I used her kids as "pedophile bait." She had still been at work when I finally brought Darcy and Davy home. Fortunately, their dad was lying on the couch watching a cable show on bass fishing, not the news. One of Robyn's friends probably saw my niece and nephew on Channel 3 and ratted me out; more likely, the kids couldn't keep a secret.

Thanksgiving dinner could be tense this year.

AND NO MENTION of Halloween would be honest without disclosing a horror that had been haunting me for the last week. I tried not thinking about it, and I definitely didn't say it out loud. As if denial would keep it from happening and shield me from blame.

If there was a Susan killer, what if the publicity my story would stir up stirred him up?

Right now he didn't seem to pose a physical danger.

So the loftiest rationalization I might use to defend airing the SUSANS story—"warning the public"—wasn't quite valid. I had to fall back on "examining the competence of the police" and "bringing closure to the families." All very good and fine reasons unless the killer struck again. Or a new killer got inspiration.

CHAPTER 19

The first production snafu came when Noreen refused to air the SUSANS story on the anniversary date.

"We're not wasting it then," she said. "That's a Saturday. Our lowest-rated show of the week. Everybody's out on the town. Nobody's home in front of the tube. Especially not our younger viewers."

Advertisers particularly covet viewers in the 18–49 age bracket. For once, no argument from me. Nobody wanted a 40 share more than I did. If Noreen could scheme up some strategy to help make that happen, well, that might help explain why she was the boss. She and the promotion manager shuffled the November lineup on a wall-sized calendar and slated the story for the sixth, to kick off the first Sunday night of the book, following the network's powerhouse prime-time lineup.

"If we can build on those numbers, that will help our overall rating for the month," she said. "Also any follow-up stories will benefit us as the book unfolds. Riley, start crashing."

A deadline.

Some folks need drugs or alcohol for exhilaration. Me, I get high on deadlines. And that's good because smoke makes me cough, needles scare me, and I'm inept at swallowing pills.

For writing inspiration, I pushed away visions of viewers and concentrated on the victims. Propped against my office walls, the SUSANS boards displayed a photo of each woman. Their eyes seemingly watched as I told their stories.

Susan Redding—a doctor's wife with a secret lover who may or may not have killed her.

Susan Chenowith—a waitress who never made it in to work the next day.

Susan Moreno—a teenage hooker living and dying on the edge.

Susan Niemczyk—a schoolteacher bent on suicide. Or was she?

I was in a zone when I wrote SUSANS, or when the story wrote itself. The words fell onto the pages that easily.

>((RILEY/TRACK))
>A DEADLY ANNIVERSARY
>IS APPROACHING.

Television news scripts are typed, all caps, in a two-inch-wide column on the right side of the page. The caps allow for easy reading on the teleprompter. The width times out to about a second a line, enabling newscast producers to estimate the time block needed for the story. Novels measure in pages, newspapers measure in inches, TV measures in minutes and seconds.

A CHANNEL 3
INVESTIGATION INTO
THE VIOLENT DEATHS
OF FOUR MINNESOTA
WOMEN HAS DISCOVERED
EERIE PARALLELS THAT
MIGHT SIMPLY BE A
STRING OF STRANGE
COINCIDENCES . . . OR
THAT MIGHT BE MUCH
MORE.

The left side of the page is reserved for editing instructions, location of specific video shots, and names of the talking heads in the story. As I related the dates and facts of each case, I dropped in sound bites from the interviews.

((SOUND/MOM/TEARS))
SOMETIMES I WATCH MEN
ON THE STREET AND
WONDER, WAS IT HIM?
OR WAS IT HIM?
((SOUND/FATHER))
I'D KILL THE GUY IF I
KNEW.

SUSANS was enterprise work, not some feature story spoon-fed to the media by government or corporate

press releases. That meant the station lawyer had a
hand in vetting it, but because Channel 3 was merely
questioning the competence of the police, not pointing a finger at a specific suspect or a big advertiser,
script review went relatively smoothly.

> IS THIS MAN SERVING A
> LIFE SENTENCE FOR A
> CRIME HE DIDN'T
> COMMIT?
> SUSAN CHENOWITH
> WORE THIS RAINCOAT
> THE NIGHT SHE
> DISAPPEARED.
> WHEN HER BODY WAS
> DISCOVERED . . . THE
> RAINCOAT WAS MISSING.
> EXACTLY ONE YEAR
> LATER . . . SUSAN MORENO
> WAS FOUND DEAD . . .
> WEARING A RAINCOAT
> HER FRIENDS AND FAMILY
> SAY SHE NEVER OWNED.
> IN THE POCKET . . . THIS
> BUTTON.
> COMPARE IT TO THE
> BUTTONS ON SUSAN
> CHENOWITH'S SWEATER.

I used a split-screen effect to show the button next to a button from Susan Chenowith's sweater. Perfect match. Then the camera pushed in for a close-up.

> LOOK CLOSELY AT THIS
> CRIME SCENE PHOTO AND
> YOU'LL SEE ONE OF HER
> SWEATER BUTTONS IS
> MISSING.

For the chief, a mere button morphed into a smoking gun.

One minute after I left the news set, my desk phone started ringing. Chief Capacasa was on the other end of the line, steamed. He'd handled scandal before, self-made, family-made, and media-made. A pro at massaging negative news, he understood that the SUSANS story was potentially more damaging than the time he had deflected rumors that his cousin in Chicago used to be Mafia muscle.

The last time I saw Vince Capacasa, he was chuckling as he packed the raincoat back in the evidence box. He had assumed no match, no story. But don't forget what happens when you assume.

"We had a deal!" The chief wasn't chuckling now. He bellowed. "You weren't supposed to run that story."

"No. We had a deal I wouldn't air unless I could prove a connection between the killings. I believe I've met that burden."

"You didn't tell me about the button!"

"I didn't realize what it meant until later."

Not exactly. The moment my mind made the connection, I also knew that I'd never get that videotape out of the cop shop and back to Channel 3 if the chief sensed that the button held any significance.

"You had the same information I had, Chief. And better access to the evidence. Let's do an interview tomorrow, talking about what this means to your investigation."

"An interview? You can't be serious. I'm never talking to you again!"

"You can look like you're cooperating, or you can look like you're stonewalling."

He slammed the phone down. I leaned back in my chair, savoring the pleasant sensation of checkmate.

CHAPTER 20

The next morning the front desk phoned. Said I had a package. I bounded out of the newsroom to claim a glass vase covered in purple tissue paper. I'd received a slew of bouquets at Boyer's funeral, but none since. My sister had pressed some of the petals in the scrapbook. The perennials I'd replanted outside. The rest I'd donated to the nursing home where his father lived.

Boyer wasn't the kind of guy who sent flowers. He made his own traditions. Valentine's Day he'd walk through the door carrying a life-sized chocolate gun in a gold foil box. Once I had suggested I'd bring home the candy if he would send me a dozen roses.

But he had a fatalistic view on flowers. "Why would I send you something that's just going to die?"

"Flowers are romantic," I told him. "A sentimental gesture of temporary beauty. Besides, it reminds other men at the office that I'm taken."

"Don't they know I carry a gun? I imagine that would be more effective than flowers. Point these guys out at the next company party."

Back at my desk, I eagerly tore away the tissue paper. I gasped at a bouquet of dead lilies.

"No card?" Malik asked.

"No card," I answered.

No fingerprints either. Mine were the only ones the crime lab techs later found on the vase. The receptionist had briefly stepped away from her station and missed seeing the delivery.

Clearly someone was unhappy about the SUSANS story, but the list of suspects was long and my time was short. The middle of sweeps is no time to rest on your laurels, not even if your story delivers a veiled threat and a 37 share.

When I had walked in an hour earlier, the number was highlighted on the overnight ratings sheet posted on the newsroom bulletin board. Through her glass office, Noreen put her phone down long enough to wildly wave me over.

"Congrats on the overnights," she said. I simply nodded. Not 40, but closer than Channel 3 had come since the firebomb killed my husband. And since June wasn't a ratings month, Noreen had forgotten all about that.

She wanted a follow-up story. ASAP. "We can promote the hell out of this."

I was eager to comply. SUSANS wasn't meant to be a stand-alone piece. I was counting on new tips to push the investigation into new directions.

But first I had to chase the dog cremation story. We'd used Malik's first and middle names and his cell phone number as the contact with the veterinary clinic. That morning, one week to the day that we had dropped off Lucky, Malik received a message from Dr. Petit.

"Lucky's ashes are ready. Please call to arrange a time to pick them up."

This time Malik wore a glasses cam. A pinhole camera was concealed in the nose bridge between the plastic lenses. The frames needed to be thick enough to hide both the camera and a thin cable that ran through one arm of the glasses, so Malik looked a little like Buddy Holly. The cable then ran under his hair, behind his collar, and down his back to a fanny pack with battery and recorder.

"You're *sure* these are Lucky's ashes?" I asked Dr. Petit. His tie, featuring a chihuahua in a sombrero, distracted me for a second.

"Absolutely."

We sat around a conference table. I glanced over at Malik, who stared steadily at Dr. Petit through the glasses. The vet pushed a small cardboard box toward me.

"It's such a comfort to know Lucky's ashes are safe," I told him. Now I regretted not spending an extra fifty bucks on an urn. That would have been a nice prop on the news set.

"You have my word. It's a special service we offer our pet families during difficult times. I hope to see you again under less painful circumstances."

"I'm certain we'll meet again."

Quite certain. But I made no promises that our next meeting might not be under even more painful circumstances, once he learned we worked for Channel 3.

Our local cremation expert confirmed that, as with

Fluffy's box, the contents of Lucky's box contained no animal cremains. They were likely the same mixture of cat litter and landscape pebbles that the Texas lab had identified. We stopped by FedEx to overnight Lucky's ashes so they could be tested as well.

Back at Channel 3, I had a message to call Dusty Foster's defense attorney. He had breaking news: based on our story he'd managed to get a Duluth judge to order a hearing on whether DNA testing of some old evidence should be allowed. Exactly the kind of follow-up Noreen wanted.

We made the drive to Duluth that night, so we could roll tape first thing in the morning.

"A blood spot on Dusty's shirt was introduced at the trial," his attorney said. "The prosecution argued it was the victim's blood. Dusty testified he cut himself shaving. Lab work confirmed it was type O human blood, but both he and the victim had type O. We were hoping for reasonable doubt, but the jury went for guilty."

"To be fair," I argued, "your client did have motive and opportunity."

"Yeah, but I think the blood influenced their verdict."

"How is this test different?" I asked.

"Fifteen years ago it was too small a sample for further forensic testing, but science has improved since then and a lab might now be able to tell us whose blood it was or wasn't. If it really is my client's blood, I'll argue for a new trial."

I was skeptical. "Would you get it?"

"Maybe, but as far as I'm concerned, the best evidence of his innocence is his alibi for the other homicides."

All day Channel 3 promoted the story for all it was worth and then some.

> TONIGHT AT TEN, A NEW
> DEVELOPMENT IN THE
> SUSANS STORY . . . IS A
> CONVICTED MURDERER
> ONE STEP CLOSER TO
> FREEDOM?
> FIND OUT TONIGHT ON
> CHANNEL 3.

Even I thought we were laying on the hype a little thick, but that didn't stop me from applying more pressure on the Minneapolis police. After my set piece, the anchor turned to me on a scripted two-shot.

> ((ANCHOR/TWO-SHOT))
> RILEY, TWO OF THE
> MURDERS HAPPENED IN
> MINNEAPOLIS . . . WHAT
> ARE POLICE HERE
> DOING TO
> MOVE THE
> INVESTIGATION
> FORWARD?

The camera switched to a close-up shot of me.

> ((RILEY, CU))
> THEY AREN'T SAYING . . .
> BUT CHANNEL 3 HAS
> LEARNED THAT THE
> MAYOR'S OFFICE HAS
> RECEIVED DOZENS OF
> CALLS FROM CONCERNED
> CITIZENS . . . MANY OF
> THEM NAMED SUSAN.

That last bit of info came from our political reporter, who hadn't seen the mayor that mad since a blizzard had threatened Minneapolis the same weekend the city hosted the Super Bowl.

Both telephone lines were ringing as I walked back into my office. My flashing voice mail light indicated they weren't the first viewers trying to reach me since the report ended three minutes earlier. When a story gets especially hot, some reporters prefer to let the machine take the heat, and they'll return select calls later; but telephone roulette doesn't scare me. I picked up the receiver, hit one of the lines, and smoothly said, "This is Riley Spartz, Channel 3."

"This is Karl Skubic, mayor of Minneapolis." His voice was agitated, not smooth.

"Hey, Mayor, thanks for returning my call."

I'd left a message with his media guy yesterday,

ostensibly seeking city reaction to the SUSANS story in an on-camera interview, but really hoping to watch him squirm under the lights when I asked about his relationship to the first victim. The mayor had skillfully deflected that by declining the interview request through his press peons and refusing to take my call. I considered calling him on the secret number he'd given me Halloween night but decided to save that for a special occasion.

"Can we tape that interview tomorrow morning?" I remained cool and professional.

That stopped him, as he weighed the drawbacks to continuing our conversation.

"No. That's not why I'm calling. I just want to say, and I'm sure you're not aware of it, but it seems to me the current path you're on is less likely to help law enforcement and more likely to make our city seem unsafe."

"You're welcome to say that on camera, Mayor. We'll put it on the air."

"I really think it's better to leave it to the police to make any appropriate comments. I'm certainly not going to impede their investigation."

While he continued with a canned speech about citizen responsibility to the community, I pondered the pros and cons of bringing up his college sweetheart. So far I had left that part out of the stories. It was such a loaded fact, I knew it would make the station attorney bonkers. We were nowhere close to meeting the legal burden of actually throwing a veil of suspicion on anyone, even a public figure like the mayor. True, a politician doesn't get as much libel protection as a private citizen, but realistically I knew we wouldn't be putting his Susan connection on the air anytime soon—if ever. But that didn't mean I couldn't bring it up right now, phrasing it in the form of a question, just to make him sweat.

"Mayor Skubic, why exactly did you and Susan Redding break up?"

No answer. He was so quiet I felt sure he stopped breathing. People often confuse action with drama, but silence can be even more dramatic. I finally broke the stillness because I didn't want him to hang up. "It sounded like kind of a volatile relationship. Was it?"

I deliberately used the word "volatile." First, because I was fishing and wasn't sure what I was hoping to find. Second, "volatile" is a good bait word because it sounds worse than its actual meaning, which is "unstable or changeable." And tell me what relationship between a man and a woman isn't that?

Our phone connection ended with a click and a dial tone. A whimper, not a slam.

Sometimes, if I'm honest with myself, I have to admit I'm the kind of reporter who deserves an occasional bouquet of dead flowers.

But not twice in one week.

CHAPTER 21

This time I found a bouquet of blooms tucked under the windshield wipers of my car when I left work the next night.

"At least they're not dead lilies," Malik said. I called him to videotape the yellow petals before they wilted any further and fell out. "This might not have anything to do with our story. What else have you done to piss anyone off lately?"

"Except they're black-eyed Susans," I pointed out. "That's the name of the flower. Black-eyed Susans."

"I'm a rose man myself. A nice, safe flower, suitable for all occasions. Nobody resents roses."

Malik followed me home and walked inside with me to check things out. I scanned a couple shelves in my home library and pulled out a book called *The Meaning of Almost Everything*. It listed supposed meanings of foods, colors, shoes . . . I flipped to the chapter on flowers.

Lily meant "purity." Black-eyed Susan meant "justice."

"Hey, those are good things," Malik said. "Purity. Justice. It might not mean someone's out to get you. It might mean someone's rooting for you. Maybe a behind-the-scenes cheerleader encouraging you to keep on digging in that garden of clues."

"Except my flowers are always dead," I reminded him.

"Someone's out to get you."

I scanned the list of plants. Could be worse. Begonia meant "beware." And we all know what hemlock means.

"What kind of plant is that?" Malik pointed to some dried leaves and white berries hanging on the doorway between the kitchen and living room.

"Mistletoe. And don't ask." Boyer had insisted on year-round mistletoe, and I couldn't bring myself to take it down.

Malik left to do errands on his way home. I was in a research mode, so I grabbed the baby name book I'd given Boyer for his birthday. He had wanted a pack of kids, and even if I wasn't ready to play mom yet, he was plenty ready to pick names. I found the *S* page and learned that Susan was one of the most popular girl names in America during the fifties and sixties.

SUSAN (HEBREW) "LILY" APOCRYPHAL: AN ACCUSED ADULTERESS SAVED BY THE WISDOM OF DANIEL. *Siusan, Sosanna, Sue, Sukey, Suki, Susana, Susanetta, Susann, Susanna, Susannah, Susanne, Susette, Susi, Susie, Susy, Suzanna, Suzanne, Suzette, Suzi, Suzie, Suzy, Suzzy, Zsa Zsa.*

At the mention of adultery I couldn't help thinking of Susan Redding. Could this be a clue? While the other victims certainly weren't virgins, I didn't think they were adulterers. But I remained a little fuzzy on the nuances of adultery. If a married woman slept with a man other than her husband, that was obviously adultery. But what if a single woman had sex with a married man? Was she also an adulteress, or just a slut?

The dictionary was no help, so I dusted off the Bible and skimmed the book of Daniel for such wisdom. His episode in the lion's den was comforting. His vision of the four beasts was confusing. But I found no mention of any Old Testament character named Susan.

I tore the Susan page from the baby name book and stuffed it in my briefcase.

LIGHT SHINING THROUGH stained glass always seems heaven sent. The church across the river in St. Paul was empty the next morning except for a few devout parishioners kneeling in the back pews. I stuck my head into the parish office looking for Father Mountain.

"He's hearing confession," a middle-aged lady behind a desk told me.

I took a closer look and realized the kneeling parishioners were actually in line for absolution. I decided to wait for a few minutes of Father Mountain's undivided attention. I was lucky the whole third grade of the parochial school wasn't ahead of me.

Father Mountain had been my rural parish priest when I was growing up, overseeing life and death in the Spartz family. He'd baptized me and buried my great-grandpa Riley a couple months later. Over the years he'd been promoted to larger, more urban parishes. We'd become reacquainted several years ago when I was working on a story about charity fraud. As an adult I had fallen away from the Church, partly because of official teachings, partly because of sex scandals. But I still believed in God. That belief took a beating when Boyer died, but Father Mountain was a merry man of the cloth whose company I enjoyed. He'd forgiven me for getting married in Vegas rather than letting him do the honors, and he had repeatedly urged me to forgive myself for the guilt I still carried about my husband's murder.

When my turn for confession came, I knelt inside the small, curtained booth and put my face next to the divider screen.

"Bless me, Father," I whispered. "I talked back to my boss and was mean to the mayor."

"Riley, is that you? What are you doing here?"

"I have a question about adultery."

"Are you here to make a confession? You're overdue, but this is not the sort of sin I expected."

"No, this is work-related, not soul-related. I checked the dictionary. I checked the Bible. I'm a little embarrassed to be talking sex with a man who embraces celibacy, but I figured you'd have the answers."

"How many people are behind you in line?"

"Just one. A lady with blue hair and a fur-collared coat. She told me to go ahead, she's still examining her conscience."

"That's Mrs. Tate," he told me. "Comes twice a week. Doesn't mind waiting 'cause she likes to visit afterward. We trade church jokes. By the way, did you hear the one about the priest, the rabbi, and the minister in a fishing boat?"

"No, but I'm kind of on deadline now."

"All right, so what's your question?"

"If an unmarried woman sleeps with a married man, is she an adulteress?"

"No. Technically, she's a fornicator. Adultery is complicated. The biblical concept had less to do with the sin of sex than the sin of 'trespassing' on another man's property. It created a double standard because for the act to be adultery, the woman had to be married. So if a married man had relations with another man's wife, the Bible calls them both adulterers. But if he sleeps with an unmarried woman, he's in the clear."

"That is so unfair!"

"Keep your voice down or Mrs. Tate will think I'm doling out heavy penance today. Absolutely it's unfair, which is why Church tradition, to preserve the sanctity of marriage, considers an affair adulterous if either party is married."

"I was researching the name Susan."

"I watch the news. What did you find?"

"An accused adulteress saved by the wisdom of Daniel. But I don't know what that means. I read Daniel but couldn't find any Susan."

"Actually, it's Susanna. And the questions you're raising deal with some of the Church's most intricate theology. You shouldn't pop into a confessional looking for quick answers. You should join a Bible study group."

"I don't have the time or the heart for that level of research right now, Father. It's a long shot that this is even related to what I'm working on. How about you just give me the basics? Who's Susanna?"

"All right, but I want you back here for a real confession when this is over."

"Deal. Susanna?"

"She was a beautiful, pious wife who was lusted after by two Jewish elders who schemed to blackmail her. They threatened to accuse her of having a lover unless she slept with them. She refused, choosing to fall into their power and face death rather than sin before the Lord."

"This story is in the Bible?"

"Daniel, chapter thirteen."

"I didn't see it, and I just looked this morning."

"What kind of Bible?"

"I don't know. Probably one I took from a hotel room. Is that a sin?"

"Different faiths use different Bibles. Each believes theirs to be the true interpretation. The Roman Catholic version has more books than the Protestant one, including two extra chapters of Daniel. Stop by my office on your way out and tell my secretary I said to give you a real Bible."

"So about Susanna? Saved not stoned?"

"That's where the wisdom of Daniel comes in. Read it for yourself. It's time for Mrs. Tate now. In the meantime, give me ten Our Fathers and fifteen Hail Marys."

CHAPTER 22

My conscience was clear.

Plenty of reporters simply rush up to the target of an investigation, stick a camera in their face, and yell, "Why are you cheating people?"

That's called an ambush interview.

The ensuing chaos often results in good TV—it can certainly help the pacing of a slow story otherwise cluttered with documents and talking heads. But it seldom results in a substantive answer to the question of why people are being cheated. There's also something unsportsmanlike about playing the championship match with an opponent who doesn't realize the game is under way.

I prefer landing an on-camera/sit-down/face-to-face interview because . . . well . . . sometimes crooks say the darnedest things. Like the time I confronted a shady car dealer about lease improprieties and he blurted out, "We're not intentionally scamming them."

Why would any adversary agree to such a showdown? For some, their ego can't fathom that their trickery has been discovered. Others, deep down, think they can explain it all away with fancy words or complicated math.

On my end, it's important not to let on that the jig is up. So when I first called Dr. Petit, I didn't say, "The

Texas lab just confirmed Lucky's ashes are a fraud and I'm doing a story on what a horrible excuse you are for a vet."

What I said was: "I'd like to interview you for a consumer story on pet grief and cremation."

I hoped the hunger for hoopla might make him bite. After all, free publicity could bring a fresh menu of gullible victims. Dr. Petit, however, seemed to sense this television opportunity was too good to be true.

"Thanks, but I don't care to be included in your story."

The gang at *60 Minutes* doesn't go away so easily and neither do I.

"Oh." I feigned surprise. "Any particular reason?"

Long pause. "I'm not terribly photogenic."

"Oh, everybody says that. We have special lights that are very flattering."

"I'm sorry, I'm just a poor public speaker."

"Don't worry. This will be taped, not live. That's much easier."

"No thanks, but maybe I could give you the names of some other veterinarians."

We bluffed back and forth before it became clear I needed to show my hand. My lawyer is quite firm on this point: the story can't air unless the subject gets a chance to respond to the allegations.

It might seem unequivocal that it must be illegal to jump out from behind a bush and chase someone with a camera, but it's not, and TV crews actually do it for sound legal reasons. The best way for Channel 3 to prove (in a court of law if I were sued) that Dr. Petit was given the opportunity to respond is to show a videotape of that opportunity to the jurors. If what they end up watching is me pursuing the plaintiff down the street while he covers his face with a magazine, ignoring my questions, whose fault is that?

"Even though it was inconvenient," my lawyer would probably argue, "my client went the extra mile to give the plaintiff one last chance to explain why he was cheating people."

It might not be Media Law 101, but then I'd never been sued, either.

PETIT FORMALLY DECLINED an on-camera/sit-down/face-to-face interview to respond to allegations he was running a pet cremation scam.

"You put that on the air and you'll hear from my lawyers!" he yelled into the telephone.

So yes, my conscience was definitely clear about ambushing him. Now it was simply a matter of logistics. Clinic versus home? Clinic was better. Home ambushes make me feel like a jerk; and neighbors sometimes report vehicles that don't belong on the street. Morning versus evening? Morning was better. The clinic opened at 9 a.m. and closed at 6 p.m. Sunrise came just after seven, sunset just after five. Malik and I needed daylight for our mission.

We moved the van into position while it was still dark so nobody would notice us climbing in back, out of sight. We waited for Dr. Petit to drive up to work in his white Cadillac. The overcast day meant good light without shadows. At eight thirty he pulled his vehicle into his usual space, about forty feet from the front door of the veterinary clinic.

"Patience," I whispered. Malik kept the van door ajar so he'd be able to move quickly. I wore a wireless microphone to record my voice and Petit's in case we were out of audio range of the camera mike.

"I'll go first and approach him casually," I said. "He might say something useful if he doesn't see the camera and freak. You keep inside and shoot through the window."

"But if he bolts, I'm after him." He put a finger to his lips and started rolling.

Dr. Petit got out of his shiny Caddy and locked the door. Good. Now we had him trapped between two locked doors. Whichever direction he went, clinic or car, he'd have to fumble with a key to get away. He was halfway to the clinic when I reached him.

"Hello, Dr. Petit, I'm Riley Spartz from Channel 3. We spoke on the phone yesterday."

I stood between the veterinarian and the clinic door, careful not to block Malik's camera angle.

"I have nothing to say to you."

"Why are you misrepresenting pet cremations?" Short, precisely phrased questions edit well.

"You want my response? This is my response!"

He reached out his hand. In his grip, a small, odd-looking gun.

It's funny what things register when you're paralyzed with pain. In the split second before I crashed to the ground, I noticed Petit was wearing a necktie featuring a coiled snake, fangs ready to strike. The last thing I remember was Malik rushing past me, screaming what was supposed to be my next line, "Why are you cheating people?"

"SHOCKED IS THE word." Malik was talking to Noreen on his cell phone. "Can you believe it? The son of a bitch Tasered her."

Dr. Petit had delivered at least 50,000 volts of electricity to my body with a Taser stun gun. The impact incapacitated me. I hit the dirt flat, like a brick, with no chance to fling out an arm and break my fall. Out for only five seconds, I still felt dazed moments later. Malik picked gravel from my face and hair and helped me stagger back to the van.

"She'll be okay," he assured Noreen, before answering the question foremost on her mind. "Absolutely I was rolling."

THE ESSENCE OF vertigo still clung to me as I hobbled into the newsroom. Word of my ambush-gone-amok had spread throughout the building.

The station suits waited in Noreen's fishbowl office to watch the electrifying tape of my mouth open wide in pain like a largemouth bass.

I'd already eyeballed the encounter through the

camera viewfinder on the way back and had no interest in seeing it on a big screen. But the general manager, station lawyer, promotion director, and Noreen would have paid per view if necessary. I closed my eyes when Malik pressed *play*. I wish I'd closed my ears instead: the audio of my harrowing wail was terse, but torturous. Especially since the bosses kept rewinding the tape.

Over and over I heard: "You want my response? This is my response!" . . . "Aghhh!" . . . "Why are you cheating people?"

The fourth time through, I snapped at Malik, "Why are you asking him about cheating people? How come you didn't ask him about zapping people?"

"I apologize. I am ashamed. All I could think about was where the interview was heading next. When you went down, I didn't have a plan."

"You did great, Malik." Noreen piled on the praise. "Lots of photographers would have dropped the camera and run to help her. You kept taping, and that's what counts. If you hadn't, Riley would have been stunned for nothing."

"During sweeps, this tape is priceless," added the promotion director. "It might be worth five share points alone. How soon can we get it on the air?"

We'd finished shooting the bulk of the story and just needed stand-ups, reaction from our tipster Toby Elness, and a few fill-in shots. Write. Lawyer. Rewrite. Edit. Air.

"Three days," I answered.

"Make it four. That will give us more time to promote the hell out of this," the promotion guy said. The other suits nodded. He headed out the door, leaving the news to us while he concentrated on the marketing.

The rest of the meeting dealt with what kind of legal action, if any, the station should take against Dr. Petit.

"What do you mean, 'if any'?" I asked. "The guy shot me."

"But technically you're not hurt." Easy for Miles Lewis to say. His most physical activity is sitting behind a lawyer's desk, crossing his fingers that none of us libels anyone.

"You'd prefer if I were hurt?" I said.

"Absolutely not," Noreen said. "We need you to write the story."

"If this had happened in Wisconsin, it would be a slam dunk," Miles said. "There it's a felony to even possess a Taser gun, much less use one."

While Tasers are banned in seven states, it's perfectly legal for Minnesotans to possess one. Except in St. Paul, which joined Chicago, Washington, DC, and New York in the last couple years to pass special anti-Taser laws. There, cops are the only folks allowed to carry.

Ironically, the only known stun gun deaths nationally have occurred after cops subdued suspects. Whether the perps had bad hearts to begin with, died of a drug overdose, or whether Tasers are actually lethal weapons is debatable, depending on which side of the trigger you're on. The folks at Taser headquarters are quick to point out that no coroner has ever listed their weapon as a sole cause of death.

"I'm talking about assault charges, not conceal and carry," I said.

"Yes," Miles nodded, "but he'll probably claim he felt threatened. Juries hate the media, they might buy that."

I crossed my arms and leaned back in my chair, shaking my head. "Not after my story airs, they won't."

"No talk like that," Miles insisted. "We don't want to give the impression that you're doing the story for revenge. The story is the story. If you can't remain objective, someone else has to take over."

That got my attention. "I'm not giving up this story, too."

Miles spoke slowly, deliberately using simple language instead of legalese. "I'm only pointing out that if the station runs the tape ad nauseam but complains it was a crime, then it looks like we're trying to have it both ways, that we're also benefiting from the crime."

"I'm worried pressing charges makes us look whiny," Noreen said.

Miles disagreed. "I'm actually more worried about looking like losers if he gets acquitted. Then Petit goes from villain to victim."

"Could somebody please worry for maybe ten seconds about sending a message not to mess with reporters?" I asked.

They looked at me like I was daft.

BACK AT MY desk three messages flashed. I listened to a voice mail from Susan Redding's best friend, Laura Robins. Since my lunch with Dr. Redding, I'd left several messages for her, but until now she seemed to be ducking me.

"Hi, Riley," the message went, "I'm down in the Cities today and hoped we might get together privately. Call me on my cell."

Her wanting to meet was good news. Her using the word "privately" was bad news. That suggested no camera. But anxious to learn more about Mayor Skubic's early years and needing a breather before writing the pet cremation story, I set up a late-afternoon appointment with Laura.

Dusty Foster's mother had left the next message. So grateful for all I was doing to help her son. "I always knew he didn't kill that woman. I just knew it. Mothers can always tell."

My own mom also had called. She and my dad live in rural southern Minnesota, far outside Channel 3's viewing area. She read something in the newspaper about my SUSANS story and wanted me to know that they almost named one of my sisters Susan. And could I please send them a dub to watch.

First, sleep. Since I had a couple hours to kill, I

sacked out on a sofa in the greenroom. That's the traditional name for the cubbyhole where guests wait to be
interviewed on live shows, and where TV reporters and
anchors get fluffed and buffed prior to airtime. "Greenroom" first appeared in the sixteenth century as the-
atrical vernacular for a behind-the-scenes place for
actors to relax before stepping on stage. Why that particular color remains obscure, but Channel 3's greenroom, like most, is painted green.

Hollywood lights and a makeup counter take up
much of the space. Head shots of station reporters and
anchors hang on one wall. Celebrity autographs deco-
rate another. President Jimmy Carter. Movie star Dennis
Hopper. Tenor Luciano Pavarotti. These names are
mingled with a national spelling bee champion, the
head of the local Vice Lords gang, and a winner of the
Pillsbury Bake-Off. But because Minnesota is a huge
pro sports market—football, baseball, basketball, and
hockey—many of the John Hancocks belong to ath-
letes. Alan Page. Randy Moss. Kirby Puckett. The autograph wall, a faded green compared to the rest of the
room, is never painted over.

The greenroom is also a popular crashing place for
staff between shifts. I never reached REM sleep
because a certain floor director kept opening the door
to check if the couch was clear. Just as well, any dreams
that afternoon would probably have been haunted by
the electrifying sound from the Taser. Eventually Malik
shook me awake. Right on time. I'd asked him to play

alarm clock while he loaded video clips into the edit cube down the hall. I scrolled through the shots before heading out. By the time I had script approval, he'd be ready to record my voice track and start editing.

LAURA ALREADY HAD a table at a college snack bar a few blocks from Channel 3. From my perspective, it's an ideal place to meet a source: close and cheap, no waitresses to interrupt, students seldom notice outsiders, and there's usually plenty of room to spread out papers.

"This takes me back in time," Laura said.

"You didn't sound like you wanted to be wined and dined, and we can hang here without attracting attention. Kids aren't big news viewers, so no one's going to recognize me and wonder what we're up to."

Curious about why she wanted this meeting, I brought up Dr. Redding, just to get her talking. "He seems to have a high opinion of himself."

She laughed. "Oh, did he talk down to you? Don't take it personally. That's just his nature."

"He must be more approachable with patients."

"As long as infidelity isn't an issue."

"What do you mean?"

"A friend of mine was a patient of his. She was married and having an affair with a colleague. When she confided that during therapy, he dropped her."

"Sounds rather judgmental for his line of work."

"His ego took a bruising after Susan was killed. Not

so much that she died, but the public spectacle of murder and the shame of her doing it with the gardener. Let's just say I think he has trust issues with women."

"So he never remarried?"

"No. If a public function requires he attend in the company of a woman, he shows up with someone suitable. But they are pretty interchangeable, and I don't get the impression he considers any of them special."

I paused now to let her lead the conversation. She didn't disappoint me. "Last time we talked, you asked if I had any doubt Dusty Foster killed Susan."

"And the last time we talked, you told me you didn't."

"I do now."

She'd seen the news coverage of the protesters outside Oak Park Heights Prison the night before. They had chanted for justice and waved signs reading FREE DUSTY FOSTER and HE'S NO SUSAN KILLER. Barely a couple dozen of them, but because the camera crew shot the scene tight, from different angles, on air it looked like a crowd.

Among them, Dusty's mom. She spoke convincingly of his innocence in a live interview. "Do you think I'd be able to visit my son and look him in the eye if I thought he was a cold-blooded killer?" Our new nightside reporter covered the story with such enthusiasm it seemed inevitable the metal doors should clank open and Dusty walk free before the newscast ended.

As I watched the coverage I again recalled *Trent's*

Last Case, one of my favorite reporter mysteries, and thought about how close an innocent man comes to ruin in that classic tale. Even I found myself asking if perhaps Dusty Foster might have gotten himself in a jam so perilous even the truth could not save him.

That tableau also shook Laura's conviction and made her dial my number. Now she pulled a manila envelope from her purse and pushed it across the table. Inside, a faded Polaroid photo of a young Susan Redding with a black eye and bruised face. On the back, a handwritten note read "Karl Skubic did this." It was signed "Susan O'Keefe" and dated 1985.

"She gave this to me years ago and told me to hang on to it, just in case."

"How come you never gave it to the police?" I asked.

"At the time of her murder, it seemed clear Foster did it. I had no doubt. The police had no doubt. Why muddy the case? Why muddy Skubic's future? Susan had expressed no fear of Karl since then. They hardly ever saw each other, but if their paths crossed socially, they were both cordial. The picture was from another lifetime."

"But now?"

"But now I don't know what to think." Tears clung to the corners of her eyes. Stubbornly she blinked them back. "Karl Skubic was in Duluth the day of her murder. And these killings have continued while Foster has been locked away. I can't go to the police now; he's the

mayor of Minneapolis. I know how these things work—
he owns the police chief."

City politics aren't as inescapable as all that, but
Laura had a point. And it certainly explained why
Mayor Skubic might have wanted to get behind the
police tape at the Minneapolis Susan murder scenes. I
had written his field trips off as curiosity or ego.
Garnett had been concerned the mayor might uninten-
tionally contaminate the crime scene with his DNA,
but what if that had been his goal all along? To establish
an explanation for why his DNA might turn up?

"I might need you to do a camera interview," I told
Laura.

"Sorry. The photo is the best I can do."

It was plenty. For now.

BACK AT THE station I made a color copy of the
Polaroid, front and back, on Channel 3 letterhead,
scrawled "When do you want to do that interview?" and
signed my name. I put the sheet in an envelope,
addressed it to Mayor Karl Skubic, wrote PERSONAL on
the front, and dropped it in the mail.

I hid the original under my computer monitor.

Most likely, Miles would play heavy and nix airing the
photo. Decades old, probably unrelated to the murder
case, but still it gave me an opportunity to mess with
the mayor. That's worth something in this business.

Then I dialed the secret cell phone number he had
given me Halloween night.

CHAPTER 23

arnett admired my chutzpah with the Polaroid.

But deep down we doubted Mayor Skubic was the killer. And the station attorney was adamant about not naming the mayor in a suspect context unless we'd already proven the wrong man was convicted. Those types of perfect endings happen in books and movies, but seldom in TV news. Darn the need for facts. That's also why I had no fear about arranging a breakfast date with the mayor later in the week. The mayor had no fear either; he thought he was meeting a Halloween honey to cure his broken heart.

"You could be setting up an interesting showdown," Garnett said. "I'm just not sure if it's going to be between you and the mayor, the mayor and the first lady, or the mayor and the police chief."

I reached Garnett on his cell phone as he walked past the Paul Bunyan flume, getting a feel for what passes as normal at the Mall of America's giant indoor amusement park. Too busy to meet him, I was caught in the "chain and chase" phase of sweeps, either chained to my desk writing a script, or chasing frantically to nail a final story element.

"I'll worry about that later. Right now, I'm crashing on another script. And nowhere is it going to include the name Susan."

As I began outlining, I relived the crackle of the Taser and the crash to the ground, realizing the dog story might actually have a perfect movie ending. Write. Rewrite. Edit. Reedit. The next couple of days passed in a blur until Malik called me for what we hoped would be the final screening before air that night.

"What do you think?" I whispered as Noreen and Miles walked in. "Is it any good?"

"It's better than good," he answered. "It's done."

((RILEY, LEAD-IN))
FOR MANY OF US, OUR
PETS ARE LIKE OUR
FAMILY.
CREMATION IS
BECOMING ONE OF
THE MOST POPULAR
WAYS TO HONOR A
DECEASED DOG OR
CAT.
BUT HOW CAN YOU
BE SURE YOU'RE
GETTING YOUR
MONEY'S WORTH?
. . . AND YOUR PET
IS GETTING THE
FINAL RESTING
PLACE IT
DESERVES?

I started the story broadly, a classic consumer investigative spin designed to draw the viewer along, to make them worry "This could happen to me." Then I introduced our everyman, Toby Elness, someone viewers could relate to, as long as they didn't catch on that he was missing a few screws.

((TOBY ELNESS SOT/COVER W/ FLUFFY PIX))
I NEED TO KNOW
WHAT HAPPENED TO
FLUFFY.
((VOICE TRACK))
TO TOBY ELNESS,
FLUFFY WASN'T JUST
A DOG.
FLUFFY WAS FAMILY . . .
AND TOBY WAS
HAUNTED BY HIS
DOUBTS THAT FLUFFY'S
ASHES WEREN'T THE
REAL THING.
((TOBY ELNESS SOT))
I HAVE SUSPICIONS, BUT
NO PROOF.
((STAND-UP))
SO CHANNEL 3 SET OUT
TO INVESTIGATE . . .
WE WENT UNDERCOVER

WITH HIDDEN
CAMERAS . . . WE
FOLLOWED THE
MONEY TRAIL . . . WE
FOLLOWED THE
PAPER TRAIL . . . WE
DID SCIENTIFIC
TESTING . . .
ALL TO EXPOSE A PET
CREMATION SCAM
THAT WILL MAKE YOU
SICK TO YOUR STOMACH.

Now I was embarrassing even myself, with every TV investigative technique and cliché rolled together. I could feel viewers on the edge of their seat, waiting to see if we could deliver.

((UNDERCOVER
PIX/COUNT $$))
20–40–60–80–100–120–140–
160 BUCKS.
((VOICE TRACK))
FIRST WE PAID DR.
KEITH PETIT . . . A
LOCAL
VETERINARIAN . . .
160 DOLLARS FOR AN
INDIVIDUAL
CREMATION FOR A DOG

WE FOUND DEAD
ALONG A COUNTRY
ROAD.
HE'S THE SAME VET WHO
HANDLED FLUFFY'S
CREMATION.
((PETIT/SOT))
CREMATION IS A
FITTING CLOSURE TO
A PET'S LIFE.
WE TAKE SPECIAL CARE
TO MAKE SURE THE
ASHES OF YOUR PET
ARE NOT BLENDED
WITH THOSE OF ANY
OTHER PET. THAT'S
THE PROMISE I MAKE
TO YOU.
((VOICE TRACK))
IT'S THE SAME PROMISE
HE MADE TO TOBY
ELNESS.
((TOBY/WIPE TEARS))
I JUST HOPE NOTHING
BAD HAPPENED TO
FLUFFY.
((VOICE TRACK))
BUT IT APPEARS TO
HAVE BEEN A BROKEN
PROMISE.

> LABORATORY TESTS
> SHOW THE ASHES OF
> BOTH OUR DOG AND
> TOBY'S DOG ARE
> BOGUS . . .
> A COMBINATION OF
> PEBBLES AND CAT LITTER.
> WHAT HAPPENED
> TO OUR PETS?
> CHANNEL 3 SET UP
> SURVEILLANCE OUTSIDE
> DR. PETIT'S VET OFFICE . . .
> THIS IS WHAT OUR
> HIDDEN CAMERAS SAW.

I'd already mentioned the hidden cameras once, but repetition is an effective investigative scripting technique. Tell the viewers what you're going to tell them; tell them; and tell them again.

> ((NAT/SOT TRUCK))
> THE BODIES OF
> NUMEROUS PETS,
> INCLUDING OUR DOG . . .
> DUMPED
> INTO THE BACK OF
> THIS TRUCK . . .
> TAKEN PAST THIS
> GATE AND NEVER SEEN
> AGAIN.

SO WHAT IS THIS
MYSTERIOUS
BUILDING? IT'S NOT
A CREMATORIUM . . .
IT'S A RENDERING
PLANT . . . WHERE
ANIMAL CORPSES
ARE MELTED DOWN
AND MADE INTO PET
FOOD AND EVEN . . .
LIPSTICK.

I smacked my lips together and paused just before I said the word "lipstick."

DR. PETIT DIDN'T
WANT THIS STORY
TOLD . . .
HE WENT TO GREAT
LENGTHS TO
STOP US.

No surprise, I ended the piece with the Taser video and the "Why are you cheating people?" sound. An explosive finale to a tabloid-style investigation. I finished up with a live on set tag, reading an excerpt from a nasty letter from Dr. Petit's attorney warning what would happen if we besmirched his client's reputation.

Miles laughed when he first read the letter and said, "Bring it on."

Of course, I knew he was looking forward to the billing hours.

TEN VOICE MAIL messages awaited me when I got to my desk the next morning.

The first, a crank call with only a dog barking. Sounded like a big dog. I deleted it.

I also deleted the one from Toby Elness. He offered me the pick of the litter from his next batch of puppies or kittens, my choice.

I forwarded a blistering call from Dr. Petit to Noreen and Miles. We'd already posted his picture at the station security desk with a warning not to let him in the building.

The message from Dr. Redding sounded almost conciliatory. Bottom line: he had seen the dog story on satellite in Duluth and figured anyone who would go to that much trouble for man's best friend couldn't be all bad. He left a cell phone number and an offer to meet again. Since he was back in Minneapolis. I hit *save*.

The next two tip calls I deleted and ignored. One viewer wanted me to set up hidden cameras to catch his neighbor letting his dog crap on the sidewalk without cleaning up after him. The other complained that the media only covered bad news, and why didn't we do any stories about all the good veterinarians out there.

Garnett had called. He asked me to swing by his office later. We hadn't seen each other for a week but had been in touch daily, bouncing Susan theories back and forth.

Minneapolis councilwoman Susan Victor had phoned next. As a Susan herself, she felt confident and qualified to vouch for the safety of the city. She told me she would be fielding questions during a news conference at three that afternoon at city hall. I e-mailed the info to the assignment desk, with a note that I'd cover it.

The barking dog with the deep voice was back. Erase.

Noreen left the last message. It was an "attagirl," congratulating me on last night's cremation story and reminding me it was her idea.

Oh, and I buried the lead: dogs got a 39 share. I'd glanced at the overnights on my way in, not particularly proud that, going strictly by the numbers, our viewers seemed to care more about dead animals than dead women.

CHAPTER 24

Mayor Skubic pushed open the front door of Mickey's on West Seventh Street in St. Paul. I hid my face behind a menu, but he had no trouble spotting my big red hairdo and slipped into the booth across from me. The smell of his cologne mixed with the smell of bacon and eggs and coffee.

"Nice wig," he said.

I set the menu down and he stared quizzically at me, trying to figure out where he had seen me before, besides on his doorstep Halloween night. In his eyes, I saw confusion, not evil.

"Do you like it?" I took the wig off and dropped it on the table. "Trick or treat."

I thought there might be a chance he'd hit me so I got there early enough to grab a booth by a window facing street side. I also had Malik waiting outside in the van, rolling tape through the glass.

Mayor Skubic stood up to leave. "I don't have time for practical jokes."

"I'm not laughing," I said. "And neither is Susan Redding."

"I think I might call your boss about this little stunt."

"I think I might call your wife."

The mayor clearly didn't want to call that bluff. He straightened his tie and walked out without looking back. I finished my coffee, left a five on the table, and headed to work.

ONE WEEK INTO the November book and Channel 3 led our closest competition by nearly three ratings points, just under five share points. Mathematically we couldn't lose, or so the bosses kept whispering, because they didn't want to jinx the numbers.

"I once owned a dog." Mike Flagg kept coming up with lame reasons why he should help me with follow-ups to my pieces. "Just think how much easier it would be to catch this killer if we worked together."

His own stories this month—a rehash on auto title fraud and tips on how to clean up your credit report—had received lukewarm numbers. Viewers expect a ratings war between stations, but few realize the level of competition within a newsroom. I viewed Flagg's phony offers to help as thinly veiled attempts to steal my story and glory. Politely I declined his assistance and tried to get him to leave by slouching over my desk, pretending to review some critical notes.

"There's enough angles on the SUSANS story for both of us," he continued. "How about if I handle whether the prison guy should get a new trial?"

"How about if you develop some sources and come up with your own ideas. I enterprised SUSANS," I reminded him. "Originality attracts viewers."

"Well, that dog story came off the tip line," he said. "You just got lucky there."

"Yeah, lucky for me you turned your nose up at it." I hadn't forgotten Mike Flagg was one of the reasons Noreen had stuck me with Toby Elness. "Anyway," I told him, "it's one thing to get an idea from the tip line. It's another to know what to do with it."

"Here's what you can do with your idea." He made a gesture the FCC wouldn't approve of and stomped off.

I spent the rest of the morning researching Mayor Skubic's background, looking for additional Susan links. I looked through an old file of newsmaker newspaper clips the station librarian kept before Channel 3 joined the computer age.

Mayor Skubic grew up the eldest of five children in an abusive family on the Iron Range. His mother escaped by running off when he was ten. His father reportedly took it out on the kids, tangling often with his oldest boy. Life seemed to improve after his dad died in the mines and Skubic's grandmother stepped in to raise the kids. Karl Skubic became a mediocre student, star hockey athlete, and owner of a local sporting goods store that slowly grew into a statewide chain. Name and face recognition followed when he started filming TV commercials spoofing sports heroes.

His northern Minnesota roots made it inevitable that when he ventured into politics, it was as a DFLer. After two terms, he'd left a secure seat in the Minnesota House representing voters in the Duluth area.

His move to the Twin Cities and success there came unexpectedly. Obvious money rolled in from labor unions, but he also became a crossover candidate, able to garner corporate contributions that normally went to Republican coffers. He ran for mayor on a lark.

An old newspaper photo of him being sworn in as Minneapolis mayor while his wife and grandmother watched jogged my memory about an awkward incident involving Grandma during his first year in office. Nanna Zsa Zsa, as he called her, looked old country then; if she was alive today, she'd be damn old.

She had joined a neighborhood card club in northeast Minneapolis after moving down from the Range. Luck stuck to her like glue—okay, she was a card shark. Things got ugly when other little old ladies started complaining she was cheating them out of their social security. The Minneapolis newspaper ran a photo of the mayor with one arm wrapped protectively around her while his other arm knocked a camera away as they left the courthouse. The headline read "Leave My Nanna Zsa Zsa Alone."

Conventional political wisdom might predict voters turning against him. But senior citizens appreciated the family values he had demonstrated by sticking up for his shifty grandma, and they had supported him at the polls. The story was largely forgotten by now. Old news.

"What's the word on him these days?" I asked Channel 3's political reporter, Cara Madden. She'd covered the beat longer than I'd been at the station, and knew which politicians owed who favors. She was the only newsroom employee Noreen didn't mess with. Her core competence insulated her from many of the difficulties aging women TV reporters face. It also didn't hurt that she had married Minnesota's Supreme Court chief justice. She could stay on the air longer than Willard Scott; Channel 3 couldn't chance a legal scuffle.

She pondered my question about Mayor Skubic before summing him up. "Slick, but can be shaken."

"Ambitious?"

"Content to be mayor, so he says. Realistically, he could make a run for governor. He's got support from the Range, support in Minneapolis, but I don't think he's got the support at home."

"First lady having second thoughts?"

"Every so often we hear stuff about him and other women, but until his wife makes an issue out of it, it's off-limits unless we catch him with an intern."

"He ever come on to you?" I asked.

"He likes to let his fingers linger on mine when we shake hands." We grimaced simultaneously.

"Okay, so he's disgusting," I said. "Think he's violent?"

"Never heard that."

"Think he's got secrets?"

"They all do."

I told her Mayor Skubic was taking the SUSANS case personally, for good reason. After I shared his connection to the first victim, she promised to keep her reporter radar pointed in his direction. We bounced around a couple ideas about a good cop/bad cop scenario. I'd already been cast as the bad cop, and Cara was fine being good cop as long as the role didn't call for letting the mayor brush up close beside her.

The front desk paged me that I had a guest in the lobby. On my way, I passed Mike Flagg coming out of the audio booth. No doubt to annoy me, he softly sang a lesser-known Elvis tune. "I'd trade 'em all for just one hour of Susan when she tried."

Oh well, better than "Oh, Susanna."

LAST TIME I'D done the heavy lifting of Trying to Be Nice. Now it was Dr. Redding's turn. He'd made reservations at Zelo, a sophisticated Italian restaurant near the station and popular for business lunches. But he seemed reluctant to get down to business. I became suspicious because instead of teasing me, like everybody else, about my "stunning" story last night, he sympathized. He had clearly done some sleuthing and was treating me with deference. I realized this had nothing to do with dead dogs and everything to do with my dead husband. To steer the conversation in the direction I wanted, I mentioned Susan Victor's upcoming news conference.

He shook his head. "I just got used to your using my wife's death for ratings; now you're telling me there's someone using it for politics?"

"Yeah. But she's actually more interested in the other Susans than your wife. Minneapolis is her turf."

"And you're doing a story for tonight?"

"Kind of have to. If we ignore criticism about our work, we lose credibility. It's sort of a journalism rule."

"So if I want to blast you, you'd put that on the air?"

"I'll call for a camera right now." I reached for my cell phone, but he waved me off.

"No. I don't want my name and face all over the news. It was bad enough when Susan died."

"It was bad when Boyer died, too."

I hadn't meant to say that. We both stayed quiet for a minute, each reliving that day. The shock. The despair. The media. We shared a murdered spouse bond, but it still felt uneasy. I wished our food would arrive. All we had was ice water and crunchy bread.

"At least you were never a suspect," Redding said.

"Did they think you did it?"

"Briefly, but my DNA cleared me and they verified my alibi."

"At least you got to watch a trial. Got to look the killer in the eye. Got to watch them lead him away. I got one conspiracy theory after another. The blame never ended."

"But you don't think my wife's killer is to blame, so any comfort I might have derived from looking him in the eye is gone."

"That is shitty," I agreed. "Sorry about that."

"So you think he's really innocent?"

"I don't know. Do you think he's really guilty? Or do you just want him behind bars 'cause she slept with him?"

Lucky for me, our server arrived with plates of pasta. Redding decided to be the professional and ignore my question.

"You would be a terrible therapist," he observed. "You're too confrontational. You seem to enjoy making people angry."

"You should see me when the camera's rolling."

So there we sat: two single people, both wearing wedding bands. Pathetic, but he more so than me. After all, his wife had been dead more than a decade and he seemed unable to move forward; I had just over a year of widowhood under my belt. Also, my husband's death gave me war widow status. Redding's wife's death made him a cuckold.

Nervously, I twisted my ring. "I'm not ready to take it off. I will when I'm ready to move on, but I'm not there yet."

Redding's reasons were more practical then emotional. "It keeps patients from fixating on me if they think I'm married. It's not unusual, in therapy, for them to develop an attachment. It's called transference."

"Is that what happened with Susan?"

He tried to mask his aggravation, but he set his cup of coffee down harder than necessary and it slopped over the edge, staining the tablecloth, the way my words were staining any chance of friendship.

"Do you have any friends at all?" he said. "You really make it difficult to be around you."

Now he was touching on a sore point. Truthfully, I didn't have many friends outside of work. And I wasn't always sure the work ones counted.

"You want to be friends? I thought this was a business lunch."

Redding paused, looking me straight in the eye. "I would like to be friends."

I held his gaze, conflicted because friendship implies trust and I was reluctant to trust anyone directly involved with the murder victims; at the same time I needed him to trust me.

"Then let's get the business part out of the way," I said. "Tell me about Mayor Skubic."

Just then my cell phone rang. It was Malik. Time to head over to city hall. Redding and I both reached for the check. As our hands touched, our rings hit and made a soft metallic clink.

SUSAN VICTOR REPRESENTED Minneapolis movers and shakers. The bodies of Waitress Susan and Sinner Susan had been found in her district, long before she was sworn in. I recalled lawn signs reading VICTOR FOR VICTORY lining the streets of the Thirteenth Ward, where I lived. A lopsided race, not in her favor, until federal agents executed a search warrant for illegal gambling on her opponent's home and office three weeks before the election. Now she savored her first term as city councilwoman.

My story gave her a chance to accomplish two goals simultaneously: get on TV and ingratiate herself with the mayor. When she introduced herself before the cameras, she placed a heavy emphasis on her first name. "Ssssusan," reminding me of the hiss of a snake.

"I certainly don't think there's a Susan killer loose in our city," she said. "The media has blown this case completely out of proportion."

"All media?" asked one of the newspaper guys, going for a suck-up question.

"No, in all fairness, the irresponsibility has come over the airwaves of Channel 3."

"Do you think they did it for ratings?" the newspaper guy persisted.

"Absolutely. I intend to ask the FCC to pull their license."

Even the newspaper guy chuckled at the outlandishness of that remark. A broadcast license is essentially a license to print money forever. Yeah, the airwaves belong to the public, but everyone knows aggressive reporting isn't going to get a license yanked. Indecency, now that's a different story. Channel 3 would be dandy as long as none of us let the F-word slip during a live shot. Then *F* wouldn't even begin to describe the resulting trouble.

"We need to protect the public airwaves," Susan Victor went on to say.

"How about protecting the public?" I countered.

"This is a very safe city," she answered.

"What do you think of the police investigation?" asked one of my competitors.

"I have every confidence in Chief Capacasa. We just need to let him and his officers do their jobs. We don't need amateurs jumping to crazy conclusions."

Deep within me, maybe deep within all of us, is a precarious place I call the abyss. Reporters like to imagine being one story away from awards and glory. I never forget I'm one story away from falling into the abyss. Damned if Susan Victor was going to push me over.

I decided to up the stakes with an old reporter trick: phrasing a provocative question that puts the subject on the defensive.

"You accuse me of doing this story for ratings. You're not by any chance holding this news conference just to get on TV and increase your political visibility?"

"I am not dignifying that with a response."

I only asked because she wore a red, white, and blue VOTE SUSAN pin on her lapel, even though, technically, no campaign waged.

Usually when someone gets testy, their forehead scrunches up, but Susan Victor's forehead stayed smooth and tight under the lights. She looked youthful for a woman pushing fifty, much younger than she looked last year when I interviewed her about air pollution from the city garbage-burning plant. I'd seen enough before and after in the TV business to suspect Botox.

I pushed harder to make her lose her control. "Then what, besides being named Susan, qualifies you to speak to this investigation?"

"I represent women. And we refuse to live in fear."

"You don't represent me," I said. Even though I did live in her district, so technically she did represent me. "And you don't even represent common sense," I mumbled as I folded up the tripod.

So in summary, Susan Victor stood for safety and against the media. A clumsy production, not likely to garner much press. Channel 3 had to cover it, because we owned the story. For that reason, the rest of the media pack would shy away. The other stations might run a short sound bite trashing us just for fun, but there was no point in making the case sound too intriguing, thus tempting their own viewers to switch channels. The papers would bury the news deep inside the Metro section, although the TV critics might side with Susan Victor because it's easier to write nasty than laudatory.

And that's exactly how the news coverage played out, until later, when something happened that took SUSANS national, and got me taken off the story completely.

CHAPTER 25

ew of Minneapolis's older homes have attached garages. New construction on a teardown lot might, but my house doesn't. So I parked the car inside my garage's narrow walls, then walked outside past a high border of evergreen bushes, along a twenty-foot stone path, up the porch steps to the front door, where I found a newspaper wrapped around a cone shape.

Inside, wilted white and pink petals in a low-budget vase. My admirer was closing in on me. First my workplace. Then my car. Now my home. I contemplated what Susan connection these blooms held, but all I could see were snapdragons.

"Oh, did you get flowers?" asked my neighbor.

Mrs. Fredericks, a skinny black woman, had lived next door for the past twenty-seven years. I'd become cozy with her because she had several huge raspberry bushes growing in her yard, and being a neighborly soul she let me have all the raspberries I could reach through the fence. Besides gardening, Mrs. Fredericks was a one-person crime watch over the comings and goings up and down the block. 911 was on her speed dial, although she'd used it only twice that I knew. Once to report some kids toilet-papering a teacher's house, and once to save my life.

Mrs. Fredericks made that call about four months ago. She noticed me walk into the garage one morning, but not come out. She could hear the engine running.

It was the day after the first anniversary of Boyer's death. No objections from work when I called in sick the day before. The past year had been an unproductive one for me. I was just taking up desk space as far as the rest of the newsroom was concerned. "No problem," the assignment editor assured me. "Take your time."

I didn't make it to work the next morning either, but I did make it as far as my Mustang.

I turned the key. Instead of hitting the remote to open the garage door and back out . . . I waited. I don't remember why I waited, but it wasn't for death, despite what everyone thinks.

The fumes filled the garage and started to seep into the car. Just a little longer, I told myself. Just a little longer and I'll hit the door-open button. But I couldn't quite face daylight, and sometime during the next few minutes, as I listened to "Viva Las Vegas" on the car stereo, I fell into the abyss.

I remember Mrs. Fredericks pounding on my car door. I don't remember much else until halfway to the hospital, when I woke up in an ambulance with a mask over my face. Some things I still don't remember. Mrs. Fredericks insists that, although the police were on their way, she came out to check because she heard my car horn. I don't remember honking. I just remember waiting for . . . clarity.

Now Mrs. Fredericks was giving me widow lessons, so she claimed, but I knew she had promised my mom she'd keep an eye on me. No problem here. One person's nosy neighbor is another's guardian angel.

Mrs. Fredericks had lots of practice being widowed. I don't even know her first name, but I know her first husband, Abe, died twenty-one years ago this coming December and there hasn't been a day gone by that she hasn't thought of him. Her second husband, Herbie, died nine years ago, but she hardly thinks of him at all. Her third husband, Eugene, died three years ago, but there are days she forgets he's passed on. "Eugene, the mail's here," I sometimes hear her call on a hot day when the windows are open. Mrs. Fredericks had lots of practice being widowed.

"If you were really hard up," I told her, "I suppose you could call them flowers. But they're not in very good shape. Any chance you saw who left them?"

"No. You must have a secret admirer."

"More likely a secret stalker." I showed her the dead blooms and explained about the other floral arrangements. "So if you see anyone hanging around, make a mental note of what they look like. I also wouldn't mind a license plate number if they get in a car."

Mrs. Fredericks reached for the droopy bouquet.

"Dog flowers," she said.

"No, snapdragons," I corrected her.

"We used to call them dog flowers back when I was growing up," she explained, "because the center looks like the mouth of a dog."

"Dog flowers?" I repeated. Dog? That might change things. Was my mystery florist following the Susans or following me?

I WASN'T PARTICULARLY worried about the flowers because in real life murderers seldom come after journalists.

Reporters are most at risk just before airing a story that could put a crooked merchant out of business. You'd be surprised how quickly a small businessman can turn violent when he senses his livelihood disappearing, his reputation in ruins, or the prospect of jail time looming. My tangle with Dr. Petit and his stun gun wasn't unique. A producer colleague of mine once got put in a headlock by a shady salesman and dragged down a dim hallway until the photographer talked him down. Didn't even matter that the camera was rolling. These are the kind of folks who'll show up at the state auto licensing counter trying to pop your home address. And long after you've forgotten all about that story . . . they're the ones who'll lunge at you while you're signing autographs at the state fair or try to ram you with their pickup truck some dark night as you walk to your parking lot.

Garnett slid into the booth across from me at Famous Dave's BBQ at the mall. He wasn't happy about my cryptic bouquets, but he doubted that the sender posed an actual physical danger.

"If you were getting dead flowers from some boyfriend who wouldn't take no for an answer, I'd be a lot more worried. This might just be a creative crank. Your line of work attracts them, and you have been out of the public eye for a while."

"Well, it's a creepy welcome back."

"No argument there. And threat or not, I'd be happier if this guy didn't know where you lived."

"If you're hinting I should move, forget it." I couldn't leave the memories, but I didn't say that out loud. "Why does everyone think I should move?"

"Would you like to see a menu?" the waitress asked Garnett.

I was already halfway through a barbeque pork entrée when he finally arrived. I'd stopped by his office first, but the guys at the surveillance wall told me he was at the theater complex investigating a report about a moviegoer surreptitiously videotaping the new George Clooney film. I left word for him to meet me at the restaurant after he finished protecting the world from copyright pirates.

"I'll have whatever she's having," he told the waitress.

"*Very* funny," I said. "It was Rob Reiner's mom. I can't remember her name. *When Harry Met Sally,* 1989."

"Actually, I wasn't playing," he said.

"Yes you were."

The waitress gave us an odd look.

"Just bring me a plate of that." Garnett pointed at my meal, which was nearly gone. "To go."

GARNETT POINTED OUT some of the hiding places for the mall security cameras as we walked back to his office. While we were riding up an escalator, I mentioned seeing Dr. Redding again.

Garnett snorted. "Another big waste of time."

"Maybe not. He knows something. Something about the mayor. It's just a matter of getting him to talk."

"And you have a plan for that?"

"I might have to bat my eyes a little."

I should have put two and two together when Garnett almost dropped his take-out dinner, but I didn't.

"Don't you have some rule about not getting involved with sources?"

"I'm not getting involved with anybody." I was emphatic about that. "But I think he's interested in me, and if I have to use that I will. Nothing personal. Just professional."

"His interest in you is probably professional as well. A chance to observe a type A personality under extreme pressure. He's probably going to write a paper about you. Some continuing education for shrinks."

"No, he says he wants to be friends."

"You don't declare friendship, friendship just happens. I think he wants the inside track on the SUSANS investigation. You think you're using him for information. I think he's using you."

"Perhaps he is," I said. "But I'm using him more. And I know what I'm doing. He's clearly got issues with women. His wife's been gone a long time. There's no good reason he's still single."

Garnett tossed his food in a garbage can. "I'm not hungry anymore."

"Hey, why'd you do that? I bet the guys would have finished it off."

That's how dense I was. Looking back, he was throwing clues at me all night, but they went right over my head and right past my heart. I couldn't see that our dynamics were changing—that Garnett wanted to be a source of comfort, not news.

Then I made matters even worse.

"Redding and I have both lost someone we loved. Violently. I'm not remotely interested in checking out his bedside manner, but I feel a connection. Like he might end up being important to me somehow."

I FIGURED THE odds were better than fifty-fifty the shadow was my imagination.

It hadn't been there when I left Garnett's office. It hadn't been there when I left the ladies room. I first noticed it out of the corner of my eye when I walked through the skyway linking the Mall of America to the parking ramp. Most of the mall stores closed at nine, but the ramp was still full of cars because the movie theaters, restaurants, and nightclubs remained open. I glanced around, trying to remember where I had parked the Mustang. One of the public relations flacks at the mall likes to brag that if visitors look hard enough, they can often count all fifty license plates parked here. I didn't have time for that game, but I was more exasperated than fearful.

About four pillars away, again, I caught a glimpse of what might be the shadow. Believing it better to confront trouble than to cower, I moved in that direction.

My cell phone rang.

"Don't react to what I'm saying." Garnett's voice sounded secretive. "Someone's following you."

"How would you know?" I glanced around nervously.

"Don't look. Just pretend you're fumbling with your purse."

"Where are you?"

"On the escalators, just coming down toward the parking skyway."

"How can you see me?"

"Twiddle Dee and Twiddle Duce have you on camera. They tracked you through the mall and watched you wandering around the ramp—"

"You're spying on me?" I interrupted him.

"Voice down. Not me, them. It was all very entertaining until they spotted a guy making the same rounds behind you, back about a hundred feet. They paged me. Might be a coincidence, but I don't like it."

"Then I don't like it either."

"I'm on my way and I've also got a couple thugs heading over. Stay on the phone and see if there's somewhere you can hide. Don't go to your car. I think that's what he's waiting for."

I caught another glimpse of the shadow I now knew was not a specter of my imagination. As it ducked behind an oversized van, I dropped to the ground and rolled under a pickup truck. I lost my cell signal. I closed my eyes and wished my overstuffed briefcase held a Taser instead of a stack of documents.

Twenty minutes earlier, I'd been savoring the evening's brainstorming success, now I was groveling in grime.

Garnett and I had played an exhilarating round of Sherlock. I'd brought along notes from the SUSAN charts, interview transcripts, and calendar. Since the killer had been AWOL for the last decade, we had to consider he might be dead. Or in prison. If he was alive, we estimated he was between thirty and sixty-five. We had no conclusive evidence the killer was a "he," but strangling requires strength, so we eliminated women. Paging through the pile, Garnett thought I should check the lily bed in Susan Moreno's father's yard and see if any flowers had been cut recently. Perhaps Tim Moreno held the answer to the dead flower riddle? I was adding the idea to my checklist, when Garnett suddenly hmmmed.

"Hmmm what?" I said.

"Isn't Zsa Zsa another name for Susan?" he asked. He held Mayor Skubic's background file. "Nanna Zsa Zsa? I'd forgotten about her."

"Hmmm." I rooted through the heap until I found the torn baby name page and confirmed Garnett's surmise. Susan. Zsa Zsa. Clue or red herring? Susan Redding? Mayor Skubic? The coincidences piled up.

Under the pickup truck, I opened my eyes. I kept my breathing soft and shallow to stay quiet, and because of the heavy, unpleasant air. I smelled sweat, but realized that might be me. I smelled urine, but even though I was scared, I knew I had not peed my pants.

I considered moving closer to the mall entrance, but heard footsteps. The shadow's feet crunched closer. Then farther away. Then closer again until they stopped near the front tires, about four feet from my face. I held my breath. A shadow bent down and peered under the pickup.

"He's gone," Garnett said.

GARNETT OPENED MY refrigerator and grabbed a beer. I didn't want anything to drink. Not alcohol to dull my senses; not caffeine to sharpen them, either. I just wanted to feel normal.

Most of the petals from the dog flowers lay wilted around the bottom of the vase. The stems looked naked, more embarrassed than sinister.

Perhaps we had overreacted, but the photo from the surveillance video of the shadow gave me chills. About average height. About average weight. Caucasian. The man wore fashionable black. His hat tilted to hide his face. A nylon stocking pulled over his head. The camera unable to get an identifiable shot. The freeze-frame

reminded me of the state's most prolific bank robber—
dubbed the "fishing hat bandit" because during twenty-
three robberies he successfully shielded his face from
the security cameras. I turned the photo upside down
and set it on the kitchen table.

Garnett was just suggesting I have my boss call his
former boss and request additional patrols for my
neighborhood when the doorbell rang. I recoiled, still
jumpy from the parking ramp shadow.

"Bad guys don't ring doorbells," Garnett said. "They
either pick the lock or crash through the door."

"Don't let anyone in," I said. I'd thrown my clothes
in the garbage can the minute I got home and was
wearing a shabby bathrobe only close friends were
allowed to see. I wanted Garnett to shove off so I could
take a shower, but he didn't seem in any hurry to leave.
I figured he didn't want to leave me unguarded, but
later pondered whether he was hoping to see me in a
towel.

Garnett opened the door to a menagerie. Toby
Elness stood on the porch with Blackie, Husky, and
Shep. I glanced at the clock. Nearly midnight.

"I'm sorry it's so late. But I saw your light on and we
wanted to thank you in person."

Toby peered around Garnett and the dogs peered
around both of them. No barking or growling, but
plenty of panting. I let them inside reluctantly, not
wanting scratches on my wood floors or dog drool on
my couch.

"Now really isn't a good time for company," I said.

"We won't stay long."

The dogs reacted to my parking ramp smell like a canine love potion. Shep was especially enthralled by the odor.

"Come on, stop sniffing," I told him. "That's not polite."

"Down Shep," Toby said. "Over here. Leave her alone."

"Bad dog," I said.

Garnett laughed as he shut the front door.

"I didn't think the circus made house calls."

"She's our hero." Toby beamed. "Isn't she, boys?"

As if on cue, the three seemed to nod and slobber in unison. Shep even tried to thank me by smelling my butt.

"Could I have some water?" Toby asked.

"No, Toby. You can go home. It's the middle of the night. I'm sure the dogs need their rest."

"The water's not for me. It's for Blackie, Husky, and Shep."

Oh well, if it's for Blackie, Husky, and Shep. I am such a chump, I thought to myself, as I filled a mixing bowl from the faucet and set it on the floor. The dogs slurped water. Garnett slurped beer. Toby pulled a chair up to the table and began humming *The Addams Family* theme song.

I threw a bag of chips at them and told them to make themselves at home while I took a shower.

When I came back downstairs, Blackie was licking

potato chips off the floor; Husky had scattered the Suicide Susan papers across the room and was chewing on the box. Toby sipped hot tea and held the Man in Black photo.

"Do you think it might be Dr. Petit?" he asked Garnett.

"He'd certainly make the short list."

"Knock it off, guys," I said. "You're interfering with my sleep. Remember I work in TV? I need to look good in the morning. You are getting in the way of me earning a living, so beat it. All five of you." I opened the front door and pointed into the night. "Outside."

"Actually, Toby and I have been talking about your problem and he has a solution. I think you should listen."

"Listen? To Toby? He has a solution? Right now you guys are a big part of the problem."

Garnett closed the door and steered me back to the table. "I know it's easier not to think about it, but you've got bigger problems than us, and I'm uncomfortable with your being alone."

"So Shep's going to stay here a few days," Toby explained. "I already talked to him about it and he's fine." Indeed, a hundred pounds of German shepherd sprawled across my couch, asleep.

"That's not necessary." I tried shaking the dog awake. Instead he curled up in a ball. "Come on Shep. Be a good dog."

"See, he wants to stay," Toby said. "He likes it here."

"I'm just not convinced he's going to be much protection."

Shep buried his face under his paws and started to snore.

"He's all relaxed now, 'cause there's no danger. But if he smells danger, look out, he's a different dog."

"Makes sense," Garnett agreed. "I'm the same way."

"Sure it makes sense," I replied. "If you live in the twilight zone."

"If you'd feel safer," Toby said, "you can have Blackie and Husky, too."

"One's plenty," I said.

Toby brought in a leash and some dog food and went over the rules. I was supposed to let Shep out in the morning and at night. He'd stop by in the afternoons and walk him. We'd reevaluate the plan after a couple of days. I showed Toby where I kept a spare house key in the bottom of the bird feeder. I figured him harmless and also figured some in-and-out traffic might keep my obscure stalker off guard.

The next morning I woke up to the sound of Shep drinking out of the toilet.

CHAPTER 26

L ast night's game of hide-and-seek worried Noreen.

She took Garnett's advice and called Chief Capacasa and asked that extra patrols be added to my street. He agreed and also offered to have the city's emergency dispatch center set up their computer system so that if any 911 call came from my home phone number, they'd dispatch a squad car first and ask questions later. He was so cooperative, I wondered if he might have his own reasons for wanting to keep tabs on me.

Meanwhile, the parking ramp shadow's surveillance photo was now pinned at the station security desk next to Dr. Petit's picture. There was a certain resemblance. But to be fair, I could say that about a lot of men, even Garnett.

I drove by Petit's vet clinic on my way to work and found an empty parking lot. A CLOSED sign hung on the door. At nearly half past nine, these should have been prime office hours. If he wasn't here, where was he? And where had he been last night?

Petit wasn't the only suspect. He wasn't even the scariest. Pedophile Paul Friendly was still loose, and probably held a grudge. Mayor Skubic also deserved a place on the list. No word from him since I'd mailed the battered Susan picture. But the most frightening possibility didn't have a name. If the shadow was the Susan killer, his average, nondescript build meant I had to be wary of just about every man except those playing for the Minnesota Timberwolves.

"No walking alone," Noreen said. "And I want you parking in the station ramp until this settles down."

Channel 3 had a small underground ramp with just enough space for the news vans, live trucks, and station execs' cars. The rest of us parked wherever we could. Expensive and inconvenient. Noreen's generosity surprised and affected me.

"Well, thanks for your space. I won't forget this."

"No, not my space. Take the employee-of-the-month spot. Tell them it's just temporary."

That would make me real popular among my colleagues, especially the current employee-of-the-month. "How about if I just ride with Malik?"

"Fine. I don't suppose you have a home security system?"

"No, but last night I got a dog."

"Really? Oh, fabulous! What kind?"

For the next five minutes she gushed about her dalmatian, Freckles, and how we should get them both together for a doggie playdate. I kept my mouth shut, but contemplated setting her up on a blind date with Toby Elness.

MALIK HAD NO problem being my chauffeur as long as I had no problem doing most of the driving while he slept.

"She's not expecting me to protect you, right? I'm just transportation, right?"

"She's met you, Malik. She knows you shoot video, not bullets."

"Just checking. Want to be clear on my responsibilities."

"Admirable. Now keep your eyes open, his place is just around the corner."

I could make out lilies sticking up through fallen leaves, but couldn't tell if any were missing from the yard of Tim Moreno, father of the third dead Susan. The other lawns on the street were better groomed. I considered stopping at a hardware store and buying a rake but Malik grumbled.

"I'm like Moreno," he said. "Don't like raking until the trees are empty. Besides, what if he comes out and catches us?"

"I think you're more afraid of a few calluses," I said. "If Moreno's home we'll just tell him he's our good deed for the day."

Malik held his palms outward. "I do have the hands of an artist. Thanks for noticing, Riley. Besides, these leaves will take the rest of the morning and you told me you wanted to track down Dr. Petit before noon. Which is it going to be?"

Just then I noticed a teenage girl putting the flag up at a mailbox on the far end of the block. "Hey, how'd you like to earn forty bucks?" I called to her.

She didn't reply, and I realized she'd probably been taught not to approach strange vehicles, especially vans offering candy or money.

"I just want you to rake the leaves on that yard." I

held two crisp bills out the car window. "Don't tell any-one I paid you. If the owner asks, say you're doing the work of the Lord."

More likely it was the sight of the twenties and not the mention of God, but we made a deal and I made a mental note to come back and check the lilies later.

"I THINK WE should shoot from inside the van," Malik said. "What if he pulls out his stun gun again?"

"Oh. I forgot about that." He had a point. I didn't want to replay my last encounter with Dr. Petit.

"How could you forget something like that? You must have lost some brain cells the last time we tangled with him."

"I think I just prefer not to dwell on bad experiences."

Dr. Petit's garage door was shut. The house was dark. Two newspapers lay on the front steps. Unfortunately, his suburban street was empty, so parking and waiting in an unfamiliar van could attract unwanted attention. We'd been busted on stakeout before after being ratted out by nosy neighbors. On the other hand, anyone who'd seen our story might not be feeling particularly neighborly toward Dr. Petit.

"I'm going to circle the block once more. See if you spot any movement through the windows."

All remained still.

The phone book listed this as Petit's home address, but when Xiong had checked property records, a different name appeared, but without homestead status. That meant Dr. Petit rented. Same thing for his clinic, where he wasn't listed as the taxpayer. That would keep things simpler if he ever had to leave town in a hurry.

"I'm going to knock on the door." I clipped on a wireless microphone. "If he answers, keep rolling. I'm betting he doesn't carry the stun gun around at home."

If our veterinarian was inside, he was laying low.

I found out why when I checked my voice mail on the drive back. Four messages. The first, from the Minnesota attorney general's consumer fraud investigator, alerting me that they'd executed a search warrant at Petit's office. I could already hear the promo for tonight's story.

> AUTHORITIES SEIZE
> EVIDENCE IN CREMATION
> FRAUD CASE . . .
> VETERINARIAN ON THE
> RUN.

The next two calls came from viewers whose deceased pets were former patients. They had suspicions about the contents of their urns and what they had to say about the vet we couldn't air. That FCC rule again.

> MORE VICTIMS COME
> FORWARD IN PET
> CREMAINS SCANDAL . . .
> CALL VET A
> REAL "ASH."

Okay, a reporter can dream.

Brent Redding had left the last message. This was the first time he had called himself "Brent" instead of "Doctor." Presumably he wanted me to do the same. He hoped to resume our conversation from the other day. Fine with me, but he needed to cut to the chase about Mayor Skubic. Therapists might be willing to wait session after session for a patient to get to the good stuff, but journalists don't have that kind of patience.

I also had mixed feelings about our "friends" talk the other day and hoped he didn't envision anything beyond friendship. I left him a message to stop by my house later, much later. First I had to pick up the search warrant, grab a sound bite from the AG's office, interview a couple of outraged pet owners, and shoot a stand-up.

Geographically, Malik and I could make it back in time for the late news, but we'd have to race. I noticed an elderly man staring at us through the window blinds of the house next door to Dr. Petit's. I rang the doorbell and he answered. I gave him my business card and asked him to call me if his neighbor came home.

"I sure will," he said. "Not surprised to hear he's a bad vet. Last summer at our block party he kicked Rufus for getting too close to the buffet table."

"Rufus?"

The man whistled and a plump, pug-faced dog wobbled around the corner. "You was just smelling the brats weren't you, Rufus? Sure I'll call if that jerk shows up. I'll get Mrs. Oster on the other side to help, too. He pulled her kitty's tail for digging in his flower bed."

Rush hour was under way on our trip back, but at least we were heading in the right direction. The other side of the freeway was choked with traffic. Malik drove while I scribbled a script. Out in the field I always keep a somewhat outdated mini tape recorder in my pocket so I can roll audio on any interviews we might have to edit on deadline. That way I can save time by not having to wait until we get back to the station to pull sound bites.

For cover we had pictures of a beagle, a golden retriever, and video of their urns. I wished the AG had called earlier so we could have videotaped the investigators carrying boxes out of Dr. Petit's clinic. Malik shot my stand-up at the clinic with the CLOSED sign in the background.

> NO ONE KNOWS WHERE
> THE MISSING
> VETERINARIAN
> IS TONIGHT . . . NOT HIS
> PATIENTS . . . NOT THE
> AUTHORITIES . . .
> NOT EVEN CHANNEL 3 . . .
> THIS IS RILEY SPARTZ
> REPORTING.

Malik turned on local talk radio just in time for us to hear Susan Victor crusading against the SUSANS story. He opened his mouth, but I cut him off.

"Just think of it as free publicity," I said. "Cheaper than buying an ad."

"Tell that to Dr. Petit."

I'M ADDICTED TO checking my voice mail. So I listened to a fresh message from the county attorney. Good news. The state had revoked Paul Friendly's parole so back to prison for him. Also, the county had no intention of spending any taxpayer money investigating whether or not Friendly was assaulted. Case closed. I gave the information to the assignment desk and heard them page Mike Flagg.

"Damn," I told Malik. "They'll probably lead with that and bump us down in the lineup."

"Fine with me," Malik said. "Gives me more time to edit."

"Stop thinking of yourself. Think about my needs. I need to be at the top of the newscast. I need to be number one."

"You need to get a real life."

We pulled into the station garage after six. I recorded my voice track while Malik loaded video and sound into the edit cube. He was smiling at a shot of the retriever when I handed him my audio.

"I'm thinking maybe my kids need a dog. A dog would be good for them, teach them responsibility." I tuned out his rambling parent jabber to write down the time code for the attorney general sound bite.

"They'd have to let the dog in and out," Malik continued. "I hope it wouldn't end up being a lot of work for Missy. You never see kids walking dogs; it's always the parents. Have you ever noticed that?"

Suddenly I remembered Shep. "Shep!"

"Who's Shep?"

"Shep's my dog."

"You have a dog? Since when?"

"Toby Elness lent him to me last night for protection. I completely forgot. I have to rush home. You've got everything you need, right?"

I took Malik's van and asked him to bum a ride over after he finished the edit. The same vehicle key fits all of Channel 3's news cruisers and I always kept a copy on my own key chain. I made the trip in eighteen minutes, being careful to avoid the speed trap the traffic police like to set up behind the bushes just off my freeway exit.

Shep appeared anxious as I snapped the leash to his collar and led him outside to do his business. I'd brought along a plastic bag to clean up after him per Toby's instructions. Just as I bent over, my ass facing the street, Shep started to growl and pull toward the curb.

CHAPTER 27

hep's hair stood up and so did mine, until I was able to identify the shape peering through the darkness as Dr. Redding. Then I felt foolish. He stood at the curb next to a silver BMW—stereotypical doctor's car—no imagination. I forgot I had invited him over. I'd meant to stop by Lund's grocery to pick up some fancy snacks suitable for company. The last time I'd had company food in my kitchen was the week of Boyer's funeral when all the other cop families brought hot dishes, salads, and desserts.

Unfortunately, all I could offer Dr. Redding was a handful of hot doggie doo.

"Just a minute," I called out, on my way to make a deposit in the garbage can next to the garage. Shep continued snarling and straining the leash in my guest's direction. "It's okay, boy," I reassured Shep, who gave no sign of quitting. "He's really very gentle," I reassured my visitor.

Redding made no move to come any closer. "Splendid animal," Redding said to me. "Good dog," he said to Shep.

Shep wasn't falling for any false compliments. With a throaty rumble and a lunge of muscle, he demonstrated just how seriously he took his protector duty.

"He'll settle down once you come inside." I opened

the front door. But like a shield, Shep kept his body between me and Redding, fervently guarding the porch steps, refusing to let my visitor pass.

Mrs. Fredericks stuck her head out her door. "Everything okay, Riley? We're not used to so much barking."

"Just fine," I answered. "I'm introducing Shep to Dr. Redding, a friend of mine. By the way, this is Mrs. Fredericks."

"Nice to meet you." Redding didn't say it like he meant it.

She gave me a wink and went back inside to escape the night air.

"Let him sniff you," I suggested, "and then he'll know you're okay." Redding looked doubtful, but Shep was eager to try—for a bite it turns out, not a sniff.

"Down Shep," I pleaded, pulling his jaws back in the nip of time as Redding's jacket sleeve ripped. I apologized profusely. "Maybe we should walk around the block and let him get used to you."

That didn't work either. Shep was determined to keep his prey in sight by herding Redding down the street with his teeth. I realized Shep could outlast me, so I dragged the German shepherd back to my yard, yanked him up the stairs, and locked him in the house. I leaned back against the door, exhausted and relieved that my dog owner days were numbered.

"Had him long?" Redding asked.

"He's a loaner." No need to go into the details of why I required a watchdog. "I'm watching him for a friend."

"Must be a dear friend."

Just then a police car came around the corner, slowed, and shined its headlights on us. The cop called out, "Everything okay tonight, folks?"

"Fine, officer. Thanks."

He waved from his squad and pulled away. Mentally I gave the chief kudos for following through on the extra patrols.

"Private security?" Redding asked.

"No, the cops just like to patrol this street. His shift doesn't end till breakfast, so he might swing by again."

"That's personal service."

Rather than stand in the driveway and continue to entertain Mrs. Fredericks, who was now watching us from her kitchen window, I decided we should walk and talk. We headed toward Lake Harriet and spoke of politics and sports and the weather. We didn't speak of the Susans.

In another quarter of a mile, we would pass the house where Susan Chenowith's killer had dumped her body. I knew the exact location; I figured Redding didn't. We walked in silence until I stopped and led him into the alley. Spooky, the temperature seemed to drop at the crime scene, probably just because we quit moving, or so I told myself.

"This is it," I said.

He didn't ask, "What?" which meant he knew what I knew. I volunteered no specifics, though plenty of gruesome details never made public came to mind. I decided to show respect instead of showing off. I also didn't want Redding to think I'd turn around and gossip about his dead wife, too. Not when I needed him to open up.

"We're here," I continued.

"Why?" he asked.

Hmmm, I noted. He asked why instead of where. "I want to know who killed them."

"I hardly think I can help you there." Clouds blocked the full moon so I couldn't read his face. I'm not sure light would have made much difference. For the last twenty minutes Redding had seemed inscrutable, perhaps steeling himself for the conversation he knew was ahead.

"You know things that might help me," I said.

"Indeed?" He seemed noncommittal.

We walked toward the Lyndale Park Rose Garden. An entire acre of roses. I was disappointed park workers had already mulched them for the winter. Some lone blooms, red, white, and pink, still poked through the tons of dead leaves piled high. The air smelled heavy and sweet. Redding picked a pink rose and handed it to me.

"Thanks." I stuck it through a buttonhole on my jacket. "If I can't know who killed them, I want to know why they were killed."

"That I do have some insight about. The human mind sometimes craves evil."

What did I expect? Redding was, after all, a psychiatrist. He proceeded to explain, in great detail, the differences between psychopaths and sociopaths, until I finally had to cut him off.

"But why the Susans?" I asked. "And why November 19?"

"If you're right that it's a serialist, he's the only one who knows the answer. Find the answer and you find the killer."

Perhaps, I thought. "Or find the killer and we find the answer. Which comes first?"

He ignored my chicken versus the egg quandary and we started down the walking path again. "Your theory could be wrong on other levels," he said. "By focusing so narrowly, you could miss other leads. The killer might be just another sexual sadist out murdering victims named Cynthia and Maureen and Stephanie other nights of the year."

At least he didn't say Riley. "Then I'll never figure it out and neither will the cops."

"But if you are correct," Redding continued, "clearly the name and date have a special significance to him. The closer the date comes, the more stress he feels. However insane his motive for killing may seem to us, to him it makes perfect sense."

"How do you know so much about this?" I asked. His insight was useful.

"Sometimes I'm hired as an expert witness to determine the sanity or insanity of the accused."

"Which way do you usually come down?"

"I like to think my diagnosis is correct for each patient. While many defendants suffer character disorders, that doesn't make them insane. Criminal insanity is and should be a rare diagnosis."

"Sounds like you work for prosecutors." Redding didn't answer. "What do you make of the raincoat?" Since the doctor wasn't billing me, I decided to milk him for all I could get. "Taking it off one victim, putting it on another?"

"A trophy. He might have even worn it himself, depending on his size. A raincoat, was it? Maybe he even flashed someone in a park with it."

"Ugh. That's gross."

Redding's mind was creepy, as well as clinical. "Case studies have well documented that sex offenders can escalate from minor offenses, like window peeping, to rape to murder."

"I get that killers sometimes collect souvenirs from their victims to relive the event. But why put it on the next victim? Seems risky, giving the cops an opportunity to link the cases."

"It might be part of his game. He might be searching for a worthy opponent. If that's the case, the police aren't his adversary, you are."

"You make it sound like chess."

"In his mind, it could be."

"So if it's a game, what are the rules? Played annually on November 19 . . . Must be named Susan . . . Trophy to be moved from one victim to the next . . . That means it doesn't end with the raincoat." Sometimes rambling leads to revelation. "We should be seeing mismatched items with the other victims." I stopped on the walking path and turned to Redding. "Was anything missing from your wife?"

"Not that I'm aware of." Redding reverted to his miffed and terse demeanor, like it was one thing to talk abstractly about sexual homicide, another to talk specifically about his wife's murder. "While all this speculation is interesting, do not forget the two of us have a major point of disagreement: The person who killed my wife didn't kill the others. Your theory is flawed."

"We may find out tomorrow."

That's when Dusty Foster's defense attorney would argue before the St. Louis County Court that not ordering further DNA testing on the old evidence would violate his client's legal rights and further a miscarriage of justice. I'd be listening in court, but Dusty wouldn't. The state of Minnesota isn't obligated to transport inmates to legal appeals. Dusty would wait in prison for word on whether he'd get another crack at freedom.

"Are you going to the hearing?" I asked Redding.

"No. This whole ordeal is stirring up sour feelings. I have no desire to encounter cameras waiting for me in front of the courthouse. I thought all that attention was over years ago."

Redding was hard to figure. Usually arrogant people like him enjoy being on TV. My bet was if MSNBC called him for a psychobabble expert opinion on some important newsmaker, he'd say, "Certainly, do you have any face powder to get rid of my shine?" But this new wave of news coverage hit him deep where it hurt most. And it was my fault.

"I'm sorry." It was not just a line; I genuinely was sorry. I know TV saves lives; I know it ruins them, too. I can live with myself because the ruining part usually happens to people who deserve it. The Susan killer, if apprehended, would undoubtedly whine about how the media had ruined his life.

But sometimes bystanders, like Redding, get caught in the mess and we make their personal tragedies worse.

"Why can't you just drop that part of the story?" he asked.

"I don't have a choice. I know you're certain the right man is in jail, but if there's any chance a mistake was made, I have to follow through."

Redding nodded, but he didn't seem to buy it and changed the subject. "By the way, what's the story behind your name?"

"You mean Riley?"

He nodded again, and I felt relaxed so I gave him more than the usual spiel about my great-grandfather. I even offered to show him some old photos when we got back to my place so he could see how Grandpa Riley's cheeks grew sunken as mine grew chubby. Grandpa, like so many of the Spartz clan, moved back to the farm to die. Generations of us consider dying on the home farm good luck, unless, of course, the death results from a gruesome farm accident. My parents and aunts and uncles still click their tongues and shake their heads every time a distant relative passes away in a car crash or nursing home. "Such a shame they couldn't die on the farm."

Redding followed my digression intently, then offered his professional opinion. "I think your family does that to try to control death."

"Is that good?" I asked. "Or bad?"

"Rituals can make the unknown less frightening. Society frowns on picking the time and manner of one's death. We call it suicide. But there's nothing wrong with picking the place and waiting for nature to take its course."

The direction of our conversation made me uneasy, but Redding didn't seem to notice. Then he dropped a verbal bombshell.

"A few years after Susan's murder, I went through an erratic stretch. I even thought about suicide."

"Really?" His words stunned me. Specifically that he'd say them aloud, especially when I was around to hear. "I thought pros like you would know better."

"I checked myself into a private clinic a couple days before the third anniversary date. I checked myself out the day after. A precautionary measure. Probably unnecessary." He shrugged. "It seemed prudent at the time, but I have not felt the need since."

I filled him in on the story about me and Mrs. Fredericks, but left out the part about having sabotaged my wedding anniversary the year before. Too dark a secret to share. After all, he wasn't *my* therapist.

"More people attempt suicide than actually succeed," Redding said. "It sounds like you wanted to be rescued."

"Am I as crazy as your patients?"

"You're not mentally ill. Well, you're not bipolar or schizophrenic anyway. But that's not the only reason people try to kill themselves. Otherwise healthy people facing overwhelming trauma can behave suicidally."

"Grief and guilt?"

"Grief and guilt can make strong people weak."

"What do you have to feel guilty about?"

"That's none of your business." He said it playfully this time, not petulantly. We were making progress.

"Come on," I pushed, "what could you possibly feel guilty about?"

Redding paused and looked serious. "I used to feel guilty because my wife died while I was absent, out of town, for my work. Later, after I learned she was having an affair with her killer, I realized her own choices cost her her life."

Oh Lord, I couldn't look at him.

My hands covered my face as I explained how Boyer would still be alive today if I hadn't put my job first.

He pulled my hands down and looked me in the eye. "What happened wasn't your fault."

I turned away. "Yes, it was."

"You are not responsible for the actions of a madman."

If only I could believe that. I didn't answer, just started back in the direction of home. Besides a "murdered spouse" bond, Redding and I now shared a "toying with suicide" bond. I suppose that made us trust each other more than we normally would have. He took my hand while we walked. Holding hands with a source is a bad, bad idea. Especially in the middle of a torrid story.

Awkwardly, I joked, "You don't know where that's been," and slipped my fingers from his. "Remember Shep?"

The clouds cleared and moonlight opened up the shadows. I headed for a bench beside the lake and sat down. He joined me, pointedly clasping his hands behind his neck. Across the lake, the silhouette of the band shell stood out against the sky. We watched a small dog swimming near shore. Then, ugh, I realized it was a large rat.

"He was my patient. Not Susan," Redding said. I didn't have a clue what he was talking about.

"Karl Skubic," he muttered under his breath.

What a strange mind-game association, I thought. A rat appears and he thinks of Mayor Skubic. Later, I would ask his professional opinion about this coincidence, but I didn't want to interrupt him right now. He seemed on the verge of disclosing the secret I had suspected.

"He was a court-ordered case. Hot-tempered, even for a hockey player. We worked on anger management issues. Susan came in for a couples session. He had been charged with assaulting her. If he had no further violations for the next year, the case would be dismissed and he would have no criminal record.

"I could lose my license for telling you."

MALIK MUST HAVE picked up the news cruiser because my driveway was empty when we returned. Redding walked me to the door. Between that courtesy, the rose, and the hand-holding, the evening was starting to feel too much like a date. Thankfully, I heard a firm growl from inside.

"I'd invite you in, but then I'd hate for you to have to run to the ER for stitches this late."

"He's quite the chaperone," Redding replied.

Then I dodged what looked like an incoming kiss on the lips, receiving a peck on the cheek instead. Much too much like a date. But at least I had a missing piece of the SUSANS puzzle. Except I had traded my deepest shame to a blabbermouth shrink.

Just then, headlights from another vehicle shone on us. Garnett climbed out of his Crown Vic—once a cop always a cop—and waved as he walked across the yard, giving my guest the once-over.

"Just checking to see how you're doing," he called out.

"Fine," I answered. "Thanks for the concern, but I'm

ready to turn in." I didn't mind Redding thinking I had personal security, but Garnett appeared to be more like a babysitter than a bodyguard.

"Not interrupting anything, am I?" The jovial tone in his voice made me suspect he'd seen our bungled buss.

"Nope. Just saying good night."

I introduced Garnett as an old friend and Redding as a new friend. Then I left them alone, standing on the front porch, to size each other up.

When I got inside, I scratched Shep behind his watchdog ears, tossed him a crunchy biscuit, and whispered, "Good doggie."

Outside I heard raised voices but couldn't make out what either man was saying.

CHAPTER 28

Judge Melina Fuentes ruled from the bench in her northern Minnesota courtroom. That's fairly unusual even though she'd reviewed each side's written briefs prior to the hearing. Most judges prefer to carefully craft their orders behind closed doors. Not Judge Fuentes. Like a breezy game show host, she enjoyed an audience. And today the stands were full.

The gist of the defense argument: Mr. Foster was paying a high price for a crime he didn't commit. The state has the means to put these suspicions to rest.

The gist of the prosecution argument: Everyone is entitled to their day in court and Mr. Foster already had his. The state has neither the time nor the money to reinvestigate every conviction.

The judge picked door number one.

"Enough time has been wasted," she said. "Either Mr. Foster is guilty, or he's not. Run the blood test and let's find out. I don't like this specter of doubt hanging over a murder case. Mr. Foster's motion deals with a very specific evidentiary issue under quite exceptional circumstances. Reopening this case does not obligate the state in future criminal matters."

As her gavel banged down, I experienced an unsettling premonition of falling ratings. Absurd, because Channel 3 would be promoting yet another SUSANS lead for tonight during *Oprah, Wheel of Fortune,* and a prime-time drama showcasing thin women in thinner plots. The judge's ruling called for expedited testing. With the new state crime lab, that meant the results might be back before sweeps month ended. So mathematically, we couldn't lose.

MINNESOTA DOESN'T ALLOW cameras in court, so besides Malik and me, the assignment desk also sent a station artist to Duluth to cover the hearing. While a new pair of ears on a long road trip makes old war stories fresh again, it also means some subjects are off-limits. So Malik and I couldn't talk about Noreen, or Redding, or Shep.

While Malik drove north, our artist added shadows to her sketches and I scrawled out a script in longhand.

> A CONVICTED
> SUSAN KILLER
> IS ONE STEP CLOSER
> TO FREEDOM
> TODAY FOLLOWING
> A JUDGE'S ORDER
> THAT THE STATE
> CONDUCT NEW TESTS
> ON AN OLD PIECE
> OF EVIDENCE . . .
> AT ISSUE . . .
> WHETHER

BLOODSTAINS
ON A SHIRT WORN
BY THE KILLER
MATCH HIS DNA
OR HIS VICTIM'S.

I switched the dial to Minnesota Public Radio and heard an echo. The host was interviewing the prosecutor and defense attorney in the Susan Redding story. *My* story. If highbrow public radio was jumping onboard, that proved SUSANS no longer belonged with News of the Weird.

"But if Dusty Foster is guilty, who's killing these other women?" Good question. Damn. A semi blew by, the radio turned static, and I missed the answer. Probably just a lot of political hemming and hawing, but I would have liked to have heard the drivel just the same.

"Does the victim's family support reopening the case?"

"Definitely not," the prosecutor replied. "I spoke to her husband earlier today. He believes the right man is in prison and wants him to remain there." Thanks for nothing, Redding.

The host thanked both lawyers for their time and introduced her next guest: Minneapolis City Councilwoman Susan Victor.

"My name might be Susan, but I speak for all women, and we're tired of the media using fear to spike ratings."

"Hey," I said, "you don't speak for me."

"Channel 3's coverage has been reprehensible." She knew how to stay on message. "If they truly care about the safety of women, they shouldn't campaign to free killers."

"Hasn't she had enough exposure?" To Malik's amusement, I lost my cool. "It's not like she's up for reelection this year. Doesn't she realize how lame she sounds?"

"Maybe she thinks any publicity is good publicity," he said.

"Tell it to Dr. Petit."

But we couldn't because Petit remained missing.

His absence didn't bother Noreen. She figured with the vet bogged down under his own legal problems, he wouldn't have time to cause any trouble for us.

Over the phone I cautioned Noreen to drop that attitude. "Don't let Miles hear you talking like that." I had called her from the road to get script approval for the Dusty Foster story so Malik could begin editing as soon as he got back and shot the court sketches.

"If he sues us," I continued, "we want to maintain we were just doing our job as journalists. You don't want him to be able to cry malice."

His attorney would salivate over the chance to argue that besides doing a defamatory story about his client, Channel 3 purposely tried to create legal difficulties for him so he would be too busy to defend his reputation by suing us. I didn't really think he would come after us in court, but if he did, I didn't want this conversation coming up during a deposition. No point in giving the jury a reason to pile on punitive damages.

"You spend too much time worrying about what-ifs," Noreen said. "Why don't you worry about where your next story is coming from?"

"If I have to waste time on lawsuits, that's time I can't spend on next stories," I pointed out. "The best way to avoid being sued is to be prepared to be sued. If the vet clinic goes under, he'll try to make us pay."

SHEP INSPECTED THE front and back doors and the windows. He even checked under my bed while I brushed my teeth. His devotion impressed me until I realized he was searching for a plastic kitty chew toy.

"What do you think, Shep? Time for bed?"

I was talking to a dog. Like I expected an answer. Is this what happens when people don't have people for friends?

It's hard to sleep alone when you're used to company. I've tried a dark room, a night-light, white noise, and even a glass of wine at night. But for real sound sleep, nothing beats a big dog with sharp teeth lying next to your bed.

Shep's heavy breathing reminded me of Boyer so I slept hard and I slept deep, but I couldn't sleep through the barking and snarling that woke me a few hours later.

Downstairs, Shep growled with authority. "The

Hound of the Baskervilles" came to mind, but then I remembered "The Silver Blaze," where Holmes deduced that the significance of the hound lay not in his bark, but in his silence.

Not so with Shep. His front paws rested on the window looking onto the backyard. His lips curled back from his jaws and he barked like he was leading the Holidazzle Parade. Whoever lurked out there, it wasn't Toby Elness. I called for Shep; he wouldn't budge. I turned on an exterior light, saw nothing, even when I pressed my face against the glass. I heard Shep's toenails skid across the wood floor as he raced to a side window. His voice alternated between a menacing rumble and a frantic roar.

I deliberated whether to pick up the phone and dial 911 or rush upstairs and grab Boyer's gun from under the bed. He had never fired the weapon in the line of duty; few cops have. But that didn't mean, under the right circumstances, I wouldn't pull the trigger first and ask questions later. A .40-caliber Glock is a manly gun. I recalled the weight of the pistol in my hand. Boyer had assured me I could handle the gun because its heft absorbs most of the kick. Keeping one eye on the window, I took a step toward the stairs. Then, abruptly, as if a canine all clear signal had sounded, Shep shut up.

Whether he sensed a robber or a raccoon, I couldn't tell, but since they both wore masks, no way was I going out to check. No way was I going back to sleep either. Shep picked up a worn rawhide bone and followed me into the kitchen. He gnawed his prize while I heated a mug of skim milk in the microwave. I stirred in some chocolate mix and was just squirting whipped cream from a can when he dropped what he was chewing and stood by the front door. His muscles tensed and deep in his throat a silent growl became audible.

A few seconds later I heard a knock at the door. Probably one of the neighbors complaining about the noise. No use ignoring the knock; every light in the house clearly broadcast I was awake. Anyway, Shep, my fortress of fur and force, remained on high alert.

"It's me," Garnett called from the porch. Shep calmed, his bark turning to a soft whimper. I opened the door.

"Boy, am I relieved to see you," I said, even though he smelled like alcohol. "There's nobody else I'd prefer standing with on my porch at four in the morning, especially this morning. How did you know things were crazy?"

"I felt a great disturbance in the force."

"Damn. You know I can't keep the *Star Wars* movies straight." I let him inside. "But I don't think you drove all this way at this time of the night just to quiz me about Sir Alec Guinness, *Star Wars: A New Hope,* 1977?"

"Obi-Wan has taught you well."

"Nice transition to Darth Vader, but I've got bigger problems than figuring out whether you're quoting *A New Hope* or *Empire Strikes Back.*"

I filled him in on Shep's nocturnal sortie, pointing out the window where all the commotion had started. Hours from dawn, the night was dead black.

"Give me a flashlight," he said. "Let's have a look."

The three of us ambled outside like a trio of blind mice. Garnett shined the beam back and forth across the front yard.

"See anything?" I asked.

"Last night I lost a glove." He continued to scan the ground. "Didn't find one did you?"

"Forget it. I'll buy you a new pair."

Shep interrupted us with a joyous yelp and appeared to follow an invisible trail toward the rear of the house. We scrambled to keep up. He lifted his nose from the ground under the big picture window and barked as if to declare victory. Then the big lout picked up something in his mouth and moved away from us, chewing.

"Stop him!" Garnett called. "Don't let him eat that!"

He herded Shep my way. A piece of raw meat draped over the dog's lips. I grabbed it and jerked, breaking a fingernail as I dug into the sinewy tissue. Shep growled at me, baring his teeth, not wanting to surrender it. "Bad dog," I scolded him as we played tug-of-war.

Garnett gave his tail a sharp tug. Shep twisted to nip at him and accidentally dropped his prize. I dove for it and held the meat over my head while he jumped at me.

To Shep, it was a tasty, unexpected treat. But Garnett and I knew a Trojan steak when we saw one.

"Whoever was here knows you have a dog. And they'd rather you didn't."

"It's poisoned, right?"

"No doubt in my mind."

Shep sulked as I tossed the meat in the garbage can. "It was a cheap cut," I assured him. "Round or chuck steak at best. Certainly not a tenderloin." I'm a cattleman's daughter. I know these things.

When we returned, Garnett was bent down, examining the ground underneath the window.

He motioned me over next to him and shined the light down on several footprints. They were average in size, about a men's size ten shoe. Garnett scrutinized our tracks. Mine too small, his just right, but the mystery tracks had a smooth grid compared to his rough soles.

"Here's your company."

GARNETT HELPED HIMSELF to beer for breakfast. I was spending more personal time with him than ever before and worried he might have a drinking problem. I tossed Shep a dried pig's ear to make him forget about the poisoned steak.

I sat at the kitchen table, outlining the Mayor Skubic/SUSANS links, in case the DNA testing changed the status quo. Freeing an innocent man from prison can be exhilarating, but so is pointing the finger at a guilty one. The mayor remained a tempting target, but Garnett thought my aim might be off.

"He doesn't have the talent to get away with it. White-collar crime, yes. Nothing this dark."

"He had a relationship with Susan Redding," I insisted.

"Old news," Garnett countered.

"A violent relationship."

"Perhaps, but again, way past tense."

"He was in Duluth the day of the murder."

"That helps."

"We have the Polaroid." I set a copy on top of the file so he could look past her bruises, and into her eyes. "A handwriting analyst confirmed she wrote the words on the back." Laura Robins had given me an old yearbook with a sample. Damning words: KARL SKUBIC DID THIS. "We can't use their names, but two sources corroborated he beat her up."

"Who besides the girlfriend?"

I deliberately waited for him to take another swallow before saying, "Her husband."

"What?" he gagged. Now I had Garnett's full attention. "Maybe I *was* interrupting something last night."

"Just business."

"Looked pretty cozy for business."

I ignored his remark. "What did you think of Redding?"

"Didn't like him."

"Professionally or personally?"

"Both levels. Guy didn't feel right. Little too arrogant."

"Maybe you didn't give him a chance." I explained about Susan Redding, Karl Skubic, and the sealed assault records. Garnett's eyes narrowed. By the time I finished, he thought less of Redding than of Mayor Skubic.

"Doesn't say much about his character that he's telling you this."

"Maybe he's a fan of the truth."

"He's no fan of ethics." He banged his bottle down and pushed his chair away from the table. "He's violating a very strict professional code and I have to wonder, why? Especially since he tells any reporter who calls him up that he's satisfied with the verdict in his wife's murder."

"Maybe he doesn't want to express public doubt."

"Maybe he's looking to settle an old score."

"He's had years to do that," I reminded him.

"He's never had a vehicle for revenge till now."

"I don't think that's his motive."

"I don't either." He knocked the bottle across the table and against the wall. Shep yelped. "I think you're his motive."

No argument from me because Garnett could be right. He also could be drunk. I could see by his sagging shoulders that my silence hurt him. Maybe I should have played dumb, but pretending I didn't know what he was hinting at seemed worse. So I said nothing, still believing his dislike of Redding resembled that of a brother exasperated at his kid sister's crush. Garnett's next words changed our rapport forever.

"Listen, Riley. I've been thinking maybe you and I could have a shot together?" His sentence ended with an inflection. More like a question than a statement. It deserved an answer. When none came, he rephrased it, bluntly, so I couldn't possibly misunderstand his intention. "Do you ever see us as more than friends?"

This was bad. I lacked the courage to say no, so I continued to say nothing. The easiest way to avoid having this kind of conversation is to avoid being alone with anybody who might harbor secret, but unreciprocated, feelings. How could I have been so stupid? Looking back, the signs were there, but my mind was elsewhere. No "aha" moment when I needed one.

Shep continued crunching the pig's ear under the kitchen table by our feet. That and the noise of Garnett's beer bottle rolling around broke the silence, but didn't make things any less awkward.

"Need to check with your shrink boyfriend first?"

"I can't be with you and we both know why." An uncomfortable pause. The words rushed out. "I can't be with a cop." Then I slowed my delivery to enunciate each one.

"I . . . can't . . . ever . . . face . . . that . . . again."

"I'm not a cop anymore." Garnett's face looked flustered—maybe from alcohol, maybe from anguish.

I shook my head. "You'll always be a cop."

"And he never will. Fancy yourself a doctor's wife, do you?" Shep stopped chewing. He whined at the nasty change in Garnett's tone.

"There's nothing between him and me. I feel a

connection. Not an attraction. We understand each other's loss. I'm not looking for a future with him."

"What are you looking for?" His eyes pleaded for a response that didn't cut his chances off at the knees.

"I don't know. But I do know I can't handle another breaking news story that breaks my heart."

Most cop widows receive a personal home visit by special officers trained to comfort them with words like "hero" and "line of duty." I learned about my husband's death from an Associated Press wire report marked URGENT.

"Never again," I insisted.

We both wanted to cry, but he was too macho and I was too cynical.

"I would never hurt you," he said. "But I've got an ugly feeling about this guy. He's feeding you damning information that could land him in serious trouble, and you have to ask yourself why."

"How's that any different from you leaking stuff to me?"

A huge difference. Absolutely. The minute the line left my lips, I knew I'd done damage. Our relationship predated our bosses, our houses, and most of our friends.

I launched into a monologue of remorse, but it was too late. "Look, I'm sorry, I don't want it to be like this with us. I want us to be okay again."

He didn't answer. Shep suddenly vomited like he'd eaten something that didn't agree with him. The air turned sour, like our relationship.

"Say something," I pleaded.

"We're okay." His voice flat, his face fallen. He turned away and opened the door to leave.

"I'm worried we're not."

"Frankly, my dear, I don't give a damn!"

He slammed the door shut. I froze. Shep barked. I fumbled with the doorknob, but by the time I got it open, Garnett's car had peeled out of the driveway. I raced after him, but he shot down the block, cheating me out of the chance to yell, "Clark Gable, *Gone With the Wind,* 1939."

CHAPTER 29

Dog breath woke me. Shep crawled in bed. Too dejected to push him away, I pulled the covers over my head and slept through the alarm.

WHEN I OPENED my eyes, the clock flashed 8:24 a.m. The date flashed 11-19-07. The anniversary had arrived. Let today pass quickly and uneventfully. Let there be no news but good news.

Faint knocks blended with Shep's bored bark. Both sounded more informational than insistent. I couldn't find my ratty robe, so I wrapped a blanket around my body and staggered downstairs to see what new disaster daylight brought to my door.

Malik waited to drive me to work. I had forgotten about my personal escort. Now if I could just forget about my job.

"Not today." I turned away. "Maybe never again."

"Are you hung over?" He followed me inside.

"No, I've just lost my will to stick my nose into other people's business."

"Well, you better get it back 'cause you'll be in the doghouse with Noreen if you mess up sweeps."

He offered to take Shep for some exercise and sent me upstairs to shower. Because Malik didn't know Garnett was my secret source, I didn't mention our fight.

While I waited for Malik to return, Mrs. Fredericks showed up with a fresh loaf of homemade rhubarb bread. She claimed she had made too much and it would just make her fat, but I recognized her baked goods as a neighborly ruse to gossip about last night's excitement. I gave her the abridged version: late-night prowler scared off by loud dog. I left out all references to unrequited love.

She cleared up the mystery of how Garnett arrived on the scene so fast: he'd given her his cell phone number for emergencies.

"He told me to call him if your dog wouldn't stop barking. He told me to call him if your dog stopped barking suddenly. He also told me to call him if things seemed too quiet."

I had a feeling her calls wouldn't be high priority for him any longer. I had dialed his number a few minutes before her visit, but he must have been screening me. I simply left a message, "I'm sorry," and hung up.

"You're a good neighbor." I gave her a quick hug. "I'm lucky to have you nearby. You better live to be a hundred."

"You keep my life interesting," she said. "At my age, that's worth something."

I was walking her home just as Malik and Shep ran up the sidewalk. Both had muddy feet. Cockleburs stuck in Shep's fur.

"Nice doggie," Mrs. Fredericks said. "But where have you been playing?" She tried yanking a few prickles out, but I pulled him back so he wouldn't accidentally knock her over and break her hip. I figured Toby could brush him later.

Malik refilled Shep's food and water dishes; by the time we got to Channel 3 we were two hours late.

"Really? You made rhubarb bread for the newsroom?" Noreen seemed skeptical about my excuse for being tardy, but helped herself to a still-warm slice anyway.

Back at my desk, I listened to two voice-mail messages. Neither from Garnett.

The first message was from my mom, wanting to know if I would be home for Thanksgiving. She needed to calculate how big a turkey to have Dad kill. I liked a farm holiday dinner as much as the rest of the family, but she knew from past sweeps that I could never commit until the last minute. My dad got on the line next. "Don't tell me you got to work 'cause you need the money. You need money like sheep need wool." A strange analogy since he raised cattle. Unfair too—I hadn't used the money excuse since college.

The second call came from a low-level source at the Minnesota Attorney General's Office, suggesting I check with the Minnesota Veterinary Board but not mention where I got the tip.

So I dialed the vet board, bluffing a bit, and said I'd like to be connected to the person handling the Dr. Petit investigation. Instantly the receptionist transferred me to a female voice.

"Hello, I'm calling about Dr. Petit," I said, purposely deciding to be vague.

"Are you a patient?" she asked.

"Do you mean my dog?" I thought of Lucky and Shep and wondered if it was stretching things to call them mine. "One of them was a patient and one of them still is."

"What's your name?"

Now we were on tricky ground. Journalists aren't supposed to lie, and I hated being tripped up on such an obvious question. I pondered answering "Riley Boyer," but that really wasn't fair, because I had never used my husband's name before.

By now I had paused so long the voice on the other end was suspicious. "Who is this?"

I mumbled my name really fast. That just seemed to make her edgier. "Riley Spartz," I finally admitted and got the reaction I expected.

"Are you that snarky TV reporter?"

The conversation disintegrated after that. No closer to answers after good-bye than I had been prior to hello.

My AG source was no help. She'd simply overheard one end of her boss's talk with the vet board boss and realized that the investigation was expanding. The same second I hung up, my phone rang.

Garnett? Not Garnett. Toby.

He was mad because I'd left Shep so dirty. He was also mad because he had to take all his animals to be revaccinated. He had stopped to pick up Shep on the way, and now he was going to be late because he had to clean up the big dog first. "Thanks a lot, Riley!"

I apologized for Shep's dirty coat. "But I don't understand about the vaccinations."

"The Minnesota Veterinary Board called me this morning," he explained. "Apparently Dr. Petit watered down all his vaccines so all my pets have to get shots again and may need to be quarantined for two weeks."

"Just your pets, or all people's pets?"

"All the pets that were patients of Dr. Petit. We're supposed to bring them down to the vet board office today."

Now I knew what new direction the investigation was taking.

"Toby, wait for me!"

MALIK AND I stayed across the street in the van while Toby unloaded Shep, Husky, Blackie, and seven cats in various cages in the parking lot behind the Minnesota Veterinary Board building. The board hadn't mentioned the hamsters, so he had left them home. He and his pets waited in line behind other people with animal companions.

A freckled man and a black woman in white lab coats were immunizing the pets from a table of syringes. Malik was rolling. I was wired. I walked over to the makeshift clinic.

"What's going on?" I asked.

Immediately the woman recognized me and screamed, "She's the TV one!"

By then Malik had a camera in their faces and I was

calmly explaining, "You can either look like you care about protecting the public, or you can look like you're covering up a public danger."

The freckled man made a cell phone call and a younger guy in a suit and tie showed up and huddled with them in the lobby for a few minutes. While I waited, the owner of a Saint Bernard crowded me, begging to have his precious poochie put on television so a dog food company could discover him and cast him in a commercial.

The guy in the suit ventured over, introduced himself as the head of the vet board, and shook my hand. "I understand you'd like to do a story about the diligent efforts we're making to safeguard the public from the unscrupulous Dr. Petit. We're happy to cooperate."

I pressed *record* on my tape recorder and Malik pressed *play* on his camera as he explained how they had suspended Dr. Petit's veterinary license after the pet cremation story. Trailing in behind the AG investigators, one of their agents had been giving the clinic a routine inspection when she noticed the seals on the vaccines had been broken.

Dr. Petit hadn't just watered down the medication; he was using water as medication. Not such big a deal for feline leukemia, unless you're a cat. But a dangerous deal for rabies vaccinations. That's why the board was readministering the shots now, and urging owners to isolate their pets if they saw any signs of aggression. In fact, the board had arranged for some kennels to donate space while they sorted things out.

I called the assignment desk to tell them I had the lead story for that night.

> VET FRAUD EXPANDS . . .
> PUBLIC THREAT
> POSSIBLE . . .
> AUTHORITIES SHUT
> DOWN CLINIC . . .
> OWNERS UNLEASH
> ANGER.

Next I talked to the producer about time. Newscast producers and reporters have different agendas. I wanted as much time as possible to tell my story. Producers want as many stories as possible in their newscast, which means they want stories told in the least amount of time. Under that formula, a high story count means more than an in-depth story. This kind of conversation normally gets nasty, with me pushing for three minutes and the producer insisting on one minute, ten seconds. But Noreen, feeling a stake in the dog folo and being the big boss, had already paved the way for two and a half minutes. The producer and I did agree on something: Dr. Petit no longer deserved to be called doctor. That would shave a couple seconds off the story.

I FINISHED MY set piece on the late news. By the time I got back to my desk, my message light blinked and I listened to a tip from a law enforcement source alerting me that the Isanti County Sheriff was investigating Petit for involvement in an underground dog-fighting ring. "I'll call again if we get close to making a bust."

Meanwhile Shep waited at home, locked in my library. Toby was allowing the big dog to be quarantined with me while he monitored the rest of the pack. I wasn't worried, but Toby insisted he stay in the library until the rabies issue was settled. True, Shep enjoyed a good growl, but I attributed that to his contrary nature, not to some disease potentially fatal to him and anyone he encountered with his teeth.

Back home, I let him out for a quick bathroom break and gave him some rawhide so he wouldn't chew on my books. I glanced at the calendar over the kitchen sink. November 19, 2007. Cursed in more ways than one.

Leaving another apology on Garnett's cell phone, I felt irritated as well as regretful. "There might be enough blame to go around," I said. "Maybe you should come over and apologize, too."

I considered he might be on stakeout, this being the night of the SUSANS anniversary. Habits are hard to break. I looked at the clock. Not yet midnight. I tried to push November 19 out of my mind. For a decade the Susan killer had been quiet. Whether because he was dead, in prison, out of the country, or reformed—who knew? I was anxious that my story might aggravate his interest. I'd left instructions with the assignment desk to call me if the police scanners picked up any homicide chatter. So far, nothing. No dead Susans. I looked at the clock again.

I experimented taking off my wedding ring, but after a minute or so I put it back on. I curled up on the couch with a good book, actually THE good book, and would have appreciated a warm dog curled up at my feet. I substituted a warm fire and a generous glass of sherry.

Chapter 13 of the book of Daniel reminded me why the Bible is the best-selling book of all time—it's full of sex and violence. Definitely rated R.

A beautiful woman named Susanna is married to an important man. Two judicial elders lust after her and plot to blackmail her into having sex with them.

She refuses, saying, "It is better for me to fall into your power without guilt than to sin before the Lord." They publicly accuse her of adultery and testify they saw her with a lover under a tree in her husband's garden. She is sentenced to death.

Enter young Daniel. God guides Daniel into questioning the elders separately, out of earshot of each other, but in front of the crowd. He asks them each the same question: Under which tree did you witness the crime? Each gives a different answer, thus sealing their own executions.

Suddenly I knew what needed to be done and could hardly wait for morning.

No SLEEP. My resolve didn't mean I knew exactly what I was doing. While I had a clear idea what needed to happen, I had only a vague idea of how to accomplish my goal. So my mind raced past numerous options instead of focusing on a single solution.

For Susan suspects, I gravitated toward Mayor Skubic for obvious reasons and Chief Capacasa, probably because of that second glass of sherry I drank on an empty stomach. I also contemplated a scenario that involved the mayor as killer, the chief as orchestrating a cover-up. Looking back now, the whole thing seems dotty. But at the time the conjecture made perfect sense to my befuddled brain.

On some pretext or another I would interview them separately, asking each the same Daniel-like question. Their answers, while seemingly innocuous, would actually prove damaging and decisive. My mind raced more. Best to interview them simultaneously so they couldn't compare notes. I'd need an accomplice. I could get our political reporter Cara Madden to interview the mayor while I interviewed the chief. Then I'd take her out to dinner to celebrate after the ratings book. I could use some girlfriends other than Mrs. Fredericks in my life. That's the funny part about being on TV; half the town can know your name and you can still be lonely.

Okay, occasionally I'm a bitch, and that probably has something to do with my lack of bosom buddies, but in

TV it's hard for reporters to develop friendships with one another. For one thing, we don't work together. We work most closely with photographers, and they're usually men. Second, the competitive nature of the job sometimes pits reporter against reporter. We fret over who's better looking. We fret over who got the lead story that night. We fret over why I only got a minute of airtime and so-and-so got two. We fret over who gets to fill in when the weekend anchor is on vacation. We fret over the perks in our contracts. We fret over who gets the best out-of-town assignments. Instead of becoming friends, we become rivals. But Cara and I had both carved out our own news niches, and I didn't see her as a threat.

But what should the key question be? Reducing a heinous crime to a harmless question was the hard part. My mind kept racing. Torn notebook pages with scrawling followed by question marks lay rejected in a crumpled pile by my feet. I fought to stay awake.

Probably because I now dreaded tomorrow, tomorrow came early.

A heavy noise hammered my front door. And why not? Nearly every light burned in my house even though the hands of the clock read half past one. I recalled Garnett's earlier words, "Bad guys never ring doorbells," and deliberately walked away from the sound, opened the library door, and freed Shep.

Just in case.

CHAPTER 30

One thing I have going for me, I don't get headaches. A colleague once joked, "You're a carrier. You give them." Anyway, my lack of headaches explains the lack of aspirin in my medicine cabinet when Garnett showed up at my door.

"Love means never having to say you're sorry," he said.

That was the closest to an apology I'd ever heard from his lips. While I whispered, "Ryan O'Neal, *Love Story,* 1970," he kissed me on the mouth.

It felt . . . wistful. Not passionate, but not embarrassing either. Interesting. Until I glanced up and was immediately haunted by the ghosts of Christmas past in the shape of withered mistletoe.

Conveniently Shep broke us up and nudged Garnett inside.

"He might have rabies," I warned.

"I'll get the shots."

The fire was dead, but the room was still comfortable. During the past month Minneapolis residents sampled spring rain, summer sun, and autumn chill. Tonight winter joined the weather team with hefty flurries blowing through the door.

"Beer?" I offered. "Hot buttered rum?"

He shook his head. "Water and aspirin. My head is pounding."

Tonight he looked old enough to be retired. While I began a futile search for aspirin, acetaminophen, ibuprofen, or any sort of over-the-counter pain reliever, he stretched out on the couch. I came up empty-handed and went back to check if he would settle for a cold rag on his forehead instead. He had dozed off, his face scrunched against a pillow. Exhausted. Unshaven. Appealing in a vulnerable way. Too bad he already had a mother.

His face felt warm to my touch. I decided to make a run to an all-night drugstore a couple miles away. A sweet gesture on my part, but if I could prop him up, he might be able to help figure out the perfect Daniel question.

His Crown Vic blocked my garage door, so I grabbed the keys from his coat pocket. As I stuck them in the ignition, I noticed the GPS system and smiled. A high-tech crutch for his directional dilemma. The other homicide detectives had given it to him as a retirement present. Being a reporter means being a snoop, even among friends, so I scrolled through the GPS, checking Garnett's previous destinations. They were a road map to his day. In some ways, better than a diary.

Mine was the most recent address; I wasn't familiar with the previous one, 4801 Minnehaha Ave. S. I recognized Garnett's, Channel 3's, the cop shop's, and the Mall of America's. I clicked on "4801 Minnehaha Ave. S." and followed the car's instructions. I figured a small detour wouldn't prove too big a delay. Even though the snow was worsening, the air temperature felt relatively balmy.

"Right turn approaching," the GPS narrator told me. The windshield steamed up as the wipers wrestled sloppy flakes.

The car stereo was playing a Roy Orbison CD. I gave Garnett credit for classic rock taste. Country or rap, now that might be a deal breaker.

"Left turn in one mile." The annoying computer voice was constant.

In the background Roy sang about being lonely and knowing heartaches. I joined in the chorus. After all, I knew plenty about those themes.

"Left turn approaching." I pulled into a road leading to Minnehaha Park, one of the city's oldest and most popular picnic spots. Damn, suddenly I remembered the lilies at Tim Moreno's house. Once buried under autumn leaves, now buried under frost and snow. Damn.

"Maybe tomorrow a new romance . . ." Maybe Roy had the right idea. Maybe Garnett and I deserved a chance. Maybe that was the sherry talking.

"Destination on your left."

The park closed at ten. I wondered what Garnett had been doing here so late. Probably trying to work up his courage to face me.

Minnehaha, meaning "laughing waters," is named for its fifty-three-foot waterfall—another Minnesota reference from Longfellow's *The Song of Hiawatha*. I could hear the creek still running, but it was much too dark and snowy to see any of the park's natural beauty or historic Native American sculptures. Kids sometimes hang out after hours to smoke and drink, but not in this weather, and that crowd generally didn't include anyone over thirty unless they were buying the booze.

The parking lot near the Longfellow House was empty except for a tan SUV in the far corner. My headlights shone on its bumper as Roy sang a mouthful: "If your lonely heart breaks, only the lonely."

The license plate read SUSAN.

CHAPTER 31

Now Roy Orbison was running scared and so was I. A woman was slumped across the front seat of the SUV. Her face pale. Her eyes black. Her body limp. Definitely dead. My tracks were the only ones in the drifting snow.

Without hesitation I did the right thing: I dialed 911 before calling Channel 3.

While I waited for police to arrive, I snapped a cell phone picture of the body. Not that it would ever hit air, but just because.

Cop cars beat our news cruiser to the murder scene by eight minutes. By the time a Channel 3 van rolled into Minnehaha Park, one officer had locked me in the back of a squad car and another had roped off the parking lot with yellow tape.

"Can I go talk to my crew?" I motioned to our overnight photographer, but two street cops kept him back.

The officer in charge told me to stay put. "Chief says you're not going anywhere till he gets here."

The victim seemed familiar. I had a vague sense we had met before, but couldn't remember where. Suddenly I felt sick. I banged urgently on the window with my fists until my guard opened the door. I threw up on his shoes. He swore but left the door ajar so I could get some air, or in case I needed to barf again.

I had already briefed the assignment desk dispatcher about the crime, so even though our photog couldn't see the victim, he zoomed in on a shot of the vehicle's license plate before the chief ordered an officer to drape a cloth over the name SUSAN.

Channel 3 got exclusive video of that move, too. Perhaps a visual metaphor for a cover-up?

I watched Malik pull up next to the perimeter. Some park police kept him from entering the crime scene. My cell phone rang. I saw his number on the screen, but the officer guarding me confiscated my cell phone. I worried he might find my crime scene photo, but he just slipped the phone in his pocket. A minute later I heard the same muffled ring. This time the cop smiled and pressed the power-off button. I scowled for show, but inside I smiled, too, knowing my evidence was safer that way.

"Chief says no phone calls till he figures out if you're a witness or a suspect."

I remembered Garnett, asleep on my couch. I had an unsettling feeling I might have pulled a Philip Trent, collecting evidence but drawing the wrong conclusion. Garnett's words from last month echoed back: "Better check me out, Riley. Like I said, he might be a cop."

The killer might be a cop. Oh boy. I had a bad feeling in my stomach and it was more than nausea.

"I need to talk to the chief right away," I said. "It's important."

The cop recoiled from my vomit breath, put a

portable radio to his lips for some chatter, then stuck his head back inside. "Chief certainly wants to talk. Downtown. Right now he's got a dead body that outranks you."

He slammed the door. I pounded on the window, but this time he ignored me. Police emergency lights reflected red off his glasses.

DURING THE NEXT ten minutes news vans from all the other stations arrived. They'd heard the code for medical examiner come over the police scanners and knew that meant death, sometimes foul play. They also knew the call usually meant news, so they plowed through snow banks, hiked cameras onto their shoulders, and sprayed the scene with video. Routine, for all they knew. Could be just a drug deal gone bad. The deceased a victim of an at-risk lifestyle, worth maybe twenty seconds of airtime.

Only those of us from Channel 3 grasped that we were looking at a story that would dominate our newscasts, and theirs, for days.

"I need to stop at my house," I insisted as the squad car pulled out of the parking lot. The officer kept his eyes on the road, his hands on the steering wheel, and his mouth shut. I pounded on the divider glass. "There's someone there I need to check on."

"None of your tricks," he said. "My orders are to transport you downtown. Tell it to the detectives."

Unfortunately for the detectives, my lawyer was

waiting at the cop shop and refused to let them interview me until he and I had spoken first. More minutes passed. I pictured Garnett waking and finding both me and his car gone. A quick trip to the drugstore had turned my world from calm to chaos.

How much information journalists should share with law enforcement is a gray area within the First Amendment. The usual answer is none—we're not an arm of the police. Our job is to put facts on the air, not turn them over to the cops. The police are free to conduct their own investigations, but frequently when they go after reporter notes and sources, it's not because of an urgent danger, but because they're too lazy to do the grunt work themselves.

Media attorneys will usually insist on a subpoena before allowing their clients to reveal anything and will often take the fight to court to resist disclosing unbroadcast material.

There are exceptions: clearly a journalist who witnesses a crime has the same obligation as any citizen; also if the police truly have no other means of getting the information, a judge will usually direct the media to turn it over. That gets messy and usually takes time. But in the case of a slain city official, no judge would pause longer than five seconds before signing such an order.

So when Miles learned the details of how I'd spent the last couple hours, he caved on the First Amendment like cement on a marshmallow and made me pony up what I knew to the cops.

By then my knee-jerk reaction (that Garnett must be involved in the murder) was battling my gut reaction (that Garnett was incapable of such a crime). My gut was winning, so I tried soft-pedaling his involvement, figuring I'd sort it out with him later. But the facts of just how I had discovered Susan Victor's body were pretty damning. After all, it was almost as though Garnett had drawn me a map to the crime scene.

When Chief Capacasa heard the GPS story, he sent a police team that broke down the back door of my house, handcuffed a disheveled former homicide detective, and nearly shot a possibly rabid German shepherd.

When Noreen got the full scoop, she didn't just pull me off the case; she pulled me off the air. Even more wretched, she assigned the story to Mike Flagg.

The worst part: it got a 42 share.

CHAPTER 32

Susan Victor learned the hard way that not all publicity is good publicity. It was her body I found in Minnehaha Park. In a grisly trifecta, the city councilwoman led all the newscasts on all the television stations all day long. Being dead, she derived no political benefit.

Verifying a suspect's whereabouts is so much easier the day after a homicide than the decade after.

Mayor Skubic had hosted a fund-raiser on the night of November 19. Surrounded by dozens of campaign contributors, there didn't seem to be much doubt anymore who the killer wasn't.

It sure wasn't Dusty Foster, who had an ironclad alibi for this one, too. The next day an even larger group of sympathizers joined his mother to protest that he be immediately released from Oak Park Heights State Prison.

It wasn't even Susan Moreno's fervent father. Turns out, during snowstorms he volunteers for the night shift at his church's homeless shelter.

I was also in the clear. I may have discovered her lifeless body, but the medical examiner determined that Susan Victor had died while I was reporting live on the ten o'clock news, watched by hundreds of thousands of viewers.

The only one without a solid alibi was Garnett.

Garnett refused to talk—to me anyway. But in his statement to police he claimed an anonymous caller promising information in the SUSANS cases had offered to meet him at Minnehaha Park at midnight. He maintained he had driven aimlessly much of the evening, watching the clock and cursing me, but when he had arrived, the parking lot was empty. The caller never showed. Was he framed? A police insider told me the caller's number traced to a downtown pay phone. One of the investigators speculated that Garnett might have made the mysterious call himself, so if the cops ever checked, his cell phone records would back up his story.

But if he was the killer, why come to my house afterward? Unless perhaps to stage an alibi?

THE STORM DUMPED six inches of snow on the Twin Cities, normally not enough to cancel schools, but coupled with the cumbersome detours from the bridge collapse, traffic was snarled to a standstill.

Instead of shoveling I stomped a meager path from my front door to the road. Malik's vehicle had four-wheel drive, so while rush hour took ages, at least we didn't worry about getting stuck on a side street. After all the trouble I went through to get to work, bad news awaited me at Channel 3.

I was under orders to stay home.

"I can work on other stories," I argued to Noreen.

"I don't think so," she countered, and as usual the general manager backed her up, and so did Miles.

"This raises all sorts of legal issues," he said.

"Ethical ones, too," Noreen added. "So we want you to lay low until this settles down. Don't worry, you'll still be paid."

"I'm not worried about that. I'm worried about my reputation as a journalist. Taking me off the story is one thing, but taking me off the air implies I've done something wrong."

"Can't be helped," Noreen said. "The station's image could be damaged long term. Remember, a city councilwoman is dead. A city councilwoman who was critical of your reporting. Our role is going to be examined. If your source winds up being the killer, we could all be in deep trouble."

I hated that she had a valid point.

None of us mentioned the numbers. But the numbers hung in the back of each of our minds, and the minds of the rest of the newsroom, watching our meeting unfold through the glass walls of Noreen's fishbowl. The November sweeps were exceptional. No one at Channel 3 wanted to jeopardize those numbers.

Our competitors would undoubtedly pressure Nielsen to flag the book, which would mean placing an asterisk next to our score to alert advertisers that the number might be tainted. That usually happens only if a television station offers prizes to viewers or promotes a story about what it's like being a Nielsen family to entice viewers with ratings meters or diaries to tune in at ten. But even if the other stations succeeded, a flag wouldn't necessarily impact sales, and that's all my bosses really cared about.

"New viewers are sampling us this month," the GM said, apparently seeing a need to spell out the reality of station revenue to me since I was part of the news department and we sometimes seem obtuse about making money. "We can't chance scaring them away. There's too much at stake down the road. If we turn around our numbers, that gives us the means to do more public service programming."

"Also don't talk to the cops anymore unless I'm there," Miles cautioned. "In fact, you probably should stay away from this Garnett guy, too."

"Right now that's not a problem," I said, "since he's behind bars."

I was feeling increasingly conflicted about my role in Garnett's arrest. Had I betrayed a friend? Or had I harbored a killer? "I do consider him a friend. And I do feel somewhat responsible for him being in jail, so if he ever calls me, I'm going to answer."

"I advise against this," Miles said.

"Actually," Noreen countered, "I wouldn't mind an interview with him. He's clearly the 'get' to get. Viewers will tune in big-time for his side of the story."

"Well, he's not going to want to get got," I said. "And I won't set him up."

"Obviously you can't do the actual interview,"

Noreen said. "You have too many conflicts of interest. But you could land it and hand it off to Mike Flagg." She winked at me like we were coconspirators, plotting which cute boy to ask to the Sadie dance.

I tried explaining why I wouldn't sacrifice Garnett as a ratings lamb. "Nick Garnett has been a top source for me and Channel 3 for years. We owe him something more."

"Not if he's a murderer we don't," Noreen answered.

She had me there.

Even though I snitched on him, deep down I believed Garnett innocent. Why would he bring me the SUSANS story if he was the killer? It made no sense. Unless he wanted to be stopped. Unless he wanted to win my attention. Hadn't he warned me that a cop might be behind all this? Was he bragging when he said that? Was he playing a deadly game?

Maybe I was naive, giving him the benefit for old times' sake. But I didn't think so. The evidence was not conclusive.

If all the cops could do was place him at the crime scene, that wouldn't be enough for a guilty verdict. Though it might be enough probable cause for the county attorney to charge him with Susan Victor's murder. That would buy investigators time to develop their case before it went to trial. Right now, authorities couldn't hold him for more than thirty-six hours without charging him with something. I figured they wouldn't file any earlier than they had to, but clearly

the legal clock was ticking. Twelve hours down . . .
twenty-four hours left to clear his name before things
got complicated.

MALIK HELPED ME move the SUSANS boards and
boxes from my office to my house. As far as I was concerned, since I was still on the payroll, I was still on
the job.

Again, the eyes of the Susans—Redding, Chenowith,
Moreno, and Niemczyk—seemingly watched me as I
propped their boards against my living room wall.

Add to them Susan Victor—a politician who had
gambled her life and lost.

They didn't resemble one another. They didn't share
backgrounds. They didn't have anything in common
but the dates of their deaths and, of course, their
names. Each board listed facts about each case. Loca-
tions. Occupations. Family relationships. Clues like the
raincoat and the suicide notes. What was I missing?

I noticed something shiny stuck between the pages
of a stack of documents and pulled out Suicide
Susan's engraved pendant. I polished it on my shirt
and impulsively put it around my neck. I didn't do
anything so melodramatic as vow to wear it until
the real killer was found, but I did pledge to keep up
the search. Besides saying SUSAN, I felt the necklace
was also saying, "Don't forget us."

I was still admiring the piece in the mirror when I
heard someone outside on the porch.

Toby and Shep. I gave the big dog a big hug. Now I had to do the big sell on Toby to get Shep back. Animal control officers got Toby's phone number off the tags on Shep's collar after the police broke into my house.

"Shep could have been shot," Toby said. "I'm not sure him staying with you is such a good idea."

"Come on, Toby, nothing like that will ever happen again."

"I loaned him to you for protection, but maybe I need to protect Shep."

"It was a fluke, Toby. Besides, Channel 3 put me on leave and I really need the company."

I meant those words. As if on cue, Shep brushed against my legs, whined like a puppy, and gazed imploringly at his master with warm, brown, dog shit eyes. Good boy.

"Well," Toby relented, "he seems to feel at home with you. I suppose it's safe now that that friend of yours is in jail. Who would have ever thought he was the killer? Shep is usually such a good judge of character."

"I don't think Garnett did it."

"The police seem to."

"The police just want to close the case. It's an embarrassment to them. They don't want to look further."

"Maybe you're the one who doesn't want to face the truth. Sometimes people deceive us. That's why I stick with animals."

Toby petted Shep good-bye and left me with my

qualms and the disturbing realization that he could be right about deception.

Dusty Foster's name was written on Susan Redding's board. Even though it broke my heart, I added Nick Garnett's name to Susan Victor's. Then I wrote the latest clues under his name.

SUSPECT/NICK GARNETT
GPS
PHONE CALL?

I needed to stay objective. I needed to stay focused. Truth never comes from wishful thinking. Truth sometimes comes from eliminating what is false. I stepped back to look at the big picture. To look at the pattern.

SUSAN REDDING	1990
SUSAN CHENOWITH	1991
SUSAN MORENO	1992
SUSAN NIEMCZYK	1994
SUSAN VICTOR	2007

What was I missing? Help me, Sherlock.

OVERNIGHT MY MIND found the answer.

I was missing a Susan. For the pattern to hold, I should have a dead body between the years 1992 and 1994. So I telephoned Xiong and asked him where it was.

"Noreen says you are not on the project anymore," he answered. "She told the newsroom if anything changes on the SUSANS story we need to bring it to her, not you."

"Please, Xiong, I'm just on leave. It's not like I was suspended or fired. I need to double-check that you didn't find any unusual Susan deaths on our date in 1993."

"I gave you all I found."

"I know. But if you could look again and call me if you discover anything suspicious."

Xiong reluctantly agreed just as the doorbell rang. I looked out my bedroom window and saw Mike Flagg on my front steps. So much for Garnett's theory that bad guys never ring doorbells. I hadn't invited him over—not this morning, not any morning. I turned the shower on so I'd have an excuse to keep our meeting short.

"What are you doing here?" I greeted him in my old bathrobe, even though he wasn't a close friend.

He handed me my newspaper. "Ever think maybe I came to see how you're doing?"

"Really?"

"No. Noreen assigned the SUSANS story to me. I went to your office to review your notes and couldn't find anything." He peered behind me and saw the SUSANS boards in full display in my living room. "I see why. Mind if I have a look?"

"Yes, I do mind." I blocked his path. When he tried

to push past me, Shep lowered his ears and raised his voice. A bark, not a growl, but definitely firm. "The notes are mine."

"Those notes belong to the station," Flagg said.

Technically he was right about work product, but nothing in my contract said I had to take orders from him.

"Well, I still work there and I'm still using them. You want to take over the story, you develop your own leads. Or better yet, develop your own story instead of poaching on mine."

"I'm just doing what I was assigned to do. If you hadn't messed this story up, I wouldn't have gotten a piece of it."

"I was just getting ready to take a shower." Yes, running water was faintly audible. "You'll have to leave."

Shep interpreted my raised voice as a signal to chase my visitor outside. I didn't praise him or scold him; I threw him a doggie treat shaped like a miniature steak.

I started the coffeepot, and as it brewed I thought I heard voices. I feared I might be losing my mind to stress and fatigue until I glanced out the window and saw Mike Flagg still parked in my driveway.

"I'm telling Noreen!" He shook his fist through the open window of his car, then leaned on the horn. "I'm telling!"

By now Mrs. Fredericks was also looking out her window, shaking her head. I ignored Mike and went upstairs and showered under now cold water. I wrapped towels around my hair and body and unfolded the *Star Tribune* for news on Susan Victor's murder.

Attorney Benny Walsh was defending Garnett. Walsh wasn't a local legal legend like Ron Meshbesher, but he was on his way. Despite what viewers see on prime-time television dramas, murder defendants are hardly ever acquitted. Yet Walsh had succeeded in obtaining not guilty verdicts twice in the last two years. None were high-profile homicides so he wasn't a household name, but the legal community recognized him as a player.

I dialed his office. When I got him on the line, I asked how Garnett was doing.

"With friends like you?" he said.

"It's not the way it seems. I need to talk to him, but he won't see me."

"Actually, I've advised him not to see you. And I require my clients to follow my advice. If he disregards my advice, he can find a new lawyer."

He hung up. I hit redial. The phone rang until a polite voice came on the line and informed me that Mr. Walsh was in a meeting and couldn't be disturbed.

"WE'D RATHER YOU come downtown, ma'am."

My front porch was a happening place this morning. A couple of plainclothes Minneapolis detectives insisted I accompany them for another round of questioning. They flashed their badges to show they meant business.

"Just a minute," I told them.

I ran upstairs to change, making sure the jacket I grabbed didn't sport a Channel 3 logo. I had a direct order not to talk to the cops without Miles present. Since Noreen had heard him give the order, I called and asked him to meet me at the police station. Then I refilled Shep's food and water dishes, reminded him to be a good dog, and climbed into the back of the unmarked squad car.

The suits didn't say anything during the five-mile drive. I didn't either. So if they hoped I'd get nervous and let something damning slip, they suffered their disappointment in professional silence.

Chief Capacasa didn't demonstrate the same restraint. "You got a lot of nerve." He paced back and forth, then slammed a notebook against the wall. "Pulling this kind of stunt."

The first few minutes he'd sat quietly in the corner of the windowless interrogation room while the suits asked me questions. His outburst was directed at my lawyer, who had advised me not to answer the last three questions because they dealt with my role as a journalist rather than a crime witness. I didn't blame the chief. I figured that Miles was just playing tough to make up for being such a patsy before.

"I don't want to hear about the shield law," the chief ranted. "I don't want to hear about unaired video. I don't want to hear about reporters' notes. I just want to hear the facts of what happened."

"Garnett didn't do it," I said.

"Your opinion, not fact." He softened his approach, pulled a chair up next to me and rested his chin on his hand. "You're probably feeling a little foolish. After all, this guy was your buddy. But how about me? I assign a cop to find a killer and he becomes the suspect. I'm taking a lot of grief over this, too."

"I've already told you everything I know. You don't have enough to charge him."

Even if they found Garnett's DNA at the scene of the two dead Minneapolis Susans, that didn't mean anything. No one disputed he was there. But was he there to investigate or to cover his tracks?

"I've got more than you know."

Did he? Hard to tell. If citizens lie to the cops, they can be charged with obstruction. But no law prevents cops from lying to witnesses or suspects during an interrogation. A lying cop who lands a confession is likely to land a commendation from his superiors. I didn't worry about making a blunder because, even though the chief didn't believe me, I wasn't holding anything back because I didn't know anything.

I FELT STICKY and smelly. I had left home in such a hurry, I had forgotten niceties like deodorant. Either that or the police Q and A was more nerve-racking than I realized. I was leaning over for a drink at a water fountain near the building exit when Dr. Redding walked around the corner.

"Riley, what are you doing here?" he asked me.

"The cops just wanted to go over the other night again," I said. "See if my memory remained consistent once the hysteria died down."

"How horrible for you to find her body." He placed his hands on my shoulders as if to hold me steady, even though I wasn't shaking. "If you ever want to talk about it, I'm here for you."

Redding may have meant well, but at the moment his offer held little appeal. Reporters would rather ask a victim the standard "How did you feel?" than answer such questions themselves.

So I put him off. "I'm dealing with it by not talking about it any more than I have to," I explained. "So far that seems to be working. But why are you here? You're spending so much time in Minneapolis; it must be hard on your practice in Duluth."

"A colleague takes over my cases when I'm out of town," the doctor said. "As for today, the investigators wanted to discuss whether my wife and Nick Garnett knew each other."

This was not news I wanted to hear. "What did you tell the police?"

"I told them that to my knowledge they had never met. I also told them my wife's killer has already been tried, convicted, and incarcerated."

"Hmmm, they're probably keeping their options open till that DNA test comes back. That means they're focusing on Garnett, even in the other Susan cases."

"I'm sorry," Redding said. "You must feel terribly torn because he's a friend."

"That's the funny part." I even smiled when I said it. "I'm not torn at all. I'm totally convinced of his innocence."

"Denial can be a powerful emotion." Redding opened the door and we walked outside. "I'll drive you back to the station."

"Actually, I'm working at home now. I've moved all my notes there. And I'm not in denial. If he was a murderer, I'd be able to tell." Sure I would, just like Dusty Foster's mother.

Redding didn't answer. He reached out to touch the pendant around my neck and stroked it between his fingers. "Are you thinking of changing your name?"

"No. I just thought it might bring me luck. I could use some."

"Susan is not the luckiest name right now."

"I know, but—"

Just then I noticed a television camera across the street from us. Redding turned and saw it, too. I recognized one of our photographers, rolling with glee, anticipating that "exclusive" bug on his videotape tonight. Next to him, Mike Flagg smirked, giving me a thumbs-up, though I knew he longed to use a different finger and would have if there hadn't been a crowd.

No arguing them out of the video. The picture of Redding had news value. He had taken special pains to keep his face private. I imagined the promo.

> WHAT DID THE
> HUSBAND OF A DEAD
> SUSAN TELL POLICE?
> FIND OUT TONIGHT AT
> TEN.

Or perhaps this one:

> WHO IS THIS MYSTERY
> MAN AND WHAT IS HIS
> ROLE IN THE SUSANS
> STORY? FIND OUT
> ONLY ON CHANNEL 3.

Either way, Redding was outed. I felt like a curse on the men around me. Boyer. Garnett. Redding. I hooked my fingers through the crook of his arm, but he jerked away and dashed back inside.

Later I realized he blamed me for the photo op, thinking I'd set him up.

CHAPTER 33

Predictably, Garnett's attorney, Benny Walsh, waived the reading of the criminal complaint. Nothing to be gained by making Garnett stand in the middle of the courtroom in an orange jumpsuit any longer than was necessary.

Late yesterday the Hennepin County Attorney charged him with second-degree murder in the death of Susan Victor. Next month the prosecutor would ask a grand jury for a first-degree indictment.

Garnett had been in a courtroom plenty of times as witness and spectator, but never as a suspect. He looked scruffy and unshaven and was shifting his weight from one foot to the other. I wished he'd turn and catch my eye. But he didn't even look in my direction.

Today's hearing was to establish two things: whether the government had enough evidence to hold Garnett, and if so, what bail, if any, should be set.

"I'm going to let the complaint stand," the judge said, "but I'm warning you, you better have more before the probable cause hearing."

The complaint outlined the government's evidence. The GPS documentation was the centerpiece, along with the fact that Garnett couldn't corroborate his alibi for the night of the murder. A search of his apartment turned up newspaper clippings about the old Susan murders, plus recent ones about Susan Victor's criticism. The clips didn't seem suspicious to me—after all, he had been investigating the cases for more than a decade and I knew him to be a pack rat. The surprise: he'd apparently argued with the murder victim at city hall a few days before her death. A council aide overheard him cautioning her not to minimize the criminal dangers women face.

"The state is requesting no bail," the prosecutor said. He didn't want Garnett to buy his way out of jail while awaiting trial. Not entirely reasonable.

"In that case," Walsh said, "the defendant requests to be released on his own recognizance." He wanted Garnett released without having to post any money at all. Not entirely reasonable, either.

"Mr. Garnett is an upstanding citizen," Walsh continued. "A longtime member of the law enforcement community, he's currently employed, has family in the area, and could assist in his own defense, provided he's not incarcerated. Incidentally, we dispute that he played any role in the victim's death."

"You'll have your day for that," the judge said. "I am inclined to set bail. As for the amount—"

"Your honor," the prosecutor interjected, "the state requests one million dollars. This is a heinous murder case involving a city official."

"Mr. Garnett does not have vast savings," Walsh countered. "We would ask—"

"Bail is set at $250,000." The judge banged his gavel and two courthouse deputies led Garnett away.

"CAN HE AFFORD bail?" Walsh repeated my question. "He can't even afford me. I'm giving him a cut rate, basically defending him for the publicity."

"Aren't you simply awesome," I said.

"Yes." He checked the daybook on his desk. "And talented." He scribbled the date of the probable cause hearing. "And brilliant."

Garnett had two kids in college and was paying alimony to his ex who still lived in their house and probably wasn't inclined to take out a home equity loan to spring him from jail.

Bail works two ways: Garnett could either put up $250,000 in cash or property until the end of his trial or pay 10 percent for a bail bond. The first way he would get his money back, provided he didn't skip town. The second way cost a nonrefundable twenty-five grand.

I called my accountant and told him I needed a quarter of a million bucks. I figured Boyer wouldn't mind. He'd always liked Garnett.

FOUR HOURS LATER we faced each other for the first time since our jinxed kiss.

"I didn't do it," Garnett said.

"You don't have to tell me. I got two hundred fifty grand that says you didn't do it."

"Thanks."

Garnett was sore that the jail wouldn't return his gun when he bailed out. The clerk gave him a receipt instead, explaining that the authorities aren't in the business of rearming accused murderers. "Come back when you're acquitted," he sneered.

"Let's just go," I said. "Your attorney can sort it out. You're not going to need your gun anytime soon."

Minneapolis City Hall and the jail share the same turret-towered stone building. Garnett waited inside while I hailed a cab. To find one I walked across the street to the Hennepin County Government Center. Taxicabs are not plentiful in Minneapolis. Bus routes are inconvenient. Light rail limited. We're a city of commuters who like driving alone, even though gas prices are edging three bucks a gallon.

"Where to?" the cabbie asked.

Once word leaked out Garnett had made bail, the media would stake out his south Minneapolis apartment. He'd be stuck without a car because the police had confiscated his Crown Vic for forensic tests. I gave the cabbie my address.

"You don't mind?" Garnett asked.

"Not at all. My accountant insists I keep a close eye on you."

Shep greeted my houseguest with a generous slobber. Clearly the big dog didn't sense danger from Garnett. A flashing light on my telephone told me a message waited. I hit *play* and heard Noreen's voice on a day-old message.

"Mike Flagg tells me you won't share your notes.

Now listen, we've been through all this. The next time he comes to your house I want you to hand everything over to him. Don't think I won't suspend you, either!" The call concluded with a slamming noise.

Garnett and I looked at each other. I held my palms upward and raised my eyebrows. "Welcome to the inside world of TV news."

He started to crack a smile when the phone rang again. The caller ID read UNKNOWN, so odds were it came from Channel 3. I decided to screen it. Good thing because I heard Noreen's voice once more.

"Hey, there's a crazy rumor you bailed Garnett out. That better not be true. Don't think I won't fire you, either!" Another slamming noise followed.

"I'm on administrative leave myself," he said.

"Administrative leave sounds lovely this time of year."

Garnett had been jumpy since he left jail, still watching his back. As he walked over to the SUSANS boards, he slowly reverted to detective mode, reviewing each, pausing longest at Susan Victor's, where his name was listed.

"Sorry," I said.

"Don't apologize. It's a homicide war room."

"Ready for battle, or do you need a prewar nap?" I handed him a marker.

"I don't want to discourage you," Garnett said. "But serial killers are seldom caught by detective work."

I paused to glare at him suspiciously. "What do you mean?"

"They're much more likely to be caught by something like a routine traffic stop or a victim who escapes." At least he had the decency to look sheepish.

"You waited until now to tell me this?"

He sort of shrugged, but started writing. "No reason we shouldn't keep trying." He wrote one word on the Susan Victor board:

SUSAN VICTOR
COPYCAT?

"Copycat?" I said.

"Yep, we may have a copycat killer. It's certainly possible because all the angles—method, date, name— were publicized." He added the words PRIOR MURDERS PUBLIC to the board. "It's easy for a copycat to imitate a serialist's MO," he said. Neither of us said anything for a minute or so. Then Garnett continued, "But there are a couple of key differences between this murder and the others."

"There are?" I asked.

Garnett pointed to my earlier notations. "I see you heard about my anonymous phone call."

"You're not my only police source," I said. "So is it true? Did someone give you the address of the murder scene ahead of time?"

"Yeah, Riley, but the parking lot was empty when I got there. The killer must have moved the SUV and body there after I left in order to set me up. Which means our culprit is making this personal between me and him. He didn't try to influence any of the other investigations."

Garnett stared at the Susan Victor board and pondered whether the killer and he might have met, and added another line: PRIOR MURDERS PUBLIC. KILLER/GARNETT PERSONAL CONNECTION?

I pondered this theory, but it didn't seem to fit with any of the other Susan homicides. I told him so.

"Perhaps," Garnett said, "but the killer also broke pattern with his last victim. Susan Victor was somebody. Unlike the others, she would be missed. This murder guaranteed front-page headlines."

"So you think we have a new killer?"

"I think we have to consider that possibility. Would anyone else want her dead?" Garnett next wrote POLITICAL ENEMIES? under her name.

"Politics doesn't usually end in murder," I said.

"That's why we're also going to look at her personal life. Would any relatives benefit from her death? They might want to use the Susan anniversary to cover their tracks."

"I'm not convinced it's not the same killer. We have to consider she practically dared him to come after her."

"So he was showing off?" He added SHOWOFF KILLER? to the list. "Interesting. I always felt a showoff factor was involved."

I opened a box of files. "Help me look through

these. If the station takes them back, I want to be sure we didn't miss anything important."

Giving a source, much less a suspect, free access to reporter notes is highly taboo, but minor compared to some of my other recent journalistic infractions. What I lacked in ethics, I made up for in organization. Each murder had its own file, plus I had transcript interviews, death certificates, and police records. We spread the mess across the floor and started on one end, preparing to work the documents for inscribed clues.

Garnett's stomach growled a few minutes later. He checked the refrigerator and cupboards, but came up empty-handed.

"I'll call for a pizza," I said.

"Not that. All they fed us in jail was heavy carbs. Pizza. Spaghetti. Mac and cheese. I need steak."

"We don't have time for steak. We'll celebrate with steak once we get your charges dismissed."

We compromised on a neighborhood Chinese takeout place.

"Do you want to come with me or wait here?" I grabbed my car keys.

"I'll come along. I need some air. And I can't hide forever."

A little voice deep inside told me it probably wasn't smart to be alone with him without protection, and since Shep loved car rides, I grabbed his leash. After all, trusting Garnett with my money was different from trusting him with my life.

CHAPTER 34

The restaurant owner didn't give Garnett a second glance, but because she recognized me from TV, she threw in an extra handful of fortune cookies. Usually I decline perks, but today the fuss didn't seem worth the effort.

Garnett scolded me when we stepped outside. "You were always on my case for mooching free food when I was a cop. What's the difference here?"

"Oh come on, this can't be worth a dime. And besides, turning down fortune cookies might bring bad luck."

"Well, okay, I can't risk any more bad luck."

Shep welcomed us when we returned to the car. Or maybe he was welcoming the beef lo mein. Our take-out order tempted him to try climbing into the front seat. The weather was too cold to distract him by opening a rear window.

"Give him a cookie," I suggested. "I can't drive with him crawling over the console, and I don't like dog drool in my hair."

Garnett unwrapped a cookie, but stopped short of breaking it open. "I don't know if I can handle hearing my fortune just now."

"How do you know it won't be mine? Or how do you know it won't be good? Maybe something like, 'A personal wrong will be righted.' "

He considered the possibility, cracked the cookie, and handed the two pieces to Shep, who crunched them enthusiastically. Garnett hit the dashboard in a melodramatic drumroll, unfolded the fortune, and read, " 'A stranger will befriend you.' It's for you, Riley. Must be talking about your doctor buddy."

"Forget him. I certainly have. Try another."

Garnett obliged. " 'An old acquaintance will reenter your life.' "

"Touché. Probably talking about your ex-wife."

"Fat chance. If she didn't call when I retired from the force, she's not going to call now. Most people shy away from murder suspects."

Another question had remained on my mind since Garnett's arrest: If he killed the Susans, could he also have shadowed me in the Mall of America parking ramp or lurked outside my house? My gut said no. But my brain reminded me how quickly he had shown up to play hero in both instances. As I broke down the play-by-play of each night, I acknowledged he had had time for a change of clothes and shoes. Foolish to bring it up now, I stayed on the subject of his ex.

"Do you want her to call?"

"I'm not sure. I'd like her to have regrets. I'd like her to second-guess herself."

"Yeah, and I'd like a 40 share."

Shep whined and stretched his big head over the seat again. Garnett opened another fortune. " 'Be careful what you wish for.' "

I laughed as I turned onto my street. "That covers a lot of ground for both of us."

"We'll read the rest inside."

I pulled into the garage, grabbed Shep's leash, and picked up today's stack of mail from the box. I dropped a copy of *Car and Driver* straight into the garbage can. A monthly reminder that life is too short to buy a three-year magazine subscription, no matter how good the price. The rest of the mail was mostly junk, but a couple of envelopes held promise.

"What do you think about offering a reward?" I asked.

"The chief will say it's a waste of money; they already have their man."

The three of us walked side-by-side, Shep's nose monitoring the bag of kung pao.

"Well, it's my money to waste."

Garnett shook his head. "I just wish I could have seen the crime scene."

I suddenly remembered the cell phone picture I had taken of Susan Victor's body. "Maybe you can." I stopped, opened my phone, and called up the ghoulish image.

The next events seemed simultaneous, but I know fractions of a second actually separated them. The whole conflict takes longer to explain than it played out in real time. The sensation of pounding feet. Panting breath. Garnett knocking me sideways. Mail scattering as I landed facedown in the snow. A growl that didn't come from Shep. And a cry of terror unlike any I'd ever heard.

The cry came from Garnett.

When I looked up he was twirling like a bloody helicopter, a pit bull attached to his shoulder. A kaleidoscope pattern of red decorating the snow around them.

Shep lunged back and forth slashing at the rust and tan beast. The other dog weighed less but had muscles like a prizefighter and survival scars to prove it. Garnett crashed to the ground and the pit bull seized his neck. Blood seeped from Garnett's throat. When Shep's teeth ripped into the pit bull's back the creature dropped its hold on Garnett and attacked Shep. Both animals clashed together, oozing blood, but my dog was in trouble: the pit bull locked its teeth around Shep's jaw and held tight. My Shep, pinned to the ground, couldn't fight back.

I would have given everything I owned if Garnett's gun could be here right now instead of in the jail property room.

Several years ago pit bull panic swept Minnesota after two of the brutes killed a teenage boy delivering newspapers. An animal control expert I had interviewed about dangerous dogs explained that a pit bull's jaws exert more pressure than a lion's, and that the best way to get one to release its prey is to grab the back legs, push like a wheelbarrow, and hope it doesn't turn its jaws of death on you.

Adrenaline took over. And I don't remember much

except that somehow I managed to fling the dog and then force myself to stand very still. Instead of charging back at me, it raced halfway down the block to an SUV with the back hatch open. I hadn't noticed the vehicle before.

Garnett had been mauled badly. I crawled to his side and pressed my hands against his wounds, trying to slow the bleeding while I fumbled for my cell phone on the ground. My bloody fingers kept slipping from the key pad as I tried to dial 911. A tortured wail came from the direction of the SUV.

"Officer down." No two words bring police force faster. Garnett wasn't a cop anymore, but I didn't hesitate to use them anyway.

"Officer down!" I screamed into my cell phone. "Officer down! We need an ambulance!"

Panicked, I was losing my grip faster than Garnett was losing consciousness. 911 calls from landlines give emergency dispatchers an address, even if the caller can't. Not so with most cell phones, and mine was an older model that still allowed me to pick up an analog signal in rural areas, but didn't display my position.

"What is your location?" the dispatcher asked.

I couldn't remember where I lived. Garnett's life depended on me reciting my address and I couldn't spit out the magic words needed to make help appear.

"Where are you?" she shouted. I couldn't make out her words because snarling and screaming continued to come from the SUV.

"Tell them I'm sorry," Garnett said, coughing. His skin turned gray; his breathing turned shallow.

"What? What?" I asked him. "Who?" Sorry he was an indifferent husband? Sorry he was a forgetful son? Or sorry he was a monstrous serial killer? His mouth moved but Shep's painful whimper drowned out the words. That's when I realized the other screams had stopped.

"I need your location," the dispatcher reminded me. "All units prepare to respond to a 10–108."

The mail. I left Garnett to grab an envelope from the snow.

It read "Occupant."

I snatched another letter, recognized my mom's handwriting, and slowly read my address out loud.

"Got it," said the dispatcher. She read it over the air. "All units respond to a 10–108." She repeated my address. "That's a 10–108. Officer down.

"Please stay on the line," she instructed me. I heard sirens approach from different directions. Faster, I prayed. I looked over at Shep. The tip of his ear was missing. He had a jagged rip on the side of his face. He tried getting up, but his knees buckled.

I held Garnett in my arms, cradling his head. The snow around us turned crimson.

"Stop it. Stop dying," I pleaded. He tried to speak and I put my ear to his lips.

"Houston, we got a problem." He stared into my eyes for a couple seconds before his own fell shut.

By then I was sobbing too hard to say, "Tom Hanks, *Apollo 13*, 1995."

"WHAT HAPPENED?" THE first officer on the scene was assessing the carnage.

"A pit bull," I told him.

He looked at me skeptically, then knelt by Garnett, checked his condition, and shook his head. "He's shutting down." He started CPR.

An ambulance siren grew closer. Ten seconds later, paramedics pulled up. Another ten seconds and they were wheeling Garnett in the back. I watched as the crew stuck tubes in his arm and started wrapping his injuries.

I begged them to take Shep, too. "He's a police dog," I lied. "He saved our lives." That part wasn't a lie. "You can't let him die!" But the ambulance peeled away like it was racing death.

"Put him in the back of my squad." A paunchy, middle-aged cop motioned to his unit parked across the street. "He deserves a chance."

He helped me carry Shep over, and I tried to climb in with them, but another officer insisted I stay for questioning. "I'll take care of him," the first cop assured me. Every second counted for my dog, so I didn't argue. The cop made good with a wicked U-turn, lights and siren blaring.

I telephoned Toby, screaming for him to head to the U of M Vet Hospital and meet Shep. I know I sounded hysterical.

I overheard another officer on his radio talking about Garnett; he seemed to be saying "likely to die."

Other squads arrived and moved toward the mysterious SUV. One cop turned on a flashlight. Raspy snarls grew louder, warning us to keep back. An officer reached for his semiautomatic. A large metal cage fit snugly in the back of the vehicle. Outside the SUV the pit bull stood his ground over the curled body of a man dressed in black—who looked a lot like my Mall of America parking ramp shadow. The dog's face and chest gleamed with blood. Some his. Mostly his victim's. Gaping flesh wounds showed through the shadow's torn clothing. A mask obscured his face.

The animal tensed and growled even more. "Easy boy," the officer said. The beast stuck its muzzle in the shadow's back and started chewing. The cop aimed and fired until his weapon was empty.

Another officer removed the shadow's mask and checked his neck for a pulse. None. They canceled a second ambulance and requested a medical examiner.

Petit lay dead in the trampled, bloody snow, a Taser just out of reach.

NO ONE KNOWS what torture Petit had inflicted on the animal to turn it into such a savage. And why the dog turned on its master, instead of me, also remains an enigma. Perhaps, on its blood-inflamed rampage, it merely went for the next moving body it saw. Or perhaps it had been hungering to take a chunk out of its trainer for some time.

CHAPTER 35

For the second time in less than a week, Minneapolis police took me into custody.

Fortunately, Channel 3's assignment editor heard the 10–108 over the police scanners and immediately dispatched all crews to the vicinity. Not until the first photographer arrived did they realize my house was the crime scene. He sprayed the scene for video, got shots of Petit's covered body and of me being placed in the back of a squad car. He alerted the desk so Miles would be waiting for me at the cop shop when two officers, one short and one tall, escorted me down the hallway.

"Don't say anything," Miles warned me. He grabbed my hand with a force that surprised me and led me to the men's bathroom. I presumed for a private conference on legal strategy, since I didn't have to go. The women's room was on the opposite side of the building.

"You can't go in there," the tall cop said.

"I need a moment with my client." Miles pushed me inside. A tubby officer faced one wall, doing what he had come to do. "Can you excuse us?" Miles asked.

"What the hell?" The cop noticed me, zipped his lip and his trousers and left.

Miles took off his suit jacket and tie. He began unbuttoning his shirt. "Take off your sweater."

I almost echoed the cop's parting line until I realized Garnett's blood saturated my clothes. Feeling a wave of nausea, I grabbed onto a urinal to steady myself. The reflection I saw in the bathroom mirrors looked like I'd been cast in a slasher flick. I shifted around, careful to face the stalls, away from the mirrors and Miles, and pulled my formerly white sweater over my head. I unhooked my bra and sponged myself with some scratchy paper towels, which quickly turned pink. Miles handed me his dress shirt and threw my clothes in the bathroom waste-basket.

Not many lawyers will give you the shirt off their back, so I appreciated the gesture. I also borrowed Miles's jacket because the shirt fit a bit snug and I didn't want the cops staring at my nipples. When we stepped outside, an officer insisted he needed my bloody clothes as evidence.

"Help yourself," Miles said, gesturing toward the bathroom.

Great, I thought, now the cops will know my bra size.

"We need to get a statement about the mauling," the short cop said.

"Fine, but I'm going to stop her if I don't like the questions," Miles said.

"Just let us do our job," the tall one said.

"As long as you let me do mine," my attorney countered.

All this back and forth wasn't getting me where I wanted to go: to the hospital to check on Garnett and Shep. "Can we take care of this later?"

Chief Capacasa interrupted our hallway stalemate. He glanced from me to Miles but didn't ask why my lawyer wore an undershirt and I wore a man's suit. "I'm all for speeding this up. I'll concede, she's a witness, not a suspect. All better? Talk."

I filled them in on the events leading up to tonight: my strange stalker, the dead flowers, the poisoned steak. Then I explained the pit bull assault.

"I was the target, but Garnett got between me and that creature. Shep fought to save us. Have you heard how they're doing?" My voice cracked with worry.

The chief ignored my question. Maybe because he didn't know the answer. Maybe because he did.

"Were you worried this vet might get violent?" he asked. "Was he why you wanted extra patrols?"

"Not exactly. If I imagined Petit seeking revenge, it was by making me bleed in court, not on my front lawn."

Chief Capacasa ushered us into his office, shut the door, and cut to the chase.

"Did Garnett say anything?" he asked.

"He wasn't making a lot of sense. Just 'tell them I'm sorry.' "

"And he was sorry for what?"

"I don't know."

"Who were you supposed to tell?"

"He didn't say."

No one else said anything either. I stared out the window. The weather looked as bleak as Garnett's prognosis.

"Did he know how bad off he was?"

Chief Capacasa wasn't asking out of empathy. Dying declarations can be used as evidence in a crime if the injured believes he may not survive.

"How do you make holy water?"

Father Mountain waited with me at Hennepin County Medical Center, interceding with the nursing staff for updates on Garnett's surgery, even though I wasn't a relative.

Between prayers for the sick and dying, he tried distracting me with church jokes. "Come on, how do you make holy water?" he insisted.

"I give up," I replied.

"Boil the hell out of it."

Even though Garnett wasn't a cop anymore, blue uniforms dominated the hospital corridors. Friends who shied away when he became a murder suspect now gathered as word spread he might become a murder victim. The police administration handled all media inquiries and notified his next of kin.

Garnett's father had died several years earlier. His mother lived in a senior care center. Garnett's arrest had hammered her already frail heart and the nursing staff were monitoring her carefully after receiving word of the mauling. His ex-wife, Janie, came to sit in the waiting room with his oldest son, Jack, the one who looked like him. His other boy, Jeff, away at college, was trying to book a flight home.

I offered them my condolences. We had never met, but Garnett had talked plenty about his family. The long hours he spent obstructing evil cost him his marriage. He used to tell Janie, "You can't control crime; crime controls you." That premise didn't soothe her frustration or ease the worry any police spouse faces. Finally she'd had enough.

Janie might even have been bitter that Garnett had waited until after their divorce to retire and take a job with bankers' hours. I decided to go out on a limb with her.

"Nick's wounds were meant for me. I held him while we waited for the ambulance. He wanted me to tell you he was sorry."

"Really?" Her eyes grew moist.

"Really." If he didn't make it, it wouldn't matter. And if he did, they could sort it out later.

THE STATUS QUO prevailed for the next couple hours. In a surgical suite off-limits to us, Garnett was fighting for his life. I was fighting to stay awake. It wouldn't be fair to sleep while he suffered. And every time I closed my eyes I saw the monster.

Toby punished me, too. He called earlier from the vet hospital to tell me to stay away from Shep. "He's not your dog, he's mine. If he dies, it's all your fault."

Nothing hurts more than the truth.

"WHY DID THE Pope cross the road?"

I tuned out Father Mountain.

"Come on, Riley." He nudged me affectionately. "Think about it. Why did the Pope cross the road?"

"I give up."

"He crosses everything."

I couldn't bring myself to even laugh politely. "Your humor isn't working for me right now, Father."

"I can see that." He nodded sadly. "And since we're being so honest, I don't like your outfit."

His reference to Miles's suit did make me laugh.

"Maybe you should try confession, Riley. Remember, you owe me one."

"My sins aren't the kind you can absolve." I started crying in front of everybody, but I wasn't embarrassed; my tears felt more like an accomplishment. A relief. Something normal people did.

Just then a woman in blue scrubs approached us. I wiped my face and braced myself lest her first words be "I'm sorry" or "We did all we could." Father Mountain squeezed my hand and made the sign of the cross. The surgeon kept a poker face as she asked Garnett's family to come to a briefing room for patient confidentiality. Good news or bad news, hospitals don't like breaking either in public settings. Janie motioned for me to come along. I tugged on Father Mountain's sleeve. A convoy of hope and dread, we followed the woman down the hall to hear the outcome.

Each of us carried some guilt in our relationships with Garnett. But in a contest, I'd win easily. I'm the one who almost got him killed. The key word: "almost."

Garnett didn't die.

And neither did Shep.

I LEFT THE hospital ahead of the others to draw the news photographers away from Janie and Jack. A reporter shoved a microphone in my face and shouted, "How is he? Is he stable?" I resisted admonishing her that "stable" is not a medical condition. After all, dead is the most stable any of us can be. Garnett remained in critical condition, but they could wring that out of the hospital PR folks. The cameras swarmed me as I raced toward a cab.

I felt some relief because the danger was over; some shame because I hadn't identified the real threat. My reporter radar had gotten it so damn wrong. The thing I feared most, riling up an unknown slayer of Susans, had nothing to do with my creepy stalker. My old buddy Garnett almost died for a measly consumer investigation.

At home my message machine flashed full. Mike

Flagg wanted an interview ASAP. I hit *delete*. Matt Lauer wanted me to be a live guest on the *Today* show. I hit *delete*. I couldn't listen anymore so I unplugged the phones, climbed upstairs, and cried myself to sleep. Odd how tears that once eluded me now came easily. The only witness to my meltdown: a mounted deer head hanging on the bedroom wall, Boyer's wedding present to me.

CHAPTER 36

I dreamed my husband wrapped his arms around me and held me against his chest, and I felt safe. We laughed about all the fun things we would do when we grew old.

Once we talked about buying an RV and driving across America. We'd get one of those colorful U.S. maps with the stick-on states and glue it to the side of the camper, adding a new state each time we crossed a border. We debated whether we could count states we'd already visited together, or whether we could only count ones we'd visited in the RV. Would the map be a record of the RV's travels or ours?

"You know what's been my favorite state so far?" Boyer teased me.

I shrugged, expecting him to say Nevada.

"The state of arousal." He reached his hand under my shirt. "Followed closely by the state of undress."

I reached for him and kept reaching until I reached the edge of the bed and realized I was alone. I drifted in and out of sleep, contemplating the states I had visited without him.

The state of shock. The state of denial. The state of despair.

I burrowed under the blankets and slept hours and hours more until the next morning when I untangled myself from the blankets, fumbled for the TV remote, and clicked on the news. I scrambled out of bed as soon as my brain comprehended what my ears were hearing.

> ((MIKE/LIVE))
> THAT'S EXACTLY WHAT
> THE DNA TEST MEANS . . .
> THE BLOOD ON
> DUSTY FOSTER'S
> SHIRT BELONGED TO
> SUSAN REDDING . . .
> THAT MAKES HIM
> HER KILLER . . .
> SO MUCH FOR HIS
> CUT-MYSELF-SHAVING
> EXCUSE.
> ((DOUBLE BOX/ANCHOR))
> WHAT ABOUT ALL
> THE PROTESTERS
> WE'VE HEARD SO MUCH
> ABOUT . . .
> ARE THEY STILL
> OUTSIDE THE PRISON?
> ((MIKE/LIVE))
> NOPE. AS YOU CAN SEE,
> THEY PACKED UP AND
> LEFT AS SOON AS WORD
> GOT OUT THEIR CAUSE

WAS LOST. THIS IS
MICHAEL FLAGG
REPORTING LIVE FROM
OAK PARK HEIGHTS
PRISON . . . BACK TO YOU.

I rushed downtown to the newsroom to see Noreen.

"What do you mean, why didn't we call you?" Noreen fumed. "You weren't answering your home phone, your cell phone, or even your door."

She had a point. "I'm sorry," I said. "Things have been crazy. I've been crazy. I couldn't think about news."

"Tell me about it. Since your buddy was arrested for killing one of our city's elected leaders, our ratings have plunged. The target of your vet investigation was mauled to death outside your house. No telling what the viewer backlash is going to be. Plus, us playing up that innocent man behind bars crap is going to hurt."

True, the numbers were down the last few nights, but it was too early to panic. After all, viewers are fickle. These salacious developments could actually increase our ratings. Then Channel 3 would face criticism for tabloid journalism and profiting from tragedy.

"It can't always be about ratings, Noreen. Sometimes it has to be about our search for the truth."

"In November ratings are the truth. This is a news station, not a philosophy class. I should never have listened to you about those old murders. You've mangled this whole investigation, so don't lecture me about truth."

Noreen's ranting was more off the charts than usual, but what hurt most was Miles, sitting in her office, nodding his head. "We're way out on a legal limb here, Riley. Your bailing out Garnett won't help matters if Susan Victor's family sues us."

"Viewers think you're in cahoots with the killer," Noreen said. "I'm about ready to fire you."

"We can't fire her," Miles insisted. "That could make things even worse for us in court. Like admitting we're screwups. We need to wrap ourselves in the First Amendment and argue the public's right to know."

Miles's presence while Noreen chewed me out was deliberate. If opposing counsel ever deposed her or me over this mess, we could claim attorney-client privilege for anything being said right now.

"The problem," Miles continued, "is that you've gone from being an objective journalist to a subjective newsmaker. You're part of the story now, so you can't cover it."

He lifted his hands in a gesture of regret just as Noreen snapped her fingers in a gesture of inspiration.

"Newsmaker?" she said. "That gives me an idea. Viewers expect to hear from newsmakers. Maybe keeping Riley quiet has been a mistake. We might win them back if they get the inside scoop straight from her lips." She came to a decision. "You'll do a live on-set interview tonight."

"I thought I was off the story."

"Oh, you're not going to conduct this interview. You're going to be on the receiving end. You'll answer the questions put to you, just like any other news-maker. Other than that, you'll keep your mouth shut."

She picked up her phone and dialed the promotion department.

MY DESK PHONE rang. A woman's recorded voice said, "You have a collect call from Oak Park Heights State Prison—"

I slammed down the receiver.

About thirty seconds later the same voice gave me the same spiel, but when she got to the part about accepting the charges, I reconsidered, what the hell, and answered yes.

The only words out of Dusty's mouth: "You can't blame me for trying." Then he laughed and hung up.

I tried thinking about whiskers on kittens, but all I could think about was what a chump I was.

Then I realized that I still had a mission: to clear the name of an innocent man. Except the man's name was not Dusty Foster. His name was Nick Garnett.

Unless I was wrong about that one, too.

LOOSE ENDS.

Even though technically I wasn't covering the SUSANS story anymore I still wanted to find a clue that would break the case wide open. So, back home, I scanned the SUSANS boards looking for promising loose ends that might unravel other secrets.

Sometimes journalists get lucky, like buying gas across the street from where a bank robbery is under way and filming the getaway scene. But I usually make my own luck by reverting to the basics: rechecking documents and going back to the same sources over and over and over one last time. Competitors and colleagues who find that part of the job tedious often gripe about my "luck." But sometimes the result is such a doozy that a B story is elevated to an A story. Right now, I was just hoping for a passing grade.

I moved the Susan Redding board away from the others and determined some anomalies: aside from being the only Susan murdered by Dusty, she was also the only married Susan, and the only one who hadn't been re-dressed by her killer. Clearly she was a false lead and not the victim of any supposed serial killer. Her name had led us down a false path. Dr. Redding had been right: his wife's homicide was not connected to the others.

Waitress Susan's and Suicide Susan's families had been cooperative. I didn't think they were holding anything back. But when I got to Sinner Susan's board, I stopped. Her fanatic father might be worth another visit. He was definitely a loose end.

THROUGH THE KITCHEN blinds, I saw Tim Moreno with his head bowed over a table for lunch. He saw me outside and opened the door before I even knocked. Not because I was the answer to his prayers, but because he wanted to get rid of me as quickly as possible.

"You're back, TV lady. What do you want?"

I was happy to keep our conversation on the front steps.

"Good morning, Mr. Moreno. I was doing some further research on your daughter's death and . . ." I often used that line when approaching people. No big deal. Just doing some research. Nothing to get excited about.

Except he did get excited. "Where did you get that?" His voice dropped a notch, sounding almost hollow.

"I was talking—"

"No. Where did you get this?" He ripped the Susan pendant from around my neck, breaking the chain.

"Ow. That hurt. You can't have that." I tried grabbing it back, but he clutched it tightly in his fist.

"It belongs to me. This was my grandmother's, then my mother's, then my daughter's." His eyes bulged. "I'm sure the whore pawned it. How much did you pay?"

"Wait a minute. Your daughter used to wear this?"

"I gave it to her when she turned sixteen. It was against my better judgment, but she insisted it was her due."

"Did Susan wear it often?" I asked.

"She promised never to take it off. But when she died, it was nowhere to be found. It wasn't on her body, or in any of her belongings. God has returned it to me."

He crossed himself. "I'm not giving it back." He grasped the pendant and held it next to his heart. "Ever." He went inside and turned the dead bolt. "Go away, TV lady," he called from the other side of the door.

I drove toward the cop shop, not to report a jewelry theft, but because the Susan pendant was suddenly important evidence.

Could Tim Moreno be the killer? His daughter was a murder victim and his family pendant had shown up on the body of another victim. Moreno might be looking like a prime suspect if not for the fact that the killer had also played musical raincoats. And now musical necklaces.

When I looked in the rearview mirror, I noticed a nasty red welt where the chain had cut across my neck.

CHIEF CAPACASA SMIRKED as he waved me into his office. "Sounds like you're on the skids with that Duluth appeal." Once again he wore the obnoxious checkmate expression on his face.

"I understand, Chief," I said. "You need to rub it in. So get it over with. Feel better."

"I told you." He leaned back in his chair. "What you're searching for doesn't exist. There's no single killer stalking Susans."

"What about the raincoat? That actually ties Susan Chenowith with Susan Moreno. And that's why I'm here. Was Susan Victor missing any personal item? Or was any clothing item found with her that didn't belong to her?"

The chief froze as if that question was the last thing he had expected from me. "How did you know? Did Garnett tell you?"

Now I was the flustered one. "What are you talking about?"

"Garnett. Did he tell you about the glove?"

"What glove? Was she missing a glove?"

"We found a man's glove in Susan Victor's car. Next to her body. The matching glove was in Garnett's car."

Suddenly I knew what a splitting headache felt like.

"So don't worry your pretty little head about raincoats and buttons," he said. "It's much easier solving one murder at a time. And this one's nailed. Garnett's going down. Careful you don't go down with him."

I recalled the image of a flashlight in my front yard and Garnett mumbling something about missing a glove.

"Maybe he lost a glove and . . . maybe the killer . . ." My stammering sounded lame, even to me.

"All right, that's it. Beat it. I've had enough of your conspiracy and framing theories. Sometimes the most obvious answer is the answer."

I tried telling him the reason I had come downtown: the Susan pendant. But the chief wasn't in any mood to listen further. In truth, he didn't need to; if the "smoking glove" evidence was everything he claimed, his case was closed.

"Beat it," he repeated.

When I got home, I added MATCHING GLOVE to the

growing list under Garnett's name, then kicked the board hard enough to sail it across the room.

So much for clearing an innocent man's name.

Just like the O.J. Simpson case, this one was all coming down to a glove. Remember the defense line "If the glove doesn't fit, you must acquit"? Well, I could hear the prosecutor already practicing this closing, "If his glove's the mate, guilty his fate."

The glove made all my "evidence" seem amateur hour. The glove represented the difference between corroboration and conjecture. The glove was just the kind of clue that could break the case wide open. But because technically I wasn't covering the SUSANS anymore, I didn't bother to tell Channel 3 about this latest twist. Let them source the damn story themselves.

"Do you still have that photo-enhancing software?" I asked Xiong.

He nodded and continued working on his computer, not bothering to make eye contact.

"I have a project that I need ASAP." He nodded again, indicating he had heard me, but nothing I said merited a verbal response. "It's a cell phone picture. I'm hoping you can sharpen it up a little."

I pulled a chair next to his desk and e-mailed the photo from my phone to his computer.

He opened it and gasped in disgust, as if I had videotaped a despised dictator hanging from a noose. "I hope this is not what I think it is."

"It is," I answered. "But I needed it as evidence."

"Does Noreen know?"

"Not yet. It's not like we're going to put it on the air. In fact, I'd forgotten all about it until the the other day. I don't want to freak her out unless it ends up being important."

"Do not bring me into this. This is not a project I want involvement in."

"I just need a little help. The quality is sort of dark and blurry." Not so dark and blurry that Susan Victor's eyes didn't seem to pop spookily off the screen. "I need to see more detail on her clothing and surroundings."

Xiong closed the screen and didn't answer.

"Please," I whispered. "It might be crucial. I can't go to anyone else."

He pressed his lips together tightly. "Come back in an hour."

WHEN I RETURNED, Xiong had pasted a small black bar over Susan Victor's eyes. I liked it. He had pulled the photo full screen. Not perfect, but a clear improvement.

"Cell cameras do not take the best pictures," he explained. "Especially not in low light."

The victim, like the other Susans, was clothed. I didn't see any sign of a glove. But that didn't mean one wasn't there. If I had framed the shot wider, it might have been visible on the seat beside her. What drew my attention was a large earring on her left ear. Her right ear was bare.

"Can you make that earring any clearer?" I asked Xiong.

He cropped and enlarged it. A distinctive silver dragon looped around her ear. A long dragon neck stretched over the rim while a curved tail hugged her lobe. In between, flared wings.

An unusual selection for a conservative politician. Raincoat. Pendant. I wondered if the killer might have planted the dragon on Susan Victor's body as part of his trophy game. That might mean there was another dead Susan out there somewhere.

"I've never seen anything like it." I pointed to the strange jewelry. And then I remembered the flowers on my porch. Dragon. Snapdragon.

"It's an ear cuff," Xiong said. "It clips on the side of your ear. My girlfriend wears some."

"She wears dragons?"

"No, she has other designs, but she purchases them at an uptown store called Eternity Piercing."

I didn't know whether to be more surprised that Xiong had a girlfriend or that she was funky. But I suppose plenty of enterprising chicks might be looking for the next computer genius to found a Microsoft or a YouTube.

An idea was forming in the back of my mind. It hinged on a lot of things going right.

"I need copies of this photo, plus the one with the dragon cropped tight."

Xiong hit *print*.

———

I ENTERED THROUGH a doorway under a neon sign reading BODY PIERCING, and walked into an alternate world.

A young man with a shaved head, a ring in his nose, two studs through an eyebrow, several earrings, and a silver loop through his lower lip greeted me with more scorn than enthusiasm. When he spoke, a metal ball flashed from his tongue. Clearly he was not just a sales-clerk; he was also a model.

I'm no matronly suburban mom, and while I certainly appeared tamer than his usual clientele, I am curious and by trade like to ask questions.

The piercing parlor behind a closed door was off-limits to all but patients, he explained. Was I interested?

I shook my head. My ears were already pierced. "Maybe later."

So he obliged me with a brief tour of the jewelry counters. The "above the chin" section took up the most room. He pivoted and motioned to the "above the waist" selection.

"Navels?" I asked.

"And nipples." With a naughty wink, he pulled a flat box from under the counter and offered to show me the "below the waist" inventory.

"Toes?"

He looked at me with exasperation. "Higher."

Lower than navels; higher than toes. He seemed to be staring at my crotch. My eyes dropped to his belt, but before he could model any of his more intimate inventory, I gave him my shopping agenda.

"I'm looking for an ear loop that doesn't require actual piercing."

"Amateur." I could tell he didn't think I was worth the bother. But since I was his only customer, he was stuck with me.

"I'm looking for something exotic." He directed me to a corner shelf. And then I saw it, displayed on black velvet, under black light. The dragon. Exactly like the one in Susan Victor's death photo. Except for one small detail. This dragon was gold, not silver.

My finger shook as I pointed. "May I see that piece?"

He shrugged and opened the case.

"Do you carry it in silver?"

"No."

A minute later the dragon was wrapped around my left outer ear. Head and wings framing the top, tail clinging around the bottom.

"Do you sell many?" I asked.

"You're the first. Just got it in stock."

It was time to decide whether to implement my plan. Susan Victor was my most recent link to the killer. My gut told me the dragon might be key to smoking him out. If I could spook him, he might make a mistake. Unhinged, he might be easier to identify.

I looked away from the mirror and reached for my purse. "I'll take it."

None of the jewelry had price tags, which left the

salesclerk free to gouge me more than three hundred bucks, after emphasizing that the piece was genuine 10 karat gold. I figured the odds of expensing the dragon to Channel 3 were nil, but paid anyway. At my next stop, the local hardware store, I purchased a can of silver spray paint.

WITH TEN MINUTES to air, I clipped the now silver dragon to my ear. As the newscast went to a commercial break, I walked to the set, took my chair, and waited for my debrief.

"Stand by!" the floor director called as he pointed his hand toward the anchor and me. That's our cue to sit up straight and pay attention 'cause we're going live in ten seconds. I used the time to push my hair behind my ear so as to boldly display the dragon.

A red light on one of the three studio cameras turned green, so I knew I was unstoppable. Our anchor, Tom McHale, read an intro reminding viewers, without making it seem too braggy, that within the last week I'd found one dead body in a park and another down the block from my house—the first strangled by an unknown assailant, the other mauled to death by an attack dog. Both victims connected to two stories I'd broken earlier this month.

((ANCHOR TWO-SHOT))
CHANNEL 3 REPORTER
RILEY SPARTZ . . .

AT THE CENTER
OF ALL THIS
CONTROVERSY . . .
JOINS US NOW . . .
LIVE . . .
TO ANSWER
QUESTIONS.

Tom was startled when he turned to interview me. He couldn't help noticing the dragon since it was practically breathing fire in his face. He stammered his first question, then started over.

((ANCHOR TWO-SHOT))
RILEY, THE STATION HAS
RECEIVED TONS OF
VIEWER CALLS
WANTING TO KNOW
ABOUT YOUR
INVOLVEMENT.
WHY HAVE YOU
STAYED SILENT UNTIL
NOW?

Miles had helped me craft this answer.

((RILEY CU))
AS A WITNESS . . .
I NEEDED TO

SPEAK WITH LAW
ENFORCEMENT
IN THE EARLY DAYS
OF THESE CASES.
THE STATION FELT
IT BEST NOT
TO GO PUBLIC
WITH INFORMATION
THAT MIGHT
IMPEDE THE
AUTHORITIES'
INVESTIGATIONS . . .
SO EVEN TODAY . . .
I AM LIMITED
IN WHAT
I CAN SAY.

The floor director couldn't speak because we were on the air, so he frantically pointed to his ear, trying to alert me about the odd jewelry on my ear and get me to remove it while the camera was on an anchor close-up.

I knew he was following orders from the control booth. But I couldn't hear all the fuss myself because I had neglected to put in my IFB—interruptible frequency broadcast—a small custom-molded earpiece reporters and anchors wear so they can hear the newscast while sitting on the set or so the producer has a direct way to yell at them out in the field without the viewers noticing.

Every time the tech crew switched cameras to mini-mize my left ear, I would awkwardly tilt my head to bet-ter display the dragon. Tom and I continued the interview. I explained that, yes, I had bailed Nick Gar-nett out of jail and thus wouldn't be able to cover the SUSANS story as a journalist anymore. And that, yes, the pit bull attack had actually been directed at me for exposing a corrupt veterinarian. I didn't bring up the significance of the dragon; that would be something only the killer would know about. I wanted to taunt the killer. I wanted him to know I knew about the dragon and was upping the stakes. But I didn't want anyone else to guess the importance, because that would make it impossible to weed out copycats, thus tainting the police investigation.

The four minutes passed quickly. The floor director gave me time cues by hand, since it was obvious I either wasn't receiving or was ignoring the audio cues. As he twirled his hand to give us a wrap—meaning we needed to stop talking NOW—I realized I needed to say one more thing and unfortunately it was the one thing Miles warned me not to say.

((RILEY CU))
OUR BEST CLUE
TO CATCHING
THE SUSAN KILLER
MAY BE THE NAME
AND THE DATE . . .

> THEY LIKELY
> HOLD A SPECIAL
> SIGNIFICANCE
> TO THE KILLER.
> SO IF YOU KNOW
> SOMEONE FOR
> WHOM THE NAME
> "SUSAN" AND THE
> DATE "NOVEMBER 19"
> HAS A
> SPECIAL MEANING . . .
> CALL OUR
> TIP LINE.

Tom wasn't just a news reader; he knew enough to follow up with the obvious.

> ((ANCHOR TWO-SHOT))
> BUT RILEY,
> HAVEN'T POLICE
> ALREADY ARRESTED
> AND CHARGED
> NICK GARNETT?
> IT DOESN'T SOUND
> TO ME LIKE THEY'RE
> REALLY LOOKING
> FOR NEW
> SUSPECTS.

By now the floor director was waving his arm like an eggbeater. Since this wasn't the Academy Awards and news producers aren't used to cutting off the talent midsentence, the folks in the control booth sat helplessly as the seconds turned to minutes and I explained that accused is not the same as convicted, and that I personally did not believe the city had seen the last of this particular serial killer.

Without any music, without any tease, the newscast slammed to black. The tape room rolled a commercial, and the control room went out of control. Our meteorologist took my seat, but during the break I could hear Tom arguing, "What did you expect me to do? Rip it off her ear on live television?" The producer and director were screaming that the only way to get the news off on time now was to cut most of weather and half of sports.

THEY ALSO HAD to dump a thirty-second car dealer commercial. That move meant losing serious money, so I knew I'd be in serious trouble the next morning. And as the news producer recited a litany of my TV sins, it seemed quite probable that Noreen would indeed send me straight to broadcast hell.

CHAPTER 37

"Some of them even think you're in a satanic cult!" Noreen waved the call sheet in my face the next morning.

The station receptionists have the tiresome task of logging each viewer call into categories. Some viewers call to rant that we're too politically liberal; others call to criticize us for sucking up to the president so blatantly. Too much sex in prime time is also a frequent complaint. But last night I was the only category, and the calls continued this morning from viewers who couldn't get through last night to register their complaints. No one called to compliment me on my interesting ear accessory.

"How could you wear such a thing?" Noreen continued. She threw the dragon in her wastebasket and it made an angry clunk. I made a mental note to definitely try expensing it as a set prop. "What were you thinking?"

"I was just trying to attract younger viewers with some funky jewelry."

Noreen paused, weighed my defense, then discarded it. "I don't believe it. You're up to something. And where do you get off putting that thing on and forgetting your IFB?"

Of course I claimed to have forgotten it. Better that they think me inattentive than insubordinate.

"And you ignored your wrap cue," she continued.

"I'm sorry, I just felt more needed to be said."

Miles decided it was time to speak up. "Unfortunately, it was the part we agreed you'd stay away from. You promised not to publicly criticize the police investigation. We had a deal. I'm not sure I can trust you."

"I'm sorry, Miles. I feel real bad about that."

"Bad? You feel bad?" Noreen said. "You're going to feel worse than bad. You're going to feel fired."

Fired was Noreen's favorite F-word. But I'd already apologized several times and didn't want to grovel further, so I kept quiet, betting she wouldn't actually fire me until sweeps ended, especially since the numbers had been up last night.

"Right now, you're off our investigative team. Hell with it, you're off our shows altogether. Don't come back until I tell you to come back. And don't hold your breath for that either."

"Maybe I should just quit." I folded my arms over my chest and leaned back in my chair, gambling she wouldn't call my bluff.

"Maybe you should." Noreen stretched forward, across her desk, in a silent, powerful dare. I know a defining moment when I face one. I also knew if I folded she would own my soul. She already owned my body and mind, sixty-plus hours a week, bought and paid for in bimonthly checks. As our eyes locked, I realized my soul was not for sale.

"Fine." I spit out the word. "And they're called newscasts, not shows!"

My last words as I stomped out of her office were not as satisfying as I had long imagined they might be.

I'D JUST PACKED a couple of Emmy awards in a moving box when Chief Capacasa bypassed the station switchboard and called my desk directly to scream about obstruction of justice.

"How did you know about that dragon?" he yelled.

"I found the body, remember?"

He launched into a tirade about tampering with evidence until I assured him I had removed nothing from the scene.

"I went out and bought my own dragon, Chief. And we wouldn't be having this conversation if you didn't agree there was something suspicious about the earring."

He listened without interrupting as I explained the raincoat, the Susan necklace, and how I viewed the killer's game. "He's taking a souvenir from each Susan and one year later placing it on the next victim. It's actually quite clever. This way if he's ever caught for one murder, there's not a whole drawer of trophies tying him to others."

But Chief Capacasa called my theory "murder psychobabble" and wouldn't back off from the suspect he had already charged: Nick Garnett. As further punishment for publicly criticizing his homicide investigation, he yanked the extra cop patrols from my neighborhood. After all, he explained, the Susan killer was lying in a local hospital bed, not a threat to me or anyone.

I ALMOST DIDN'T pick up the phone when I walked through my front door and the caller ID showed Redding on the other end, making an audio house call from Duluth. I changed my mind for two reasons. First, I hoped to smooth over the misunderstanding about the camera outside the cop shop the other day. Second, without Garnett, without Shep, and now without work, I felt isolated.

That outlook lasted only about thirty seconds because, of course, Redding wanted to revel in the Dusty Foster disaster.

"I never had a doubt," he gloated. "But I'm a trained professional in these matters; you're simply a TV reporter."

"Trained in what? Murder investigations?"

"No, human psychology."

Over the last forty-eight hours I had listened to numerous people telling me I told you so. What was one more? Apparently, one too many.

"I've had it." I guess I sort of snapped. "For somebody who is supposed to be tuned in to other people's feelings, you are incredibly self-centered."

"Why? Because all I can think about is my deceased wife?"

Oh right. I had run him through the wringer on that. "Please, I'm sorry. I guess I'm just a little punchy with everything that's happening."

"Yes, I heard about that pit bull business. Nasty. How is your friend?"

"He and Shep will recover. But actually I buried the lead. The cops found a glove by Susan Victor's body. They found the matching one in Garnett's car."

"That certainly complicates matters. Or uncomplicates them depending on where you stand."

"That's the thing. My reporter gut still tells me he's innocent. Why would he tip me to the SUSANS story if he's the murderer? And if he's a killer, why save my life? Why put himself between me and a pit bull? Why not use me as a human shield and escape without a scratch? You're the psychiatrist, you're the one who understands human behavior, you tell me."

"Human behavior is seldom as simple as all or nothing," he explained. "It's not unheard-of for a serial killer to be a good family man or a respected professional. And denial helps us protect relationships we value. We block out things we don't want to see. Or hear."

I knew he was referring to me. So I changed the subject.

"Garnett mentioned something a while back about losing a glove by my house. You didn't notice one that night you were over?"

"I'm afraid not."

"I think the killer planted it to set Garnett up. Just like luring him to the murder location with the phone call."

Redding gave an impatient sigh. The kind of sound effect I sometimes made when I had a viewer on the line who wouldn't give up about some dubious conspiracy theory she wanted Channel 3 to investigate.

"What do the authorities say about your hypothesis?" he asked.

"That I'm nuts. Hey, remember when we talked about the killer playing a game? Putting items from one victim onto another? I think he used the Susan necklace I was wearing the other day."

"Indeed?"

"But the chief's too mad to listen. He even pulled the police drive-bys from my house."

"Are you concerned for your safety? Would you like me to drive down?"

"No. I'll be fine."

"I saw your interview last night. I don't remember much of what you said, but that was certainly a mesmerizing earring you wore."

"I don't want to talk about it." I had just logged on to my computer and was looking at the very image Redding referred to on the Minneapolis newspaper Web site. Me, on set, the dragon clinging to my ear. I wrapped up my conversation with Redding and turned my attention to the paper's local gossip columnist.

Please, I thought, let it say something like this: "Fire-breathing news director Noreen Banks overreacts as TV reporter Riley Spartz models a medieval look in contemporary times."

Instead, I read: "Channel 3 reporter Riley Spartz reportedly fired for violating the station's on-air dress code."

Hmmm. I didn't even know we had a dress code. And I really should demand a correction. After all, I hadn't been fired. I had quit.

ON DEADLINE, I file by pile. So piles of SUSANS notes lay scattered across the floor of my living room. As I bent down to pick up the Suicide Susan stack, I noticed some papers that must have slid under the couch earlier. I pulled them out and read the education conference schedule for her doomed trip to Rochester.

Susan Niemczyk had marked some of the panels specializing in adolescent behavior. "Talking Them into Learning" dealt with motivating teen study habits. "Education Funding at the Local and State Level" seemed like a boring, but job-required seminar. She had circled and starred one titled "Outreach Techniques for the Street-Savvy Teen." Listed among the panelists: Dr. Brent Redding.

I almost dropped to the floor.

I didn't need Sherlock Holmes to connect the dots for me. And I knew just how Philip Trent felt when his dinner companion casually revealed he had shot Manderson.

I grabbed a marker and started a new suspect board, with a new list of clues.

SUSPECT/DR. BRENT REDDING
NIEMCZYK CONFERENCE SPEAKER

Seems like the kind of thing Redding might have mentioned during our nighttime stroll around the lake. Unless he had something to hide.

What did I know about the Susan killer? *The date November 19 is significant to him. The name Susan is also significant.*

And I realized Dr. Redding was someone whose life had changed forever on November 19. And to whom the name Susan meant something very special.

I added those clues to Redding's suspect board.

NOVEMBER 19 SIGNIFICANT
SUSAN NAME SIGNIFICANT

Next I wrote CHENOWITH/MORENO ALIBI? because I realized that after the presence of Susan Redding's DNA had confirmed Dusty's guilt, Redding's whereabouts for his own wife's murder no longer took him out of the suspect mix for the other homicides.

Susan Redding's murder might be related after all. Perhaps the case did start with her, but in a manner I had never envisioned. Perhaps her death had triggered an annual chain reaction of violence.

Then I scanned the rest of my notes, pausing at the 1993 Susan gap—no body found. I tried to remember if that was the year that Redding had claimed to have checked into a clinic . . . was it to avoid killing himself, or to avoid killing another Susan?

I recollected his intense interest as he had reached

for the Susan necklace I wore. His fingers inches from my neck. Maybe he wondered if I was now playing a game with him. More than victory might be at stake. If that was the case, I needed backup.

I set pride aside and dialed Noreen.

"Why are you telling me this?" she said. "You don't work here anymore. So stop trying to build a criminal case against everyone you meet. You're seeing suspects under every rock. And you better not go around repeating this wild innuendo about Dr. Redding. He'll sue us from here to eternity!"

"But he was in Rochester at the same conference Susan Niemczyk—" I tried repeating the headline news. "He had opportunity."

"Big deal. Fifty psychiatrists probably spoke there. He probably can't even remember all the conferences he speaks at, especially going back ten years. You were wrong about the mayor. You were wrong about Dusty Foster. You're probably wrong about this Garnett guy you have a blind spot for. And you're wrong to think we want to touch this story ever again."

Noreen hung up.

I felt a little foolish. Opportunity means nothing without motive. Why would Dr. Redding kill women? Maybe I *was* seeing suspects under every rock. After all, barely a week ago I'd built up a fairly convincing scenario around Mayor Skubic. My headache was back. I walked to the bathroom and opened the medicine cabinet. I knew from the other night it was not well stocked. Behind the Band-Aids and shaving lotion I found an outdated bottle with a couple of prescription painkillers left over from when Boyer had sprained an ankle playing hoops with his jock buddies. I turned the cover until it clicked and it was like a light clicking on in my head.

The container fell from my hand and the pills scattered across the tile floor as I raced back to Redding's board to add another note: DOCTOR/PRESCRIPTION DRUGS. None of the other suspects was a psychiatrist with easy access to barbiturates, the kind of prescription drugs that had killed Suicide Susan.

CHAPTER 38

The list of clues might not be enough for a jury to convict on homicide charges, but they were more than enough to make Dr. Redding a person of interest to the authorities. Except the authorities remained disinterested in anyone beyond their prime suspect, Nick Garnett.

The hospital staff wouldn't let me see him. And an armed police officer guarded his room. They had moved Garnett from intensive care that morning, and he was heavily sedated, in no condition to hear about the latest developments or help me land irrefutable proof that Dr. Redding was a serial killer.

"Come back tomorrow," the nurse told me.

So I spent the afternoon escaping to the movies, though it wasn't the same without Garnett. I nearly turned back when I saw *Wait Until Dark* advertised on the Lagoon Theater marquee, but I told myself sometimes it helps to be reminded there are people worse off than you. Like Audrey Hepburn's blind character, Susy Hendrix. At least I didn't have to worry about going home and playing cat and mouse against a psychopath with matches.

But when the smooth thug told our heroine, "Damn it, you act as if you're in kindergarten. This is a big bad world, full of mean people, where nasty things happen," the 1967 movie line sure resonated with me.

In the dark, in the back of the theater, I mouthed Susy's words as she replied, "Now you tell me."

I had just pulled the Mustang into my garage when my cell phone rang. The phone number was unfamiliar, but I answered it anyway. Sam Fox, Susan Moreno's old street boyfriend, said hello back. Working the floor at Best Buy, he was calling to tell me he had just watched me on the late afternoon news on more than a dozen giant HDTV screens. I wasn't impressed because, one, I no longer worked at Channel 3. Two, because TV ratings are determined by televisions in households, not televisions in hotels or businesses, so no matter how many Best Buy sets are tuned to a particular show, it has no impact on a TV station's bottom line.

"Lucky I still had your card," he said. "I'm calling about the guy walking next to you in the shot." The man he described sounded a lot like Redding, probably from the tape Mike Flagg had snared the other day.

"What about him?" I unlocked the back door, walked inside, and threw my purse on the counter. I'd just spent the last couple hours watching a blind woman fight to survive by concentrating on her other senses to discern the odors of cigarettes and cologne and the sounds of squeaky shoes and rustling window shades. Like Susy, I almost felt someone was watching me. I shrugged my paranoia away and repeated my question to Sam, "What about him?"

"He was some county shrink Susan went to before she died."

"What?" I dropped to a chair at the kitchen table and gave him my total attention.

"Yeah, as part of her probation the judge ordered her to visit him every month. She brought me along once to sit in on a session. Seemed like an okay guy."

"You're sure?"

"Yeah, he seemed okay to me."

"No, I mean are you certain it's the same man?"

"Absolutely. Hey, I got a customer now. Gotta go. He's stroking a sixty-inch plasma." Sam hung up, clueless, not realizing he had just scored a big one for the knuckle-heads. A jury would likely convict on his evidence.

In most murder mystery novels, the heroine doesn't figure out who the killer is until he points a gun at her head. I silently congratulated myself for being smarter than most fictional protagonists, then smiled as I walked over to the SUSANS charts, wrote this latest clue on the Dr. Redding board and starred it.

I still regret not having had adequate time to relish the special "aha" nature of the moment because it turned so quickly into an "oh shit" moment.

First, I spied newly delivered flowers arranged in a crystal vase on the center of my living room table. Bleeding hearts.

Then Redding stepped between me and the door and held out a key. *My* spare key. "Bottom of the bird feeder." He winked.

As I reached for the key, he reached for my cell phone, hit *power-off*, and put it in his shirt pocket. "Let's take your mind off work. Doctor's orders."

If Garnett were here, he'd turn to me now and say, "I got a bad feeling about this." And I'd reply, "Harrison Ford." But I'd probably fumble the actual movie title since Han Solo was in almost constant peril throughout the first three *Star Wars* films and it was easy to confuse them. Of course, if Garnett were here, neither of us would have a bad feeling about anything, because we'd outnumber Redding two to one and Garnett would be packing a light saber, I mean a gun.

I sensed danger, but I'd been alone with Redding before and nothing lethal had transpired. Although now, thinking back, plenty of witnesses had seen us together that night outside my house. That certainly could have cramped his style. So I put on my smile with teeth and decided to play dumb.

"You didn't have to drive all the way down from Duluth." I patted his arm. "I told you I'm fine."

No role-playing for Redding. He picked up Shep's leash from the table and flexed it. "It is regrettable. You were a worthy opponent. Too worthy I'm afraid."

"Brent." For the first time, I used his first name. "You don't need to do this."

"Unfortunately, I do. You're too close. And you talk too much. The necklace, the earring, I can't risk your speaking with the authorities again. Especially not now." He gestured toward the SUSANS boards leaning against the wall. The one with his name and clues stood in front.

SUSPECT/DR. BRENT REDDING
NIEMCZYK CONFERENCE SPEAKER
NOVEMBER 19 SIGNIFICANT
SUSAN NAME SIGNIFICANT
CHENOWITH/MORENO ALIBI?
DOCTOR/PRESCRIPTION DRUGS
DR./PATIENT CONNECTION TO SUSAN MORENO

Redding tapped the last line, the one I'd freshly written after my phone call; the "aha" one. "This list is not something I can allow you to share with anyone outside this room."

He pivoted, quickly looping the dog leash around my neck and yanked, but I ducked and deflected before he could tighten it. Slowly he advanced, and slowly I backed up, so neither of us made much progress toward our ultimate goal: him homicide, me escape. I broke the pattern, darting past him to where the Bible lay on the coffee table next to my portable phone.

"Have you read chapter thirteen of Daniel?" I tried distracting him.

For centuries leaders have debated whether it is better to disarm one's enemy with a Bible or with a sword. A metaphor for persuasion versus force. Philosophy aside, if a sword had been handy, I would have reached for it. Instead I grabbed the Word of God. The Bible can and has been used as a psychological weapon. Today I used it as a physical one.

I smacked the cover hard against Redding's ear. When he stumbled I used that second to grab the phone off the table to dial 911. The average police response time in my neighborhood is about three minutes. For a true emergency, I knew they could cut the time in half without my even uttering a word. All I needed to do was hit four buttons and squad cars would race to my address. One push to turn the phone on. Then 9 . . . 1 . . . 1.

Nope. He had taken the kitchen phone off the hook. Instead of a dial tone I got a useless beeping noise. I threw the telephone at his smirking face. He remained between me and the door, so I took the stairs, two at a time.

Even though the hardware was flimsy, I locked my bedroom door. I didn't bother going for the window, I knew it was stuck. Painted shut by the previous owner. Redding was cracking the wood off the hinges just as I rolled under the bed, reaching for my dead husband's Glock.

I moved my hands along the carpet in every direction. But the light was dim, and instead of metal, all I hit was dog hair, dust bunnies, and lost socks. I squandered the tiniest microsecond regretting not keeping the gun under my pillow.

Redding dropped to the floor after me. His eyes

stared at mine. He looked like Jack Nicholson in *The Shining.* I half expected him to yell, "Here's Johnny!"

Instead he clawed at my face, so I bit down on his hand, breaking the skin. Redding swore. His vocabulary didn't sound so academic now. My teeth clenched hard against his knuckles until his fingernails ground into my nose. He pushed himself up and moved to the other end of the bed. There he grabbed my foot and tried dragging me out. My sock slipped off in his hand. I used that brief interlude to clutch onto the bed frame and kick. Hard.

Unfortunately, I kicked the gun out from under the bed.

CHAPTER 39

Redding had a head start so he beat me to the weapon. By the time I was even part of the race, he was pointing the barrel at my chest. We both breathed heavily. My heart pounded. His hand was bleeding, so was my nose.

"I'm not going to die on the home farm, am I?"

Redding didn't answer, but his eyes narrowed.

Now seemed a good time to try lying. "I told the news desk during that phone call if they didn't hear from me in an hour, they should call the cops."

"You're bluffing." Psychiatrists can always tell.

Now seemed a good time to try establishing a dialogue.

"Killing other women won't bring back your wife."

But I had seriously misjudged his motive. That was understandable, because murder motives are sometimes learned only after the perpetrator is identified and questioned. I never anticipated his next words.

"I don't want to bring her back. I want to be the one to kill her. For betraying me."

Susanna . . . an accused adulteress . . . Oh my God, he was executing women for the sin of adultery—his wife's adultery—under the biblical law of woman as property of man. Talk about objectifying women.

"You're killing other Susans because your wife cheated on you?"

"It was an insult to my skill as a therapist. Do you think I didn't see my peers snickering behind my back?"

I don't think he actually expected me to answer, which was good because I couldn't. All I could think about was him seeking out surrogate Susans to strangle for revenge against his philandering mate. That she was already dead didn't seem to satisfy him.

"I fantasized about what her last breath sounded like. I deserved to know. She belonged to me."

He described first seeing Susan Chenowith waitressing at the diner one year to the day after his wife's murder.

"She brushed against me while pouring coffee. On purpose. I noticed her name on her uniform. It seemed a sign: a Susan sent to me on the anniversary my Susan was taken."

I disliked blood or I could have shot myself with Boyer's gun months ago and no one would have challenged the medical examiner's ruling of self-inflicted. But as I listened to Redding's homicidal ramble, I realized I wanted to live and was willing to fight for tomorrow. If Redding wanted to stage my death to look like suicide, he could fire only one round and his aim had to be perfect. Should I gamble my life he couldn't pull it off?

"On a whim," he went on, "I waited outside for her shift to end."

I nodded in what I hoped he would take as compassion and rushed him for the gun.

I had the advantage of surprise, but he had the advantage of having a finger on the trigger. He fell backward as I struggled to turn the weapon away from me. A loud blast halted our wrestling match. Blood seeped into the carpet around our bodies. I remember praying, let it be his blood, not mine.

It was.

Redding bled from a stomach wound. Although his face clenched in pain, his fingers still clung to the semiautomatic.

"So much for making it look like suicide," I said.

"Actually, I was leaning toward a botched burglary."

Uneasily we chuckled, but the laugh hurt him. He didn't seem so crazy anymore. Now seemed a good time to offer help. "Let me call an ambulance."

He shook his head and pointed the weapon at my chest.

"Okay, you're the doctor," I said. "What's your medical opinion?"

"The patient will outlive you." I didn't like that prognosis, but I knew better than to argue with a man holding a gun. Besides a bullet in the gut, I tried to gauge Dr. Redding's other weaknesses. By trade, he liked to listen and talk. I also knew he liked to show off.

"Tell me about the raincoat."

"I already did."

"That was very clever of you. I bet you laughed about our late-night walk for days. Did you know about the blue button? That's what broke the case open."

"No. The button surprised me. Quite impressive on your part. That's when I decided to get to know you better."

Garnett was right. I was a dolt. Redding had wanted to stay close to the investigation.

"So you put the raincoat on Susan Moreno's body and took her necklace."

"I took a special interest in that patient because of her name. As the anniversary date grew closer, I determined she was the next one. For her therapy, I offered to meet after hours, to coach her on how to stay straight."

No surprise she had walked into his trap. After all, look at me.

"That phone call I had earlier," I told him, "it wasn't the station. Her old boyfriend recognized you from that news clip of us together."

"Now you know why I'm camera shy."

I didn't know much about stomach wounds, but I hoped if I kept Redding talking, he might bleed to death before he could pull the trigger.

"Were you lying about your own suicide watch? When you checked yourself into a clinic?"

"That made me realize I didn't really want to stop. I just didn't want to go to jail. I decided to vary my method. To pass off a murder as a suicide is an accomplishment." At his reference to Susan Niemczyk's homicide, the corner of Redding's mouth curled up, like a cross between Mona Lisa and the Big Bad Wolf. "That's when I knew the police would never catch me."

"But ultimately you did stop." I tried stressing the positive. "Until Susan Victor."

"No. I didn't stop." He sounded proud. "You just didn't find the others."

The others. No one would probably find me either. The blood stain on Redding's shirt was spreading, and he had to be growing weaker. I knew it. He knew it. He needed to pull the trigger soon, before he passed out. I silently debated how much longer I could play Scheherazade with the most important interview of my life.

"Come, I have something to show you," he said. "You drive."

Leaving the house was riskier for him than for me. Usually an abductor takes his victim from a public place to a more private setting. That spells trouble for the victim because more privacy means less chance of rescue. Redding might have a secluded gravel pit in mind, but he'd have to get me there first. Past other people. With his bullet wound, he couldn't carry my body. Damn if I'd end up like that TV anchorwoman in Iowa. Ten years later, still missing. Better closure for my parents to bury me in a marked grave. Whatever plan Redding had before, I felt certain he was now improvising.

"Can't we take your Beemer?" I asked. "I don't want blood in my car." A joke might catch him off guard. Nope.

He wobbled as he stood, pressed the gun against my

back, and pushed me toward the stairs. "I purposely took the bus so no one would notice my car parked by your house."

When we got downstairs, he made me fold up the SUSANS board with his name on it. "Put it in the backseat."

I picked up my purse off the kitchen counter while he stuffed some dish towels in his shirt to absorb the blood. He grabbed his coat and we exited through the back door. The sky still held a half hour of daylight, but the street and surrounding yards were empty. Where were the paparazzi when I needed them?

If ever I wished Mrs. Fredericks would peek out her window, now was the time. Most likely she was tuned to *Desperate Housewives,* oblivious to her own desperate neighbor.

CHAPTER 40

My car keys were caught in the clutter of my purse. As I groped for them, my fingers brushed against my mini tape recorder. Surreptitiously, I pressed *record*, to make an audio record of our drive, or at least the first thirty minutes of it. As we got inside the Mustang, I slipped the recorder on the floor under my seat. If the police found my car, they'd find a concrete clue that pointed to a specific suspect. I made a special point to call Dr. Redding by name, so the cops would know the identity of my abductor.

"Where are you taking me, Dr. Redding?" I asked.

"Fasten your seat belt," he instructed me. I don't think he was concerned for my safety; he was concerned I might leap from the moving vehicle and leave him to die in a fiery car crash. "Keep your hands on the steering wheel."

My right hand had powder burns and my thumb knuckle had suffered a small gash from the gun's kick. I was in considerably better physical shape than my captor, riding shotgun, bleeding like an ulcer. But he had the confidence that comes from being armed and dangerous.

"Here, put this on." He handed me a VOTE SUSAN campaign button. I didn't need to ask where he got it.

"Please, Brent, not that. I didn't even vote for her when she was alive."

"Put it on now, or I'll put it on you later."

Obediently I pinned the button to my sweater. "You know journalists aren't supposed to support political candidates."

"I offered to make a contribution to her campaign," he said. "When I explained who I was, she understood why I wanted to meet in private and avoid publicity."

No use thinking ill of the dead.

"Now give me your wedding ring." He said the words calmly, like he was asking me to pass the salt or the sports section.

"No. You can't have it."

"But I insist." He emphasized the seriousness of his request by waving my husband's gun. "I might need it next year."

The emotional response would be to spit in his face. The rational response would be to hand over the ring. Boyer's gun. Boyer's ring. Boyer would want me to buy time.

I wished my knuckles were swollen, but the ring slid off easily. Redding placed my gold band on his left pinkie and held up his hand, fingers spread wide. When he pressed his fingers together, my wedding ring and his touched each other, making a soft, metallic clink.

"Now start the car."

I backed out of the driveway and pulled up to the stop sign on West Fiftieth. "Which way? How about the hospital? They could stop the bleeding."

"Head to the freeway," he said, "35W South."

That gave me just over a mile of residential streets. Once we got on the freeway, I'd have fewer options. I needed a strategy fast, because having hope is not the same as having a plan. I recalled Garnett saying something about how most serial killers are caught either during a routine traffic stop or when a victim escapes.

Redding's blood dripped on the dark carpet of my car. Between those splotches and the congealing pool in my bedroom, the forensics team would have plenty of evidence. Little chance his DNA would be on file, but fingerprints might eventually point them in his direction, if I couldn't.

"And you lured Garnett there?" An idea took form in the back of my mind. A long shot, but right now what wasn't?

"Yes. That was a nice touch. It turned out better than I had dreamed. I thought I'd have to call some anonymous tip line and report seeing his vehicle in the park late that night. You were a big help."

I ignored his verbal jab as we approached Nicollet Avenue. "How'd you get his glove?"

"He dropped it that night when we met outside your house. I thought it might come in handy."

I stopped for the light. A traffic sign warned no right turn on red, and that bought me valuable seconds of plotting time. The windshield was starting to steam up. I made a big point of wiping the windows to improve my visibility. Redding scowled and hit the defrost button.

"So what do you want to show me?" I asked.

"You'll see soon enough."

I hit the gas a bit to drive uphill, then inched the speedometer higher as we cruised downhill, over Minnehaha Creek. I accelerated until I was fifteen over the limit and hoped that would be enough as we passed a bank of trees at the end of the bridge. I was counting on one of Minneapolis's finest still being on speed trap duty.

"Did I ever tell you I'm afraid to fly?" I changed the subject to distract him from our change in speed.

"A good therapist could probably help you with that."

The squad clocked me. I saw police lights in my rearview mirror but didn't slow down until he gave me a shot of his siren.

"How fast were you going?" Redding's voice cracked.

"I don't know. Not so fast. I'm nervous is all."

The patrol car stuck tight to my bumper as I turned onto Diamond Lake Road. We were almost at the freeway entrance. If I didn't stop now, we'd be in a slow speed chase like O.J. Simpson.

"Pull over. But play it very cool, or I'll kill you both. How'd you like another cop widow out there?"

That perspective changed things.

The officer had either run my plates, memorized them, or was a loyal Channel 3 viewer, because he greeted me by name. His smile stretched so wide, I imagined the euphoria he would experience when he waved my ticket at Chief Capacasa to claim his reward. He gave my passenger only a perfunctory look. Redding's coat was draped over his lap, hiding his wound and his weapon.

"Going a little fast, Ms. Spartz?"

"Was I, officer? I'm so sorry."

I fumbled with my wallet and purposely dropped my driver's license onto the floor. I unhooked my seat belt to reach for it, scraped it back and forth against the bloody carpet, handed it to the officer, and watched him head back to his squad.

"Why's he so smiley?" Even Redding noticed the young officer's enthusiasm.

"Probably just excited to be ticketing a TV celebrity. Something to brag about at the precinct."

But the bounce in his step slowed as he reached his squad door. I figured he must have identified the sticky substance on my license.

"Don't make him suspicious," Redding said. "If he asks you to step outside the vehicle, I will shoot him. And then you will have two dead lawmen on your conscience."

This was his first reference to my guilt over my husband's death since I had confided in him that night in the park. I decided not to remind him that I'm not responsible for the actions of a madman. And for the first time since Boyer's murder, I believed those words.

"Stay calm," I said. "I'm just going to take my ticket and apologize. Don't freak if he asks for an autograph."

"I'll bet he has kids. Maybe a little boy with a toy badge who wants to be a cop when he grows up, just like daddy."

Shit.

I kept my eyes on the side mirror, watched the cop rest his hand on his holster and glance backward. It was now or never. I slammed my purse against Redding's stomach and the gun while jerking the car door open with my other hand. The next three seconds felt like thirty. Everything seemed to transpire in slow motion. By the time I heard the shot I was rolling on asphalt. Screaming in pain. Or was it fear?

The officer, on one knee, yelled, "Drop it! Drop it! Drop it!"

More gunfire. Breaking glass. Hysteria. I swear the cop fired at the car. But later Chief Capacasa told me Redding blew his brains out against my dashboard. I really wish we had taken his BMW.

CHAPTER 41

heard a soft bark and opened my eyes. Shep stuck his big head into my hospital room. Bandages covered his jaw and left ear. But the big mutt was smiling anyway. Toby was right behind him.

"Wake up, sleepyhead," I called over to my roommate and fellow patient. "We have company."

Garnett had been drifting off from the meds last night when I was admitted for overnight observation. We both wore hospital gowns, but he had an IV bag full of antibiotics and painkillers attached to his wrist. Numerous black stitches tattooed his shoulder, neck, and ear. I filled him in on the latest SUSANS developments but wasn't sure how much he remembered. When he started to snore, I'd helped myself to a cup of red Jell-O sitting on his tray table since I couldn't remember my last meal and since he hadn't mentioned anything about being hungry.

He couldn't speak yet, but he gave a brief wave to our canine visitor.

"I'm so sorry," Toby told me. "I shouldn't have said those things I did. Shep's going to be fine. He's got the heart of Rin Tin Tin. It wasn't your fault. I'm the one who got you started with Dr. Petit. If I hadn't called your tip line, none of this would have happened."

"That's nonsense, Toby. It's Petit's fault. Put the blame where it belongs."

Garnett motioned for a dry-erase board on the counter. "Petit?" he wrote.

"Dead," I answered.

He kept writing. "Redding?"

"Dead, too. You weren't dreaming. Or high on your morphine drip."

He shook his head and leaned back on his pillows. Shep climbed onto the foot of my bed and I wrapped my arms around his furry back, being careful not to squeeze too hard.

"How did you get him in?" I asked Toby. "Hennepin County Medical doesn't allow dogs."

Toby tapped a finger against his sunglasses. "My trusty Seeing Eye dog and I have busted through tighter security than this place. Nobody wants to risk discriminating against the disabled."

Unfortunately a nurse chose just that moment to check Garnett's vitals so she overheard enough to evict the trespassers. But she also brought more Jell-O, and this time Garnett finished his.

Then he reached for his board and started writing. When he held it up it read ELEMENTARY, MY DEAR WATSON.

I smiled and answered, "Basil Rathbone, *The Adventures of Sherlock Holmes,* 1939."

EPILOGUE

((ANCHOR, TEASE))
PSYCHIATRIST SERIAL
KILLER STALKS SUSANS
FOR MORE THAN
A DECADE . . .
TONIGHT AT TEN.

had no regrets that I never saw what Dr. Brent Redding had wanted to show me. Chances are, it would have been my last memory.

His final words are nightmare aplenty. The police tagged the audiocassette from my tape recorder as evidence. When Chief Capacasa returned my wedding ring, he let me listen . . . Redding's voice was barely recognizable after my escape from the car. I expected harsh words directed at me; instead he spent the last thirty seconds of his life blaming the mess he had created on Susan—his murdered wife—whom he castigated for his degeneration into evil. His ranting also gave some insight into their marriage vows.

"I warned you, Susan, what would happen if you ever cheated. That I'd kill you. So I did." Not exactly, but in his mind, close enough. He sounded haughty, his narcissism overpowering his logic.

He called her a bunch of names like "whore" and

"bitch" and vowed to see her in hell. Then he released a wail of "Suuussann!" and pulled the trigger.

The tape continued to roll, silent, then sirens, faint at first, growing louder. I hit *stop* when I heard the cops approach the vehicle and open the door. I didn't care to hear their description of the physical scene.

Redding's pledge of where he would meet his wife in the afterlife seemed overconfident. While the Bible condemns both adulterers and murderers, there was no doubt in my mind who was more worthy of Satan's company.

When police searched Redding's Duluth town house, they found neatly organized folders of newspaper articles documenting the Susan murders, plus the cases of four other missing women named Susan whose bodies have never been recovered. The most recent: a punk chick with a dragon tattoo on her hip. The most heartbreaking: an eleven-year-old Nebraska girl who had disappeared after soccer practice. She was last seen walking home on November 19, 2003, wearing a red team uniform with the name SUSAN printed across the back.

The composite sketch of a stranger seen near the field earlier in the day strongly resembled Dr. Redding.

Our computer search hadn't popped these cases because, since no bodies were found, no death certificates were ever issued.

Authorities also found lilies, black-eyed Susans, and other flowers growing in a small greenhouse porch attached to Redding's home.

The calendar in Redding's kitchen had a thick red circle drawn around November 19.

Experts on Court TV declared the killings classic revenge/fantasy homicides. They speculated that Redding had transferred the anger against his wife to the other Susans and derived sexual satisfaction from killing them.

Funny how I had once thought Redding and I shared a bond of spousal grief. Grief almost drove me to suicide. Grief drove him to murder. Possibly his problem wasn't grief, but a lack of grief. He never mourned his wife's death; he only mourned her infidelity.

THOUGH HE CERTAINLY had earned the right, Nick Garnett never once said, "I told you so."

He fully recovered from his dog attack injuries but would sport some wild scars for the rest of his life. Authorities dropped the homicide charges against him and awarded him a civilian medal of valor. He boycotted the ceremony, so they mailed it to him. He uses it as a coaster on his desk.

Garnett predicted the SUSANS case would be featured in homicide textbooks as an example of the symbolic value of victims to serial killers. Researchers have long speculated that Ted Bundy murdered college-age women with long brown hair parted in the middle as revenge against the upper-class fiancée who had rejected him. Bundy always discounted this theory and insisted he killed simply because he enjoyed it.

My whole experience with the Susans soured me on Hollywood thrillers. I refused to go to the movies with Garnett unless we watched musicals. We hit a stalemate because the only musical he wanted to see was *Chicago,* and I couldn't bear to sit through "We Both Reached for the Gun."

SHEP JOINED THE St. Paul Police Canine Unit where he became Minnesota's top drug-sniffing dog.

DUSTY FOSTER'S MOTHER stopped visiting him in prison because she couldn't bear to look at his face anymore, though she continued to send him birthday cards. That didn't bother Dusty much; he married a woman named Susan he met online who didn't seem to mind having an incarcerated husband.

PRURIENT CURIOSITY ABOUT the psychiatrist serial killer caused a ratings rebound, so Channel 3 won the November sweeps by nearly three points, becoming the top news station in the Minneapolis–St. Paul market for the first time in more than twenty years. In recognition for her leadership in turning the newsroom around, the big bosses gave Noreen Banks a nice fat bonus.

MIKE FLAGG DUBBED the SUSANS story onto his résumé tape, bragged about the numbers in a cover letter, exercised an out in his Channel 3 contract, and landed a national correspondent job with FOX News. He died while doing a live shot during a hurricane when the street sign he was clutching to demonstrate the gale force winds blew loose. The clip went viral on YouTube. Bill O'Reilly delivered his eulogy.

EVEN THOUGH MY sins didn't violate the traditional Ten Commandments, I confessed to Father Mountain anyway. After all, a deal is a deal.

"Bless me Father, for I have sinned. I almost freed a guilty man. I almost ruined an innocent one. And I almost helped a serial killer escape."

Just like my inept literary detective role model Philip Trent, I'd gotten it all wrong. If I were writing my memoir, I'd have to call my adventure *Riley's Last Case*.

Sorry, Sherlock.

I understand now that not all crimes can be understood. Life would be easier if murderers resembled monsters, as in Mary Shelley's *Frankenstein*. Then we'd know who to fear and who to suspect when bodies started piling up in the morgue. Instead most killers are normal people living secret lives. Clearly I had obsessed on the wrong crime classics. The answer to the Susan murders sat within reach on my bookshelf: *The Strange Case of Dr. Jekyll and Mr. Hyde*. Robert Louis Stevenson's examination of the dual nature of man—good and evil fighting for control—summed up Dr. Redding as neatly as any of the FBI profilers at Quantico could.

Noreen pretended my quitting was all a big misunderstanding, so with heavy misgivings I signed a new two-year contract with Channel 3. With no misgivings I sold my house in south Minneapolis because my most vivid memories there were mostly bad. True love can't trump dual brushes with death.

I packed up my dead husband's belongings. Some I kept, some I gave away. While cleaning out Boyer's sock drawer, I found an envelope addressed to me, in his handwriting. Inside I found two letters, each dated the eve of our anniversary, different years. I set them side by side, reading the first one first.

Babe,
You have no business snooping in my sock drawer unless I am dead. So if you are reading this, it's not a good sign for us. But us is the best part of me. Always know there is nothing you can do that I won't forgive, and in the course of a marriage, snooping is only a misdemeanor. I will penalize you with long, deep kisses.
Love, Hugh

Darling,
I hope you never read these letters. But if you do, I hope there are dozens to bring you comfort and symbolize our years and years of life together.

By now you probably won't even remember

that night we fought about when to drive to Chicago. Already I'm sorry. But none of our fights are deal breakers. This one barely a blip on the radar. A speeding ticket vs. a DUI. Remember our biggest fight so far? Where to hang the deer head? I guess I lost that one, too. I leave you never regretting a minute of our marriage. The best part of fighting is making up. Good-bye, Riley.

Love, Hugh

"Thank you, darling," I whispered.

I put his letters back in the envelope, along with my wedding band, sealed it with a kiss, and stuck it in one of the moving boxes.

ACKNOWLEDGMENTS

The list of people who made *Stalking Susan* a better book is a long one.

My dear friend and first reader, Michele Cook, was supportive and encouraging.

My fellow author and last reader, Steve Thayer, was critical and discouraging.

Both approaches improved my manuscript.

My readers in between, Kevyn Burger, Caroline Lowe, Alan Cox, and Trish Van Pilsum, kept my story sound, my characters honest, and me sane.

I'm grateful to all the people in television news I've worked with or covered these many years, along with my friends and very large extended family spread far and wide. You all inspired me. But keep in mind, this is a work of fiction, and the characters on these pages are not you.

Thanks to Vernon Geberth, the smartest cop I know and master of *Practical Homicide Investigation*.

Garrett Young for his skill behind the camera.

My debut colleagues at International Thriller Writers for their fellowship, as well as the veteran authors there, for their generosity.

I owe enormous gratitude to my agent, Elaine Koster, for taking me on as a client, giving me confidence as a writer, and finding my novel a home with

Doubleday. Her associate Stephanie Lehman, an excellent author herself with a genuine fondness for television, worked with me on revisions to improve my plot.

When an editor the caliber of Stacy Creamer wanted my book, I felt like I had won the literary lottery. Special appreciation for Stacy's patience with a novice and the enthusiasm she expressed toward me, my protagonist, and my novel; assistant editor Laura Swerdloff for her remarkable attention to details; production editor Sean Mills; Jean Traina for cover design; Maggie Carr for copyediting; Rachel Lapal for publicity; Adrienne Sparks for marketing; Elizabeth Schraft and Tom Lacey for proofreading; and the rest of the Doubleday team. As a television news producer I realize much of the work in launching a book involves behind-the-scenes people whose names don't appear on the cover. The least I can do is mention them in the credits.

The same goes for the paperback team at Vintage/Anchor. Among them, my editor, Zachary Wagman, who made me feel quite welcome and whose confidence is contagious; my production editor, Vanessa López; and publicity manager, Lisa Weinert.

And as a journalist, I respect accuracy and have thick skin, so thanks to the eagle-eyed readers who corrected fact and spelling errors in the hardcover edition of *Stalking Susan*. They are, in the order in which they spoke up: Don Shelby, Esme Murphy, Col. Richard Kramer, Karen Pearce, Gina Smith, Scott Libin, Bill Follows, and Cherie Hanson.

The following folks didn't have anything to do with my book but are hankering to see their names in print. Some have been vocal about their desire; some have been subtle; and some have politely kept their mouths shut. But they're family, so here it goes: Ruth Kramer; Katie and Jake Kimball; Joey, David, and Aria Kimdon; George and Shirley Kimball; Michael Kramer and Christina; Bonnie and Roy Brang; Teresa and Galen Neuzil, and Rachel; Richard and Oti Kramer; Mary Kramer; Steve and Mary Kramer, and Matthew and Elizabeth; Kathy and Jim Loecher, and Adriana and Zack; Steve and Moira Kimball, and James, Paul, and Craig; George Kimball and Shen Fei, with Nick and Huan; Mary and David Benson, and Davin; Jenny and Kile Nadeau, and Jess, Becca, David, and Daniel.

Hugs to my sons, Alex and Andrew, for allowing me time on the computer and not laughing when I said I was writing a book.

And deep, personal thanks to my husband, Joe, for his love and understanding. He is indeed my soul mate.

An excerpt from

MISSING MARK

By JULIE KRAMER

Available in hardcover from Doubleday, Summer 2009

PRELUDE

The bride wept—not from happiness.

She threw her bouquet—in the garbage.

The bridesmaids looked helpless. The grooms-men looked sheepish. The mother of the groom looked like she'd rather be anywhere else. Finally, the minister made the announcement to the three hundred waiting guests.

Then the mother of the bride unzipped her daughter's gown and drove her home.

CHAPTER 1

My past sold quickly, despite the down market.

Of course, no one actually died under my roof. Just a couple of near-miss murders that my real estate agent assured me didn't need to be disclosed to potential buyers. But now I needed to move fast and she promised me this was the place. "I have a feeling about you and this remodeled bungalow," Jan Meyer said. "The owner is anxious to leave town and just dropped the price twenty grand."

Jan enjoyed playing matchmaker between buyer and seller. Especially since she knew I'd made a killing on my own real estate deal and had plenty of cash to put down. So she took the key out of the lockbox and prepared to give me the tour.

"You might just fall in love with the kitchen," she said.

Not love at first smell. The house had a definite odor. And it didn't seem to be coming from the kitchen.

While Jan went to open some windows, I followed my nose to a closed door where the smell seemed strongest. Journalists prefer open doors. So I turned the knob and peeked inside. Then quickly slammed it shut before any flies could escape.

"What is that horrible smell?" Jan asked.

"I think it might be the owner."

"Is he dead?" she gasped.

I nodded as I headed back outside to call the police from my cell phone.

"Did he have a heart attack?" Jan followed behind, anxious for details.

"In a manner of speaking."

I hadn't gotten close to the man on the floor. But I could see the congealed pool of blood around his body and the knife sticking out of his chest.

That's when I decided to keep renting.

CHAPTER 2

Some days I wish I could just write about sweaters. After all, sweaters never hurt anyone. And no reporter ever got kidnapped, blindfolded, and paraded in front of Al Jazeera's audience writing for *Vogue*. Of course, no sweater ever got a gold-medal 40 share in TV ratings, either. Except perhaps Kathleen Sullivan's figure-hugging crew necks during the Winter Olympics in Sarajevo.

Sweaters are the mashed potatoes and gravy of a woman's wardrobe—the ultimate comfort clothing—unless gravy accidentally drips onto a pricey cashmere. But I was nowhere near the kitchen, so I could safely curl up in a hand-knit sweater of scratchy wool looking out an upstairs window at a narrow view of White Bear Lake. I don't actually live on the lake, but if I angle my chair and crane my neck just right, I can watch the whitecaps and fishermen on the legendary water.

I'm Riley Spartz, an investigative reporter for Channel 3 in Minneapolis. Close to five months ago I fled my highly sought-after urban neighborhood for a fresh start after a TV sweeps story went bad. Lakeshore homes in this northern Twin Cities suburb go for a million bucks plus, but the rest of the town is quite affordable.

My landlord recently moved out, listing this place for rent because his next-door neighbor held perpetual yard sales that attracted traffic at annoying times. Always looking for a bargain, I'd even checked out the inventory myself, but found only overpriced junk.

Today I paged through the weekly *White Bear Press,* delighted by irksome crimes that wouldn't merit a mention on a major-market TV newscast. Nothing makes a woman living alone feel safer than reading police reports about teens caught smoking behind the school and bicycles stolen from open garages.

A want ad for an item I definitely wasn't looking to buy caught my eye and my imagination.

FOR SALE: WEDDING DRESS. NEVER WORN.

Mystery and emotion, all in one line.

Forget sweaters. A wedding dress is much more likely to garner a 40 share. Viewers love weddings. The research proves it.

In the world of television ratings, two weddings stand out. And both brides would probably have been happier if their wedding dresses had never been worn.

In 1969, when Miss Vicki married Tiny Tim on *The Tonight Show Starring Johnny Carson,* 45 million viewers made that episode the highest rated in talk-show history.

That was nothing compared to the wedding of the century. A dozen years later 750 million viewers worldwide watched as Prince Charles and Lady Diana promised to forsake all others. That royal wedding delivered royal ratings, but ultimately royal scandal. The bride and groom learned (as I reluctantly learned from my own brief marriage) no "I do" guarantees happily ever after.

When it comes to TV weddings, happiness and ratings may be mutually exclusive. While Prince Charles's sequel ceremony to Camilla Parker Bowles tanked in the ratings department, the marriage seems to be thriving in the happiness arena.

Now TV weddings are typically interactive events, like the *Today Show* where viewers choose gowns, cakes, rings, and honeymoon destinations for the happy couple, or reality shows, like *The Bachelor,* in which grooms propose marriage before our voyeuristic eyes.

I circled the "Never Worn" want ad with a red pen and pondered whether the story behind the wedding dress might be worth a television news story.

Perhaps a lesson about love and loss, if I could sort through the he said/she said of a broken engagement. Was the big day called off because of a tragic parachuting accident? A philandering groom caught with a bridesmaid after the rehearsal dinner? Or perhaps a wedding guest revealed a juicy secret when the minister inquired whether anyone knew any reason why this man and this woman should not be joined in holy matrimony.

Doubtful that the truth would prove as irresistible as the scenarios in my mind, but maybe the story could be a lesson about second chances if the gown made it successfully down the aisle on the back of a new bride.

As an investigative reporter, I seldom get a chance to tell love stories.

The May ratings book loomed, just on the fringe of the June wedding season. A tantalizing tale of doomed courtship might spike the overnight news numbers. The Channel 3 bosses were always anxious this time of year because the May sweeps were arguably the most important—Christmas holiday ad rates are based on those figures. Jingle all the way.

I had no blockbuster investigation up my sweater sleeve this sweeps. I'd sat out the February ratings book because I was a mess personally and the November book remained an unpleasant reminder of my blood, sweat, and tears.

My hypothetical wedding-dress chronicle was unlikely to require a major investment of time or money, so if the backstory was compelling, Channel 3's news director, Noreen Banks, would probably give me a green light. Another reason: we had a mandate from the suits upstairs to attract more women viewers because advertisers think they control the household cash.

In May, Minnesota ladies also control the TV remote, because fishing season opens and their menfolk flock to boats like ducks to water. Noreen might certainly seize this wedding-dress opportunity to throw the big bosses upstairs a bouquet . . . I mean a bone.

So I reached for the phone to dial the number in the "Never Worn" newspaper ad to find out who dumped who.

"You look beautiful," Madeline Post said, as I twirled this way and that in front of a full-length mirror in her little-girl-pink bedroom.

I hadn't intended to try on the gown. But when she insisted, it did occur to me that it would be harder for Madeline to kick me out the door when she learned I was a reporter if the garment was literally on my back.

The dress looked even better up close than on the e-mail fashion photo she'd sent me the previous night. The kind of dress a fairy-tale princess might wear. Satin. White. Strapless. Fitted at the waist with a ball-gown skirt that flared at my hips. Interesting sparkles around the bustline. The dress accentuated my figure, decent but not voluptuous. And it contrasted nicely with my brown shoulder-skimming hair. I'd checked the designer's reputation online and knew this almost bride had spent nearly fifteen grand on her dream dress.

Not exactly. Her mother had actually written the

check. Because, according to Madeline, it was her mother's dream dress.

"She wanted me to look like Cinderella," Madeline explained. "But I wanted an outdoor wedding and would have been happy wearing a sundress or even jeans."

"Why didn't you tell her?"

"The big wedding meant the world to her. Because she compromised on having the ceremony outside, I compromised on the dress. And she's done so much to raise me and my brother after our dad died."

Because I was trying to pose as someone other than a reporter—a self-absorbed bride, in fact—I didn't follow up on that nugget, though I was quite curious to learn more about her father's death.

Besides checking out Madeline's dress, I'd also checked out Madeline and her fiancé, Mark Lefevre. Or rather, I had Lee Xiong, our newsroom computer geek, check them out with a crime database he'd assembled from several law enforcement and court agencies. Xiong came to the United States as a toddler refugee from Laos. He flourished in Minnesota, despite his parents' poverty and the state's winters, and became a respected producer at Channel 3.

His cyber report showed the bride had a clean record here in the state, while the groom had been picked up on a minor marijuana possession charge a decade earlier that netted nothing more serious than a small fine and the requirement that he attend drug education classes.

Madeline's place was not far from mine. I'd left her name, phone number, and address with Xiong along with instructions for him to call the cops if he didn't hear from me in three hours.

Normally I wouldn't have hesitated answering her ad alone, but the recent Craigslist nanny murder—in which a disturbed young man posed as a local mother in need of child care before killing the coed who answered the ad—did cross my mind and made me more cautious than usual about meeting strangers in nonpublic places.

Those precautions might not save my life, but they'd make it easier to find my body if things got ugly. And this way my parents could console themselves with the knowledge that at least they were able to give me a decent Christian burial. And I could console myself that at least my murder would lead the late news, although I wouldn't put it past Channel 3 to bump me down to the second section just so the station had something lurid to tease at the top of the show and again at the first break to hold viewers into the second quarter hour of the newscast.

I'd found Madeline and Mark's engagement announcement and photo online. At twenty-four, she was ten years younger than her fiancé. Her face pretty, not stunning. Her most noticeable feature, her splendid golden hair, long and flowing.

The first thing I observed about Mark was an odd, diagonal scar across his forehead. Not a lightning bolt like Harry Potter's, yet still mysterious in this age in which plastic surgery can fix most facial flaws. Mark's hair was dark, frizzy, and shoulder-length, and he had black Groucho Marx eyebrows and mustache.

She was beauty to his beast.

I read that he was a comedian and I wondered if that was supposed to be a joke or a euphemism for unemployed. Especially when I saw that Madeline came from M-O-N-E-Y. Big money. Old money. Trust-fund money. Her great-great-grandfather on her mother's side had been a founding partner of one of Minnesota's Fortune 500 companies—a maker of countless useful office products and industrial items most folks take for granted. Her mother was sitting on an impressive pile of family money and company stock. So when Madeline spoke of all her mother had done to raise her, well, she wasn't describing working a shift job and stretching a baked chicken over an extra meal.

Which made me mildly curious just why she was selling her never worn wedding gown. And extremely curious why it was never worn to begin with.

"So what do you think?" Madeline asked, startling me out of my internal dialogue. "How about two thousand dollars?"

It was a steal at that price. But my bridal days were over and it was time to level with her.

"You see, Madeline," I began.

"Okay, fifteen hundred."

While she came from money, it was quite possible

the young Miss Post might not have actual access to it yet, or might even have run through her share already. But she clearly wanted the dress gone. And a minute later, after I explained who I was, she wanted me gone, too.

I'm generally considered among the best-known TV reporters in the Minneapolis–St. Paul market, so I was surprised, yet pleased, when Madeline didn't recognize me right away at the door. Not everyone watches the news, I reminded myself, as she now fumed visibly.

"You're a reporter?" Madeline's voice trembled with outrage and her wide blue eyes got wider. "I thought you were interested in the dress."

"I am interested," I assured her. "I think the dress might make a great story."

"A *story*?" She threw open the door and waved me out of her condo with all the gusto I had anticipated. I turned and asked if she minded unzipping me first.

"Think of it as a free television ad," I said. "Soon as we get that dress on the late news, you'll have a bidding war."

That image stopped her. She shut the door.

"Do you think I care about the money?"

Madeline buried her face in her hands and started to cry. Tears made her engagement ring sparkle like the diamond it was—a real big one, at least two carats. Between sobs, she grabbed me like the sister I wasn't and dripped wet splotches all over the expensive satin dress that still clung to my figure.

I generally don't like people I don't know touching me. But I didn't say anything because I sensed Madeline's embrace meant she would soon share her deepest secret.

READING GROUP GUIDE FOR
STALKING SUSAN

1. Serial killer novels are numerous and can feel stereotypical. How original was the premise of a serial killer targeting Susans and killing one each year? Because name origination becomes part of the plot, do you think the story would have been entirely different if the book had been *Murdering Mary* instead of *Stalking Susan*? Are any of you named Susan? With references to famous Susans and song lyrics, did reading this book make you feel special or creeped out? Did those of you not named Susan feel any chills?

2. Does learning Riley Spartz is a widow change how you feel about her? What do you think of how the author unveiled that part of her backstory? Would you feel differently if the book had been written in third person rather than first person? At what places in the story did you find yourself rooting for her?

3. At the time the Susans were murdered, the cases didn't get a lot of media attention. Why do you think that was? In real life, could you ever envision a mayor or police chief trying to keep quiet news of a possible serial killer? Do you think every murder deserves to

lead a newscast or be on the front page? Do you find some murders more interesting than others?

4. Does understanding how decisions are made in a newsroom make you distrust reporters or sympathize with them? Does knowing what's at stake in the ratings game make you feel differently as a TV news viewer? Did the author's use of scripting copy in teleprompter style make the story more interesting or was it distracting to you as a reader?

5. One of the story's underlying themes is how grief changes people—from the heroine to the villain. Discuss grief in relation to Riley Spartz, the families of the dead Susans, and Dr. Brent Redding. How does the loss of each of their loved ones affect their motivations and actions?

6. Have any of you known bosses like news director Noreen Banks? Did you find yourself wishing Noreen would die? What did you think about Mike Flagg and the competition within a newsroom?

7. The novel incorporates several subplots, one involving a pet-cremation scam. In real life, do readers and viewers sometimes care more about animals than people? Why?

8. Dusty Foster introduces the possibility that an innocent man had been wrongly convicted. Were you

surprised when Dusty turned out guilty as charged? In real life, how often do you think prison inmates serve time for murders they didn't commit?

9. Having so many characters with the same name— Susan—can make a story complicated. How successful was the author in keeping each victim distinctive? What techniques did she use? Is there anything you think would have been helpful to you as a reader?

10. How did you feel when Nick Garnett became the prime suspect in the Susan killings? Riley's relationship with him is problematic because she is a journalist and he is her source. What would you like their future to be? What did you think of the author's use of movie lines as part of their shtick?

11. How did the author keep the reporter-with-cop-sidekick plot from becoming cliché? How about the final confrontation, sometimes known as the "talking killer scene"? Did you feel any pity toward Dr. Redding?

12. What did you think of the use of an epilogue to tell readers what happened to the characters after the action wraps up? How necessary to the story was the scene in which Riley reads the letter from Hugh?

Q & A *with Julie Kramer*

Stalking Susan deals with a serial killer targeting women named Susan, killing one on the same day each year. Do you have a special enemy named Susan?

No. *Stalking Susan* is not a tale of personal revenge. And I apologize to any Susans out there. I was inspired by two cold cases I covered as a WCCO-TV journalist a decade ago. They involved two women in St. Paul, Minnesota, both named Susan, strangled on the same day, two years apart. I hoped doing a story might shake loose some new tips and lead to a break in these unsolved murders. It didn't. The first homicide is now twenty-five years old and the killer is still out there. When I sat down to write a novel, I first created my character Riley Spartz but then needed an adventure for her. It's the unresolved cases that stay with journalists years later. Somehow the Susan story came to mind; you see, I never forgot them. I changed the city, the time of year, the women's last names . . . and I almost changed their first name, but I wanted to keep something of them in the story. As you know from reading it, name origination becomes part of the plot, so if I'd called them Mary, it would have been an entirely different story.

How would you describe *Stalking Susan* to someone you met on the street?

It's a cross between *The Da Vinci Code* and "Oh Susanna." Seriously, I hate simplifying things like that. I think *Stalking Susan* takes readers inside the desperate world of TV news in a classic serial killer thriller that involves the Bible, the calendar, and a smart heroine pitted against a smart antihero. I don't like stories in which the protagonist stumbles across the solution. I like them to work for it. What I think makes this story so memorable is the subplot of how grief changes people. Riley is a victim of grief, but so is our villain. In some ways, grief is an equalizer in life. How we deal with it says a lot about who we are.

Did you know who the killer was when you started writing your book?

No. I sort of made it up as I went along. I was just as anxious to see what would happen next. For a while I wanted to come up with a believable scenario in which Nick Garnett was the killer. I thought that would be real cool. But I also believed that for justice to prevail, the killer needed to die. And I grew too fond of him to kill him off. I also wanted to keep him around in case there was a sequel. He seemed like a character with a lot of potential.

You weave some real-life news stories into your novel, like the collapse of the Minneapolis bridge. Why did you do that?

After the book was sold and in production, the bridge fell. I was there, working through the night, covering the story for the *Today Show* and, in fact, was the only journalist to get a live interview the next morning with one of the rescued kids from the school bus that fell in the river. Since my novel was set in Minneapolis, I felt I had to include some references to snarled traffic and detours in order to be realistic. My publisher allowed me to make these changes. I also refer to other bona fide news stories in my novels because I think it's fun, and I think it makes the made-up stuff seem more realistic. Here's some evidence: several readers have told me they don't remember the big explosion on the Iron Range that killed so many people, and asked me why it didn't get more news coverage. I've had to remind them that even though *Stalking Susan* is written in first person, it's a novel, not a memoir. Most of what's between the pages is all fiction. But I take it as a compliment that readers buy into the world I've created.

Are TV newsrooms really so obsessed with ratings?

Yes. Sometimes people ask if I exaggerate the flaws of the profession for dramatic effect. I suppose that's possible. But really no more than John Grisham does with the legal world. Critics say one of the strengths of *Stalking Susan* is that it really does show how decisions are made in television newsrooms. Some of my news colleagues think I gave away a little too much in the way of newsroom secrets. Did you really have to tell them, "If it bleeds, it leads"? But I felt that for the book to work, I needed to come clean about some of the flaws in my profession.

Do you dislike your day job?

No. I love it. There is nothing like the exhilaration, unpredictability, and desperation of live TV. I want readers to feel the wild competitiveness and satisfaction that comes from nailing a big story against the odds.

Stalking Susan is a finalist for several awards, including the Mary Higgins Clark Award, which honors books featuring women whose lives are invaded and who must use their own courage and intelligence to get out. Another criteria is that the story contain no explicit sex, violence, or strong language. Was that a conscious decision on your part?

Not really. I didn't start out with that on my mind. I've read books in which sex and violence advanced the plot. But I've also read books in which sex and violence seemed to get in the way of the story. As if someone told the author, sex sells, better put some in. Some people suggested I add a sex scene to jazz things up. Certainly my characters have sex. And some die violently. But that action happens off screen. I'm not saying I wouldn't ever write a sex scene, but as the story unfolded, that's just how it played out. Perhaps I was influenced by the fact that I have teenage sons and want them and their friends to be able to read my book without being embarrassed. I don't think readers are missing out on anything by me not naming specific body parts. There are places in my story where people cry. There are places where people cheer. Those were conscious decisions on my part, because I feel a book needs to move readers emotionally for them to connect with the characters.

What was your writing process like for *Stalking Susan?*

Solitary. Very few people knew I was writing a book until it sold. My kids knew because I kept kicking them off the computer. I kept quiet about it because I have a large extended family (seven siblings) and I didn't want them constantly asking me what page I was on, or "whatever happened to that book you said you were going to write?" Now they all want to be in my next book, and that creates its own problems. Everyone wants to be the hero. Nobody wants to be the villain. And they all want to be cute, with toned bodies and interesting jobs. No one wants to be flawed, get fired, or be killed. So I tune them out.

Stalking Susan was your first book. Any advice to other aspiring writers?

Yes. Never give all the characters the same name. That was a major pain.

What other challenges did you face in sitting down to write?

The year before I started writing, I concentrated on reading. I knew I wanted to write a series, so I read all my favorite authors' debut books that resulted in successful series. Kathy Reichs, Linda Fairstein, Sue Grafton. John Sandford. Patricia Cornwell. I tried to read as both a critic and a fan, and focus on why readers embraced their characters.

In reading books, I tired of fictional TV reporters always being portrayed as annoying secondary characters, who could be killed off when the plot started dragging. So I wanted to make one in which the TV reporter was the hero. A close friend, who I really respect, said a reader has to fall in love with a story's protagonist, and she worried that people hate TV reporters so much, it's not possible to make one likeable. So I always had that worry in the back of my mind as I wrote. I knew I was going against stereotypes. That's why I'm so pleased when reviewers say this is a series we want to see more of, and readers tell me how much they enjoyed getting to know my heroine, Riley Spartz, and want to know what's next.

What is ahead for Riley?

In the sequel, *Missing Mark* (Summer 2009), Riley answers a want ad reading, "For Sale: Wedding Dress. Never Worn," and is drawn into a dangerous missing person case during sweeps month. All my life, I've been curious about such ads. A wedding dress is the most emotional item in a woman's closet. What would make her part with it—anger, grief, economics? I've often been tempted to call them and ask, "What happened?" Here I was able to use my imagination. Oh and yes, Shep makes another appearance in a subplot about a meth cartel out to assassinate a K-9 dog for its powerful nose for drugs.